THEY ONCE HAD NAMES

THEY ONCE HAD NAMES

VOLUME II OF THE GIFTBORN CHRONICLES

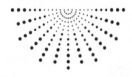

DREW BAILEY

FALSTAFF
BOOKS
WWW.FALSTAFFBOOKS.COM

For every voice and every gift that ever inspired my own. You are many. You are mighty. And you are well prized.

DRAMATIS PERSONAE

HOUSE LANIER

Aiden Ashborough/Prince Desmond Lanier, the eldest son of King Whitman II and Queen Larissa Lanier, the true heir to the Throne of Lancastle, twenty-three cycles old

Princess Marsea Lanier, the eldest daughter, twenty

Prince Rembrandt Lanier, the youngest son, eighteen

Larissa Lanier, Queen of Lancastle

Whitman Lanier II, the last and former King of Lancastle, died during the coup of the Midnight Men at the age of fifty

COURT OF LANCASTLE

Merillion Casilvieri, a man of questionable character, and Marsea's mentor

Effie Cavendish, a cloth maiden, and friend to Princess Marsea

HOUSE HARVER

Raelan Harver, General and High Commander of the Lancastle Royalguard Regiment, Larissa Lanier's husband

Pion Harver, Raelan's son, twenty-two

Julia Harver, the daughter of Raelan and Queen Larissa, nine

Vaustian Harver, Viceroy of Lancastle, the middle Harver brother

Sylvie Harver, Vaustian Harver's wife
Aeralie Harver, the daughter of Vaustian and Sylvie, fifteen

ROYALGUARD
Rhymona Curie/Morgandrel Tully, an ashaeydir battle-magus with a violent past
Yurien Tenbrooks, a battle-magus of some repute
Bromas Aldridge, a Captain in the Royalguard, stationed in Lancastle

HOUSE DALIVANT
Drezhal Dalivant, Emperor of Courowne
Magwyn Lanier, Empress of Courowne, Dalivant's wife

COURT OF COUROWNE
Rhonyn Waldgrave, Ambassador of Lancastle, Queen Larissa's older brother
Ender Visbane, Commodore of the warship Belisarius
Marlowe the Younger, a Captain in the Emperorswatch

SOUTHLANDS
Stella Ashborough, Aiden's step-mother (deceased), a storied magus, and former archivist to Lancastle Library
Vincent Ashborough, Aiden's step-father, a winemaker
Autumn Ashborough, Aiden's younger step-sister, fifteen
Valestriel Alyfain, an ashaeydir soldier that befriends Aiden
Xavien Ledgermaine, a barkeep at The Heart House in Port Tavern-mast, a magus and blademaster
D'Anna Hex, the Captain of Blackhall's Banshee
Keats, the Quartermaster of Blackhall's Banshee

RAVENHOLME
Elsymir Beldroth, a y'deman huntsman
Broenwjar, Beldroth's wolf companion
Yongrin Tarboril, a magus loyal to Ravenholme
Davrin Tarboril, a soldier loyal to Ravenholme

FURTHER PLAYERS

Dagmara VanLandingham, a former loyalist to Ravenholme, Beldroth's friend, Klaus's wife

Klaus VanLandingham, a councilman for the township of Vinth, Dagmara's husband

Solindiel Alyfain, Valestriel's eldest sister

Dysenia Luiryn, an ashaeydir assassin

Tetherow, a magus and author tangled in rumors

WHAT HAS COME BEFORE

THE ROYAL NOTHINGS: Fifteen cycles past, the throne of Kingdom Lancastle was usurped by a rebel faction led by the turncloak Vaustian Harver. The King, Whitman Lanier II, and heir apparent, Prince Desmond, were both murdered during the coup leaving the remaining royal family members, Queen Larissa and her young children Marsea and Rembrandt, little more than heartbroken prisoners.

Last cycle, upon his eighteenth birthfall, Prince Remy Lanier abandoned his father's kingdom of Lancastle for the dogs and drear of The King's Wall. Amongst the soldiers of the Kingswatch, he quickly discovered just how cruel and ruthless the world outside his family's posh chambers and heavily guarded courtyards could be. However, despite these hardships, he chose to remain amongst the lowly. Preferring his shame, to the fiendish games of House Harver.

While Remy and Black Stag Company are on duty in a hamlet named Brymshire, the township is invaded by a lich who has resurrected the nearby grave-ridden and ordered them to attack the townsfolk, adding to its undead legion. To further complicate matters, an ashaeydir assassin is also in attendance—the ashaeydir are darkly creatures from the cursed moon of Ashira known to summon lichlords to do their bidding. This onslaught would only serve as the beginning of the nightmare to come.

Narrowly escaping the sacking of Brymshire, Remy meets a mysterious huntsman that forces a grimoire upon him and bids him to take it to a woman named Tarboril in the nearby kingdom of Palatia. Once inside the kingdom, Remy and Captain Rhymona Curie seek an audience with Tarboril only to find that there are two of them and they are loyal to a rogue guild known as The Covenant. Heeding Rhymona's warning, Remy decides to keep the grimoire and the pair find themselves on the run with The Covenant in pursuit. The following day, the blight descends on Palatia. The ashaeydir assassin once again finds Remy, but he manages to elude her blade a second time. By the favor of the fates, during the fall of Palatia, Remy and Rhymona happen upon a portal that returns them to Lancastle.

Back in Lancastle Proper, Princess Marsea Lanier prepares for a dark task. For the past cycle, in the absence of her brother, she has trained with the usurper Vaustian Harver and his bladehand, Merillion Casilvieri, to prepare for her trials with Ravenholme. During this time, her relationship with Vaustian has grown more complex and intense as she develops a strange attachment to her captor. These feelings lead to her murdering Vaustian's brother Ganedys at Ravenholme's behest. However, during the ambush, one of her hands becomes severely mutilated.

As she recovers, tidings from the north arrive regarding the return of a lichlord and the dreaded blight. Vaustian promises Marsea safety through his connections to Ravenholme and decides to expedite her call to trial, requesting she meet him in the courtyards after nightfall.

This meeting is interrupted by Remy's homecoming. The Prince, having harbored an unyielding hatred for Vaustian over the cycles, finds the Viceroy alone in the courtyards and they duel. Vaustian defeats Remy in the clash, but he becomes distracted by Marsea's arrival and her potential conflict over him stabbing her freshly returned brother, that he never notices Rhymona in the shadows, allowing her to murder him without contest.

Minutes later, Remy drops out from his wounds and Marsea realizes Remy was run through during his duel with Vaustian. As Remy bleeds out, the horns of war sound and arrows light the sky, marking the approach of the blighted legion.

Meanwhile, in the Southlands, Aiden Ashborough is an archivist at Perciya University's storied archives. Since graduating, he has made a drunken mess of his life, exacerbated by the sudden passing of his mother a few months past. Sodden once more in the pit of his sorrows, he is joined by a sellsword named Val. She brings a spark to his life not felt since his romance with Rhymona Curie some cycles back.

As young lust blossoms, Aiden and Val take a trip into The Spellbind—a magical realm out of time and space where one can heal, refresh, and bask in the unparalleled magnificence of the gift. Only they come to find that something wicked has passed unto her tranquil fields. A magus named Solomon Darrow is there being eaten alive by an alien parasite. He tells them that The King's Wall has fallen and instructs them to warn the high kingdoms and the Oathsworn of this approaching horror.

Afterward, they search the university archives for any insight into the Oathsworn and are steered to the port of Tavernmast. In Tavernmast, Aiden learns that an ancient entity known as the nether has returned from beyond The Pale and will soon devour the moon of Vaelsyntheria as it did Ashira centuries before. He also learns that he is Desmond Lanier, the crown prince and true heir of Kingdom Lancastle, and that he was resurrected after the coup of the Midnight Men and his identity concealed when his memories did not return.

When the location of The Spellbind is revealed to be near Nocthun, a city in ashaeydir territory, Val decides to admit to her familiarity with the region and confesses that she is ashaeydir. This upsets Aiden, but Val's sincerity and willingness to explain herself earn her a tentative compromise. They make plans to travel to Lancastle and then to Nocthun.

CHAPTER ONE

U nbe-fucking-lievable.

"I'm losing him," Rhymona growled, the words tearing from her throat as she pushed her mind into the opening folds of The Spellbind's rift, focusing her attention on restoring Remy's lost blood. And it was all she could do just to manage that bit.

You little silver spoon cunt. You're not getting out that easy. I didn't run myself ragged and nearly die twice just for you to bite it the second I get you back here.

But, at least, The Spellbind was actually responding to her again. Still, the dead Palatian she'd stocked from must have been remarkably ungifted to produce such a poor result as this. Sealing the wound would have to come later.

And the gods knew, Remy was a horrid gusher too. It was coming up quick, fighting her pressure. And through their blood bond, she could feel his vitality waning. Fucking Shit-for-brains stuck him but good too, hadn't he? And for that, Harver had earned every iron-hard inch of Fucker's wrath. But this could have been avoided. And it should have been avoided. She should have known better. She did know better.

This is on you, Morgan. This is what happens when you involve yourself.

She knew men like Harver. Plenty of them. Killers. Pit dogs. Bastards born with a blade in their hand and a nasty penchant for dealing death.

And Remy wasn't that. He was anything but. But fuck all if the soft little tosser hadn't wormed his way into her stupid fucking heart. She knew he wouldn't have the talent to take on a practiced swordsmith as was Harver, and yet she let him have a go anyway. And mayhaps worse, she let him believe he could win.

You brought this one on yourself, fuckwit. She could taste death's kiss inside him. *Now fix it. No more running.*

"Marsea, figure it out!" she screamed into the swell of snowfall as the sister collapsed to the stones next to her with Harver's body in her lap.

"What the hells?" Marsea rasped.

What's the fucking problem now, Princess Prim?

"You're bloody ashaeydir?"

Rhymona glanced down through the riven binary at her lilac skin and her golden orbs widened. *Well, ain't that about a bitch mother...*

It was only then that she felt Toff's hand against her neck. *Baka.* He had grazed her trezsu implant. And he had her blood inside him, didn't he? *Fucking bollocks. Fucking this one up shite proper then, aren't you?*

"I will explain later," she scrambled for anything resembling actual words, emotions dashing to and fro about her countenance. "Right now, I need more blood. I have to go deeper."

"Tell me what to do, then?" Marsea answered.

Curtains of sleet came slicing into the arcade, but Rhymona was too far in to feel it. She was caught somewhere between the physical world and the astral plane, and she knew if she yielded by even the thinnest of margins, Remy would be lost.

"It's going to be messy," she said, her voice sounding as an echo from within The Spellbind's cry.

"And I'd say we're well past messy at this point," Marsea quibbled, pulling her girlish frame out from under Harver's body.

Proper lady, my left arse cheek. This one here bared a wholly different aura from the walking cry for help Rhymona met last cycle. An intriguing prospect, that. She might have even pressed the girl about it were there any time left to them.

"All right, first run Shit-for-brains there a red smile," she responded, "and keep it pouring over my hands." Rhymona had no doubts Harver would provide substantially better stock than the Palatian soldier. One did not make such a grand societal leap without possessing at least some significant measure of the gift.

Marsea wrestled Harver's corpse against the balustrade next to Remy and retrieved her dagger.

If there was any one thing in the world Rhymona loathed above all else, it was a pull of raw magic. They ravaged the bloodstream and burned like ruddy hellfire. All the way down. But it was all she had left to work with. And really? What the fuck did it matter in the end, anyway? All the times she had sought after ruin, begged The Hood to take her from this miserable turd of an existence, if *this* of all things was what turned out to be the death knell, why she would count her fucking luck stones all the way to the maker's rosy, pink gash and give her a sloppy wet seeing-to.

"Once I'm inside The Spellbind, it's on you to keep the blood flowing, yeah. I will be in a fugue of sorts so I won't exactly be able to respond or help you." Marsea nodded. "And it's going to get fearsome dodgy for a bit. It's going to look shite bad for the pair of us. Corpse bad, yeah. But no matter what you hear or see, just keep the blood running. When the neck runs dry, start severing limbs. Use Fucker if you have to."

Her breathing slowed and her words began to drift away from her as Marsea maneuvered Harver on top of Remy so his head hung over the wound.

"And Marsea," Rhymona began as the princess placed the blade's edge against Harver's throat and let it taste of flesh, "remember…"

Harver's blood was still warm as it trickled atop her hand, into her open wound, and began to coalesce with their bond.

"He's only a man…"

Sound fractured into abrupt silence and her eyes rolled back in her head as she felt her body jerk rearward away from Marsea and the material plane…

A heartbeat later she found herself behind Remy inside the pale endless ash pit encompassing The Dragonsfall.

Remy was hunched over at the edge of a cliff, facing away from her, clutching himself tight around his belly.

"Remy," Rhymona said.

Slowly he turned toward her voice. "Who the shit—"

"Steady on, Toff, it's me."

3

"Curie? Bloody hell, why do you look like that? Where in fucknation are we?"

"We're in The Spellbind. Obviously," she replied as she approached. "And you enter how you left. You disabled my trezsu implant. Cheers by the way. Royally fucked my little social experiment, didn't you? Cycles of hard work right down the shitter."

"I disabled what?"

She exhaled. Explaining herself to children was about as high up her list as raw-dogging another Spellbind rift. "I'm bloody ashaeydir, Remy." She let the confession cogitate for a breath. "This is what I truly look like." She thought about adding a jig and a wink for good measure but figured the cheek would be wholly lost on a dour joy-fuck as was His Royal Pain in the arse.

"No, you're not," came his eventual response and his eyes widened as if in realization of something significant.

"Starting to make sense now, is it?"

His face fell, and she could tell he was mulling something over. "You're not lying, are you?" By his dumbfounded expression, she could see the puzzle pieces from the past few days slowly clicking into place. "You're actually one of them."

"And there it is, yeah. Cat's out of the bag. Whatever I am, I'm done lying. How 'bout that?"

"You're done lying?" he scoffed. "And did you know the other one then? The one that tried to murder me in Brymshire and then again in Palatia?"

"More than like," she answered honestly. "There aren't too many of our kind that bother over The King's Wall these days."

"The Stranger take me." He raked a hand through his hair. "You were one of them this whole time?" He gave her another confounded once over. "And you didn't try to kill me?" His gaze altered from daft fuckwit to something almost respectably inquisitive.

"Quite the opposite, I'd say," she replied. "And you don't make it easy, do you?"

"And what is that supposed to mean?"

"It means I should have thought better about all this Harver business, yeah. He was clearly your better. Could've had you a dozen times over in the arcade alone." She meant the words to frighten him.

4

"And yet he did not," Remy argued. "I wonder why that was."

"Obviously, he was toying with you," she countered. "I bet you didn't even see the blade that bit you."

By his soured expression, she knew she had the right of it. And not surprisingly he reacted poorly, throwing up a hand and muttering something under his breath as he stormed off.

For the hundredth time since their meeting, she asked herself how this petulant little shit-stain and Aiden could possibly be brothers. She reckoned being raised well didn't necessarily mean being raised right. And thusly her respect for Stella Ashborough's quality of mothering solidified that much more.

"Sorry, not sorry, Toff," Rhymona called as she followed, brushing bone-white bangs out of her face, "but we don't have time to attend one of your little fucking episodes just now, yeah."

"One of *my* little episodes?" He halted and spun about crossly, flakes of ash drifting down around them in stones and chunks. "You're one to talk. The queen sprawling clusterfuck you are, Rhymona. Every second in your presence is a fucking episode."

"Tut, some gratitude there, yeah. We can't all shit rainbows and unicorns as his Royal Highness, now can we?"

"Oh, piss off, why don't you?"

"Oi, don't take it out on me because you went and got yourself fucking stabbed to death. And you better not turn your fucking back on me again. The only reason you aren't a mindless corpse already is because of me."

"Oh, we all know I fucking owe you, Rhymona." He spread his arms out wide. "Fantastic. Brilliant. Huzzah. Rhymona fucking Curie, everyone. Honestly. If I must hear about how much I fucking owe you every single time you step up then all told you can keep your bloody charity."

"I never said anything about you owing me, Remy. You did that yourself."

"Come off it. I know—"

"You know what?" she snarled. "What do you know, Rembrandt Lanier? You think you know fuck all about me? You think I'm just like the rest, yeah? *Still.* Even after all the bullshit."

"Fuck off."

"Because if you knew even the faintest inkling about me you would know—"

A memory of Aiden stopped her cold. Hard as an open palm slap to the face.

He was cauterized into her brain, stubborn as a brand of hot iron. Aiden. Ash. Borough. Desmond Lanier. The gods know. She hadn't a clue what she was getting herself into when she took assignment in The Lanier Objective…and that was putting it real fucking kindly.

She and Aiden drifted down the pier in Lower Kanton, hours into eventide, pissed to the nine, as was their wont, the salty breath of the sea coursing wildly through their hair and he issued her a smile, innocent as fuck, as was ever his guise, snickering at one of his own gods-awful japes once again, and—

He'd been here recently. Inside The Spellbind. She could sense the wander of his phantom's aura.

"I would know what?" Remy inquired.

You would know…

You would know your brother yet lives.

And you would know your sister loves you enough to make stupid, shady deals with filthy degenerates just to see to your wellbeing.

You would know…

A splintering sound like a crack of thunder ruptured their brief silence, and a long, miserable wail of agony chased its echo across the ashen plain.

Rhymona gazed out toward the source of the horrible sound and discovered a giant pitch-black mass in the distance, looming over the monolithic elder tree like a mourner at a wake. How had she not noticed it before? The creature was tall as a citadel tower and grotesquely corpulent, with a series of tentacle-like appendages slithering about its immense silhouette.

Fucking Toff. It went without saying really, but if Prince Fuckwit excelled at any one thing in all the world, it was throwing her off her game. No doubt it would serve her a handsome grave, ass up like Shit-for-brains back in the court of courts. And sooner rather than later, the way things were. But that was the Lanier Luck in all its shining glory, wasn't it? Horrid fucking rotten. And yet somehow just enough to get by.

"What the hells is that thing?" Remy asked.

"An answer to a question," she responded grimly. "Think I know why I had such trouble reaching The Spellbind back in Palatia."

Rhymona had seen all manner of monster over the cycles, from land and sea both, wngar, kraken, oni, hauntlings, but never anything quite like this, never anything quite so large. Its torso appeared human in form, but its lower parts were akin to that of an octopoid creature, and its head bore a snout and antlers in the vein of a dracari.

"It's starting at the source," she found herself saying, lost in her own inspection of the impossible creature. "It's leeching her dry, absorbing what little remains of her life force."

"Her?"

"Yvemathira."

The dracari's voice, more sensation than sound, was a song in requiem, and Rhymona let the pain burrow within. As though there was any other choice in the matter.

"She has been expecting us." The magus glanced over to the dying prince, eyes aghast, and her heart broke for the both of them.

Yvemathira's pain hurt worse than her own, tenfold worse. Worse than any pain she had ever known before, including the loss of her family. It too was an emotional pain. A psychological pain. A pain of deep sorrow. A pain for her and Remy and all the world around them. It was a pain Thira had fought to avoid for many, many cycles. But finally, inevitably, it had caught up to her.

A sudden rumbling in the distance returned their attentions as the giant creature shifted, and it felt like all in existence shook right along with it.

"It knows we're here," Rhymona said, feeling the entity's awareness through her connection to Yvemathira. And with the thought, it was there with them, inside her mind, cold as a crypt, twisting its dark, inky tendrils around what woefully little remained of Yvemathira's aura.

Dread turned Rhymona's stomach in knots as she began to understand the fiend's intentions. She'd sensed a similar presence before, but only once. That night with Aiden when they summoned the dead man's rift.

Concurrently, the creature's head shrank into its torso and the shifted mass burst from its chest as though it had just been disemboweled and its tar-like entrails snaked out toward them across the great ashen landscape weaving itself within a pair of its tentacles to form one fantastically large appendage. It moved, slick as a serpent, spiraling and slithering about, and yet there was nothing comparable this side of the Vael.

"We're running out of time." Rhymona focused on Thira's instructions as the entity strove to muddle it. It too was attempting to pass through the doorway Thira had opened up inside her. "She says she can help us. She says she can bring us back. Bring you back. But you must be willing to sacrifice."

At her words, the gash across her palm began glowing bright cerulean, a brilliant beacon in an otherwise pallid sea of gloom.

Yvemathira's sickly voice resounded from within, and through their shared torment Rhymona echoed the dracari's message. "I am dying, highborn. So too is my connection with this world. And soon the parasite will consume all you see before you, The Spellbind itself and all the magic left in this place. But it will not stop there. It will scour the countryside, from coast to coast, devouring all in its path, without discrimination, taking on a thousand, thousand forms to remake what was once stolen. There is nothing to be done about this. It is written. It will—"

Rhymona collapsed to her knees and screeched like a wounded animal as the entity choked Thira's words from utterance.

"Rhymona!" Remy sank with her.

"I can feel her spirit fading," she said, cradling the arm of her glowing hand, and her appearance suddenly reverted back to that of her Midaran mask.

"Whoa!" Remy cried. "What the hells?"

"What?" she managed.

"You changed back."

"You must have brushed my implant again," she explained before crumbling over. It felt like her arm was on fire.

"Shit. What can I do? Tell me, Rhymona! Tell me what to do!"

"Accept her," Rhymona said. "She wants you to accept what little remains."

The Spellbind began to darken around them as though taken by an eclipse.

"She wants you to accept her into your vessel."

"*My* vessel? But you're the bloody giftborn. I'm just…"

"She says it must be one housing the maker's ichor."

"The maker's…what?"

"She can marry her essence…ungh!" Rhymona doubled over again. She could feel the entity's presence spreading inside her, its disease like a ravenous beast in hunt of a long-awaited repast. "She says they will sense her through you. They will return...to aid us."

"Who?"

Rhymona's mind returned to the last time her world shattered. To the night she left Aiden. To the black of the wood outside Kanton, when the drink wouldn't quiet the voices and she punched her knuckles to the bloody bone. When her tears and screams refused to stop, and her heart nearly burst shrieking from her chest.

"The others," she answered, pushing down the entity's attempt at distraction.

And the image of her sister flickered into memory to replace it. It was from the day before the coup. The day before her world would shatter for the first time. They were nestled away happily inside their secret place. Fia was giggling and reading to her as Morgan braided her sister's hair. She always liked it better when Fia read. Fiandrel always had a certain knack for the arts, especially literature, and spoke far more eloquently than any girl of her youthful age ought.

I am but a leaf on the wind.

A stone on the earth.

A spit in the flame.

A wave in the sea.

I am nothing.

I am all things.

"The Eldnumerian," she continued.

The monstrous creature was nearly upon them now, and her consciousness was beginning to betray her. Blood thundered in her ears as though she was physically there, and her head began to pound like her brain was boiling in its fluids. The fiend's dark influence was proving far too powerful to contend with. Its company relentless, like a hundred prying fingers rummaging through her past, plucking from it the absolute worst of the horrors that had found her, as though they were but hairs upon her scalp. She tried to steel herself against the snap images, against the overwhelming emotions they conjured, but they were becoming longer and more brutal the deeper the entity plundered.

Her father...

The beating...

Her mother...

The shaming...
Her sister...
The cutting...
Her newborn...
The passing...
Her beloved...
The sacrifice...
Val-shan...
The withering...
Desmond Lanier—

"We're out of time, Remy." The grotesque alien glow of Rhymona's hand spilled out from her clutch, shrieking untold sorceries, bright as shimmering star fire. "Look at me."

Obediently, his gaze rose from the cry of magic between them to meet hers, his face pale as old bones.

And there it is. That 'I just shit myself' look. Right on cue.

"I'm sorry," she said, the entity's voice bucking around inside her skull like a fever-mad oni on spriteling dust. "If I could take this on for you, I would. But it has to be you. Her choice, not mine."

She raised her hand up toward him.

No more running.

CHAPTER TWO

A slab of meat, Marsea finished, staring past the blood-matted split in the back of her dead love's skull to take in the catatonic ashaeydir killer kneeling before her.

"Rhymona?" she uttered, unwanted tears scalding the backs of her eyes.

No.

No more liquid eyes. She blinked them away, her vision chasing out into the spiraling snowfall, sinking to the contrasting trails of bright red gore Vaustian and Remy had made from her draggings.

Oh, but how the maidens know, if given the proper time to it, she could cry the entire Commonwealth below the tides. And even then, it still might not be enough to quell her anger and sorrows.

Suddenly Vaustian's streaming blood began to slow, coming to a trickle.

Her breath caught. *Shit.* Panic set in as she tried to position him at different angles to restore the flow, even yanking the side of his sticky hair back to widen the gash in his throat, but it made little difference. The neck was dry and she was left gagging from the putrid stench of his awful head wound.

It's on you to keep the blood flowing, Rhymona's words came back, stronger than the stink.

I know, I know...

Frantic, Marsea worked one of Vaustian's sleeves up, exposing his lower arm, then moved it over top of Rhymona's hand, and slit it longways from wrist to elbow, letting it gush anew.

This wasn't how it was supposed to go.

She swallowed down the hurt of further mutilating the man she'd at times adored, and watched numbly as the last of his lifeblood coated her friend and younger brother.

Yet how else could it be?

The Omedran Canticle returned to her at that and she began praying, though it came more out of habit than actual faith...

Maidens, make me thine instrument
Where doubt may dwell, may I find faith
Where despair may haunt, may I find your hope and grace
Where hate may tread, may I find your gentle love
Where the nether grows, in blackest dark, may I find your light

Silence pooled in response and it felt like a thousand, thousand leagues of dead space now lay twixt her and another normal, living, breathing soul. The image of Effie Cavendish flickered into place at the thought. She could certainly use one of the cloth maiden's warm, tender hugs now.

A second full volley lit the heavens in the distance and her lungs paused, breath catching quick at the base of her throat. She watched in awe as the wave of flaming arrows arched high and disappeared behind the other side of the courtyard. She had to remind herself to breathe out and then back in again.

Stay here, girl.

Stay present.

Rhymona began to twitch before her.

"Rhymona?" Marsea whispered again, her glasses sliding down her nose, and it was in that moment the princess realized she was no longer alone. Her attentions fell to Rhymona's hatchet, but before she could reach for it, a creeping numbness devoured all prospects of movement.

Rhymona's hand began to pulse with a bright cerulean glow under Vaustian's dwindling blood spill, and Remy's eyes burst open next to her, his orbs white as the snow that bespeckled his dark curls.

The stars save me.

Wind swept up from a snow-drift at the courtyard's edge, and a figure began to form from its gust in the arcade just behind Rhymona, spawning with it a ghoulish dark energy and the sickly-sweet stench of embalming fluids. And what began as numbness fastly progressed into a state of total paralysis. Nothing of her body responded to her behests. Helpless, her heart began to batter against her ribcage as more figures emerged all around the courtyard, their eldritch, uneven, ever-shifting forms bleeding through the snowfall as inky tempests, little more than thin, fitful smears of movement, like daggers cutting about a sea of vapors, before assuming a more corporeal form.

They were hooded, each of them, once materialized, their cowls long and deep, and black as the belly of an endless chasm, denying her access to their identities. However, within each cowl she felt the scrutiny of a thousand beady eyes, most clever and cutting, like glinting razors, staring back out at her. It was of such a powerful glower that she could practically feel each one of them crawling about underneath her skin.

Ever closer the specters crept upon her petrification, like leeches to a bruise, their whispers growing louder and more determined—

"Ignore them," a voice commanded from behind. "It's all bleed through."

The winter's kiss came back to her at that, raw and furious, and she inched forward, grasping the hatchet with her good hand.

"Fucking hells, Scraps," the voice said as he approached.

Cas. His mere appearance rejuvenated her confidence, if only faintly, and something of her training burrowed forth from the back of her mind. *Focus on what you know you can control.*

"Just out and open for anyone to see. You've truly lost your shit, haven't you?"

"Cas," Marsea managed. "What's happening?" *And why don't you seem surprised at the presence of an ashaeydir?*

"They've taken the outer hamlets. Illery, Fountain Head, Mythris Pointe—"

"You know her?" Marsea said as she pushed up to her feet.

"Did you hear what I just said?" he replied dismissively. "We've got bigger problems just now."

"You *do* know her." She knuckled her gran glasses back up to their proper placement.

More phantoms began to form around them as the snowfall thickened and a third volley ignited the gray expanse above.

"Bloody hell, is that Harver?" Casilvieri questioned, studying the mass of bodies closer.

She nodded. Her love's death still hadn't sunk in quite enough to permit words, apparently.

"Reckon it was unavoidable in the end, wasn't it?"

"You reckon it was unavoidable?" Marsea said, raising the hatchet up at her mentor. "My brother is dying because of all this! And what in vael-nation are these...these things?"

"Hauntlings. From the place Morgan took your brother to."

"Morgan?" She swerved the hatchet at Rhymona. "Is that the creature's name then?

"Marsea."

"Don't lie to me, Cas. That is an ashaeydir. A fucking ashaeydir. In the upper courts. And you didn't even bat an eye at it. You know her, don't you?" The answer was written plainly on his face, try as he might to conceal it. "How?"

"A tale for another time, that," he said. "But that's the real world for ya, isn't it? Ten pounds of shit for a two-pound sack."

Rhymona's twitches intensified to violent convulsing and a long, otherworldly shriek, like nails dragging down steel, poured out of her.

"Bugger all," Cas grumbled as he came to the ashaeydir's side.

"What's happening to her?"

"Fuck if I know," he answered, studying their connection to The Spell-bind. "I've never seen anything of this nature before, though the magic she's holding appears as that of Eldn fire, yeah?"

"Eldn fire?" Marsea dared a closer assessment. "How is that possible?"

Cas shook his head as he turned his inspection to Remy, waving a hand before her brother's vacant white orbs and lowering his fingers under Remy's nose. "Nothing."

"Are you saying he's dead?" It was a painfully daft question, but she had to ask.

"Appears so," Cas confirmed. "But if anyone can bring him back its Morgandrel. She's mastered The Spellbind's influence as well as any magus I know." He pressed Remy's hand against her neck, and her appearance shifted back to the one Marsea was accustomed to. "She was something of a shaman before—"

"How did you know to do that?" Marsea inquired. "How do you know all this? How do you know her?"

Something sparked to life in the courtyard's epicenter, bright as a struck match, and a scar of golden light dragged away from it across the snowy ether, expanding outward in jagged lines and half-moons to form what Marsea knew to be named a ward. She had seen the symbol before, in her father's writings, though she was by no means proficient in the language of runes.

What now?

In short order, a rippling puddle of water materialized around the glyph and a moment later a pair of figures stepped out from behind it. The first was male and clad in crimson armor, and the other a female wearing a strange ensemble of dark leathers and magian robe attire. They both appeared several cycles her senior.

Marsea was almost certain she had never seen either one of them before. No doubt she would have remembered such a striking pair if she had. And yet, all the same, something was eerily familiar about them.

"Stay behind me, girl," Cas warned as he stood and passed through a hauntling into Alistair's Courtyard, iron appearing in his hand as if by magic.

Marsea maneuvered herself in front of the heap of bodies to conceal them as much as could be had, hiding the hatchet behind her back in the process.

"Fiveknives," the knight in crimson greeted as he crunched forward and scanned the surroundings. Marsea rather thought him handsome in a rugged, woodsy sort of manner.

"Tarboril," Cas returned with a noticeable lack of enthusiasm.

"We were expecting Harver," the knight said as he followed the trails of gore past Casilvieri to Marsea. By his accent, Marsea knew him to be of northern blood.

"He is engaged elsewhere, I'm afraid," Casilvieri answered. "You understand."

"Mmm, yes, it appears we have come about at a rather inopportune time, haven't we?" the magus said, swiping a hand through one of the smoky apparitions. She had the superior air of a lifelong noble; chin up, purposeful, proud. She quite reminded Marsea of her mother, long sparkly blond locks and all. The northern lot, even the peasantry, had a certain inimitable way about them, after all.

"And who is this pathetic creature?" the knight inquired; his gaze having settled on Marsea.

The scar on her upper lip began to itch under his quizzical scrutiny.

"Don't be thick, Davrin, this is our charge, of course," the magus replied. "I hope you will prove yourself less troublesome than your brother, milady."

Marsea's tongue held, and she toed back a step. *My brother? What could a Ravenholme sorceress possibly have to do with Remy?*

"Come now, Yongrin," the knight began, "you mean to say this drowned rat is Marsea Lanier? The Princess of Lancastle? What Vaustian has been falling apart over for the past cycle?"

The preening jackass. Marsea dropped her gaze to hide her offense and felt her grip tighten about the hatchet's haft.

"Yeah, about that," Cas began. "There's been a change in plans, yeah."

"Is that so?" Yongrin said. "I wonder. Would that have anything to do with The Spellbind summoning, by any chance?"

"More or less," Casilvieri shrugged.

"Mayhaps I can be of assistance then," she murmured. "I'm quite acquainted with the dark arts, as you well know." She craned her neck to view what lay behind Marsea. "And what have we here?"

"That's far enough," Cas trained his blade on Yongrin.

Yongrin's pleasantries faded in an instant. "You dare raise your blade at me, heathen?"

"We're all set here, yeah," he grumbled. "You both can fuck off back to whatever festering shithole you crawled out of."

"You are brash, aren't you?" the magus replied icily. "Honestly. All coarse language aside, I'd be more than happy to oblige, but we've orders, haven't we?"

"Don't care."

"Hand over the girl, Merillion, and we'll be on our merry. What more do you care about a disposable royal wantaway besides?"

"I could ask the same of you."

"Cas," Marsea whispered. Without a doubt, she was horribly miscast by comparison to the rest of this bunch. They each looked dangerous and doubly devious, and she appeared about as harmless as a lost little school-girl, even with a hatchet in hand.

"The girl stays," Casilvieri declared.

"Like hells she does," the knight spat, "this order came directly from Tetherow."

"Then tell Tetherow he can bring his wrinkled old arse out here himself, he wants her so bad. I've got a few things I'd rather like to say to his face, all told."

"The gods know," Yongrin hissed, turning to Davrin, "I swear these Lanier brats are more trouble than a pack of riled wngar."

A fresh volley from beyond awakened the heavens once again, and the magus flicked a wand into her possession, directing it at Casilvieri. It was ivory and thin, mayhaps made of shaved bone or antler, and displayed two distinguishable knuckles in its finger-like shape, one a third of the way down separating the curved grip, and a smaller notch another third down nearer the tip.

The crimson knight unsheathed his sword in unison. "What are you hiding back there, Fiveknives?" he asked. "Whose insides have we splayed out fresh before us here?"

"I daresay, Davrin," Yongrin answered. "It appears our most darling inquisitor has gone turncloak and murdered his liege lord."

Of course, this was going about as poorly as everything else had since the new cycle began. How could it not? Marsea hefted the hatchet up defensively and both Tarborils' eyes hardened at the sight of it.

"Is that?" the knight began.

"It is," the magus answered as she sidestepped to gain a better look at what lay beyond the princess. She trained her wand on Marsea, and her eyes grew wide at what they found.

Nope, wrong again, Marsea. Now they are going about as poorly as everything else had.

"Lower your wand, Yongrin," Casilvieri bade.

"Curie!" the magus snarled. It was the ugliest face Marsea had ever seen beauty make.

And for the thinnest moment, the night went still, moving as though in slow motion. The hauntlings wavered but faintly in the cut of snowfall, the torchlight from the arcade guttered in their sconces, and the last embers of magic yet crackling about the ward's sigil paled to dust. Then another volley, notably fewer in number, kindled the heavens above, and with the loosing, The Hood's dance tossed Alistair's Courtyard into absolute chaos.

Casilvieri sprang to life first. The blade that appeared like magic in his hand only moments before disappeared and reappeared an arm's breadth before the sorceress, forcing Yongrin to snap it away with a flick of her wand, her reaction devastatingly quick. The dagger turned end over end away from her, clattering into the stonework somewhere inside the arcade's shadows. A second longer blade appeared thereafter in Casilvieri's offhand and raced for the knight's throat.

Davrin was keen to the attack and deflected, but just as swiftly, Cas was on him, smashing a vial against the crimson knight's pauldron causing an explosion of smoke.

Marsea remained frozen all the while, straining to map the lunacy of magic thrumming about her and the others, struggling to find a method of usefulness to her mentor, but finding herself hopelessly incapable. The scene flashing around her formed something from a different reality entirely, a reality far beyond her proper comprehension. And Casilvieri's cruel words came back to her at the realization.

In this, the world of magic and combat, she was every measure a housecat amongst strays.

There was a sudden brightness in the obscurity of smoke and snowfall as the mage chanted in a strange devil-sounding language and a coil of magic, like a screaming comet, coursed into the place she knew both Cas and Davrin to be.

What is this? What are we doing? Hadn't there been enough death already?

A second flash cracked into the stonework across from her, and she heard a groan and the ring of steel cry out against its own.

Wasn't there more than enough to come just beyond these walls? Why are we killing each other so needlessly?

As skilled as Cas was, these two would prove too much for him. Marsea knew this in her heart. The spellslinger alone might prove too much. But what help could she possibly offer with an unwieldy hatchet and a bum hand?

What could she possibly do against a knight and a sorceress? How could she be even marginally useful against such practiced adversaries?

Her brain refused to cooperate. She may as well have been half the moon away for all the good she provided. She may as well have been a statue, or a hauntling, or a corpse right alongside Vaustian and Remy and father...

Wake up, girl! her other screamed.

It was her rancorous half, come to rear its ugly head again. Come to convince her she was worth half a shit. Come to keep her head above water. Come to save itself. Her plucky, confident, vengeful half. The half that kept her from stepping off her bedchamber windowsill all those many quints ago. The half that kept her from running a blade down her arms night after night. The half that kept her from downing half the poisons in Old Man Abernathy's apothecary every chance she passed. The half that trains with slitthroats and strikes deals with wandering sellswords. The half that murdered a man in cold blood and tortured another.

The half she was absolutely terrified of...

The half to which she owed every breath she now took...

You have to help him, Marsea. You have to think of something. You can't just let him die. Not like this. You have to do something. If Cas is killed, who knows what may happen next? And she recalled Yongrin's reaction to Rhymona's presence. It was downright disturbing. Mayhaps she was being desperately hopeful in all this, but housecats had their advantages too did they not? *The maidens keep me.* She could still save them all, couldn't she?

Marsea watched in white-faced horror as Cas parried a dig by the knight and spun away, out of the smoke cloud, and into Yongrin's sights.

Do something, Marsea! Anything!

Yongrin took aim. She would not miss this time.

Now or never.

A bead of magic blistered hungrily at the tip of her wand.

Truly, Marsea wanted anything but this. She was utterly terrified of leaving Lancastle. Still. But this was what it had come to, hadn't it? It was her only play. At least the only one that came to her in the time she had. And she had to protect the ones she loved, didn't she? The maidens knew, she'd done her best over the cycles to portray the elder sibling for Remy, but she'd never been much good at it. It turns out surviving middle children proved a rather poor substitute for their first-born counterparts, and doubly so in her case. But maybe, just maybe, this was her chance to finally make things right. If leaving was what it took to save her brother and mentor, and the stars only knew who else from these two dodgy miscreants, then so be it.

Now!

Father, protect me.

"Stop!" the princess howled, closing her eyes and stepping out between Yongrin and the dueling pair.

Her breath held. But her heart beat full.

Amazingly she was still alive. Another beat and her eyes cracked open. She found Yongrin standing before her with an expression of unbridled fascination painted across her face, the tip of her wand still hissing angrily between them.

"I'm going with them," Marsea said, staring the spellslinger straight, releasing Rhymona's hatchet to the snow at her feet.

"Good girl," Yongrin said, her lips quirking up in a vile pink smear.

"They're fucking cockroaches, Marsea," Cas spat.

Marsea turned to her mentor. Casilvieri's hair had come loose from its wrapping, and for the first time since his arrival, he actually looked the part of the heathen she knew him to truly be. Davrin appeared out of breath only a few feet away from him.

"It's my choice," she argued. *And you're losing your mind.* She braved Casilvieri's iron glower longer than she ought. *But they are underestimating you. They always underestimate you.* "If I go, you'll let them be?" she asked Yongrin over her shoulder.

"Of course," the magus agreed, lowering her wand. "Orders are orders, after all."

"All of them." Marsea added, shifting her attentions to Davrin.

"Hand to heart," he said.

"You can't trust Covenant," Cas argued.

And who can I trust anymore? Truly? "I'm doing what I can," she found herself saying. "I'm being useful."

Famous last words.

"However," Yongrin began. "There is but one more matter just now. I'm assuming one of the lot over there is Harver, and I'd venture a guess by your rather unexpected overprotectiveness that the other is your meddlesome brother?"

The princess glanced at the pair of corpses and frowned, the cold cutting her lungs like a knife.

"Your brother took something from us," Yongrin continued as she advanced, "something quite valuable. And we will require its return just as well. Inside the satchel there."

Marsea located the satchel tossed carelessly down in the arcade across from the bundle of bodies. She remembered Rhymona bringing it over with her when she dropped the torch. *What were you doing out there, Remy?* Slowly, Marsea approached it, knelt, and opened it as though some horrible creature lurked inside and might leap out to attack her.

It may not have leapt out at her but indeed nestled there within lay a horrible creature. A black leather-bound tome chained in barbed wire that appeared about as old as the Vael itself. Marsea retrieved it and stood, holding it up for Yongrin to inspect.

"Be a doll, Marsea dear, and bring it along, would you?" the magus ordered, cordial as you please, as she snapped her fingers and the ward's glyph came pulsing back to life followed by its watery portal.

Beyond the rippling mirror-like plane, Marsea could faintly distinguish a large fire-lit chamber on the other side.

Davrin, sword extended at Casilvieri, backed up into the courtyard to meet them at the portal's mouth. "The lady first," he said as he came to her side.

"Marsea, you're making a mistake," Cas called to her as he pursued Davrin into the wintry bluster at a fair distance. "You go through that portal, you're dancing with devils."

"It's what must be done," she said as she gazed over at the bundle of bodies one last time. "Make sure she brings him back."

And without giving her mentor the chance to respond she turned her cheek, crunching forward a step, and once more into the ward and instantly farther away from Lancastle than she had ever been in all her life.

CHAPTER THREE

The princess held her breath as she entered the portal, and after a momentary resistance, she was through it to the other side, as though she had simply passed through any old ordinary open doorway.

Yongrin and Davrin surfaced through behind her, and the ward evaporated, leaving them to a darkness like the night devoid of stars.

Four massive wrought iron braziers blazed in the far corners of the great hall, though despite their size they did little to light the chamber's vast expanse. Initially, the braziers were all she could see, but after a few more deafening heartbeats, her eyes began to adjust to the room's pitch-black submergence. It smelled dank, and she suddenly had the terrifying sensation of being entombed alive. Stalagmites and stalactites rose and hung in jagged rows that resembled the fangs of some colossal beast. Tiny noises like dripping water and creeping critters echoed hither and yon. But still the place lacked most manner of proper definition. Truly, they could be anywhere. The highlands. The southern shores. The Morrigar Mountains. Beyond The Scar. Anywhere.

Anywhere but where she had always been.

Marsea remembered the first time she walked outside Lancastle's kingdom walls, clinging to Vaustian's arm like some poor frightened child, her heartbeats thundering with violent excitement inside her chest, her breath clouds erratic and wanting, her body tense as a board under layers of leather and fur skin, every slight sound a potential danger, the pastel morning sunlight clawing between the sea of rimy spruces and pines in bright pink slivers and patches.

"Leave us," a voice spoke from seemingly all around her, racing along the walls, cascading into the far, esoteric yonder. It was how she imagined a god might sound. And nothing at all like the image of the quaint little stroll she and Vaustian had taken that tranquil morn last new cycle's eve.

She heard Yongrin and Davrin shift away without a word, their steps echoing long into the formless dark behind her.

In their absence, the braziers' flames gradually intensified, rising high above their cinders, impossibly high, bringing the chamber into a fiery, phantasmagorical glimmer. Marsea's eyes flickered about like those of a wild animal until enough light filtered through to bring some measure of clarity to her surroundings—though the clarity the towering flames restored brought little comfort to her nerves.

In the distance before her arose a series of steps to a throne every measure as impressive as the vast hall that housed it. Marsea's jaw lowered. The maidens knew, it put the throne of Lancastle to utter shame. It was cut into a massive stalagmite that hooked forward, high over the seat, in the form of a harpy's talon. A hunched figure stood before it upon the top stair watching her.

"It's been a long time coming, Marsea," the figure greeted.

He was already being far too familiar, but any manner of response she might have had, whether defensive or proper, jammed right up in her throat. The Lanier princess found herself stuck somewhere twixt petrification and awe. And with the way he condescended to Yongrin and Davrin without contest, she had little doubt of his standing. He had to be one of the masters. He simply had to be. There was no two ways about it. His aura emanated, almost like a lightning storm, practically drinking all the air from the chamber.

"You are no doubt wondering who I am," he continued. "And why I am being so forthright."

"You are Malthus Tetherow, are you not?" Marsea dared, clutching the grimoire tight to her chest. Vaustian had described him to her during one of their midnight meetings some months past, though admittedly even he had never seen Tetherow's true appearance before. It was said Tetherow rarely left the shadows, and when he did, he wore a mask to spoil any study into his identity. The rumors were countless as to the purpose behind the masquerade.

"I am what is left of him," the figure said as he descended the steps toward her.

He was quite tall and strapping, but walked queerly, with a bit of a slumping limp, not unlike Pion. Though he did not stagger a cane, nor did he strike her as being crippled. Rather, his hobbling appeared to be the result of a freshly found injury. Marsea couldn't help but wonder what could possibly bring harm to such a daunting presence as was this fellow. Normally she might have offered assistance, but she didn't dare risk offending him. Instead, she remained perfectly still, her tongue pressed firmly against the insides of her clenched teeth.

As he neared, she found beneath his cowl that his entire face was wrapped in linens. It seized her breath for a beat. And the memory of her father came flooding back over her, his mutilated face masked beneath similar wrappings, his battered body barely able to stand under its own power.

But this version could talk. And this one still had eyes between the gaps of bandaging.

Tetherow halted three steps away, and his head tilted in consideration of her. "There is no need for you to fear me, Marsea," he said. "This place is a temple for folk like us."

Folk like us? "And what manner of folk am I, pray tell?"

"A dangerous question, that." The lower half of his bandages shifted into something Marsea took for a grin. "Take no offense in the coming words, but you are quite obviously an outcast. Woefully misunderstood." He descended another step. "Taken advantage of." Another step. "Overlooked. Underestimated." She could see his eyes perfectly now. They showed a strange, mystical shade of violet, like fully bloomed wisteria. "To come from everything and yet have nothing. It is a path I too share some familiarity with. And, so what do you do?"

And the question hovered between them as though a mist in a glen.

"You make yourself invisible, don't you?" he said to the wandering silence. "Small as a pebble. Insignificant. But even still you cannot snuff it out completely, can you? That voice. That curiosity. That power simmering inside you. That undeniable understanding that you are meant for something far greater than what has presently found you." He stepped down onto level ground with her and shuffled past. He was one of the tallest men she had ever seen. Taller than Bromas Aldridge. Taller than Vaustian and Gan. Taller than even Raelan. True, she was shorter than most folk fully grown, but even with him noticeably hunched over she barely reached his shoulders. "That's your father's work there."

My father?

"Your father understood. Far too well."

"You knew my father?" She followed behind his plodding, delicate as a petal on the wind.

"I did. Whit Lanier was one of my brightest students," he returned. "Of course, this harkens back many cycles. As I recall, he was around your age when we first met. I daresay, you quite remind me of him."

"I do?"

"Oh, yes. You are just as inquisitive, anyway. I can already see that much. Your father was a sponge. Always reading, always thinking, always pushing his mind. If you want my personal opinion, his manner of brilliance was rather wasted on a kingship. He was far better suited for the academics. He would have made for a remarkable professor, or better yet a physicist or alchemist. Though, it would seem, for some, they are only what the world allows them to be." Tetherow cleared his throat. "But I digress. Verily, I did not invite you here to reminisce about your father's accomplishments. Make no mistake, princess, you are here because of your own efforts."

The great hall led to a long, twisting, torch-lit passageway. They passed a handful of unusual closed doorways as they progressed. Behind one she could hear grunts and the sounds of iron clashing. From another, within the slivers of space surrounding the crude wooden door shone a bright, unnatural, cerulean glow. The passageway became narrower the further they traversed until it opened up to another large, sparsely furnished chamber that itself opened to an overlook of the countryside.

A murky shade of winter starlight spilled across the floor.

Tetherow closed the door behind them.

The wind howled, and Marsea hastily crossed the room to gain a clearer view of her whereabouts. She discovered they were high upon a mountainside. If she weren't utterly terrified of her present situation, she might have even found the spectacle breathtaking. Furious Ashira had made something of a gibbous moon of her corpulent sister Y'dema, but Marsea could still make out a river in the starglow, and the lights of a dozen some odd dwellings, and leagues upon leagues of blackened wood-lands beyond that. It was not so much different than the view from her bedchamber back in Lancastle—it felt just as isolated, anyway.

"Where are we?" she asked.

"The township you see below is named Vinth," Tetherow answered as he poured a bright green liquid into a pair of goblets at a stone platform in the chamber's corner.

Vinth? This meant she was still in the highlands and only a few days travel south of Lancastle by horseback. Or so Vaustian had once told her.

Marsea watched Tetherow as he took a taste from one of the goblets.

"Marsea," he began with an easy lilt a heartbeat later, "where is Vaustian?"

The princess stared at him as though stricken and swallowed hard. The answer couldn't have been more obvious.

"I see," he said before taking another slow, deliberate sip. If he was surprised at all by her reaction, he certainly didn't show it. "And was it you?" He took up the second goblet and approached her. "I wouldn't blame you if it was. It seems only fair, after all." He offered the goblet.

And for the first time since her arrival, Marsea lowered the grimoire from her chest. It was only then that she realized just how hard she had been clutching it, and she winced as a pair of barbs came away from the skin beneath her shirt. She took up the goblet in her good hand.

It seems only fair?

She wanted to slug him. She wanted to scream. She wanted to grab him by his ugly yellow robes and thrust him over the balcony balustrade. "I loved him," she said instead and chased it with a swallow from her goblet. It tasted like licorice.

"Did you now?"

"'Twas an ashaeydir that killed him, if you must know."

"An ashaeydir?"

Had she actually surprised him with that one?

"He was protecting me," she lied, recalling their last moments together. Vaustian knew he had done something she would never forgive him for. She could see it in his eyes. The guilt and regret. And maybe he was set to explain himself before Rhymona intervened, but she found out soon enough anyway, hadn't she?

"Is that his blood you have on you there?"

She glanced down at the smears and splotches of red now dried upon her shirt, jacket, and trousers. It hadn't registered in the frenzy that was Alistair's Courtyard, but she looked an absolute shambles, like some disfavored poppet out of a hearthfire haunter.

To think only an hour ago she'd been in her bedchamber pulling Remy's old hunting jacket on, judging the quality of its cut in her vanity mirror. How naïve she had been even then.

She brought the goblet's rim to her teeth and inched it up so that the absinthium slowly trickled into her mouth.

Of course, she had been planning to tell Vaustian the truth. That she had no intentions of leaving Lancastle despite the encroaching dangers. That she had no desire to join Ravenholme. That she would refuse the trials. If only she hadn't dallied so long getting ready. If only she hadn't become so lost in finding the right words. She focused on the contents of her cup as it fastly dwindled to nothing. If only she had known about Remy's return. If only she had found him first. If only...If only...If only...

"No matter," Tetherow said in lieu of awkward silence, "Vaustian was a pawn. For all of his promise. All of his precision. All of his bravado. It was all a front. A fool's charade. A delusion he convinced himself of." Marsea thought the words unnecessarily cold. "My apprentice was a clever tactician, mind you, and an equally skilled swordsman, but he was also quite prideful, Midaran to a fault at that, and he made the mistake of relying too keenly on those gifts. You may not want to hear the words just now given your affections, but let Vaustian's indiscretions act as a lesson, Marsea. In the end, preparation and talent only go so far. I warned him of such arrogance on numerous occasions. That there are things in this world one cannot prepare for. Little fragments of minutiae that slip through the cracks."

Hard words. Heartless words. But that did not make them any less true.

Even still, anger coiled itself upon her tongue ready to strike.

"What is the old saying about the flame that burns twice as bright?" he asked.

Her Uncle Rho came to call. And Marsea stayed vigilant in spite of her growing crossness. "It only lasts half as long." Her answer came as a dry whisper.

Tetherow nodded. "And so it does. And you should prize just as well, those two self-serving lickspittles you came here with, they are no different. They are parasites just the same. Glory hounds. Carrion crows. Vermin. Less than vermin. And they won't hesitate to put you in the ground if it means gaining another notch in the pecking rung."

A litany of questions immediately began to form at the fore of Marsea's stream of consciousness, but her head suddenly felt like it was spinning and she found she couldn't quite focus her vision. The shadows dimmed and drew ever closer. "Oh my," she uttered as she listed forward, her legs like jelly.

"I've got you," Tetherow said as she sank into his chest.

"What's happening...?"

"The feeling will pass," Tetherow assured. "It is the effects of the ward catching up to you. Puddle-jumping usually takes some experience getting used to. All told, I was surprised it had taken this long to sink its teeth in. Though I suppose it speaks to the nature of your abilities, doesn't it?"

"My abilities?" Marsea could smell the forest on his robes and feel the sinewy shape underneath as he eased her into a chair at the table.

The taste of candy licorice fattened along the walls of her mouth and expanded down her throat as she breathed it in and out. Her eyes closed and she explored the blank space behind her eyelids following a tiny green spot that fluttered this way and that.

Breathe in, breathe out.

Time folded in on itself.

Breathe in, breathe out.

When she opened her eyes again, she found Tetherow sitting across from her. He had removed his cowl and was lighting a candelabrum at the table's edge with a marble-sized cerulean flame formed at the tip of his index finger.

Breathe in, breathe out.

Her head tilted to the side and the table seemed to stretch on and on away from them until it smashed into the chamber door that appeared an eternity away from her grasp. She just stared at it for a beat, trying to comprehend the impossible distance.

Breathe in, breathe out.

Rhythmic movement drew her fuzzy attentions back to Tetherow, and she found him unwinding the bandages from around his face.

He was y'deman. But, of course, she had known that. Malthus Tetherow was arguably one of the most fabled y'deman figures to ever grace the annals of Midaran history. His long, pointy ears still somehow took her by surprise, one considerably shorter than the other, having taken some manner of ghastly trauma beforehand that left it misshapen by mounds of scar tissue.

The scar on her upper lip itched at the sight of his deformities.

Breathe in.

Quickly, it became clear why he chose to hide his visage. His face shown a mangle of shifted bones, burn marks, lumps, bruises, scar lines, and scabs that made her bad hand look like a holiday by comparison. Their severity had rendered the original shape underneath nearly unrecognizable.

Breathe out.

Tetherow drew a fresh sip from his goblet and shifted into the candle-light to face her directly.

She knew it was bad form, but Marsea refused to turn away from him. He appeared like one of the grotesque creatures described in one of Ingrid Ashmead's Penny Horror tales. But the maidens knew, did that somehow make her the damsel in all of this? She thought of all the damsels in those chilling tales, Princess Prue from *Widow Bride and the Hungry God*, Nancy Moon from *A Tale Half Told*, Tanil Thomasyn from *Heretic Harvest*, each one of them more helpless than the last. *The stars save me, I hope not.* By one fashion or another, it usually ended poorly for the heroine in those stories.

"I hope you don't mind," he said.

"I don't."

The grimoire lay between them. It bore a bitter and dangerous aura, doubly cursed under the rippling cast of firelight.

"And here it is. Right on schedule." Tetherow turned up his goblet, took another swallow, and set it back down in the exact same spot. The dark gash across the bridge of his nose began to ooze a black ichorous fluid between fresh fissures in the crusting.

It was painful to take in.

Marsea winced. She had never seen anything like it before. For certain, it looked like nothing that should be leaking from a living being. "Does it hurt?" she couldn't help but ask.

"Not presently. It's more of an annoyance than anything else." He dabbed the end of a bandage against the inky trail seeping down the crease of his nose.

"I hope you do not think me rude in asking, but what is it exactly?"

"To the contrary, I'd think you a fool if you didn't ask," he replied, holding the cloth to the gash. "It is an infection. Nether-rot. It's eating my leg away too."

"How did you become infected?"

"No, Marsea," he removed the cloth and regarded her with a piercing expression. Though, truth be told, the ghastly state of his face, it was nearly impossible to judge any of his expressions with any measure of accuracy. "This is not how we begin. The gods know, you remind me so much of your father. Always leaping ahead. Head over heart. Caution cast heedlessly to the wind. Too curious for your own good. First things first, if we're to begin on quality terms, you should properly know who you are speaking with, wouldn't you agree?"

"Well, I..." *What?* "Yes, of course. I only thought—"

"You thought *I* was Malthus Tetherow," he finished, sharp as bladed obsidian. "Suffice it to say, I am not he. At least not in the manner you believe me to be. Though I meant it in earnest when I told you I am what is left of him. What is left of his teachings, anyway. I will explain all of this in due time, of this I promise, but for now, I hope you can accept this for truth."

Marsea didn't move an inch. She remained keenly fixed on her strange host that only grew stranger by the minute.

"My true name is Elsymir Beldroth."

The hairs rose on the back of her neck and a shiver forced a crooked path down the length of her body from shoulders to toes as a series of words, words she had recited a thousand, thousand times before, snapped into place.

Frayed are the threads that cast shadows. Lush is the drear in their unforgiving wake.

Instantly the pages of her father's *Kingstome* came back to her as though they lay right there before her, as though she were tucked away inside the cramped candlelit stacks of The Cupboard once more. And her mind paused on one particular page about midway through. Marsea had always thought that page quite peculiar by comparison to the rest. It was one of the only pages devoid of an ascribed date or any additional context. And it was the only page written in modern Midaran script, scrawled hastily as though it had been jotted without proper time for structure. Unquestionably, it was authored in the style of her father's hand, though it lacked the concentrated perfection that comprised his typical form.

It read as:

> *Elsymir Beldroth x Malthus Tetherow.*
> *The faceless man. The man of a thousand faces.*
> *The Master. The Apprentice.*
> *The Stranger. The Whisperer in the Wood. The King in Amber.*
> *The Wandering Madness.*
> *Of She Who Dawns the Endless Night.*

"You were the one in Lancastle this morning," Marsea uttered; her voice woefully scratchy. And just as she spoke the words, she became aware of a third presence in the chamber peeling away from the shadows behind her. The maidens know, but it was ungodly large.

Breath choked up inside her.

"*Broenwjar, thae quolo ma,*" said Elsymir Beldroth.

Stiff as a stone, Marsea glared at Beldroth, her eyes wide as the sister moons and shimmering with undisguisable fear.

"Broenwjar is my familiar," Beldroth explained. "I assure you he will not bring you harm."

Marsea felt an immense weight lingering directly behind her and then its hot breath upon her shoulder before its snout arrived beside her followed by its massive head. Slowly she turned to take it in. It appeared like a wolf, but it was significantly bigger than any wolf she had ever heard of. Its fur was mostly black, but there were hints of gray in places marking the beast's age. The eye that faced her was scabbed over from injury and clouded with cataract. Similar to Beldroth, it too reeked of forest and snowfall and some bit of animal savagery. It lowered itself into a sitting position just inches away from her and somehow topped her height.

"I think you've made yourself a new friend," Beldroth said as he stood, goblet in hand. "Care for another?"

"N-no, thank you," Marsea managed.

"There's cider wine, Old Crow..."

"No, that's quite all right."

"Very well," Beldroth hobbled across the chamber to the tonic table. "And so now you have my true name," he said as he poured a fresh cup. "You are the only one, Marsea. The rest yet believe me both. Yongrin, Davrin, all of them. And I'd rather like to keep it that way for the time being. Savvy?"

"Savvy," Marsea echoed.

"And yes, to answer your question, I was in Lancastle earlier. I tried to warn your people. Of course, Vaustian was already aware, but I thought I might try to give the rest a fighting chance. We are all running short of time now. And we're all in this thing together like it or not."

Broenwjar shifted toward her, lowering his head, and nudged his big, nightmarish snout against her arm before resting his chin in her lap. Marsea let him have his way without complaint, though, honestly, she didn't feel she had much choice in the matter. As big as he was, he could've had her in pieces at a moment's count.

"Hmm, how about that? I would say he definitely approves of you." Beldroth eased back into his creaky old chair. "Old Boy has a soft spot for the fairer sex. Always has."

Riding the fade of her unraveling nerves, Marsea lifted her bad hand and grazed it gently over Broenwjar's long dark mane before allowing her remaining fingers to wander into the depths of his fur down to his skin. His hair was thick and coarse and his body scabbed and bumpy. She actually felt sympathy for him in that moment. She hated that he should have to live such a rough life.

"I'm curious, Marsea. You have knowledge of Covenant affairs, but I wonder, are you familiar with the Oathsworn as well?"

"I've heard the name in passing," Marsea replied. "I know my uncle had some business with them before."

"I should say so. Your uncle *is* one of them," Beldroth said. "And do you know what the Oathsworn are? What they represent?"

Marsea shook her head, trailing her hand down the back of Broenw-jar's long, muscular neck. She found an unexpected comfort forming within the beast's friendly company.

"They are the protectors of this side."

Her hand paused just below one of Broenwjar's great pointed ears.

"There are two worlds that inhabit the shell of this moon. The one you know. The surface world, we'll name it. The one created by the gods or whatever daft happenstance that occurred millennia ago to bring us forth to this most grisly chapter. And then there's the darkness we bought. The foul, twisted reflection created twixt the gaps of our shameful, depraved evolution. The one that exists because of our neglect and greed. The one the dracari tried to warn us about an age ago before your ancestors revolted and brought about The Dragonsfall. The one responsible for this shit here," he motioned to the wound across his nose. "There have been those of us that have tried to keep the other world at bay, and we are named as the Order of the Oathsworn. But our numbers are dwindled to the throes of extinction. One of our own has betrayed his oath in service of a new master and now hunts those of us that remain."

"Tetherow," Marsea said.

"Tetherow," the name was now spoken with utter contempt. "He was once my mentor— many cycles past. Before the ashaeydir invasion. Before even the Southland secession. But in the end, Malthus and I did not see eye to eye. He became obsessed with the other side—with soul magic. Black magic, as the Ministry names it. He believed it a far more powerful form of the gift in comparison to blood conjuring. And so, his continuous dark-dabbling perverted him, scrambling his mores, and with every sacrifice turned him further against his proper nature. And it wasn't long after that that he abandoned his own teachings and abandoned me just the same." Beldroth turned up his goblet. "Some months later I finally worked up the stones to confront him about it, though by this time I hardly recognized him any longer. His appearance had altered to match the many dark deeds he had committed since our last meeting and he drew his wand on me at the slightest opposition. He gave me no other choice but to defend myself. And, so it was that I drew upon him, and with more than a little favor in stow, I bested my mentor. Only…"

"He didn't die, did he?"

'Twas but a fair few cycles ago that Marsea had fallen into a period of

33

giftborn obsession and thusly gobbled up every page Lancastle's library had to offer on the subject, and though there were scant few accounts of necromancy to be had amidst the bunch, she found enough morsels to cobble together something of a rudimentary understanding.

"He did not," Beldroth grumbled, glancing into the flames of the candelabrum. "I killed the body, but by this time his body was merely that —a vessel, a temporary skin. His soul persisted elsewhere."

"He forged himself a phylactery," Marsea said, nudging her glasses back up to a more comfortable placement, bumping her elbow against Broenwjar's noggin in the process. Somehow, she had momentarily forgotten he was still there. "Sorry, love," she found herself saying in response, though it didn't appear to bother him in the slightest.

"I think it began as that, yes," Beldroth replied, offering an arched eyebrow. "Color me impressed."

"I'm not a complete simp, you know." *Good gravy, Marsea!* Had she truly just said that? Apparently, the beast's company had made her a mite too comfortable and doubly bold. "Father rather had a fascination with soul magic as well," she added in recovery.

"Mmm. You found his hideaway, I take it?"

He knows of The Cupboard? The skeletons are endless with this one, aren't they? "My older brother Desmond once showed me when we were little," she confessed.

"I suppose I shouldn't be too surprised, now should I? Your father knew of my studies into the like. And he knew of my past with Malthus."

"Was father an Oathsworn too?"

"He was not. The objective of the Order was to operate in the shadows, unswayed by politics, capitalism, and public opinion. Such would have been a difficult task for even the noblest of kings, wouldn't you agree?"

"I suppose."

"He was never far from us though. He named his Hand, your uncle, to the post in his place. And there was scarce a secret kept between those two."

Oh, what I would give to have Uncle Rho at my side just now, she thought.

"There was a time when our ranks were many, generations ago, but now there are only a handful of us left. And the two worlds are beginning to merge. It's all so much bigger than the Oathsworn now. Vaelsyntheria as we know her is changing. The old rules, the rules of our ancestors, no longer apply. Mortal will means next to nothing in the world to come. Hope is a fantasy. Escape is an illusion. And the more you try to fight that truth the more it will take. The dead are a reminder of this. They show us for what we really are. A blight. A curse. A malady on this land. And yet—"

He stole another swallow from his goblet.

Marsea glanced at her own, rather wishing she had taken him up on his offer of cider wine. Hells, at this juncture, she might even stomach a dram or two of Old Crow.

"We must find a way. We must endure. We must adapt. You must adapt, Marsea. Very soon you will have to choose a side in all this. We all will. Or we'll have it chosen for us. It is for this very reason that I have invited you here. You have a unique position in all of this. You are born of the old blood, the royal blood, the purest blood left on this moon. This means that you carry weight in what's to come. Your namesake carries weight."

"You mean the namesake that's been dragged through the mud and spat at since I was in nursery?"

"It's no secret you and your kin have been spurned by the fates. I won't deny you that. But you've got to put the past behind you now. You've got to rise above the tavern songs and the barmy gossipmongers looking to drag you down on their level. It's all useless chuffa in the end, isn't it? Not a mite of it will matter in what's to come. And that's a bloody promise. Folk know the name Lanier, and desperate times are coming. And in desperate times, folk are always looking for a savior—a leader to step up and take the reins—a voice to follow."

"And you believe that's me?"

"I believe it can be you."

"I'm no savior, sir. I'll tell you that right out. I can't even save myself from captivity inside my own family's court—"

"Stop right there." He held her gaze, eyes hard as gravestone. "No more of that now. No more naysaying. No more doubting. That rot went out the window the moment you stepped foot through Yongrin's ward and into this place. Is that understood?"

"Yes." *Maiden's mercy, another fresh scolding?*

35

"You don't think near well enough of yourself, Marsea. And you mistake your own merit."

"Well, you'll have to forgive me in that. For I've beheld more than enough of what happens to those that think too well of themselves."

"I suppose you have. But that was before. Here, you define who you are. Not them. You *were* a royal once. You *were* a victim. Once. You *were* a captive. Once. You have been humbled by these circumstances. But, of course, you have. You're only human. Who wouldn't be, fettered to the throne of a thieving maniac for as long as you were? But because of these cards, you also have an understanding of what it means to be both highborn and low, concurrently no less. It is an understanding very few are ever granted access to. Now you must choose who *you* want to be. You are free here, Marsea. You are free to decide. I won't force you to do anything you don't want to do. You can walk away from this if that is your wish. But know there is great potential in you. Just like your father and your father's father and on and on across the Lanier line before you. You house the maker's ichor inside you, which makes you quite powerful. More powerful than most if properly tended. Powerful enough to make a difference even in the darkest of times."

"Pardon my ignorance, but I've never heard this term before. The maker's ichor..."

"It is the blood of the gods," he expounded. "The gift doesn't come from study or skill as the Ministry would have you believe. True, they both help as with all things, but they are not the source of its potency. The gift comes from within." He drew a fist to his chest. "There is this misconception that you're either born with it or you're not, but that is all Ministry propaganda. The highborn can't have everyone believing they are special, now can they? They can't have everyone believing they can become something. There's only so much room at the top, after all. Only so many shelters to beg under. Only so much food and drink for all the mouths." He scoffed. "But the truth is we are all born with it. We are all wells for it. And we all have different triggers to untangle that which lies within. For some, it is manifested by love or faith. For others, it might be pain and loss, or abandonment. For many, it resides just beneath the surface, ready to expel itself upon the world at the softest spark. But there are those for which it resides deep within. Those that would necessitate the direst of scenarios to draw it forth. And then of course there are the scabs. Charlatans, that require the assistance of an outside source to bring it to fruition."

"You refer to blood candles and wax bags?"

"Something of the like," Beldroth replied, a certain measure of irritation in his tone. "Blood candles are about the worst of it, if you want my opinion. They are a most heinous perversion of the gift. I'm sure you've heard the term warlock before?"

"Of course." And, indeed, she had. All the old tales had them.

"And do you know what they are? Truly? Not the ridiculous storybook parodies, but the real thing? Do you know what they do?"

"I believe so," she answered, though his sudden hostility certainly made room for pause. "I know they practice the sort of magic that is greatly frowned upon by the Ministry."

"Frowned upon by the Ministry," he muttered. "The Ministry frowns upon anyone and anything that takes coin away from their bloody coffers. Warlocks are betrayers of their own kind is what they are. Oath breakers. Corpse-rats. Giftborn that hunt other giftborn. Some for sport and trophy, but most for trade and a habit of their own making. They murder those housing high contents of magic in their bloodstream, exsanguinating them, and then they bottle the drained lifeblood to either consume or barter. And the chandlers and apothecaries have only made the market that much more rampant over the cycles. Fashioning waxes and oils and elixirs from the supply and exploiting the effects of its addiction. It's absolutely deplorable. All of it.

"But you—you should never have this hindrance, Marsea. You are blessed by the Masters' seed. You have the maker's ichor pumping through your veins. Your gift is as pure as magic comes this day and age. You only need to find your trigger to unleash it."

"And how do I do that?"

"No doubt you've experienced something of it before. Only you didn't know what it was. Most describe it as a voice in the back of their head, a voice that wants to guide, prepare, and protect."

Other. She could almost hear its fiendish cant now.

"I can see by your reaction you have. You must go deeper into this. You must ask yourself the proper questions. When have you heard it? What was happening? How did it sound? What did it say?"

"I thought it was a demon at first." Her eyes flickered tungsten horror.

"Or some sort of hauntling whispering about just over my shoulder. Then I thought I was suffering some bout of sickness. I thought I was going mad."

"You're not going mad, Marsea, I assure you. That voice, it is your gift calling to you. I know it goes against everything the world has taught you about what is proper. But that's all Ministry conditioning. Control tactics. Highborn rubbish. You should try listening to the voice, even if it sounds like The Hood itself. Now try to remember. What did it want? What did it say when it spoke to you?"

"Little things." Her heartbeat began to hasten. "And it was always condescending." Mistress Veranski's dance lessons came to mind. "Like a strict classroom tutor." Her breathing became heavier, and a sudden razor-sharp pang surged across the arches of her feet.

"Good. You're on to it now. Go with this. Slow your breathing." His eyes flitted down to the beast. *"Broen, vasjte po mai."*

The wolf slowly lifted his head from her lap, gave her one last doe-eyed glance, and padded away into the shadows.

"Now, loosen yourself," Beldroth said. "Sit upright, arms on your lap, and try to relax your shoulders as much as possible."

The princess obeyed.

"You will want to breathe in through the nose. Long, slow inhalations. Hold it in for a three count. Then out through the mouth, equally as slow. Concentrate only on the process of breathing, on the air going in and leaving, nothing but the process itself. In through the nose, out through the mouth."

In through the nose.

Her eyes shifted from Beldroth to the candelabrum's flames.

Out through the mouth.

In. One. Two. Three.

"You're doing great. Now when you're ready close your eyes."

Out. One. Two. Three.

And the world went dark behind her closed eyelids. *Head in the breeze, heart on the sleeve.* Though, she supposed, if Beldroth meant her any harm, it would have certainly come by now.

In.

"Are you comfortable?" he asked.

"Almost never," she breathed out.

"I can appreciate the candor," he said. Marsea sensed an unexpected amusement in his response. "Just follow your gut."

In. One. Two. Three.

"Visualize the place you are most at peace."

Out. One, two, three.

"Now, where are you? What do you hear?"

In.

"I hear..." It was a gentle, fluidic motion, accompanied by the sounds of swelling and contracting. *Waves.* "...the ocean." And the darkness began to melt away around her like tears of paint running down a canvas revealing her endless internal ocean. It glistened brilliantly in the pale astral starlight above. She drifted about in a circle, taking in her surroundings, searching the starry heavens. "It runs as far as the eye can see," she whispered, "in every direction."

"Good. Concentrate on the song within. Let it resonate." Beldroth's voice was distorted, as though spoken from the ocean's depths beneath her. "Center on the last time you heard it. What is the last thing you remember the voice telling you to do?"

A strange tingling sensation joined the ocean's soothing ebb, and she gave all her focus to it. "It was always pushing me forward. Whenever I got scared."

She could hear something in the distance. A humming sound. Faint and ethereal. Barely there at all. But decidedly female.

"Whenever it got to be too much. That's when it would find me."

"And what did it tell you?"

"It told me..." Marsea listened closer. *I know this song. How do I know this song?* "It told me whatever I needed to hear to keep going, whatever it took to keep me alive. It's the reason I came here. The reason I..."

"What is it?"

"I can't..."

"Marsea?"

"I can't move," she gasped. And her breath held.

"Stay calm. Stay focused. Tell me what you see?"

"Someone else is here," she uttered, as a blackened humanoid silhouette appeared against the horizon, its shape crouched atop the ocean's surface, bent down on all fours like a mongrel, its body and movements snapping and contorting about in a most unnatural manner. "Oh no," Marsea gasped, her limbs still numb and unresponsive.

"What's happening?"

"It sees me," she rasped, though try as she might to move away, she found she could not. She stuck firm, like prey in a spider's web, squirming in vain. Pathetic squirming. Useless squirming. She couldn't even open her eyes from it. The creature's presence had somehow taken control of her.

"Keep talking, Marsea. You have to keep talking."

"It's coming toward me," she answered. "I...I can't move. It won't let me."

"Yes, you can. You can do anything it can do."

"How?"

"You must accept it. You must accept that part of you."

"I don't understand. What part of me? What does it want?"

"It wants you to stop running."

"It's almost here!" *The stars save me!*

"Accept it, Marsea."

"I can't," she whimpered. The thing was choking the life from her with every inch it neared.

"It won't hurt you, Marsea. It only wants to be let out."

"Let out? What does that mean?"

"Let it out, Marsea."

"No! I can't!"

"You must!"

"Father, help me!" Marsea cried out and her eyes burst open, like waking from a nightmare. Skin damp, her heart thundered, and her muscles ached, and her throat felt raw and bruised as though someone had tried to strangle her to death.

"Maiden's mercy..." she panted, nearly breathless.

"You're all right, Marsea," Beldroth said. "You're all right. You did well."

"I did well? Are you mad? What the hells just happened to me?" The tears would not be denied this time; slow, fat crawlers cycles in the making.

"Just breathe—"

"What was that thing?"

"It's never what we expect it to be, is it?" His voice was vexingly calm.

"It? I saw *Its* face behind the sludge and the hair." She managed between gasps of breath. "It looked like me."

"Because it is you, Marsea—a part of you at least."

"But the way it moved."

"Your gift is feral."

"My...what? Feral? What do you mean feral?"

"It happens. I have seen it before, numerous times, in fact."

"Yeah? And what does it mean exactly?"

"Take no offense in this. It harkens back to our most base nature as survivalist creatures. We can lie to ourselves all we like, but we can't hide from our own natural instinct, can we? And if there is any one part of us the gift is tied to, it's our natural instincts. Dress it up all you like with posh bedchambers and fancy meals, but we're all animals in the end, aren't we? A cage is a cage is a bloody cage and that is where you've lived all of your life. You have been oppressed all of your life, Marsea. And what's worse is you've been made to believe that you haven't by the folks that were supposed to love you the most."

Suddenly, the slow, fat crawlers transformed into free-flowing rivers. To hear someone else speak on her life in such a brazen manner. To hear the truth of it all 'twas quite overwhelming, indeed.

"You've had to live inside this bubble, this delicate façade, with enemies you could not hope to defeat, much less understand, where you were taught disobedience could mean pain, the suffering of others, or even death. So, you did what you had to, didn't you? What you thought was right. You did what your mind told you. But your heart was not so forgiving, was it? It knew something was deeply, horribly wrong. And it's been my experience, in differences between the head and the heart, for better or worse, the gift will always fall on the side of the heart." He glanced over to the balcony, out into the nightfall. "And so now, this part of you that has been locked away and neglected for cycles, only peering out in bits and pieces, has finally begun to show itself, because you are finally in a place to listen. But you must understand it has lived inside your fear for as long as it's been sequestered. It has lived with your anger and your resentment and your despair and has taken on the image of those personality fragments."

Marsea removed her glasses and wiped the tears away as best she could.

"Honestly, all things considered, you did quite well for your first attempt."

"My first attempt?"

Beldroth turned back to her and she could almost make out an actual expression in the ruin of flesh.

"You want to become better. You want to rid yourself of how you feel right now, of all the hesitation and helplessness. You will need to accept her."

"You don't understand."

"But I do. All too well, mind you. Just as she is half a thing, so too are you. And pushing her away will not make you whole. To the contrary, a gift as powerful as yours left to the rot like it is will only grow more and more volatile."

"But she is a monster. A killer. And that's not me. That's not who I want to be."

"No, Marsea. You have it wrong. You have said it yourself. The things she has done. The dark deeds. They were to keep you going. They were always to aid you. You must understand. The gift will do anything to protect its host. Anything. As I said before, it is bound to the heart...to your natural instinct...to a part of you that cannot be ignored or willed away. But it can be reasoned with, and it can be reshaped and forged anew if tended to properly. There can be balance between the head and the heart.

"I can help you with this, Marsea. I can help you repair the split. I can prepare you for what is to come. I can help you adapt to the world outside of Lancastle. I can help you reach your gift. And I can help guide you back to some semblance of your true self."

"And why in all the moons would you offer this to me?" Her voice was sloppy inside the swell of emotions, but in the least, she wasn't blubbering. "What do you ask in return for such charities?"

"As I've said, the old guard is fallen. And I am not long for this world. This infection will consume my body and scruples sooner rather than later, just as it did Malthus, and my legacy will become forgotten like yesterday's breakfast. But I made a promise once. A promise that I foolishly turned a blind eye to. Chased with a betrayal that I can never make fully right." His eyes lightened. "But the gods be merciful, with the days I have left, I can certainly try. I only ask that should you give my charity a chance, you take it seriously and you put the lessons to quality use, to good use, to survive and to help others when able."

The maidens know, what have you gotten yourself into, Marsea? She couldn't imagine how mad her face looked just now, stained with dirt and blood and tears and the maidens only knew what else, but her answer had been a long, long turn in the telling.

Far too long.

From some rest deep within, Other echoed the sentiment. **I will not let my past define me**.

"And so, I ask you plainly, princess. What's a doddering old fool's charity worth to you?"

CHAPTER FOUR

S he could taste the adrenaline in the back of her mouth as she gasped back to life.

Fuck. Not adrenaline.

Fuck all. Not adrenaline at all.

Rhymona wilted away, collapsing onto her side, the snow-dusted stones beneath greeting her hard as a driving fist as she felt the tickle of something crawling upward inside her throat. A coughing fit swiftly spiraled into dry-heaving as she crawled forward, trying to regain some measure of composure.

The fuck?

And before she could even think to somewhat comprehend the source of the burning sensation inside her chest, her stomach cramped up, contracted, and a clump of muddy black bile surged up out of her like one of old Grandpa's nasty ass hairballs. (The gods only know how she missed that furry little fuckhead).

"Scraps?" a voice called from behind her.

A familiar haunt, she thought, *face down on the floor.* She lay there staring at the puddle of foamy black sick before her, crimson bubbles like spider eyes blinking up at her as the bile squealed in agony and withered to ash.

"Bloody hell." She heard a second voice.

Toff.

Reality settled in, constricting about her neck, taut as a hangman's noose.

"Scraps," the first voice echoed as it knelt beside her and placed a hand on her arm.

She glanced up at him, and her watery eyes grew wide. "Rill?" She could never forget that ugly mug, no matter what shade it took.

"Small fucking world, yeah," he grumbled. "Casilvieri in the courts, then."

"Curie," she said, forcing herself to sit up, wiping slobber and sick from her face with the back of an arm.

"I heard," he said glancing at Remy as the princeling lifted Harver's corpse off his lap. "Got yourself in a lovely little shitshow here. Even by your standards."

"Harver was a fucking wanker," Rhymona hissed. "He nearly killed the boy. Far as I'm concerned, he had it coming."

"Be that as it may, you effectively severed my sole connection to Ravenholme."

"Honestly? Fuck your connections, Rill. And fuck Ravenholme just the like. Bunch of dodgy tomfucks, you ask me."

"Aye. Same old Morgan then."

"Yeah, I'm the arsehole, we all know," Rhymona said, coming to her feet. "And, so where's the sister?"

"Gone with said connections."

"Yeah?" She fought back a clawing dizzy spell. "And how's that?"

"How do you think? Fucking Covenant lackeys. She actually agreed to go with them, if you can believe it. Damned girl's always running head-long into peril."

"And you let her go?"

"I didn't have much choice in the matter. The Tarboril bitch had me at wandpoint. And the brother—"

"Gods damned Tarborils," Rhymona snarled as she grabbed up Fucker by its worn wooden scruff and choked it tight inside her fist, just the way he liked it. "I should have put those two fuckwits in the ground when I had the chance."

"Aye, you should have."

"And, so where did they take her?" Remy cut in as he inspected the stab wound that was miraculously no longer there.

"To Tetherow," Casilvieri answered.

"Tetherow?" The watchman returned as he brushed down the blood-dried ruffles in his hideously stained uniform. "To what end?"

"She is to undertake the trials for initiation into Ravenholme. Or so Harver claimed."

"Trials? And what could Ravenholme possibly want with Marsea? She's never even been outside the kingdom before."

"Aye, she has," Casilvieri corrected. "And you should well prize, she's nothing near the same bookish walkover you left here to rot last cycle."

"I'll agree to that," Rhymona granted. *We madwomen can sense our own, after all.*

"Her hand," Remy said.

"Case in point," Casilvieri said. "Earned every bit of that one, she did."

"She really killed Ganedys?"

"Aye, she did. Gutted him like a fish at market."

"Fuck me," the prince uttered.

"Made a damned foul mess of it too, but she saw it through in the end. She's a damned sight tougher than she looks, I'll give her that."

"And, so where's the bloody grimoire then?" Rhymona barked, lifting the empty satchel.

"Where do you think?" Casilvieri answered.

"No!" Remy ripped the satchel from her hands. "You can't be serious."
Fucking Tarborils. What a pain in the arse.

"They've broken through the upper quarters!" someone shouted from outside the courtyard.

"Seal the castle gates!" howled another deeper voice from a different direction.

"And so how do you two know each other?" Remy asked.

"Long story," Rhymona answered.

"One we haven't the time for just now," Casilvieri appended.

All three turned toward a Royalguard soldier that came dashing into the courtyard, his face dark and haunted.

"You, sir," Remy hailed, but the soldier paid them no mind as he scrambled through the snowfall down a passage away from them.

"I've seen that look before," Rhymona said, voicing what they were all thinking.

"Seal the damned gates!" the deep voice called again as a fresh volley lit the sky above them, the arrows falling over the courtyard's other side to the tier below.

"We need to be inside the citadel," Casilvieri said before following after the terrified soldier.

"You good to go, Toff?" Rhymona asked.

"As if there was a choice in the matter," he muttered as he took off behind Casilvieri's footpath.

Rhymona glanced back at Vaustian Harver's corpse with an ugly sneer as a man and woman dressed in highborn fashion hurried into the courtyard from the next over and followed after Remy. She gripped Fucker tight as the war horns cracked through the chaos over the courtyard's walling and she pushed herself in the direction of Lancastle Citadel, once more into the great wide unknown.

About midway down the passageway, the flood from the lower quarters poured into Alistair's Courtyard like a ruptured dam, some of it streaming into the walks behind her, blocking any chance of return. There were screams close enough to bottle, the sounds of steel warring, bodies struggling, flesh tearing, and the familiar clicking death song of the ghoulish horde.

Fuck. She dared a glance over her shoulder. The fuckers were moving fast, much faster than the ones in Palatia, and they were gaining. And for good measure, they brought the creeping mists along with them, thick as storm clouds.

Effortlessly, Rhymona caught up to the highborn couple, passing them by, the throng of madness not a stone's throw behind them. "This way," she shouted over her shoulder, hoping the couple heard and followed. She hurdled over a balustrade, back out into another courtyard, the grass slick under patches of fresh snow, another cascade of arrows passing overhead, as she came to another dark passageway. They were coming on endlessly, the courtyards and passages, but the citadel was gaining taller and ever nearer. One more corridor and she would be on it. One more corridor and there was safety or, in the least, some measure of defense.

"Hurry!" Remy called from an open doorway across the last courtyard.

Rhymona halted at the other side and glanced behind for the highborn couple. "Here!" she shouted as they came into view. "Over here!"

And just behind them one of the blighted, clad in the navy and gold colors of the Royalguard, came scrambling wildly after their tracks, looking more demon than ghoul.

Dammit. She took a step toward the couple. *Determined little fuckstain aren't you?* They weren't going to make it. "Come on, Morgan," she muttered. "Don't do this. A couple of posh geezers ain't worth your life."

She pushed off anyway.

"Rhymona!" She heard Remy yell.

Baka. You're actually doing this, then. Everybody's favorite little fuckup fast at the grave again. So fucking be it.

She rushed back headlong into the previous courtyard, a growl loosing from her innermost depths, knuckles white on Fucker's spine as she reared back and clubbed the ghoul with an overhead swing mere seconds before it would have reached the couple.

Shit!

There was something different about this one. Something almost intelligent. She aimed for the head, just as she had done a dozen times before, but the creature somehow predicted the strike and she hit shoulder instead, Fucker feasting through cloak and clothing into shoulder blade and lodging deep into the flesh beneath, forcing Rhymona to release or come crashing down into it.

The rabid bastard had baited her in.

She let go and rolled away from the creature's immediate reach, but the strike only proved a momentary hindrance. The creature was after her anew before she could even get her feet back under her, Fucker protruding from its mantle like a fresh layer of battle armor.

Fuck!

At least, she had given the couple enough time to reach the others. But the blighted soldier had her dead to rights.

Fuck me.

She turned toward the impact, her eyes slamming shut.

And she could have sworn she saw Fiandrel a second before the darkness set in. From the corner of her eye. Fiandrel. Clever little Fia.

Her haunter. Her guardian. Waiting in the snow-covered courtyard.

Sister.

And she heard a distant voice repair the quiet in between, as though in answer.

"...Thas'kon ech vira dhu leckt!..."

It was Toff's voice, though it carried a cadence both ancient and arcane and decidedly un-Remy-like. And just as she caught a whiff of the ghoul's horrid stench it was fastly replaced by a spatter of warm, thick fluid (amongst other unsavory things), like slop flung from a cauldron on the pit of an over-sized ladle.

Emyria's cock!

She was sodden in a literal bloodbath. But, somehow, still standing. Her head lowered as she swallowed her terror back down.

Well, at least my fucking mouth wasn't open.

She wiped a hand down her face to clear the chunks of cartilage and viscera before opening her eyes. She found the blighter's torso was missing entirely above the abdomen and the lower half had crumbled to the snow beside her still writhing and kicking about with its prior momentum. Her vision rose from the spectacular explosion of blood, nether dust, and ghoul guts to Remy at the courtyard's other end, a glowing palm still held out toward her.

Her lips curled madly skyward as she retrieved Fucker from the pool of gore and advanced. "Son of a fucking cunt, Toff, I don't know whether to hug you or pound the ever-living shit out of you right now."

"I have no idea where that came from," he answered in his typical chicken-shit monotone as they hurried toward the citadel door.

"You know exactly where it came from," she said, nonchalance at its finest, the ghoul's insides still dripping down her face and chin.

"The boy speaks Dracthonir now?" Casilvieri grumbled as they entered the castle's outer ward, and he bolted the door behind them.

"Evidently," Rhymona returned.

"Brilliant, that. Anything else you might want to clue me into?"

She spun around on him, orbs like tiny, little knife cuts, walking backward as they kept on pushing inward. "As it happens, his soul might yet be bound with Thira's."

"How's that then?" Casilvieri questioned.

"You heard me, you miserable old fuck. Bloody hells, five ticks in and you're already boring my tits off." She coiled back forward, following Remy's shape toward the torchlight.

"Yeah, I heard you," he groused. "Thira? As in Yvemathira the fucking Undying?"

"As in…"

"Knowing the consequences of soul magic? The gods know, Scraps, I know you get off on recklessness, but—"

"Oi, that'll do right there then," she spat over her shoulder. "Do me a favor and lose the fucking slave name when you address me, arsehole. And while you're at it, you can cram the bloody lecture just the like. I'm well aware of the consequences of black magic. Besides, I didn't really have much of a choice in the matter, as I recall. Toff was a rotter. And Thira was dying. They needed each other. And we need them. So I did what needed doing, yeah."

"And what in this world could possibly kill Yvemathira?" Casilvieri asked. "She's been alive for ages."

Remy lifted a torch from its iron sconce and turned back to them, his irises cut like that of the dracari, burning the azure ruin of untamed Eldn fire, and answered.

"…Malthus Tetherow…"

CHAPTER FIVE

Without realizing it, Remy repeated the voice in his head, and after a moment of gut-wrenching terror, he understood precisely who it belonged to.

Yvemathira.

Her voice sounded every measure as ancient as it ought, given the count of centuries she'd burned through. It was sharp, calculated, and undeniably clever. But there also resided a certain reptilian coldness within its intelligence, one that would exude intimidation from even the meekest of hosts.

In the torchlight, Remy studied Curie and Cas. The gods knew, he wished he had a burning glass of the expressions they presently wore. If only the circumstances weren't so damned dreadful.

WE ARE AS ONE, Thira answered.

Dweir ta ka'le du alé rinza. The words made perfect sense to him now, roughly translating to *the death crone is returned* in Midaran proper.

And the creature in The Spellbind, that was Tetherow? He asked the voice in his ramshackle head.

IT WAS A MAGUS NAMED SOLOMON DARROW THAT ONE OF TETHEROW'S MINIONS INFECTED. FROM WHAT I UNDERSTAND, TETHEROW USED HIM TO REACH ME AND TURNED HIS GIFT

AGAINST HIM. FORTUNATELY, YOU AND YOUR DARK-DABBLING FRIEND CAME ALONG WHEN YOU DID.

You mean to say that miscreation was once a man?

YES. NOT SO VERY LONG AGO. BUT TETHEROW MADE OF HIM A CREATURE NAMED A GNAUDRYLAX.

And what in the nine hells is a gnaudrylax?

IT IS AN ABOMINATION OF THE NETHER. ONE I THOUGHT TO BE OF FICTION BEFORE IT FOUND ME. SUCH WAS A HORROR OF A DIFFERENT AGE. AN AGE THAT PREDATED EVEN MINE OWN ANCESTORS.

Right, but what is it?

AS I UNDERSTAND, IT IS A LIVING BEING THAT IS CORRUPTED WITH A COLLECTION OF NETHER-DAMNED SOULS THAT THERE-AFTER BEGIN TO MELD AND MUTATE THEIR HOST FROM THE INSIDE OUT.

The hells...

THERE WERE OTHERS WITHIN DARROW'S MASS. I COULD FEEL THEM THERE, SUFFERING, TRYING TO RIP FREE OF THEIR IMPOS-SIBLE CURSE. ONE AMONGST THE LOT WAS OF MINE OWN BRETHREN. I FELT HIS PAIN THE DEEPEST.

The image of an enormous obsidian-skinned dracari slithering across the storm clouds flashed before his eyes. Remy knew without asking that the vision came from Thira's memories. Memories he apparently now owned too.

How is this possible?

THIS I CANNOT SAY. TETHEROW HAS SOMEHOW UNEARTHED KNOWLEDGE I BELIEVED ONLY THE GODS POSSESSED. I HAVE NEVER MET A CREATURE THAT CAN BEND THE NETHER TO ITS WILL.

What exactly are we saying Tetherow is? Is he a god?

I CANNOT SAY.

Thira, he has my sister! You must know something.

DOES HE?

You heard Cas.

NOT ALL THINGS ARE AS THEY APPEAR, YOUNG ONE. IF YOUR SISTER IS WITH WHO I BELIEVE SHE IS THEN SHE IS IN CONSIDER-ABLY BETTER REPAIR THAN WE ARE.

And who do you believe she is with?

The vision of a man in amber robes danced through his mind from another one of Thira's memories. He was inside The Spellbind before the elder tree. The man dropped to a knee and pulled back his cowl revealing a face Remy would not soon forget.

Beldroth?

YOU KNOW THIS MAN?

He saved my life. Remy shared a memory of the same y'deman ranger appearing from the woodland shadows outside Brymshire. *Though if I can be quite candid, I found him a rather unseemly fellow in the after.*

HE TOO HAILS BY THE NAME OF TETHEROW WHEN IT IS NECES-SARY. THERE IS GREAT POWER IN A NAME, AFTER ALL. AND NONE KNOW THIS BETTER THAN THE EXILE ELSYMIR BELDROTH, LAST OF HIS NAME.

"Oi, you care to walk that back, Toff?" Curie's voice hacked into his internal dialog.

"Thira says Marsea is with Beldroth, not Tetherow."

"And so we're back on Marsea again then are we?" she questioned. "Wait a tick, did you just say Beldroth? As in archer from the wood Beldroth?"

"As in," Remy confirmed. "And the horror in The Spellbind, she believes to be a creature named a gnaudrylax."

"Chuffing hells, you mean to say the mind-fucker has an actual name then?"

"And Tetherow, the real Tetherow, may be a god, or in the least, may possess god-like abilities."

Curie and Casilvieri shared an anxious glance before turning back to him.

"Right. Hi, Thira, Rhymona here," Curie began, cheeky as ever, stepping forward, arms tucked behind her back, staring the watchman deep. "I rather like my poison straight, yeah. So if you don't mind my asking, just to confirm, exactly how fucked are we here? Cause I'd rather like to get on with the drink then if there's no point left to it."

Care to comment?

WE NEED TO FIND YOUR UNCLE.

"She says we need to find Uncle Rhonyn."

"Waldgrave left for the swamps weeks ago," Casilvieri said. "He is Lancastle's acting ambassador in the Courowne Summits."

"...*Brummit, Goss, Ledgermaine...*" Remy repeated Yvemathira's words.

"Dead. Who? And your guess is as good as mine," Casilvieri answered in short order.

Who are these people?

THEY ARE OATHSWORN. THE GUARDIANS OF THE MORTAL REALM. ASK THE UGLY ONE...

"So, who is in charge here?" Remy finished.

"Fuck all'd be my assumption," Casilvieri returned. "Last I checked it was the corpse Old Girl here brained to bring you back."

And at that it all hit him. The last words he could remember of his discussion with Marsea. *Two out of three.*

Vaustian was dead.

Ganedys was dead.

"Where is Raelan?" Remy asked.

"I left him back at the battlements to seek out Vaustian. About an hour past. Given the blight's press, he could be anywhere now. He may well be a corpse just the same."

If only.

"What's your thought, Toff?" Curie inquired.

"I need to find Mother. And Jules."

WE DO NOT HAVE TIME FOR SUCH SENTIMENTALITIES, PRINCE.

They are my family, Thira. I have to make sure they are safe.

I AM SURE THEY ARE WELL GUARDED.

As am I, but I have to do this. I have to know. Please allow me this one thing, Thira, and then I'm yours to command.

He could sense Yvemathira's discontent.

VERY WELL, BUT WE MUST MAKE HASTE.

A SONG LATER, they found Queen Larissa and Princess Julia inside the King's solar overlooking the madness below from the grand balcony's high perch.

They were accompanied by other high standing members of the noble court. Houses deemed important enough to warrant such protection. There were nearly thirty heads in all. Most of which Remy recognized. Half noble standing, a third Royalguard, and the rest serving staff.

The absolute absurdity of this rotten bunch. The nobles were all mingling and nursing goblets and eating fruits and cheeses as though it were a bloody holiday festival.

Captain Bromas Aldridge appeared equally as agitated by the affair. He was the only one of the knights that Remy recognized.

A collective gasp rose as Remy and company came to the center of the solar and the firelight caught their horror.

Hands dropped to hilts, save Captain Aldridge, and Larissa turned to behold the ghastly spectacle. She and Remy linked eyes.

"Rembrandt," the Queen uttered as she drifted back in from the night. She portrayed the very essence of regal perfection under heavy mink fur and an elegant satin dress. Shrieks and horns and ringing steel were a distant chorus in the lower quarters behind her.

"Mother," Remy greeted. "You look as though you've seen a ghost."

"And you very well brandish the part, don't you?"

Remy's azure Eldn fire gaze advanced past his mother to not-so-little Julia who came striding up to him a river of raven-black hair only to punch him squarely in the gut.

"Ow!" He clutched his stomach. "Hey, what was that for?"

"For being an idiot and leaving. You didn't even say goodbye."

She made to sock him again, but this time he caught her fist and knelt before her, turning the back of her hand up to him and pressing it against his forehead.

"I made a mistake in leaving. Trust it true, it's never been clearer to me. And you're absolutely right, I should have told you. I should have. But it was never going to be for forever." The frightened father and daughter from the alley in Brymshire came back to haunt as he knew they would if he ever saw Julia again. He still hated himself for turning his blade at them and warning them away. The gods know, he wished for all the moon he could have had that moment back. But in the end, he had been just as frightened and all the more craven.

"Promise you won't leave again?" she asked with a watch mother's sternness.

BOWING TO A CHILD? WE DO NOT HAVE TIME FOR THIS.

"You know I can't make that promise," Remy said as he stood, ignoring Thira's complaint.

"Remy," Aeralie whispered bashfully as she approached from the crowd of onlookers, wrapping him in a perfumed hug despite his unsightly appearance. He kindly returned her affections with a light there-there on the back, careful not to offer too much. Marsea had made him painfully aware of Aera's little crush in the days before his abscondence. *Would that the world were fair*, he lamented for her.

"And who is this..." Larissa began, eyeing Curie with unbridled revulsion, "this..."

"What?" The magus started in hard. A mite bit harder than she ought, given the company. "This what, milady? And don't be shy on my behalf. I know what you all bloody well think of me. Don't know shit about me and you're already tossing about all of your fucking judgments."

This barefaced insolence drew a fresh round of gasps from the gathering.

"Excuse me?" Larissa retorted. "I daresay, Rembrandt, what wretched dung heap did you readily pluck this ill-mannered piece from?"

"The one that saves prince's lives apparently," Curie grumbled as she shifted her scowl in the hearth's direction, slicking back her hair from out her eyes, ghoul blood splattering the surrounding floor. "By the way, I thought you should know. Desmond is still alive."

"Desmond?" Larissa echoed.

Another collective gasp rose from the group followed by light murmuring. *Nothing quite like a fresh bit of scandal for this lot*, Remy thought.

"You know, your first born, the rightful heir to the Lanier throne. The one you thought they buried."

"How dare you," Larissa hissed. "Honestly Rembrandt, all these months rubbing elbows at The King's Wall, have you not yet taken the time to learn this heathen her place?"

"My place?" Curie shifted about. "*My* fucking place? Prize well, you'd be two birds short if I'd simply kept my fucking place, Highness."

"Rembrandt," the Queen aimed a puzzled glance his way. "What in vaelnation is she talking about?"

"Desmond is still alive?" Remy returned, still trying to wrap his mind around what fresh bollocks had just arrived.

"Sorry, Toff," Curie shifted away with a shameful look stretched across her guise. "I meant to tell you. I—"

"You meant to tell me?" His ears began ringing. "How? How do you know this? Where is he now?"

Curie glanced toward the doorway at Casilvieri, who was noticeably cross, even for him, then back to Remy. "We were mates...at university... in Kanton."

"You were mates?" Remy nearly laughed. Truly? She might be the most ridiculous person he had ever met. And just when he thought she couldn't possibly become anymore absurd. "You and my dead brother...were mates at university? The gods know, Rhymona, you do realize how barmy you sound right now?"

The murmuring of the attending nobles had come to a definitive halt. As well did the fire's crackle. An age crawled by as the entire party watched them.

"Tell him." Curie pressed through gritted teeth at the Queen of Lancastle.

"Mother?" Remy implored. But the answer was written quite plainly on Larissa Lanier's face. To wit, he had never seen his Queen mother so horridly fraught in all his days. Impossibly, Curie was telling it true. Somehow his elder brother yet lived. Instantly, he couldn't help but wonder if Marsea knew.

No.

Marsea was many things, misleading and a thousand layers of madhouse on her best day, but she would never keep such a secret from him. Not after all their pining and promises. Not after all those hours spent haunting the castle crypts and praying together behind the abbey proper. Praying to father and Desmond and the maidens many. He had to believe that. The gods know he wished she was here. He wished—

REMY. The sudden terror in Thira's voice rattled against his very bones as a tendril of mist began to spread across the balcony floor and into the King's solar.

And a bloodcurdling screech followed from some rest just beyond, ringing throughout the entire chamber like a knife across glass before clattering out amidst the vast lordly labyrinth of Lancastle Citadel.

IT'S HERE.

CHAPTER SIX

"There are two types of folks in this world," Vaustian slurred from the dregs of another bottle of red. "There are scars. And then there are stitches."

"Scars and stitches," Marsea echoed playfully.

"That is to say, there are folks who cause injury and folks who mend that which the scars dispense."

"And *that* is meant to be the meaning behind your house motto?" Marsea asked skeptically, glancing back over a naked shoulder at her heart's desire.

The chamber was aglow with dozens of trembling flames. It was the first and only time they had ever shared her bed. She was the little spoon. Her favorite place on all the moon, (save mayhaps The Cupboard's stacks).

"That is what I know of it, at least," Vaustian answered, pressing his lips down gently upon her shoulder's edge. "Something my old man used to say." He kissed her again a few inches closer to her neck, and the tiny hairs upon her nape rose. "But then again, my old man was a compulsive liar and a drunkard that liked to beat on women and boys half his size." He let out a heavy sigh. "Never quite figured out why my father was so bloody hateful. I suppose you could say he had a sickness. That would certainly make it all easier to stomach, wouldn't it?" Her love's sorrow was practically palpable. "I suppose I've made something of my own definition of the words ever since."

Marsea swallowed. "I'm sorry."

"There's nothing to be sorry about," his wine-thick breath tingled across her skin. "It's nothing you did."

"But still, you didn't deserve—"

"What's done is done," he interposed. "There's nothing more to be done about it now. Varymus Harver died how he lived. Penniless, unloved, and alone."

Maudlin stillness.

Breaths small as dust motes.

"You, however," he began again after a few sonorous heartbeats, "I have not yet decided on."

The princess squeezed her fingers between his, his long muscular arm draped around her, warm as the coziest winter blanket. "Oh, I'm stitches all the way down," she declared.

Kept close, she felt the chuckle rise up within him. "Is that so?"

"Naturally. That's my story, and I'm sticking to it."

His smile was disgustingly handsome inside the merry kiss of candlelight. "So it is, love. So it is."

Gently, he placed his fingertips against her cheek and led her swollen lips to his. Her tongue pressed into his mouth on instinct. She couldn't help it. Vaustian had always had a way about him. He always made her hungry for more. Especially when he took control. And so she settled back down onto the pillow, lying flat before him, looking him proper, and she opened for him like a flower.

Fingers roamed down her throat, over her breasts and ribcage, across her navel, and between her thighs before a pair found their way inside her. Synchronously, his mouth came down and crushed against hers, their tongues colliding once more.

She'd resolved to let him just have his way from there. He knew impossibly well how to tend to her body and all the places that mattered most.

He rolled atop her, his weight measured, his hardness lingering against the inside of her thigh. "I need you to do something for me."

And I need you to do something for me. She nearly breathed the words to life.

Marsea had always found that where sex was involved, the anticipation was always better than the act itself, though by her estimation, Vaustian had mastered both.

"I have taken from you." His words felt awfully calculated.

Her eyes came to his, fluttering like butterfly wings.

"I need you to acknowledge this." His voice sounded injured, which strangely only heightened her arousal.

"You've taken from me," she whispered, her breathing heavy.

"I murdered your brother."

The princess swallowed. *What?* Knuckled sickness jabbed at her stomach.

Say it, he commanded with a dominating gaze.

"You murdered my brother." Her craving was now running down the inside of her leg and onto the bedsheets, though Vaustian was apparently doing everything within his power to spoil it.

"We should be even, if we're to be together." He said the words slowly, with intentional seduction. And once again she was putty in his arms. Stupid, useless putty.

Before she could conjure a response, his tip grazed her and the shaft pressed slowly, deeply inside her wetness. At once, her eyes rolled back into darkness, her skin became flushed, and her heart began to race as the first moan escaped. He pulled out, nearly fully, before he thrust himself back in. Hard and harder still. She cried out as he fell into a vigorous rhythm and had to bite her bottom lip to keep her pleasure from drawing unwanted guests.

He knew how she liked it. He knew what got her excited. But, of course, he did. He knew everything about her. Far too well, in fact. She was his, after all.

He stopped, his manhood lodged inside her up to the base, and gently eased himself out. And Marsea couldn't help but wonder. Was he every measure hers as she was his?

His palm pressed against her waist, gripping the whole of her hip before sliding down beneath her buttocks, and he turned her over onto her stomach, entering her again, deep as she had ever felt him. She gripped a pillow in her fists as he drove himself into her. Deeper and deeper still.

She raised her haunches, coming up on all fours as a hand brushed across her belly, rising up to cup a breast, forcing her up before him. He nuzzled inside the depths of her loose, honey-gold locks and nibbled softly on her earlobe.

"Marsea," he whispered.

"Yes, my love," she returned with an ache in her voice, nearly breathless.

"I want you to kill my brother..."

―――――――

MARSEA CRIED awake with a jolt and the tome tumbled from her lap. For a beat she was petrified between worlds, her heart pounding for escape, her skin heavy and clammy, and between her thighs, she had become tender and sticky. She could almost feel the heat of him still inside her.

Vaustian's face flickered within, his left eye drifting unnaturally sideways, blood leaking from his nose.

"Ma...Ma...Marsea."

Another heartbeat later and the dream released her.

Good gravy! She sucked in a great lungful of musty air. *The maidens wept. Even dead, I still can't say no to you.*

Deep down, she had always hated that about herself. But then again, deep down, she hated most all things about herself.

A sigh crawled out of her from somewhere black and buried and long since disregarded.

―――――――

SHE'D BEEN READING BEFORE, unable to quiet her mind after her encounter with Other, nestled deep in a surprisingly comfortable antique reading chair. The maidens knew she felt a proper nan about it too, snuggled up in a throw before the old crackling hearth with a bevy of books and scrolls for company, but she could barely contain herself. She had become giddily enthralled the very moment Beldroth introduced her to the Ravenholme library. Finally, some new material! And the way her affairs were lately, this went over like all of her birthfalls rolled into one. Sure, the archive was quaint and woefully thin by comparison to Lancastle's gargantuan collection, and the pages had a funny and decidedly unnatural smell to them, but it hardly mattered. They were all fresh to her. Some bit of goodness in all the gloom, she supposed. And a passable distraction from dwelling on Vaustian and Remy and everything else that had happened over the past few days back home.

It went without saying, really, but Ravenholme was nothing at all how Vaustian had described it. He'd always made it sound similar to a university, or at the very least a military order, not unlike the Royalguard. However, thus far, it appeared more akin to a cult for killers and dark-dabblers. Cas had tried to warn her, hadn't he? The stars save her, but she should have read the signs long before. Here, there was no comradery, no common room for socializing, no tutors to fall back on, not even a storybook rival to keep her on her toes. Moreover, there were no other apprentices at all that she could discern of, only strategically placed sconces and a sea of hoods hiding dark, hateful scowls with even darker intentions.

She sidled up in the chair, wearing her loneliness like armor, and flexed her bad hand, turning it from front to back in the firelight, studying the lines of jagged black thread laced throughout. The horror of it. She was already beginning to forget how it used to look. But all the same, she was also forgetting to care. If she didn't know any better, she might almost say she was getting used to life as a grotesque.

"Stitches all the way down," she mocked the memory, wiggling the remains of her ring and pinky fingers. *Dreadful little nublets, aren't you?* There was simply no getting around that bit, was there? The fat, ugly scar lines were not so much a bother and would fade with time, but the half-missing ring finger might one day prove quite the hideous affair for a wedding band. Marsea snorted. *All that's going on and you're still concerned about a marriage? Good to know your priorities are in standing order.*

"So this is how we're dealing with all of this, hunh?" a voice spoke from the library's entrance behind her.

The princess tensed up immediately. *Speaking of storybook rivals.* The mere sound of Yongrin's voice froze the blood in Marsea's veins.

"You poor dear thing, I do hope you are settling in all right," Yongrin Tarboril added as she approached all cherry lips and perfect teeth.

Brave face, Marsea, she told herself as she came to her feet and knuckled up her smudgy gran glasses, the throw blanket falling to the sheepskin rug around her ankles.

The maidens knew, but the magus appeared an absolute vision in red. Her beauty was of the sort that inspired bards, and her voice was every measure as smoky and dangerous. She was Kinzi Kincaid from *Devil Cake*, only taller and more intimidating, and just about everything Marsea was not.

"I daresay, how long have you been cooped up in this stuffy old cupboard for?" Yongrin asked as she came into the full of the firelight.

Good question. "Not long," Marsea returned and wondered if the magus could tell how much her voice was shaking. The fewer words the better, she decided.

"My, my, my, you are practically a doll come to life, aren't you?" Yongrin eyed the princess up and down. It was the first time they had seen one another since Alistair's Courtyard. "Hopelessly girlish figure. Precious, porcelain skin. Impossibly soft, delicate features." Her vision dropped to Marsea's rag doll hand. "Well, mostly."

Marsea tucked the eyesore behind her back.

"Apologies," Yongrin repaired, "how needlessly rude of me."

It was quite possibly the worst offered apology in the history of their like. *So much for fast friends, then.*

Awkward seconds trickled by.

"I understand we haven't begun on the best of terms," Yongrin started again, "but I was rather hopeful you might still be open to a chat."

"A chat?" *Or do you mean an interrogation?*

"Oh, but I've seen that look before."

Marsea shifted toward the flames. She felt the scar on her upper lip begin to itch again, and her nose scrunched up in response.

"The 'I'm better than you' look," Yongrin expounded. "If you've seen it once, you've seen it a thousand times."

And here we go again. Truly was there no end to the line of folk trying to tell me about myself?

Marsea shook her head, fighting to maintain a neutral demeanor. "You're mistaken."

"I'm mistaken, am I? You want to play at this little game then?"

The stars save me. This one was all over the place. "I'm not playing at anything."

"What did his Lordship want with you then?"

"We spoke about my training, of course." *Keep it simple.*

"I'm sure that wasn't all you spoke about."

"He told me he once trained my father." *Harmless.*

"Hmm, did he now?" Yongrin drifted toward the flames alongside her, brushing loose strands of blond behind an ear to gain a better view of the Lanier princess. They stood side by side in the firelight's flicker. "And did he tell you he had your father murdered as well? By your dearest Vaustian, no less. How positively cruel." She pouted, putting on a real show of it. One that might have even put Marsea's mother to shame.

We all know. I'm the bloody poster child for domestic dysfunction. Marsea had the sudden overwhelming urge to bash Yongrin's bonny face against the mantle and shove her screaming into the fire.

"And, so after everything, knowing what he took from you, you still went about shagging him anyway? Your own father's killer?"

"That's none of your damned business." She regretted the words immediately. *Let it be.*

"Oh, but it is my business. Everything that happens in this place is my business, and you would do well to remember that."

Marsea couldn't hide a scowl from forming and immediately felt the fool for having been so obvious about it.

"Look me ugly all you like, but you don't belong here, Marsea Lanier, try as you might with these dirty rags you're sporting."

Marsea refused to take in Yongrin properly. She was nowhere near prepared for a war of words with this woman, and she was certainly no match were it to escalate beyond that. She had to choose her actions carefully from here on. She had to be smart.

Though she could now feel Other boiling ever so near the surface.

"It used to be you want to survive in this world, you want to get on and be something, then you had to be perfect. And so that was what I strove for. For cycles on end. That was how I lived. Knowing good and well perfection was a lie. But that is how I had to be. Because that is what life is truly like outside of court. You see, Davrin and I came from nothing. Backwoods, low-cut northern stock as we were. A couple of misbegotten foundlings from a dreadful little haunt named Bask. Doubtful you've ever heard of it."

Marsea hadn't. But she had heard a similar tune before. A tale once written twice told, carved in stones of silver and gold. This was her mother's story, dazzling and dull. Of the poor beautiful servant girl from the sticks who against all odds would one day become queen. The maidens know it took everything within her not to feign a yawn.

"As such, do you know how many filthy toes I had to press mine lips to? How many greedy, lecherous slobs I had to serve and bend the knee to? How many lies I had to tell? How many hearts I had to break? How many necks I had to run red? How many bastards I had to bury and betray just to barely sniff the echelon of living you were quite randomly born to?"

Fe, what you don't know about me could bloody well fill the ocean. The words were perilously close to drawing breath, but Marsea forced herself to swallow them back down like a cut of poison apple.

"Civility is an illusion," the magus continued. "Savagery is the true face of humanity. Pretty it up all you want. Verily, what does it say about this fouled up abortion of a world if a lowly hick like me can gain such powers? And if that lowly hick can create such fear in folk who were born to rule?" Yongrin glanced sidelong at the Lanier princess and split a pretentious smile. "Have you ever felt another's fear of you, Marsea?" A vision of Wils Gilcrest guttered within the princess, his bones crunching, the hammer's handle vibrating in her aching palm. "I can assure you it is the most intoxicating feeling in all the moon."

Marsea concentrated on the flames, forcing them to bear the brunt of her mounting hostility.

"You are doing your best to conceal it, but I can still feel your fear of me, Marsea. And yet still you believe you are somehow different. That you are somehow above the rest. Above me."

"You know nothing about me," Marsea returned.

"I know everything about you, girl. I was once a royal myself. Not so very long ago. A queen, mind you. Though my kingdom, sadly, was not nearly as fortunate as yours. Nor was my husband. Be that as it may, I know what it is to live with the expectations of others...with the weight of a city. To be forced to hobnob with idiots and yet be made to feel as the outcast. I know precisely who you are and I can assure you, whatever deceit Tetherow is feeding you, I have heard it all the same."

"Think what you like."

"I bet he told you that you were special, didn't he?" She turned to Marsea and waited this time until the princess returned her look. "Prize well, he told me the same once. And Davrin. And probably a hundred more undesirables before us." She sighed. "Though I do so wonder in what way he tried to convince you."

Marsea remained silent.

"He is a liar, whatever it was. His Lordship is not nearly as clever as he thinks. You see, I know a little secret about our illustrious Malthus Tetherow." Yongrin's lovely face was chocked full of contemptuous horrors at the claim. "And you should know he is not the man he pretends to be." Her voice lowered slightly. "Change is coming to Ravenholme, milady, sooner than you might think, and you would do well to consider your options." The magus suddenly shifted toward the doorway, and Marsea followed her fiery glower.

A moment later the unmistakable figure of his lordship cut a deathly shadow that spread long into the stony black behind him. The amber hood was drawn low to conceal his face. A strand of linen cloth hung from inside the cowl's mouth like the end of a winter scarf.

"Milord," Yongrin lowered her head.

Marsea did her best to mimic the act. She noticed something dark in Beldroth's hand.

"Leave us," he ordered, his voice noticeably changed from before. Mayhaps by some alteration spell.

Yongrin shot Marsea a knowing glance and took her leave without another word.

They both waited until her footsteps faded and Beldroth closed the door behind them, reciting some bit of incantation under his breath. Some manner of blocking magic, no doubt.

"I have something for you," Beldroth said, removing the hood from his bandaged head and offering the curiosity in his hand.

It appeared similar to a soldier's leather gauntlet. Marsea studied it in the firelight. She had never beheld anything quite like it. On the surface, it was hardened dark brown leather and yet underneath, it was somehow impossibly soft. The fingers had been cut and modified to fit her injuries and there was an extra layer of leather padding stitched across the knuckles forming a row of four X's.

"I molded it in boiling water to firm it up. And that's deerskin inside. Should give it a decently comfortable fit. A bit of guesswork as to the sizing, but I reckoned it was close enough to give her a try and make alterations afterward if need be."

Marsea untied the lacing at the wrist and slipped her bad hand inside. It actually fit snugly. She closed her hand into a fist inside it and released. She couldn't hide the smile a moment longer. "It's surprisingly light."

"Aye, and it should offer a fair complement of support while you try to build some strength back."

She closed her hand up into a fist once more and looked Beldroth proper. "Thank you. It's absolutely perfect."

"I am glad you approve." He glanced at the chair and the mound of tomes and scrolls next to it. "You read like just your father did."

She shared his gaze, blushing at the clutter. "And what does that mean, exactly?"

"He was a messy reader, just the like. Hardly knew what a shelf was. He would take a tome, devour it, and when he was done, he'd feed it to the stones. That is, unless he liked it. If he liked it, he would keep it and treasure it like it was part of his own soul." Beldroth eyed the two books stacked neatly atop the mantle, clearly kept apart from the others. "And none other, save himself, would ever see those very pages again."

Marsea couldn't help but take delight in the tale. "I promise I will clean up when I am done."

"All told, I am just glad this old haunt is finally getting some use again. Though I hope you've gotten in a decent fill. We set out for Vinth in an hour."

"An hour?" Her heart danced. "So soon?"

"I'm afraid time is not on our side, princess."

"No, I suppose not. What time is it anyway?"

"Nearly noon," he said with a groan.

She studied his slumped form. "How bad is it?"

Beldroth shook his head, and Marsea noticed some bit of darkness that had already bled through the fresh bandaging. "Today has been manageable. But my bones and vitals are beginning to give under its growing pressure. It's all my gift can do to contain it. And the Chandii tonics are having diminished effects. Even now I can feel it feeding and expanding."

"You were going to tell me how this happened to you."

"I was, wasn't I?" He hobbled on to the hearth and placed a hand against the mantle as he glared down into the flames. "You mentioned an ashaeydir in your court. The one that murdered Vaustian."

Rhymona. "An ashaeydir did this to you?"

"Mmm, a particularly nasty one too. One with the sort of past that would likely produce such a vindictive devil."

"But Tetherow is y'deman. I thought the ashaeydir turned up their noses at the y'demans."

"They typically do, but Tetherow is not your typical y'deman. And the one that came after me was not your typical ashaeydir. She is the last of her house. Betrayed by her own and left to the rot. The sort of damaged wretch Tetherow has always had a keen eye for exploiting and empowering. Suffice it to say, there was a time I too became seduced by such promises.

"She found me outside of Brymshire during the lichlord's incursion and we crossed blades. But she didn't mean me death in the duel. Not yet, anyway. She meant me suffering. She meant to slight me in her master's name. She meant to use me for their cause. The fool I was, adrenaline pumping a mad fever, I never even felt the poisoned blade cross my thigh. It was only in the after that I deduced what had actually happened." He grunted in pain, ironing a fist into the top of his bum leg.

Marsea took a step closer.

"Stay back," he gritted. "It'll pass."

"My eye it'll pass." It tore at her to see anyone in such agony. "Surely there is something more I can do."

"You can start preparing yourself for the trek," he answered flatly. "You must stay committed, no matter what happens to me."

"And what, pray tell, is going to happen to you?" Her hands fell to her hips.

"Nothing good, to be sure." His orbs were like twin pools of violet nightmare. "Nether-rot is the complete death. And once it sets in, there is no way to stop it, at least not a way that I've become privy to. It is beyond the abilities of the gift and that of blood-based magic. Hells, I'd wager it's beyond anything this side of the Vael. The gift can slow its feasting to a degree, but it is merely a small hindrance. The nether will find a way to adapt and continue to alter until it has eventually taken over both the body and the mind."

"And so what happens then?"

"You know what happens."

"You'll become one of those things out there?"

"Possibly. Probably. But given what I've seen the nether do to most highly attuned giftborn, it could be something much worse. Prize well, I have already begun to experience hallucinations and hear voices. Echoes trapped within the nether that racks my body. I have begun to see memories of lives I have never lived from the perspectives of creatures I could never hope to emulate. They are mere distractions. Little horrors called forth to propagate its seed of madness. I won't be fooled so easy, but as the creature digs deeper inside my soul, it will begin to surface the absolute worst of my own fears. Keep this close, Marsea. It is a bridge we'll cross when we get there. But it is a bridge, nonetheless. At some point soon, we will part ways. And there may come a time when I ask you to turn on me."

What? She could hardly believe what she was hearing.

"Which brings us 'round to your pick of poison, doesn't it?" he went on.

Wait, what? She thought. But the words wouldn't come.

"I know Vaustian was always keen on the Helanderan short sword. I presume that was what he was training you on."

"I...yes, he was," she managed, shifting with the turn of conversation despite her concerns. "Or he tried to at least. Though I rather preferred my father's steel, if you must know. A proper knight's sword. Straight and narrow. Double-edged. Twenty-seven inches of starbright singing silver. Two pounds or less."

"You know your hardware."

"A blade well measured is a blade well brandished," she rattled off a line from Howland Baylet's treatise, *The Wise Man's Blade*. It was one of her favorite quotes; one that she certainly never expected to be saying aloud in any sort of meaning circumstance. *My, how the times have changed.*

"Indeed. I don't suppose you've had much exposure to wand work as well?"

"You mean outside of your favorite lickspittle's rather forceful display last night?" A poor attempt at humor. "None at all. Sort of new to this whole giftborn thing. By the way, did you know she was once a queen?"

"Tut, Yongrin was once playing at a queen. Truth's witness, she is no more an actual queen than an actress performing the part in a royal theatre."

"Whatever she is, she doesn't think much of you. If I didn't know better, I would say she means you trouble, and soon. Just before your arrival, she told me she knew some things about you. Namely, that you are not who you pretend to be."

"Did she now?" he grumbled. "You let me worry about Yongrin. Is that clear?"

"Crystal."

He started for the door. "Make sure to pack those two books you set aside on the mantle up there."

"You can count on me," she found herself saying.

"The grimoire as well," he called back to her before returning to the shadows.

CHAPTER SEVEN

Valestriel leaned against the starboard rail of Blackhall's Banshee, staring out into the endless sea. The wind was an absent lover this night, pushing them along at a snail's pace, and lulling most of the ship's crew belowdecks and into an early slumber.

A pluck of lute strings began from The Banshee's bow, and Val's attentions drifted to the musician. By the starlight's cast, she was an older woman, mayhaps in her forties or fifties, donning a tricorn hat, a worn leather vest, and a rag for a shirt to match her patchwork trousers. In spite of her threadbare disposition, she fastly proved herself quite the talent at the song. Strumming what Val could only imagine was a right tavern turner 'round the ports. It started slow, as did they all, but swiftly gained in intensity. The woman hummed in place of words, her expressions fierce and full of pain, quite reminding Val of her Morgandrel.

Val's lips puckered in the ballad's wake, and a smile of pure sadness settled somewhere within as her mind wandered to the past.

"You've cut your hair," she exhaled at last.

Valestriel had not spoken to Morgan in months, nigh on a full cycle, watched her get her ass handed to her in a back alley brawl the night before, and this of all things was what she landed on as a proper greeting?

It was midsummer, the cycle of the Hound, and hot as the bloody nine. Hot enough that the Kingswood's shade provided little relief from the midday sun's imperious temper, though, the air, reeking of dew and earthiness, whispered of a coming storm.

"I did," Morgan replied. She lit a half-smoked shufa stick and took to a cool lean against a maple tree. "What do you think?" To no one's great astonishment, she was still pissed-rotten-trollied.

"I don't know," Val muttered. She hated it, and Morgan knew it. But Morgandrel Tully always knew these things about her.

This Morgan, in her human guise, looked more androgynous than a coffeehouse dandy—and not a particularly fetching one. Valestriel remembered running her fingers through *her* Morgan's long silky hair, back when their kisses were hungry and their auras were entangled, and she missed it terribly. She would never forget how perfect it felt against her touch. How right it felt. How right they felt. Together.

"And yet your face says it all," Morgandrel answered.

"I said I don't know, all right. It's different."

Everything about her was different. Her swagger. Her accent. Her smell. It all niffed of Midaran pomp, Southland surliness, and days-old whiskey. The gods know, she appeared considerably older now too, having somehow added cycles to her guise she hadn't yet lived. Val had no doubts her continuous dark-dabbling had been at the root of all that. And she noted immediately that Morgan had already mended the shiner and busted lip from the night before. Gift bought, they were. Though the manner by which she mended her many wounds seemed completely at random. Some came from the gift, others were seen to the old-fashioned way, and more still were left to their spoil and would more than like never fully heal (at least not properly).

"You can't lie to me, Val. The point is that I look ugly as fuck, yeah. Put the creep boys off me as much as can be had. They outnumber the women thirty to one at the wall, probably worse. You do the sums there."

"Well, you're certainly acting more and more like one of them, aren't you?"

"Am I? Reckon I'll take that as a compliment then."

"Don't do that." Valestriel's expression soured.

"Don't do what?"

"You know what."

"The fuck am I supposed to say to that, Val?"

A tense moment ticked by. And with every broken second a freshly whetted invisible dagger twisted itself deeper inside her heart, severing each subsequent beat in half.

"Soli says you've even taken up a new burn name," Val's voice came out ghastly misshapen.

"Rhymona Curie." Morgan's lips thinned to a jagged smear. "My little social experiment."

"And, so you're wearing their colors now too, I see."

Morgan shrugged. Her eyes in her human guise appeared quite dark and empty.

"Right. And, so when are you coming back then?" The question couldn't be helped. Valestriel found she could no longer hide her deepening sadness. Her soul ached something terrible inside this Morgandrel's presence. Somehow, impossibly, it was even worse than within her absence.

Morgan took a long pull, as though the answer lay within her burner, and blew it out.

Another silence, thick as molasses, pursued.

Valestriel watched her former mentor, drinking her in, unable to pull her eyes away. "At least tell me why."

A breeze riffled through the treetops at the request, and a pair of leaves, rusted red and parchment yellow, drifted down between them in a twirling dance.

"I'd figure that would be painfully obvious at this point," Morgan sneered.

"I still want to hear it." A memory of courage.

"No, you don't."

"Then mayhaps you would like to explain last night to me?" A flint to steel.

"Last night?"

"I've seen you down goons tenfold harder than that one."

"Oh, that." Morgandrel simply smiled, crooked as her bottom teeth. "Saw that, did you? Reckon the drink got the better of me then, didn't it?"

"Rubbish, that. Drink or no, you wanted the pain. You barely even lifted a finger against him."

"Didn't I?" Morgandrel's eyes narrowed to a pair of razorblade nightmares. "And, so what's this then? You wake up with a case of the fuckarounds and decide to bring me out here and scold me about like some disobedient daughter?"

"No. I brought you out here because I needed to see you. I needed to talk to you. I miss you, Morgan." Her mouth was dry as the blasted-plains and yet somehow, impossibly, a nose to the north, white-hot tears burned away at the backs of her eyeballs. "But all this—how you are now—I can't understand it. I can't understand you. I can't understand this life you've chosen. As much as I want to. I just—"

"The gods know, Val, find a ruddy point already."

"I know how Father treated you." It felt like those words had sat on her forever. And yet the weight remained in spite of their divulgence. "How they all did. Only I didn't rightly understand it back then."

Morgandrel looked at her deadly serious and the air withered about them. "You'd best leave that box of bullshit closed." Despite all the outward changes her scowl was still in fine form.

"So, this is how it is, then?" Val asked. "You're just going to shut me out? Like all the rest?" If she had learned one thing about Morgandrel Tully over the cycles, it was her singularly awful ability of cutting folk out. "Fine." Valestriel placed a fingertip against the newly embedded trezsu implant behind her ear revealing her human skin. "But you should know. I came prepared."

This pulled Morgan from her shell.

"You joined?" She actually sounded surprised. And maybe a little hurt by it.

"Of course, I joined," Valestriel said, reaching out her tattooed arm and studying her own unfamiliar swarthy skin. "What did you expect I would do? We're all in it now, like it or not. And the other houses only grow bolder by the hour. But, prize well, I would just as soon leave it all behind—"

"Val, we've discussed this."

"You don't have to be alone, Morgan. Not anymore. With me, you'll never walk alone."

"But I do have to be alone." Words choked in barbed wire. "I've always

74

been alone. Always. I'm fucking meant to be alone, yeah. It's how the fates designed me. And I'm well past spent fighting with it."

"What is this truly about?" Val probed. "Is it Halion again?"

"No, it's not fucking Halion again. Halion's in the ground. His choice. And, for the last fucking time, I've made my peace with it."

Val swallowed. "Well, what is it then?"

"You need to let it be, Valestriel."

"I will not let it be. Not this time. Just fucking talk to me, Morgan. I want to help you."

"You can't fucking help me, Val. No one can."

"And so why don't I get a say in all this? I'm just as much in this thing as you are."

"There is no *thing*. We can't be whatever you think this is. Please get that through your thick fucking skull. I've already told you—"

"I wanted it, all right!" Val cried. "I'm here too, yeah. You can't just throw me away. Not after all this. Not after Rhesh. Not after Skagaten. I won't let you."

This unlocked something from deep within her old mentor. Something she knew Morgan was struggling to keep at bay. Some morsel of madness, she supposed. Or mayhaps it was a bit more akin to despair.

"You know I love him, right?" Morgandrel said and she glanced away. "Did Soli-shan tell you that bit? I know it was her that told you. Goodness knows I fucking hate him for it, but I can't just deny what's there, now can I?"

"I don't care," Valestriel said sullenly.

"Yes, you do. Don't be a fucking child." Morgan pushed away from the tree and flicked the roach of her shufa stick as she ambled drunkenly past her former apprentice, still working through yestereve's debauchery.

"*I'm* the child?" Val followed after her, the welling wetness stinging her false-colored eyes. "I just want to be with you. In whatever way you'll have me. And you're quitting everything."

Morgandrel stopped cold, swaying a bit. "Oi, I'm not quitting, yeah. That is not what this is."

"Then what is it?" Valestriel dared.

"I don't know, Val," Morgan murmured, her back still turned. "Think of it as more of a holiday. Hells, think of it whatever you like. I really couldn't give a toss."

"A holiday? A bloody holiday? Are you serious? The King's Wall is a fucking madhouse, a place for exiles and rejects, scarcely better than a dungeon cellar—"

"Right up my alley then, some would say."

"Scraps." Val's chest became tight at the calling. The name slipping past her tongue in her mounting anger. A name her family forced upon Morgan all those many cycles ago. A name meant to belittle. A name meant to mock. A name meant to constantly remind her of her rotten place in this world and all that she had lost from before.

"Don't you dare fucking speak that shit at me." Morgandrel turned on her heel and snarled. "I hate that gods damned name and you know it."

"I'm sorry." Val had never been so frightened of anything in all her life.

And what was left of their world began to shrivel up like parchment set to the flame, crumbling to ash around them.

"I won't be easy, Val. Not for you. Not for anyone."

"Please, don't do this."

"It's already done, yeah," Morgan said crossly. She was pigheaded as ever. "I'm finished with the ashaeydir, with House Alyfain, with being named fucking Table Scraps, and you're not going to change my mind about it. Accept that."

Emptiness consumed.

Agony bloomed.

And dissonance pulled up a chair.

"Can't I be finished along with you then?" Valestriel had never heard her voice so ruined and desperate before. "Please." By now, she should have known better, but try as she might, the lesson just wouldn't keep.

Trying to tame Morgandrel Tully was like trying to capture lightning in a bottle.

"You can be finished with whatever you like." Morgan started away again. "But I have my path to haunt. And you have yours."

"You don't mean that. You still love me. I know you do."

"But I do mean it, Val. And love's nothing to do with it. Trust me, I'm doing you the favor here."

"Fuck you, then!" Valestriel seethed, her agony molting away from a new skin she had never known herself capable of. "And fuck your favor if that's all I'm worth to you. You spoil everything good in your life, you know that? The fates didn't design your bloody loneliness, Morgan. You did!"

"Reckon we all have our own shit to smell at one point or another," Morgandrel sneered over her shoulder.

"All this for a boy?" Valestriel hollered out after her, tears blistering down her Midaran mask, "a fucking human boy."

CHAPTER EIGHT

V al turned from the musician to that very same human boy who sat just inside the messdeck of Blackhall's Banshee leafing idly through his codex in the pitiful gutter of lantern light.

He appeared a boney thing, corpse-like, especially when one considered his past tribulations. His hair ran long and untidy, his beard uneven and patchy, and his robes torn and faded. He was still quite young, at least his features were anyway, underneath all the poor hygiene, and yet at the same time he somehow portrayed a very old thing, almost as though he were from a different era altogether.

"What in the bloody nine are you doing, Valestriel?" she muttered in Ashaeydiri tongue as she watched him.

She liked Desmond—Aiden—truly she did, for a human or a haunter or whatever the hells he was. On the whole, he'd shown himself a surprisingly tolerant and empathetic sort. Still, she couldn't quite wrap her head around Morgan's undying fascination with him. True, he proved a decent lay, but there were plenty of those about without anywhere near the baggage. He wasn't especially smart or charming either. And in terms of general attractiveness, he was middling, for a Midaran. Foiled in large part by an apparent allergy to proper grooming and fashion etiquette. Oh, but if he only had a clue.

Her head shook.

She could certainly see him cleaning up nicely if he put even a modicum of effort to it.

At least, she supposed, he made her laugh on occasion; though, to have it honest, it was mostly at him.

Flaws notwithstanding, he'd come around to her being ashaeydir well enough in the short time since the unveiling. Yet, she could still feel a reticence between them that did not exist before. And fucking Ledgermaine certainly wasn't doing her any favors in all that. Though, she could hardly fault him, considering. She knew what the humans said about her kind. She knew the folklore— the absurd old nans' tales. The ashaeydir were named as demons and monsters amongst the Vaelsyn commonwealth. Horrible creatures that hunted the countryside butchering and devouring those wandering out too far alone. And that they wore the skins of those they consumed to haunt effortlessly amongst them. Sadly, as ridiculous as the stories sounded, the Midarans were not too far off.

She sighed, tucking a stray ashen curl behind an ear.

They had already been at sea for the better part of a day, glancing the cape of Six Ports in route for Dorngar, and to have it from Ledge, it would be at least one more before they arrived upon the Vinteyaman coastline, and that was if they caught no trouble from Dalivant's war fleet.

She and Aiden had agreed on something of a plan before joining in with The Banshee's crew. First, they would journey to Lancastle. Aiden said he had to see it for himself. He had to see these people that were apparently his real family. And, truly, she couldn't blame him for that. No doubt she would feel the same were their roles reversed. Then they would head for Nocthun—for The Spellbind. What they planned to do once they arrived there was a different story altogether. But they had to do something. They had too much information just to sit on their hands. And Valestriel even more than he. Or so she suspected.

Though, just the thought of seeing her own kinfolk again sent a shiver up her backside.

She could pick them out the second she saw them, her family. Her Uncle Merillion, her sisters, Solindiel and Nym, and the dozen or so some odd others in their cadre. She hadn't the faintest inkling what guises her sisters presently wore, but she knew Rill's. His was a nasty bastard. A pauper turned bladehand named Fiveknives. And she knew he had been working on Aiden's sister for some many quints since The Lanier Objective began. Marsea Lanier was a vastly important piece, he had told her. As the only female heir, she was the best option for expansion into another house. Initially, he'd wanted Val in on it. She would play house servant for the Lanier princess, learning her mannerisms and cadences to gain her ear. But that was before she convinced him she would be better utilized resuming Morgan's assignment in bringing Prince Desmond home. Someone had to see to it, after all.

And somehow, in spite of everything, all the awkwardness and bungling, all the strange, unsettling distractions, the original plan remained miraculously on course. Valestriel had never been one to dally in talks of fortune and prophecy, but the longer this business with Aiden carried on, the more it began to assume an undeniable air of destiny.

She strolled over to the archivist's table and quietly sat across from him. He did not bother to greet her. Verily, she expected as much.

Her attentions fell to Ledge across the mess, who appeared to be in a rather profound discussion with The Banshee's quartermaster. Beside him at the table's edge lay her ka'rym chii nestled silently inside its obsidian coffin. She couldn't help but glower at the sight. The gods help her if her father ever found out she willfully relinquished her blade to a Midaran, especially a dodgy old geezer as was Ledgermaine. And she might never live it down if either Soli or Nym caught wind. But what other choice did she have? Surrendering it was the only way Ledge would keep her secret and accept her company. And Aiden had told her he needed her. That they were in this together, come what may. It was an impossible situation, and it pissed her off to grant it thought. Suddenly she had been reduced to little more than a sad little tour guide. But she knew the risks beforehand. She had thought them over a thousand, thousand times since that drunken night at the Brass Lantern when they fucked like a pair of wild rabbits. She could have kept her secret a little longer and affairs might have been different, but this was where she landed. She had taken the high road, the road of honesty, and it had burned her. But she decided, in the end, it would be better than holding on to the lie. In this, she had to believe.

"Anything interesting?" she offered, swallowing her pride back down, cobbling together something that resembled a smile.

"Mmm," he returned, flipping a page.

Baka, she scolded herself in Ashaeydiri. *No doubt he's read the thing a thousand times over by now.* Her false cheer evaporated. *Just give him what he wants already. Someone else may as well share in your devastation of her.*

"Morgandrel Tully was born in 1788 on the new cycle's eve to High Lord Refyn Tully and High Lady Caladria Luiryn," Valestriel began.

Somewhere a bow went off its violin strings, and their eyes collided.

"She also had a twin sister named Fiandrel. Or so it's been said."

Slowly, the grimoire cracked shut. It was the book version of an old man working his way up from bed in the morning.

"The device behind my ear and hers is called a trezsu implant. It allows us to alter our appearances. Not physical structure, mind you, but skin tone, hair color, eye color, and such the like. The implant surgery is performed on all soldiers enlisted in the Ashaeydir Guard after The Trenches."

"The Trenches?"

"It's similar to what the Royalguard name basic training."

"What is this?" he asked bluntly. "What are you doing?"

"I'm coming clean." *Or sullying myself further. Tough to tell much of a difference these days.* "No more secrets, yeah?" She had to gain some semblance of Aiden's trust back, especially with Ledge seemingly plotting against her. In the least, she had to try.

Aiden leaned forward, elbows on the table, icy blues ravenous with quizzical intent. "She *had* a twin sister? As in..."

Valestriel winced but maintained eye contact.

"Was it by your family?"

"My House was involved. But all of that was before I was born. Well before. Suffice it to say, I do not know all the details."

"She never told me she had a twin," Aiden said, glancing away in frustration. "She never told me much of anything about her family, all told."

"Morgan can be quite secretive, can't she?" *And wasn't that the damned truth.* It actually made her feel better to know that Morgan had maintained her same caginess around Desmond too.

"88'...that would make her..."

"Forty," Val answered.

Aiden's face wrinkled in contemplation.

"But we age much slower than your kind," she added. "Some of us live centuries. Most of us do, in fact, when left to our natural lifespans."

"And so how old are you then?"

How old am I? She was genuinely stunned that he would venture a personal question of *her* given all that he could have about Morgan. "I'm twenty-seven by the Midaran calendar."

There was a light in his frosty eyes, bright as a high noon sun.

Stay honest.

"I was in a Lancastle hamlet named Illery in a shithole named The Sparrowhead when tale came of a snow-haired madwoman the next town over drinking lads under the table and challenging their mates to fist-fights," she found herself saying. "Evidently this had been going on for some time and had become quite the nightly spectacle. And somehow, instantly, I knew it was her. Something in my gut just told me. And, sure as shit, when I arrived, there she was, in her Midaran skin, lip fat, eyes swollen, knuckles up, taking a punch from one of the ugliest goons I'd ever seen. Morgan went down hard and I nearly ran to her. My hand dropped to my hilt and a current of violence trembled within. But then she started laughing. And it was like nothing I'd ever heard before. It came out sad and angry and frail and broken and ghastly wrong, as though laughing had somehow become her own fucked version of crying. And somehow despite it all, she pulled herself back up to her feet..."

"And the cuts and names?" he asked.

"Those too came before me." *Mostly.* Val recalled how the screaming white lines felt against her caress. "She could make them disappear if she wanted. I've seen her mend some nasty gashes before. Hells, I've seen her mend wounds down to the bone. It might take her a few candles to see it through, but..."

"She doesn't want to."

"It's how she honors her House. Or so that's what she's told me. I can't say I fully understand it either. I do know she views her gift as a curse. As such she hates giving any power to it at all. Even still, she will almost always use it to help others in need, but rarely will she spend it on herself."

Aiden's mouth opened as though he was about to say something, but the tolling of a bell from beyond the mess kept the words at bay. Together, they turned toward the main deck as harried footsteps clamored about the aft deck overhead.

"All hands!" a voice cried from a nearby rest. And a second echoed the order from just outside.

"What is it?" Aiden asked.

"Nothing good," Ledge grumbled as he passed them by, her ka'rym chii in hand.

"Gold sails," the quartermaster announced as they came to The Banshee's starboard edge, the waves lashing up at them from below.

"Twin birds," the lookout called from the crow's nest above, "clippers."

"And more than like the mothership isn't far behind," the quartermaster added.

"Can The Banshee outrun them?" Ledge asked with troubling concern.

"Doubtful," the quartermaster replied, craning his attentions to the helm where the galleon's captain stood with foot to taffrail and spyglass to eye.

No one knew her ministry name, but according to Ledge most folk amidst the ports, depending on station, referred to The Banshee's captain as D'Anna Hex. Hex was built like a lady, though portrayed herself as anything but. Over the past decade, she had forged herself a reputation as one of the toughest scrappers sailing the high seas and for the most appeared the part. She was tall and carried about her an air of confident authority. Her head was shaved and her face was marked by an assortment of inks and scars including a fresh, angry cut across the right side of her lip. As for the rest, she wore dark, frayed leathers crossed in varying places with shiny metal horrors, and a simple wine-colored cape that hung down low to her booted ankles. All told, Val rather thought she gave Morgan an honest run for the most terrifying woman she had ever met.

"Keats," Hex called the quartermaster in a deep, smoky voice. "How long do we have?"

"Half day tops," Keats responded, fishing a compass from his vest pocket. "If they push us, mayhaps half that."

Hex's face creased. It was clear she was weighing their options as she approached.

Valestriel stared out at the two dark shapes painted innocuously against the velvety starlit horizon.

"If we pull to port, it may buy us a bit longer," the quartermaster continued. "At least, the wind would have us, but it may send their raiders all the quicker. Either way, if they want us, they'll eventually have us. There's just too much sea twixt us and shore."

"And what are they sending?" Hex asked.

"Most clippers hold about thirty men, forty at maximum, and most will be capable. So roughly sixty, seventy total, if they send both, forty, fifty worth a shit."

Keats sounded like a man in the know. By his attire and attitude, Val had already pegged him as a Royalguard deserter and this only bolstered that hunch.

"I'm sorry, what exactly are we discussing here?" Val couldn't stop herself.

"*We* are not discussing anything," Hex rasped contemptuously.

Val's eyes wandered to her ka'rym chii in Ledge's possession then over to Aiden.

"No doubt they will pick us clean this time," Keats said. "And you will stand trial for your actions in Samulda, D'Anna. That is, if they don't decide to feed you to the depths first."

Val took Aiden by the cuff of his robe and pulled him back within the mess.

"What the hells, Val," Aiden quibbled.

"They mean to war," she said. "They can't risk capture."

"I gathered."

"We can't align ourselves with this."

"And what exactly would you presume we do?"

"Desmond," Ledgermaine called as he joined them.

"You!" Val hissed, stepping in the old man's face. "What the hells have you gotten us into?"

"Steady on." Ledgermaine brought her ka'rym chii between them and pressed it against her chest. "The high seas are lawless territory. This was bound to happen." He waited for her to take hold of the scabbard. "Obviously I had hoped for smooth sailing, but that would've been too easy now wouldn't it?"

"Too easy?" Val grumbled. "Are you serious?"

"Come now, ashaeydir, where is your sense of adventure?"

Her lips pursed and her eyes narrowed. The fool had just returned her blade and then had the stones to risk outing her. She had a right mind to be done with him right then and there. *He's testing you*, her rational side reminded. *Keep your bloody wits about you.*

"And, so what," Aiden chimed in, "we're pirates now?"

"We are what we are," he answered cryptically.

84

"Ledge," Val grumbled, issuing a hard, irritated look.

"Listen, I know this isn't ideal," he said, stroking his beard. "Nothing much is these days. In fact, at this juncture, assume the more ideal it seems the less it actually is."

"Is this your attempt at a rally on then?" Val scoffed.

"I need you to trust me, Val." His expression remained calm and composed, "both of you."

Trust you? It was all Val could do to stay her fury. Ledge was a schemer and a cheat, of this she had no doubts, and their current predicament reeked horribly of ambiguity and betrayal. But what other choice did they have? They were literally in the middle of nowhere surrounded by strangers and now enemies. Given all that, sorting Ledgermaine had quite suddenly taken a plunge on her ever-growing list of shit to solve.

She gripped the leather hilt of her mae'chii revealing four fingers of steel from the scabbard's mouth before sliding it back in place.

At least, she had her biter back. She could only pray she wouldn't have to use it any time soon.

CHAPTER NINE

Nearly a day gone to the lichlord's offensive and the creeping mists were now inside the castle halls, The Hood's subtle reminder, hovering about in pockets and patches like prying haunters. As good fortune faired, for whatever that meant in this freshly fucked iteration of the world, the blighters had not yet caught up to their dreary make of deathly sunshine. Though it was only a matter of time...

Rhymona waited outside the council chamber with arms crossed and a nervous eye twitch, wishing she had a shufa stick to burn, moreover, wishing she had two, or in the very least some shithead alky she could readily drive her fists against.

It felt like it had been hours that the small council, or at least what was left of it, had been in session, but she knew that it was only her impatience at work. She had trudged back and forth, up and down the corridor upward of a thousand times, sharing ugly looks with the pair of fuckwit bluecoats standing sentry at the council chamber door every time she passed. It was a small bit of pleasure. Though weren't they all so small these days?

Her mind dashed hither and yon, unable to settle. Bad as it had ever been. Bad as after Halion's death. Bad as forsaking Aiden. Bad as losing Fiandrel. The Spellbind creature's cruel leavings. Dredging up every little poxy gremlin memory that had long since been locked away before leaving her to tear herself apart all over again.

So, she paced. Like a wife awaiting the widow turn. Floating up and down the corridor with her shite fucking past for shite fucking company useless as a gods damned turd and smelling little the better. But all the anxiety had to go somewhere, didn't it? For now, she reckoned, this had to be enough.

She lightly traced fingernails down the sleeve of her left arm, over an old scar that ran from wrist to elbow.

No, she scolded as her fingers curled into a ball.

TABLE SCRAPS TULLY had been a horrid cutter in the cycles to follow her captivity, long before Rhymona Curie came to haunt. Though, as woeful an affair as cutting could be, in young Morgan's case, it turned out to be something of a blessing. For it was by her awful penchant for self-mutilation that she would eventually come to find the depths of her gift.

It began innocently enough. In the least, as innocently as something like cutting one's self could. She was slicing vegetables for yet another banquet, as she had done a dozen, dozen times before. However, on this occasion, something within shifted slightly—a phantom shudder, as it were—and she cut a chunk of flesh from her index finger. She wagered most folk in such a situation might scream or make a fuss or rush to find a spigot and cloth to clean and dress the wound, but not Morgandrel Tully. Morgandrel Tully stood there staring dumbly at the blood spill, studying it, as it oozed out of her staining the onion a deep, dark crimson horror.

The feeling never left her.

After a time, she found herself pocketing little pins and razors from around the Alyfain's manor, and in the dark of nightfall, chained like a beast in the stables, she would apply them to her body. Initially, it was simple lines that only drew little wisps of red. *A scratch a day, keeps the demons away*, she would tell herself. Most were straight and even, but some ended up jagged if she took a fright mid-cut. The barn owls were a particular bother back in those days. But it wasn't long before the lines arched and curled into letters and words and elaborate symbols.

The first word she ever carved was FIA, etched with care by starlight into the outside of her right thigh. Then came her father's name, REFYN, a few inches higher and a few letters longer. And then her mother's just above that. CALADRIA.

A series of names followed, those of her fallen family, and she became something like a walking memorial. Then came the symbols, so many symbols, culminating with her house sigil, a three-scored X dug deep into the space between her neck and breasts.

This was the one that got her caught, and the Lord and Lady Alyfain had her stripped bare for inspection, turning away in disgust with what they found beneath her dirty rags. A cycle's worth of hidden markings. It was at that point, seeing the repulsed looks on their faces, she knew she would never stop. Not as affairs remained. Not until she was either free or dead.

She had finally found her weapon against her most hated Lady and Lordship.

'Twas not a month later, her new-found weapon nearly found her an early grave. After a particularly nasty whipping, in a blur of tears and snot, she went too deep over the inside of her left arm. Blood bubbled up and gushed from the wound like a city fountain, far more than she had ever given before. And it just bled and bled. She felt woozy almost immediately as she collapsed into the pile of hay she called a bed, the stable spinning violent circles around her.

She closed her eyes and began to pray as she clasped a hand over the wound to stem the bleeding. Her light was fading fast.

Then something else began to rise up within her, something desperate to stay alive, something beyond mere prayers, something that was calling her name. She opened her eyes and found a figure in the stable's pitch. Somehow it didn't spin like the rest of the world. It was arcane, untouchable, immovable, and black as the inside of a closed coffin. Even the sister moons were no match for its darkness. But Morgan recognized its shape. It was a shape she could never ever forget. A shape that nearly matched her own, but for the cycles they had spent apart.

Fiandrel.

THE VERY MOMENT she thought her sister's name, the door to the council chamber yawned open and Merillion appeared, looking more irritated than usual. Rhymona could hear Remy and Queen Deadbeat still going at it behind him, and she couldn't be prouder of her barmy little Toffy-woff. It sounded like he was in a devilish sort of mood to be sure.

Merillion Alyfain closed the door behind him and offered her a grim expression. "On me," he grumbled.

They marched away, through blotches of mist and torchlight to the end of the corridor which lead to a stairwell. Without word, they ascended until the winter air found them and the starlight came to call. Merillion stopped just before taking to the battlements.

"Antagonizing the queen is not a good look," he said, pressing her up against the wall, his breath reeking of foreign tonics.

"Much to your make, I gave up on good looks long ago." She smiled madly at the busted mug her mother had given him all those many cycles ago.

"You need to smarten up," he kept on, turning his back to her and stepping out into the night. "This isn't The King's Wall or some dodgy back hollow drinking hole you're in here. That woman, despite your opinions, can have you in a noose at the snap of a finger."

"Tut, I think it's fucking adorable you still believe I fear death." She fell in behind him, skinny as the shadow's sister.

Screams and the sounds of the blight echoed from the ruin below. The lichlord's army was knocking at the door now, and there were those still out there scraping and scampering about.

"Enough with the japery and nonchalance, this is all quite serious now, isn't it?"

"I know what it bloody is, yeah. In case you forgot, I am the one that saw the thing in The Spellbind. The one that had it burrowing around inside my skull like a fucking rat on holiday. The one that fought through the fuckwit convention in Palatia, only just surviving. And all this time, what the fuck have you been up to, Rill? Save whoring about these useless poshers and tugging at Harver's itty bitty cock like a—"

"Oi, you can shit on me all you like, Morgan, but I am the one that got you out, yeah. Remember that. The one that gave you a chance at a new life. Everything you do, everything you have ever done out here, everything you think you've changed, everyone you've ever helped is because of me."

"Delighted to know your ego is still driving the old carriage then." She dared a peek down below, between breaks in the clouded mist and watched from a bird's eye view as a bluecoat archer passed through a courtyard into the next over, a trio of ghouls in fast pursuit. They looked about the size of little toy soldiers from this height. "Where are the others?"

"The others," Merillion scoffed. "You mean where is Valestriel?"

"Don't be a shit, Rill." The archer plunked the nearest blighter and it dropped. But his next nock wasn't near fast enough, and he had to ward the second ghoul off with his bow. They both disappeared under an arcade.

"That's hilarious coming from you," Merillion said. "What's the matter, Morgan? Don't like the taste of your own medicine?"

She turned away from the parapet. She couldn't help a shit from up here anyway. No use feeling bad about it. "First off, fuck you," she started. "Secondly—"

"Kanton," he interjected, clearly over any measure of riposte, "She's in Kanton. Or Gallea's Grace. Or wherever the boy is."

Rhymona's face fell. "The boy?"

"She took up your old gig, hadn't you heard? Practically begged for it in the end."

"Tell me you're joking." Her eye twitch put in double time.

"And why the fuck would I be joking?"

Gods dammit, Val, what were you thinking? "She has no idea what she is dealing with," Rhymona huffed. "Aiden Ashborough is a danger to everyone and everything, himself included. Didn't you think there might be a very good reason for why I left him to memory's rot?"

"Hmmm, might have been worth mentioning if it were that bad, yeah? I'm not a fucking mind reader, now am I?"

"Fuck off."

"Yeah, fuck off, is it? Isn't that what you did, yeah? Abandoning us. Abandoning your duty. You're just as bad as that brat Remy."

"Fe, I abandoned my jailors and somehow I'm the villain?"

She remembered how harsh she had been on Val the last time they had been together. It hadn't been her intention to turn the girl inside out. And it was certainly never her intention to steal away her heart. She tried to be careful with Valestriel. She tried to be considerate. But it happened anyway. They happened anyway. Because she was weak and Val was so damned kindhearted and lovely and relentless.

She had meant well outside Fountain Head with her cruel words. She thought the less she gave about Aiden the better. That if she told Val she loved him, it would make her hate him and stay away. But even her best laid plans somehow found a way to bite her in the arse these days.

"Go on then. Let's have it." Rill groused. "What happened?"

The winter winds began to whisper, and she felt a chill run up her backside. Drunk as she was that night, she could still recall near everything about it. It was her own fault in the end. She shouldn't have pushed him into it. But wasn't that ever her way?

"I tried to reach Fia," she mumbled, bracing for backlash. "And I knew if I convinced him, given his bloodline, we might be able to open a ward."

"Baka!"

"I know—"

"You know? This is twice now you've fucked about with soul magic. You'd be caged if the Ministry found out, and that's if they didn't fancy a burning for it."

"I said I know."

"Coins to cobwebs, that's what's put us in this shite fucking predicament with the blight in the first place. The gods know, Morgan, what in the nine hells is wrong with you?"

"You couldn't possibly understand."

"Try me."

"What's there to try?" It was all coming back up now, like it or not. "She was my sister, Rill. My twin. My second half. Together we made a whole. That's how it was. And then your cunt fucking House took her from me. Eleven cycles old, sweet as could be. Never did a thing wrong. Never sassed back. Never once said a hurtful word to anyone. And gone!

"I was the firebrand. I was the poxy little shit-stain. I was the bratty punk." Her face screwed up from the swell of emotions. "It should have been me."

"Morgan, we've discussed this. Fia's not—"

"No, Rill, you let me fucking finish. You let me fucking have this. You said try you. And I know you've heard the tale a thousand times, but you'll have it again, yeah." Her voice cracked. "It's like a part of Fia still lives inside me, calling after me. Always. Even now. And it only grows worse the longer I try to ignore it. No matter where I go or what I do, the weight of her remains. So, you're damned right I tried to communicate with her. I decided I was going to be selfish for once. I was going to have some answers. I was going to see her again. I was going to hear her real fucking voice again. And I nearly did. I was so close. Inside the rift, I could almost feel her there…"

Dread filled her throat and mouth like ash from a tapped shufa pipe.

"But then I felt something else behind me. Something wrong. And so, I turned to check and that's when I saw his face…" She remembered the expression Aiden wore. It was an expression she had never seen before, almost as though he were wearing a mask. "It was only there for a second. But the power I felt in him. It was immense. And it was unnatural. And nothing at all in resemblance of the gift. It wasn't just hungry. It was starved. Ravenous. And it tried to bury me inside the rift. I could feel arms like tentacles begin to curl around me and hands like hooks tearing at me as I clawed back out. All the while, I could feel the withering begin to set in. It couldn't have been more than a few seconds."

"Is that what happened to your hair?"

"And why I look old as Grammy Alyfain's fucking nan?" she added. "Yes. And afterward, he bore no memory of it at all as he came rushing to my aid. And this was immediately after. Truly, I don't know which disturbed me more. The fact that he possessed such terrifying powers or that he couldn't remember anything at all about them." She crossed over to the other side of the battlements and glanced out over the empty churchyard below. "Days passed into weeks and he never once showed signs of the same change from that night. Yet still my fear of him grew. I wanted to help him, but at the same time I wanted to be as far away from him as I could possibly get. I became convinced I would trigger it again. You know, typical Morgan mindfuck bullshit. And, so I fought with leaving and staying for weeks. Until one night, I finally worked up the nerve to pack a bag and run. And I just kept pushing 'til morning. And then I did it again the next night. And again the following. And I found the further away I got, the better I began to feel. The more like the old me I began to feel.

"I felt this same presence earlier in The Spellbind. The creature we saw there. The gnaudrylax, as Remy named it. It had the same ravenous aura as Aiden did that night."

"And you think they are connected?"

"I know they are. And I know they are both somehow connected to Tetherow." She spread an arm out to the madness below. "All of this is. Back in Palatia, a magus had one of the blight in his laboratory. The fucker spoke to us. Been dead a full day and it spoke clear as you and I here. Said we were wasting our time. Said some other useless shit too. But I am now convinced that voice was Tetherow."

"Tetherow," Rill spat. "It would be a fucking y'deman responsible for all this, wouldn't it?"

A bright white explosion of blinding light ignited the sea of mist in the distance and they both shielded their eyes to it. An eerie silence ensued.

"The lichlord," Rhymona said and a clicking sound from below responded.

She peered over the edge, and a bloodied hand shot up at her, squeezing at her neck, as the whole of the ugly fiend followed. With inhuman strength, it lifted itself onto the crenellation and atop her. It had no regard whatsoever for its own wellbeing. Rhymona struggled against the bastard's grip and weight as its drooling, blood-smeared mouth gnashed at her face, flailing at it to the best of her ability before she felt it go limp and collapse upon her.

A moment later, Merillion ripped the knife from out of its skull and hurled it at a second ghoul that was pulling itself up onto the battlements down the way. It stuck inside the devil's heart, barely worse than a bug bite.

"Shit," he grumbled as Rhymona shoved the first blighter off her and came to her feet. "They climb walls now?" he questioned.

"They do whatever the lichlord commands," she said, hefting Fucker from its short-lived slumber. "Aim for the head or don't bother."

"This way," Rill ordered as more of the devil's army clambered upon the ramparts, blocking the path whence they had come.

The pair picked their way along the battlements as the creatures poured onto the stonework behind them. Theirs became a game of inches as they barely stayed ahead, step by gambled step, knowing one little slip-up was all it would take to become a blighter party platter.

A ragged ghoul with half his jaw dangling loose lifted itself onto the parapet ahead of Rhymona, forcing her to take action. She took no chances, clocking it across its temple with Fucker's flat end before it could find proper purchase, sending it clicking back over the other side. An instant later, another braindead fuckwit came up to take its place behind her.

Onward she pressed, a footstep behind her old mentor's coattails, a second bright white explosion flashing and rumbling from the courtyards down below.

"Hells, they're everywhere," Merillion barked as they scrambled toward the open stairwell at the other end.

And just as they came within spitting distance, a fire-haired girl in alabaster linens appeared at the stairwell entryway chanting, her fingers moving rapidly.

There could be no mistaking what the movements were. And there could be no mistake in the change of air around them, nearly wrung free of all its prior oxygen.

Is she?

"Wide berth!" Merillion howled.

Rhymona tossed Fucker ahead as she dove into a forward roll, as far away from the center walk as possible. A comet of Eldn fire coursed between them into the horde of chasing ghouls, its cast torrid as dragon's breath, singeing after her wasted shadow. Loon-eyed, she bounced up in full sprint, smoke pouring off her, collecting Fucker as she scurried passed the Chandii girl whose hands were now roaring in crackling blue flame.

Holy shit. Holy shit. Holy motherfucking shit. She never thought she would ever actually see one. Not in a hundred lifetimes. Hells, not in a thousand. Though she reckoned Thira had promised they would come if Remy took her in. And sure enough, here one was. And not a moment too soon. Every measure as breathtaking as the fables made them out to be.

Rhymona dared a glance back over her shoulder as she and Merillion came upon the stairwell entrance, and she watched as the Eldnumerian sorceress, her long tail of ginger hair floating impossibly behind her, splashed a second wave of azure conflagration across the battlements, easy as you please.

It hit her about halfway back down to the inner corridors that she recognized the girl. She was the cloth maiden Marsea was constantly palling around with before all the corruption began.

And a name swiftly followed the recollection.

Effie, she was called.

Effie Cavendish.

CHAPTER TEN

T hat one is not to be trusted," Larissa said a breath after
Casilvieri vacated the chamber. "Between he and Vaustian, they
have just about ruined your sister."

"Wrong again," Remy remained confrontational. "The gods know, it
absolutely astounds me how little you truly know about your own
children."

"I told you to mind how you speak to me, Rembrandt."

"And you should well mind your ignorant ways, Mother," he said as he
stood at the foot of the table. "If that monstrous pair have accomplished
anything decent in all their time here, it would be that they have made
Marsea stronger. She's the one that sacked Ganedys in the Kingswood, by
the way." He turned his attentions to Sylvie and Aeralie, "and she was
there for Vaustian's deserts just as well."

"And what is that supposed to mean?" Sylvie questioned.

Admittedly, he could have gone about the confession with a touch
more empathy. Though over the past half hour his mother had near quibbled to death what little he had to begin with. "I'm sorry you've had to
find out like this."

"No!" Sylvie Harver cried out. "I won't believe it. You're lying."

Her eyes were hard, hard as he had ever seen from her before, which

96

honestly wasn't saying much given her largely diffident demeanor, but his were of another world altogether and blazing with indisputable azure conviction. Conviction that gazed down another chair to Aeralie at the very moment her heart began to break. All that love and affection she held for him dashed to bits in an instant. Or so he suspected.

Now you maybe understand the smallest thing about me, he thought at her sorrow.

"And what purpose would such a lie serve?" he answered vacantly, glancing briefly from one dumbfounded face to another down the length of the long table until it came round once more to the head where his mother sat.

Not a one of the small council knew how to approach this new version of their puppet princeling. And it was a small council indeed, cut to nearly half the usual heads. Gilcrest and Adler were perhaps the most noticeable of the absentees, though Ellory, Pryce, and Cleverly managed attendance. Not a trustworthy face amongst that lot, to be sure. But given the turn of things, they hadn't much in the way of quality input anyway. They were merely faces of titles that were fastly growing useless. His eyes trailed back to Sylvie Harver. "We came about him in one of the upper courtyards. There could be no mistaking it. Vaustian was one of the blight." And there it was. The lie he had recited in his head since his apparent death and improbable return from the other side. Though, it could have been argued that it was more of a twist than an actual lie. If nothing else, Vaustian Harver had certainly proven himself a blight on Remy's life over the past decade. "There was no other way. He had to be put down."

Shaking, Sylvie pushed away from the table, her chair grating roughly against the stonework below. All eyes were on her as she stood. They all just sat there for a minute, silent as a lonesome walk home after dusk. Then Sylvie cut a nasty look directly at him. "Whatever he was, I know you're responsible, you little worm. You and your whore sister." And she stormed out without another word.

Aeralie offered him a sullen glance and quickly followed after.

"Someone should probably follow her," Larissa said to the bluecoats standing guard at the room's edge.

"And might I request the remaining small council vacate the chamber as well." Remy was quite over this charade. It was practically free theatre for anyone not named Lanier at this point, and he would no longer serve as the small council's laughingstock.

"Your Highness?" Ellory questioned his Queen.

Larissa nodded her accord.

Remy ignored each one of them as they passed him by, and Aldridge closed the chamber doors leaving only the Prince, his Queen mother, and little Julia.

"You knew Desmond was still alive and you kept it from us?" he started in immediately.

"Rembrandt, you need to calm yourself."

"I will not calm myself, Mother," he huffed. "Did Marsea know?"

"Of course not," Larissa murmured. "As usual, you've missed the point entirely, haven't you?"

"Clearly I have. Why would you keep such a thing from us? He was our brother! And he is the rightful King!"

"The gods know, Rembrandt, no one knew—only myself, Rhonyn, and Ledge."

"Why would Desmond choose to stay away from us?" Remy thought twice about that question after loosing it. Had he been given the chance to leave Lancastle when he was younger, would he not have taken the chance just as well?

"He didn't choose to stay away. Your brother hasn't the faintest inkling who he really is. And we chose to leave him that way." Larissa sighed. "It is as your gutterwitch friend claimed. No one knows about him because of the manner by which he yet still lives."

That statement certainly sat ill with him. Remy couldn't imagine. Desmond's entire life had apparently carried on as some big sham. Though, in fairness, to the present, his own had proven little the better.

"Your brother died on the night of the coup. That part is true. He was dead for nearly a week. He yet lives now because he was thereafter brought back from that death. Your uncle saw to that in his dreadful madness. He and Ledge stole Desmond away to the Southlands into the care of a practiced gravedancer and somehow they managed to bring him back."

"You've seen him?"

"I have. But you must understand the dark arts are considered treason by the Ministry."

"Oh, I am well aware."

"What we did could never be known for fear of recourse. We implored the Oathsworn in this, but they would not abide our actions. So we had no other choice. We had to keep the resurrection quiet or risk the noose. Prize well, these were the actions of desperate people. We were not in our right minds at the time. Certainly, I was not in my right mind. And I let Rho convince me this was for the best. I let my emotions gain the better of me. Truly, how could I not? He was my son. My baby boy. My first born. And he was still so young. I couldn't bear having lost him so soon. However, once the deed was done, the Desmond that returned was nothing at all like the prior version. The version that returned was no longer my little Des. It broke my heart to see what he had become.

"Rhonyn convinced me that he should stay for the time being with the gravedancer. That she might be able to help him gain some fashion of his memories over time. So I agreed. Honestly, what other choice did I have? It was in his best interests, after all. It would keep him safe. No doubt the Ministry would have had him burned alive as an abomination had they found out."

Oh, they most certainly would have. "When was the last time you saw him?"

"It would have been a few cycles ago." Tears welled in her icy blues. "We watched him graduate Perciya. Your uncle and I."

"So he actually attended university?" *The gods know Marsea would have been green with sick at that.*

"He did. And not only that, but he graduated Crown of his Order. Oddly, some good did come of his foster family. He was quite happy that day." It brought the ghost of a smile to Larissa's lips. "Diploma in hand, robes flowing, a lovely highborn girl on his arm. I walked right up to them to congratulate him, but he still didn't recognize me. Nor did he know Rhonyn. We were but faces in a crowd. Two amongst a thousand randoms. The passing cycles had changed nothing about his memory."

Remy's heart sank for his mother. He could sense her hurt as he neared and wrapped her in a hug. An even stranger sensation washed over him inside the act. How long had it been since they had last hugged? She felt so small in his arms now.

"I never imagined it would be so hard," she spoke across his shoulder.

Jules, quiet as a midnight church mouse, hugged around them both and for a moment they remained tight together in an embrace. It was almost family-like. It was almost...

REMY, Thira interrupted. For an instant, Remy almost forgot about their strange union.

A nearby explosion shook the citadel, causing dust and stone to rain down around them.

"Your Highness!" Aldridge burst back into the chamber. "We must be leaving. Blighters are in the halls."

"In the halls?" the Queen inquired. "How is this possible?"

"They are scaling onto the battlements, milady," Aldridge replied. "Dozens of them. Dozens of our own. Climbing the ramparts as though they were bloody born to it."

"Take them to the King's Passage," Remy commanded the knight.

"Rembrandt?" Larissa questioned.

"I must stay," he answered. And his uncle's words came back once again for the haunt.

A king must be more than his fellow man. Always and evermore. Without complaint. A king must be able to see beyond what lies plainly before him. For a true blood king has more than himself to account for. Always and evermore. A true blood king must account for all things.

"No!" Julia protested. "Come with us."

"I can't," he said. "You know I can't."

"Yes, you can."

"I am a soldier, Jules. I have a responsibility to protect the kingdom." Remy opened his palm before her and an azure-white flame ignited inside it. "Because I have this." Amazingly, it only tingled slightly at his touch.

Julia's eyes widened in wonderment. "What is it?" she asked.

"The kiss of the dracari," he said, crushing it out inside his fist. "Now go with Bromas and Mother. I need you to keep them safe for me."

Reluctantly, Julia turned away.

"And Jules," Remy called after her, "I love you."

"You can have those words in return the next time I see you," she replied, Harver-cold.

Deserved, he thought as the father and daughter from Brymshire flickered into his mind's eye once again.

THE LITTLE ONE IS QUITE SHARP, Thira said as they stalked down the corridor toward the battlement stairwell.

Screeches echoed from the darkness within. And shadows shifted in the stairwell accompanied by an all too familiar clicking sound.

Remy gripped his watchman blade, and it sang with thirst from his sheath. *Do your thing, Thira.* And his other hand ignited in flame, aglow in the bright azure violence of Eldn magic.

"...*Thas'kon ech vira dhu leckt!*..." her words spewed forth, and the heads of the first two charging blighters darkened to blue and popped like a pair of bad blemishes, leaving a black and red mess down the walls as their bodies staggered forward, wilting to the stones below.

Remy slashed at the next ghoul, sending it sprawling awkwardly past as he jammed the point of his sword through the eye of the fourth, piercing its brain end to end, leaving the tip and a third of steel for the next. The watchman kept grinding forward, both hands at the hilt, crushed against the cross-guard, using the fourth ghoul as a shield as they rammed into the fifth, steel eating into face.

He halted the moment the fifth ghoul went slack and ripped the blade back from skull and flesh and eye socket. Swiftly, with a fluidity he had never experienced before, he spun about toward the third blighter he had let past, the magic words on his tongue again, and the left side of its body burst outward, sending its remaining half smashing violently into the opposite wall.

He shifted back as he heard a fresh clicking sound from the stairwell and watched as two more ghouls burned blue from the inside out, their skin crumbling to ash inside their clothing.

Behind them in the stairwell appeared a fire-haired girl dressed in cloth maiden linens.

Remy recognized her. But, of course, he had. There were not so many Chandii folk this far west, after all. She was a girl from the abbey he knew to be good friends with Marsea.

Effie.

But Yvemathira knew a great bit more about her. She knew the girl's truth. In fact, she knew the girl by another name entirely.

The girl had once been like him, many cycles prior. He could still sense her presence within. She'd once had a name too. She had once been her own being. But at some point, circumstance called upon her for a higher purpose and her soul was thenceforth bound to another.

"...*Myrenna*..." Remy spoke Thira's greeting. *Mercy me.*

"My Queen," the Chandii girl said meekly, bowing her head dutifully.

CHAPTER ELEVEN

Snowflakes sprinkled down in thick crumbly clumps as Marsea and her new mentor crunched along the barren cobbleways. The air was crisp creating a lovely stillness within the fanciful glow of Vinth's sundry street lanterns.

It had taken them the better part of the afternoon to trek down the mountain pass, through the Kingswood, and make the clearing just outside town. And Vinth was quite the quaint holiday gush of a hollow with its smoky chimneys, cozy thatched cottages, window candles, and fresh layer of snowfall. The sort of pleasant little country village you only read about in the mushiest of romance novels. Marsea had to believe the sight of it alone was enough to delight even the grumpiest of hearts, if by only the slimmest of margins.

It was the sort of place that seemed so innocent one felt almost ridiculous walking about with a knife at her waist.

She glanced over at Beldroth. Seeing him in the daylight had humanized him. There was something ghastly unfair about the way his life had turned out. And here she had once thought herself the most misunderstood person on all the moon. How was that bit for perspective, then? It was true. Her life had been tragic. But paled by comparison to that of Elsymir Beldroth. But wasn't that what more cycles bought you in the end, anyway? More pain. More loss. More scars.

"We're here," Beldroth said, stopping at the door of a gloomy little cottage and rapping his knuckles against it. By first impressions, it appeared the ugly duckling in town, in desperate need of repairs and a fresh coat of paint, with more than enough drear and dodginess to drum up a genuine pang of concern about the lodgers within.

"And where is here, exactly?" she asked, her teeth fighting off a chatter. They had been clenched tight for so long, simply talking was strange. Evidently, Remy's old tweed hunting jacket didn't hold quite the same warmth out in the deep, dank wilderness as it did in the brazier lit luxury of the bustling kingdom cobble.

"The nearest place I have to an actual home," Beldroth answered.

Of course.

The door opened wide, as if on cue, revealing a short, gray-haired woman.

"Elsymir?" she uttered.

"Evening, Dags. Been a while."

"Indeed, it has. Come in, come in," she mothered.

Beldroth hobbled into the hearth light, his cane digging deep into the hardwood. "Marsea, Dagmara. Dags, this is Marsea Lanier. She has taken on apprenticeship with—well, it's just me now."

"Pleasure," Marsea said, sticking to a popular greeting amongst the common folk.

"The pleasure is all mine, milady," the elderly woman returned. "Now come on in out of this dreadful cold before it catches you."

Marsea had never beheld such a deceptive creation in all her days as Dagmara's cottage. The inside was the opposite of its exterior in almost every aspect imaginable. It was warm and bright and lively and it smelled like the castle kitchens. Nay, it smelled even better. Like stew set to the boil and laced with a perfect pinch of seasoning. And suddenly Marsea felt her little belly rumble in agreeance. When was the last time she had eaten, anyway?

"I hope you two brought your appetites, then," Dagmara said. "I've put on a bit of rabbit garden stew." She had the kind of face that scrunched up when she smiled, and the kind of smile that made the eyes disappear.

"Klaus's recipe I hope," Beldroth said as he shirked off his jacket and placed it on the wall rack.

"Yes, of course," Dagmara replied from the cauldron's boil like a proper Granny Cookpot. "He should be back in a spell. Had some late business down at the Inn."

"You're in for a real treat here," Beldroth assured. "Best stew in the Vael, Klaus's rabbit garden stew."

Marsea shouldered down her backpack with a smirk and followed him from the foyer toward the great chamber. It was almost absurd that a man such as Elsymir Beldroth should ever say such things as 'you're in for a real treat here' and be taken seriously, yet here they were.

And with all that had gone on lately, she was simply amazed that something could still actually surprise her.

"Where is the beast, I wonder?" Dagmara asked as they came into the main room.

"Prowling for sup," Beldroth said. "I noticed the cobble was unusually quiet."

"Aye, ever since the rumors of the blight began to make the rounds, folk have been packing it in early."

"I can't say I blame them."

Marsea stopped dead in her tracks and stared in wonderment at the handsome white spruce decorated at the farthest edge of the great chamber. She had never seen anything quite so marvelously preposterous in all her life. It was tall as the ceiling and festooned in funny little trinkets and shiny silver and gold circlets of tinsel. And at the top, a large red ribbon was wrapped about it in a neatly tied bow.

"You've a tree in your home," the princess said.

"So I do, milady," Dagmara answered. "Bourystrom winter tradition, that."

Marsea glanced at the old woman. "You're Bourysh?"

"But of course. Half-Bourysh on my father's side. And we Bourysh hold hard to our traditions no matter what land we settle. This is part of our Yuletide's Passing. Every cycle during the cold season we take a tree in and we celebrate its life. In turn, it protects us from the haunters of the Mad Hunt."

Marsea took a step closer to the tree, giving it a keener inspection. "It's quite lovely." She studied one of the ornaments, a round red ball that returned her captivated reflection.

"Should I even bother asking about the bandages?" Dagmara inquired her other ramshackle guest. "The old masks were one thing, but this new look has me quite unsettled."

"And here I was hoping you might not notice," Beldroth returned.

"My eyes aren't so bad yet."

Marsea's smile faded at the turn of their conversation. It was in that moment she found a bond between the two that transcended the confines of mere friendship. A bond, she surmised, that could only be formed by time spent in company.

"I'm infected," he confessed.

"Mmm. I could smell the tonics on you. The girl too?"

"Just me. It's nether-rot."

Dagmara stopped stirring and took a heavy breath. "How?"

"Mal's latest rat. During the sacking of Brymshire."

"You know what must be done?" She resumed stirring.

"Of course."

"How much longer?"

"Could be days. Could be hours."

"Hours!"

"I know I've left it a bit late, but that's always been me, hasn't it?"

Dagmara's frown deepened. "Are you hearing their voices yet?"

"Yes."

"And seeing their memories?"

"Aye, all of it."

"The gods wept, Elsymir," Dagmara uttered.

"There's nothing more to be done about it now."

"At least, do you know the layer?"

"Could be wrath. Could be pride."

"And so the girl…"

"She is my choice."

Dagmara shifted her attentions back to Marsea, an eyebrow raised. "And she has agreed to it?"

"Agreed?" the princess asked. "Agreed to what?" Their serious tone had her stomach turning itself inside out.

Silence made the rounds between their contrasting expressions before Beldroth raised a side of his shirt revealing a tattoo in the maelstrom of bruises, burn marks, and scar tissue about his abdomen. Its symbol was a pair of triangles facing each other like an hourglass with a line running vertically through it. Forming a ring around the hourglass was a strange circle of script like she had never read before.

"What is that? What are you showing me?"

"It is the Mark of Shyraithka," Beldroth expounded, though by Marsea's understanding the explanation may as well have been utter gibberish. "This morning you asked how I came about Broenwjar." He lowered his shirt. "I found him outside The Scar some cycles back. He was already old as the hills then. Something got after him, something big and nasty. Gave him the pretty face he now wears. Left him for the worms. But I brought him back. This brand binds him to me and my service. And, so he lives on through my life force. The halo of script is old-world language. A spirit tongue charm. So the bond with the dead one won't let others slip inside."

"So you are like his phylactery?" Marsea asked.

"It is a similar concept, yes. However, if he is still in my service when I die—"

She took the hint. "He's worm food."

Beldroth nodded. "And I think there's still more for him to do here. I think he can still make a difference in all this. I think he can still help you, Marsea."

She thought about the big, mangy pup's hot, smelly breath and ragged coat of fur and then selfishly of the small council's expression if ever she were to bring such a wretch home. Doubtful anyone would ever try her again with such a beast at her side. And he was rather sweet in his own odd way, wasn't he?

He can be useful, Other pitched in, sending a tide of goose pimples up and down her arms.

"Will it hurt?" Marsea asked, pushing her glasses up.

"The branding isn't so bad," Dagmara answered. "But the binding ritual will require a certain measure of sacrifice." *Sacrifice, my new middle name.* "As with all things, there must be a balance. But that's what they make the whiskey for, isn't it? Lots and lots of whiskey."

"It takes someone strong with the gift for the ritual to be fruitful," Beldroth added.

"But I'm not—"

"Yes, you are, Marsea," Beldroth interjected, his expression bled earnest beneath the layers of bandaging. "I know you are. There's little else I have ever been more certain of. You only need to believe in yourself. You need to believe in your own strength and capabilities. Because, frankly, when it comes down to it, it's either you or the grave for Old Boy."

"That's hardly fair!"

"Fair? You bring up fair? There's scant little in life that's ever fair. You of all folk should know this."

"Elsymir," Dags called out his name like a reprimanding mother.

Silence descended again, and they all hovered alongside it for a stave of beats, completely motionless.

"In the end, it is your choice, Marsea," he added. "You don't have to do this. And if you must hear the words, nothing about this pleases me. Naturally, I realize how unfair this decision appears, but prize well, I wouldn't be so adamant about it if I didn't believe it was possible and for the absolute best."

Marsea nodded. She believed him. But of course, she believed him. And the words of choice were a nice sentiment too, but she had already made up her mind. There was no choice here. Not really. No matter how unfair. No matter what the sacrifice. When it came down to it, if there was even the smallest chance that her actions could possibly save Broen-wjar, she had to take it.

"I'll do it," she said, reluctance thick on her tongue. *Famous last words.* Though she couldn't quite bring herself to meet Beldroth's eyes.

"What are we doing?" a fresh voice called from the foyer, drawing the trio's attentions as he revealed himself.

"Klaus, old friend," Beldroth hailed.

"Elsymir?" Klaus replied.

Klaus was old and gray, just like Dags, with a big round belly, big bushy eyebrows, and bigger, bushier mutton chops wandering down from a mostly receded hairline. He quite reminded Marsea of a surly old sea captain. At least, how they were characterized in all the maritime tales. All he needed was a corn-cob pipe to complete the ensemble.

"No offense, but you're looking like hammered shit these days."

"Feeling like it, too," Beldroth confirmed.

"And who is the bonny lass here?" Klaus inquired as he took Marsea in. "Bit out of your league, wouldn't you say?"

"Behave, husband," Dagmara chimed in.

"This is Marsea Lanier," Beldroth introduced. "Marsea, this is Klaus VanLandingham."

"A princess of Lancastle in my own home. As I live and breathe," he murmured.

"She is the new apprentice," Dagmara said.

"That a fact?"

"Though I wish we came with better tidings," Beldroth put in.

"Hells, I've known you long enough to know if you're here, shit's gone sideways somehow," Klaus said. "Reckoned it wouldn't be long after the reports of the blight swept through town, you'd be around. Is it as bad as they say?"

"It's worse. Though, more than like, I'll not be around long enough to see it through."

"What are you on about then?"

"This is the end for me, old friend."

This last statement sapped any measure of humor left in jolly old Klaus as he read the room. "You want to be a little more descriptive, yeah?"

"I am infected with nether-rot. And before you start in, no, there's nothing to be done about it. I'm already too far gone."

"Bugger, that!"

"I'm not here to argue away my last days, Klaus. I've accepted my fate. We've all got our number, haven't we? Reckon mine's just about up. I brought Marsea with me to pass on what I can in the time I have left."

"And where is that snake Harver, then?"

"Dead," Beldroth replied. "Killed by an ashaeydir, as it were. More than like the same one that poisoned me. Again, nothing to be done about it. We move forward with what we have. And as it stands I have you and Dags and little else. And I need to prepare Marsea for what's coming as best I can. So I need you to be right with this."

"I'll get right with it when I get right," Klaus grumbled. "But whatever you need while you're here, you need only ask."

"The sword," Beldroth said. "I trust you still have it?"

Klaus directed his attentions back at Marsea. "For this one here?"

"I mean to train her to it."

"Train her, eh? Fancy yourself a fighter then?"

"Yes," she answered, sure-tongued (far more sure-tongued than she actually was).

"Hmm, you look kind of scrawny to me and twice as soft."

"Yeah? I would say to go ask the last guy that underestimated me, but that would require a gravedance for a pile of wolf leavings." *Good gravy, Marsea! Where in the devil did that come from?*

"Hah! How about that, then." Klaus glanced over at Beldroth. "I like this one here." And he kept on toward the cauldron, grabbing up a bowl. "Hope your grit's as sharp as your tongue, princess."

The maidens know, Marsea. What in vaelnation have you gotten yourself into now?

It went without saying really, but she hoped so too.

AFTER SUP, Marsea joined Beldroth out in the darkness of the VanLandingham's front porch and they waited for Broenwjar to return. It took mere seconds for the hearthfire warmth to fade away entirely. She blew lightly into her good hand to keep it thawed. The hour was late, and the snowfall had finally stopped and settled creating a most enchanting portrait of stillness. It looked like one of the idyllic paintings her mother favored so, though regrettably Marsea could never remember any of the top artists' names.

"Thought I would check up on you," she said taking a seat next to him, her breath clouds thick as they had ever been. "You've been out here a while."

"Have I?" His voice sounded gruffer than usual, like he was just getting over a long lingering sickness. "I'm still here."

"Interesting friends you keep."

"Good folk."

"That they are." Never in a thousand cycles did she ever think she would meet such a crowd and get on passably.

"Better stew, though."

"Better stew," she echoed, running her tongue along the roof of her mouth. And so it was. Good enough that she kept shoveling in mouthfuls despite it blistering her palate into utter tastelessness.

"And don't mind Klaus. He griefs everyone the first time he meets them. Just his way."

Not that she had ever really met many, but Marsea knew a good ole boy she saw one. "And here I thought it was saved special just for me."

A smirk shifted Beldroth's bandages, and there was a pregnant pause to chase it. Marsea rather found this sort of thing a common occurrence where Elsymir Beldroth was concerned.

"In all seriousness though," the mentor began after a time. "You are sure about the familiar binding?" His amethyst orbs appeared sincere, made all the more mystical by the soft hue of winter starlight.

"I am sure." The words nearly froze on her lips. She had already answered the question a thousand times over since their arrival. Though she was starting to gain a better understanding of the severity with each subsequent ask.

A small, delicate silence ensued. A silence like she had never really heard before. A country silence, as it were. Deathly set and beautifully realized.

"What does the name Broenwjar mean?" Her voice came, a hair above a whisper.

"Dags named him, actually," Beldroth said. "So, of course, it's a Bourysh term. It roughly translates in Midaran to 'black walker' or 'dark walker' or mayhaps 'shadow walker.' It seemed a fitting enough name at the time, so it stuck."

"So it did." Marsea fixed her attention on a candle in the window of the cottage across the cobbleway. "I'm sure you've seen dead animals before. Out of all creatures, what made you want to bring this particular one back?"

"You've never had a pet yourself before, have you?"

It was an innocent enough question, and yet for some reason, it upset her. More so than it ought to have for certain. "I have not," she confessed. "Father probably would have allowed for it, but not Mother. Remy once tried to keep a stray we came across in the upper courtyards when we were both still quite little. That lasted about a day before mother had it promptly run off. The nearest thing we've had to a pet ever since has been the Harver's hunting dogs."

"Hmmm," Beldroth grumbled. "Damned shame, that. There is a great deal to be had from a good animal companion. At least in my experience."

Marsea nodded.

"To answer your question, though. For most folk, there is a feeling you get about a certain animal. A sort of knowing. Not unlike the feeling you get about certain people. Where there is an undeniable yet indescribable connection. Where you know you and this creature will get on like a pair of brother scoundrels if given a chance to it."

Marsea had only felt that way about one other in all her days. Effie. Oh, and how she had disappointed her good friend. What she would give to simply explain herself. What she would give to once again find herself in Effie's good graces. She could only hope the maidens would one day be so kind as to allow her the opportunity.

"I sat with him for an hour, out in the middle of nowhere, doing my best to nurse his injuries. It was just enough to keep him breathing while I dragged him back to camp. He expired as I reached our caravan. To have it true, I thought he would have passed long before, but he was a tough old bastard. Tough as he looks. He was dead for some time before Dags and I mustered the binding spell to try to bring him back. But he was a fighter. Even in death, he still craved life. And eventually, he found my gift and well...cycles later here we are."

"Is that like the spell I'm to face?"

"To some extent. Though you should know, a blood bond is a world's difference by comparison to a mere master's bond."

"How do you mean?" The scar on her upper lip began to itch anew.

"You will be able to sense each other from long distances. And eventually, depending on your gift, you may be able to varg."

"Varg?"

"Ancient Chandii magic that allows a giftborn to enter the mind of a familiar and take command."

"You're serious?"

"I am."

"Have you done this before?"

"I have. But it requires a great deal of skill and the utmost concentration. There have been those that have lost themselves to the beast by such an undertaking. Seer madness, they name it. Prize well, Marsea, such echelons of magic are not to be taken lightly or abused. All it takes is one reckless act, and it will take everything from you. The greatest lie we giftborn tell ourselves is that we are in control, that the gift is ours to manipulate. Make no mistake about it, such beliefs couldn't be further from the truth. You remember this every time you call after yours. Every time you think you understand what it is. The gift is not our instrument. We are its."

"I will." She turned to her mentor. "I promise."

"You better."

A series of quiet breaths passed. And the maidens knew, the night had teeth at such an hour, sharp as the razor's kiss.

"I wanted to thank you for earlier," she said, "for the tracking and hunting lessons."

"Think nothing of it."

"And I apologize if I was a bit crabby at first. I confess I'm not much of a morning person most days."

"No need for apologies. All told, I thought you performed quite well. Not a single complaint. That is more than I can say for most of my past students. Honestly, you wouldn't believe some of the apprentices I have trained."

Marsea imagined Remy in the role and couldn't help but wonder what Beldroth would have thought of him. And that brought it back around again, didn't it? She had tried to put him out of her thoughts as much as could be had, but the effort was no easy task. He was her brother after all. A damned fool of a brother, but a brother nonetheless. How else was she supposed to be about it?

She sure hoped Rhymona was as talented as Cas named her. She couldn't lose Remy too. She just couldn't.

"There was something else I wanted to talk with you about," Marsea said. "The ashaeydir in Lancastle, I didn't tell you all of the truth about her the other night."

Beldroth remained fixed to his spot. "Go on."

"I knew her before she murdered Vaustian. At least I thought I did. Her name was Rhymona Curie, though she looked Midaran then. I hadn't the faintest inkling she was actually ashaeydir." The more she thought about it the more foolish she felt. "The stars save me, she looked more Midaran than I do."

"Mmm, she was one of their warriors, then," Beldroth said. "Ashaeydir soldiers are given an implant that allows them to alter aspects of their appearance. It is a contrivance not of this moon. Nor was it known to mine father's moon. It is how they were able to invade and enslave my ancestors so swiftly on Y'dema. Though I find it peculiar if she were able to infiltrate your court, as you say, that she would not ever try to harm you or your kin."

"To the contrary," Marsea said. "She and I formed a sort of alliance. We met in secret for months." *Drinking and bonding and scheming and drinking some more.* "And she agreed to return my brother home for a small fee." *We would take back the throne together. Infantile dreams.* "I only discovered her true identity just before I came here. Cas named her Morgan."

"Casilvieri knew this creature?"

"He seemed to. Though with all that was happening there was little time to question it. But the thought passed that he too might be one of them. The way he was acting..."

"That would certainly explain some things," Beldroth said.

Marsea drew the hood of her cloak over her head to cut the cold as the wind began to stir again. "But he has never done anything against me. Truthfully, and I hope you take no offense to this, but you and Cas are quite similar."

A Beldrothian quiet returned, in all of its meditative, esoteric glory. It possessed such a keen influence it was almost religious. Like abbey prayer on the Sabbath.

Under cowl, Marsea pulled at the wrist string to tighten the glove about her bad hand. At that, she felt as though she might have said enough for one night.

Sooner or later she would need to put Lancastle away. And the past would have to follow suit. Nothing had gone the way she had expected anyway and she doubted that course would suddenly change now. But there was one more subject she needed to know more about. One more subject that she needed to broach while there was still some time left for it. One more subject and she would be done with it. One more and she would try to let the rest be.

"My father," she said. "You were close back when, yeah?"

"I like to think so."

"I should like to know more about him." She focused on the candle in the window across the street again. Strangely it helped her center her thoughts. "Not his deeds. Not his talents. I know all of that. I've lived in it all my life. I've heard all the nothing little stories, all the platitudes and pleasantries. I want to know more about who he was as a person, as an actual living creature. What his flaws were. What sort of friend he was. What sort of man he was. What he liked to do aside from writing and study and taking council. I want to know what it was about my father that would have a man of your distinction wasting away his final days teaching the hapless daughter what remains of his secrets."

Beldroth let out a heavy breath. "All of this. What you are doing right now. It reeks of Whit. You are very much your father's daughter, Marsea. You don't look from the inside out. You look from the outside in. Right to the heart of the matter. No room for chuffa. Take but a small look within and you will have your answer as to most of your father's flaws. And most of his strengths too.

"As a friend he was loyal. Honorable to a fault. He never once did me wrong. Never once went back on a promise. And because of this, he began to feel like family to me. What little I remember of family, anyway. As such, I have always watched over you and your brother, Marsea. Since Whit's passing."

"Yongrin said you had him murdered." The question couldn't be helped. She caught him turning to her from the edge of her cowl.

"Yongrin knows nothing about that night save what fictions better serve her own devices."

"Then what really happened?"

Another intake of air was followed by a guilt-ridden sigh. "Your father did not approve of my actions as Tetherow. As such, he ordered me to disband Ravenholme once and for all. He believed Ravenholme to be a malefic construct of a bygone era. I did my best to explain why the guild was still necessary, but he wouldn't hear me. This argument went on for a time, neither one of us relenting. Your father could also be quite stubborn, all told. Eventually, it became clear that this row between us would result in a civil war. My apprentice at the time convinced me a coup might be the only way to prevent such a war. So I allowed it."

"Your apprentice was Vaustian?"

"Yes. We agreed your father was not to be harmed. And your brother was never supposed to be in the chamber with him. It was intended to be a peaceful occupation. And I trusted Vaustian to see the orders through to the letter. Not once did I believe such a horrible circumstance would come to pass in its place. Up to that point, Vaustian had proven himself a pupil of consummate dependability. He was as strait-laced and by the book as I'd ever taught."

Every word was a knife wound. And yet, somehow, she had already known. She had long since matched the many random pieces of that fateful night that had fallen to her over the cycles. Father's side. Vaustian's side. Desmond's folly. And yet she still couldn't let it go. How could she? It had practically defined her entire life up to this point.

Why did it have to be this way?

"As I understand it, there was a skirmish that resulted in your older brother's death. Whit became quite violent at the spectacle. What followed is where it becomes unclear to me. I know that Whitman was restrained and tortured. Though to what end, I am still at a loss. This went against everything we planned. I've since come to believe that there was some other force at play."

"Like Tetherow?"

"He was involved, I have no doubts."

"And do you believe Vaustian was loyal to Tetherow?"

"It is possible. Vaustian held very similar values. He knew Tetherow's scripts as well as any."

Beldroth stood as Broenwjar came padding up the snowy footpath. Marsea followed Beldroth's gaze and studied the beast closely as he came to heel before his master.

And here he is.

Instantly, Marsea could tell there was something different about him. After a moment of reverence for Beldroth, he came before her and nudged his wet snout against her bad hand before licking the exposed ends of her remaining fingers. Somehow, he already knew. She wondered if Beldroth had something to do with that. Some sort of intuition granted by their master-familiar bond.

So it is, pup. She looked him dead in his clever orbs—the one burning bright icy azure, the other a ghoulish reminder of his tragic first life. *It's you and me.*

CHAPTER TWELVE

The crew of Blackhall's Banshee had spent the better part of the past few hours in harried preparation. Aiden knew scant little about actual seafaring, and save for a few basic sailwarding chants he'd memorized from tomes on maritime magic his presence rang otherwise useless. Accordingly, he'd kept mostly to himself at The Banshee's prow, scratching at the infernal scar across his belly, letting the wind rip through his long unruly mane, lost in thought over the events of the past week—events that despite their passing still somehow eluded all proper nature of plausibility.

And yet—

Val. Valestriel-shan. Or whoever she was. Rhymona. Prince Desmond. The creature in The Spellbind. The rumors from the north of blighters and lichlords and fallen kingdoms. It was all connected somehow. They were all connected. The fiend in Redding's Room had been right. They were all bound by the shackles of causality, and somehow, it fell on him to sort the puzzle pieces back into their true shape. But then there was Ledge too, wasn't there? Xavien bloody Ledgermaine and his treasure trove of ungodly secrets.

There were far too many bloody secrets about these days; gnawing, gutting, towering fucking secrets.

Aiden glanced back to the old man at the ship's helm. Ledge had been in conversation with Hex and Keats for a lengthy spell now. In the shifting lantern light, the only face the archivist could see was Hex's, and it was not a cheery one by any stretch of the imagination. Verily, she appeared a woman on the edge.

Consequently, a pall of dread had fallen over Blackhall's Banshee.

Aiden browsed the sullen faces of the crew upward between the flapping black sails at the crow's nest above. Val was up there, obsessively staring out after Dalivant's warships; some measure of confidence returned with her mae'chii, but not nearly enough to dispel her mountain of worries.

"I've got good news and bad news," Ledge said as he approached. He had a bottle of black in hand, half-emptied. Or half-full, depending on your fancy. It seemed to be the going thing these days.

"Dealer's choice then." Aiden was in no mood for games, whatever his mood actually was.

"Right. Bad news first," Ledge resumed, scratching at his beard. "The pisscoats will more than like have us in firing range within the hour."

"Lovely, that," Aiden grumbled, "can't wait for the good news then."

Ledgermaine took a sip and offered the bottle. "The good news is we've still got rum and just enough time to have done with it."

"Well, there's that," the archivist agreed, removing a hand from his pocket, taking up the bottle, and sniffing its contents.

"Oh, it's cat piss to be sure, lad. But it might help for what's to come." Ledge brushed a hand through wispy gray hair. "Reckon it's about time you get what's owed you then, isn't it? We may not have another chance if this all goes to the nines. And I'm a man of my word after all."

"And I'm all ears then." Aiden knocked back a pair of swigs and grimaced. The burn was instant and oh so inviting.

Ledgermaine clutched the buckle of his belt with both hands and straightened his posture. Aiden rather thought it a soldierly stance. "You said you wanted to know who I was. Why I know what I know. How. Well, I was once an instructor in Lancastle. A sword-master, some might name it. At least that was what the King and his small council thought of me. And because of this, I became initiated into a clandestine fellowship known as the Order of the Oathsworn."

"You're Oathsworn?"

"I *was* Oathsworn. Suffice it to say there isn't much left to the once

118

lordly order. I renounced my vows cycles ago. Last I knew, it was just a handful of 'em left. The man you mentioned in Tavernmast. Solomon Darrow. He was amongst their count. An arch-mage of some repute that had taken up station at The King's Wall in one of the northern garrisons. Personally, I always thought him a bit dodgy. But his abilities were never a question."

"He said they needed to be warned, the other Oathsworn. He said The King's Wall had fallen. That Van Wyck was dead."

"Van Wyck was one of the Order as well."

"And so the few get fewer."

"A few that I know of, I should append. The gods only know how far the order has spread by now. It's been ages since I was involved."

"Who are they? What are their names?"

"Names. Let's see. There was Marlowe, Van Wyck's right hand, a magus named Brummit, a governor named Goss, your uncle."

"My uncle..."

"Aye, he is the reason your father entrusted me to your tutelage. Rho and I go back a long way. We were recruited together into the Royalguard, ran the ranks together until we both became Oathsworn, at which point I was to take the Prince of Lancastle under my wing to learn a proper set of blade work."

Aiden snorted. "And that prince was me?"

"Aye."

"The gods know, you must have been a shite instructor then."

"All told, you were rather a shite student, if I can be quite honest."

Aiden found himself smiling and loathed every fake fucking inch of it.

"You were hardheaded, rebellious, and dreadfully volatile. You hated the lessons, and you cared even less for me most days, but your father was adamant you stay the course and learn the way of the sword as he once did. Say one thing for Old Whit, say he was a man of hard convictions. Though, to your point, in terms of sword technique, I concur. You were about as graceful as an ox on your best day."

"Yeah, and fuck you too." Aiden passed the bottle back and eased himself down to the deck, leaning back against a barrel.

"I met Stella at university." Ledge took a sip. "Stella Critchlow. Of course, she just had to be gorgeous. Had me smitten at first sight, she did. But the gods know, she had such a way about her. A certain kindness that missed most folks. And given the rotten past I'd come from, she filled me like a breath of fresh air...like an impossible daydream. Something about her presence lit up every room, and—"

"Pass on this," Aiden interjected.

"Pass?"

"No offense, old man, but I'd rather like to skip the part about your raging hard-on for my mum if we could."

"Mmm, I reckon that's a fair request."

"Let's just rip the bandage off all the way, shall we? Meat and potatoes this thing. How is it that I died? Abridged version, if you will."

Ledgermaine glared down at him for a moment as if testing his resolve before nodding. "There was a coup by a rogue circle named Ravenholme. From what I know, there was no initial plan for violence with this coup. It was simply meant to displace your father as king. But, of course, affairs escalated."

"Of course," Aiden agreed for storytelling's sake.

"You were with your father when the Midnight Men came to call. I do not know the specifics. I was not there when it occurred. The dissenters were clever enough to wait until Whitman's closest were away before insurrection. But I had it in the after from a man named Gilcrest who was present for the entire unfolding. And not for nothing, but I trusted this man, Gilcrest. He was a great friend of your father's and a goodly sort, at least as far as I could tell."

Ledge cleared his throat and washed the words down with a fresh swig.

Aiden simply watched the grizzled old man. Hate raced after every single word Ledge spewed, every word that unstitched everything he'd ever thought he knew about himself. But, all the same, he could not simply ignore the unsettling feeling it gave him—

"You've a scar on your belly," Ledgermaine began again after a time, and Aiden rested a hand over its location, giving it a fresh scratch. "That was where you were stabbed. Run through by a man named Vaustian Harver. The consensus is it was self-defense. Gilcrest corroborated this. Apparently, some of the King's Own took umbrage to the insurgents' claims and grew quite testy. They said you took up your father's sword in the scrap and came at Harver's back with it. Vaustian's brother Raelan warned him of the coming attack and out of instinct Vaustian turned about, deflected your attempt, and ran you through before he realized who it was upon him."

White-hot pain boiled along his scar and up into his chest at the retelling. He could practically feel the blade inside him again. Aiden pressed down tight against the wound. And an image flickered in his mind's eye, a vision of a young dark-haired man on the other end of the blade whose face fell from hells-born fury to bedsheet white in an instant. It was a man he had seen before in fits and spells. A name for a haunter, as it were. A cure for a long-lasting fever dream. Another piece of the puzzle sorted. *Vaustian Harver.*

"And, so I was brought back?" the archivist managed.

"Aye. Six days dead, six feet under, buried in a mahogany box far too large for your tiny corpse. But your uncle refused to accept it. He returned to court a man possessed. I had never beheld my friend in such a furor. Whitman's death gutted him, but *your* death sent him over the edge. He and your Queen mother both. In the days to follow, he became convinced that you were not yet meant for the grave, that your resurrection had been written, prophesied, and he tried to convince the Order of this. But the other Oathsworn would not sanction his request. Gravedancing is a serious offense, after all, and one they could not abide, not even for a would-be king. So we dug you up in the middle of the night like a pair of pitiful damned grave robbers and transported you through a ward to Gallea's Grace."

"Gallea's Grace? Why Gallea's Grace?"

"Because Stella was there. And through it all, Stella still loved me. And by the gods and the devils and all the broken bullshit in between, Stella knew her way around a grimoire. And though I'm sure she wished she didn't at the time, she knew how to gravedance with the very best of the giftborn elite."

"Fuck me." Aiden brought fingers to his temples and began massaging.

"She's the one brought you back, lad. Against her own wishes, against everything she knew to be right and proper. Far too generous for her own good, was Stella Critchlow. And, even still, after all that, we put you on her for even longer. And we put you on Vincent, knowing they had a baby girl still in the cradle. We used her. I used her. But she took you in anyway, and she loved you just like you were her own."

"And so what does this make me then? Am I a lich?"

"Would that I could name it, but no, you are not a lich. Something like a revenant would be more accurate."

"*Something* like a revenant? What the fuck am I supposed to do with that?"

"It's what I know, lad. I don't know how else to say it. We fashioned a phylactery, meaning to bind your soul to it, but it didn't take. Something from the other side wouldn't allow for it, something that found us during the ritual. Something that had affixed itself to you in the time you spent under. Stella believed it a fragment from a severed soul."

Never more than right now did he miss his mother. There were so many questions bubbling up to the surface, and the list only grew longer. "So what does that mean exactly?"

"It means part of someone else's soul is inside yours and somehow you were brought back with it still attached."

Aiden suddenly felt quite ill. At the realization, he could almost feel that alien sliver like a cancer feasting upon what was rightfully his.

"There hasn't been any evidence to prove this, but Stella was certain it once belonged to a magus named Malthus Tetherow."

Aiden's icy blues hardened. *No.* Though, somehow, immediately, he knew this for truth. Somehow, he had always known. From the moment he had first been introduced to the fabled y'deman's works. But he ignored what couldn't possibly be. That Malthus Tetherow was somehow a part of him. That his words somehow meant something more than all the others. Such musings were a fool's charade. Fairytale folly. Nightmare material. Only...

"It is believed in some circles that in his bid to gain immortality Tetherow actually discovered a way to split his soul. Again, there is no actual proof of this. Nothing of the like has ever been achieved before."

"But there is proof," Aiden said standing.

Another image came to the fore. One he thought to be of a dream. Or rather, a night terror. But his gut was now telling him otherwise. His gut had always told him otherwise.

It was of him and Rhymona. She told him he had a connection to the nether. And what else?

He closed his eyes and burrowed deep within.

Sister. There was something about a sister. *Fiandrel! Shit, that was it!* Once again, his mind became a spiraling maelstrom. He *had* known she had a sister. But how could he have forgotten such a significant detail about someone he once bled the world for? *So many questions.* And he remembered she wanted to communicate with her sister. She had to, she said. She had become obsessed with it. And she convinced him that he was the only one she could trust to help her with such a task. And so he offered what support he could, the white knight he once portrayed, and they called a haunter's ward from the space between worlds.

Aiden bowed his head and bore his knuckles down atop the barrel.

"Desmond?"

Aiden shushed the old man as he clawed deeper into the folds of his memory. It came back in bits and pieces, as though from a collection of burning glass portraits.

It was late, crone's hour late, and unseasonably cool, and they found themselves deep inside Tyrenier Park. They had both been drinking, heavily. For warmth, they had japed all evening. Why else would two fool young scholarly types partake in such frolicsome hedonism? And the gods know, but RC looked particularly fetching that night too. Seduction incarnate, she was. Clad as she was, she could have ruined his life a thousand times over if she wished it so.

Rhymona was never much one for dressing up, but she had outdone herself in a lacy black dress that would have been far more fit for the Midwinter Masquerade than a random weekend bender. Her long, silky black hair brushed back wet, glistening majestically in the starlight. At some juncture, he had let her borrow his ghastly tatter of a cloak and they drank some more and danced between the trees.

Sometime later, he remembered something about a sister, but then Rhymona was shrieking in horror as she fell away from a dead man's rift. She rolled about and scrambled away from the ward as though it had set her on fire and eventually dropped lifeless in the distance, her skin beset with ugly scarring and her dress a gashed-up shambles. He hurried to her side, and when she gazed up at him, she was pale as chalk and her hair had become white as a fresh-born snowfall.

"It was me," he whispered. "No. Not me." He recalled the bastard twisting the ward on her as she plundered inside, the movement of his hands betraying his thoughts. "Him. Through me. He did that...he made me do that—he..." Aiden's heart ached at the memory of Rhymona's withering.

"Desmond?" Ledge echoed.

"It's true," Aiden said. "Tetherow, he's…somehow…he's a part of me."

"VOLLEY!" a holler blistered out from The Banshee's aft.

"TAKE COVER!" Valestriel called from the crow's nest above.

And before Aiden could turn to the call of chaos behind him, a body crashed against him, dropping him to the deck.

Arrows followed like whistling hailstones, shredding through The Banshee's sails, and thudding into the hardwood all around him. Ledgermaine staggered forward, collapsing to the deck beside him, a pair of arrows protruding from his back and one from his leg.

"Ledge!" Aiden shouted against the chaos.

Ledgermaine howled bloody horror and grunted as the archivist came to his side.

"Fucking hells," the old man groaned.

And then came the damning thunder of cannon fire. Three cracks, one after the other.

"INCOMING!"

"ARCHERS FIRE," Hex commanded.

Aiden lifted Ledge up from under an arm, struggling mightily. Gods know the old man was every measure as heavy as he looked. They hobbled together toward the mess hall, stepping past a series of arrow-marked bodies, the glut of their horror masked only by the dim shade of clouded nightfall.

"VAL!" Aiden shouted. There was no response.

Shit.

A cannonball hammered into the hull of the main deck behind them just as they fell through the mess hall opening. Shards of wood came lusting after them. Aiden tumbled forward into an overturned table. The blast rocked Blackhall's Banshee like a tidal wave, and ocean water flooded onto the deck. Orders and wails of agony bounded from all directions.

Aiden crawled back toward Ledge, pulling him away from the surge of seawater rising up toward the mess, and staggered back to the opening to inspect the damage. They were taking on water fast.

"BATTEN THE HATCHES!" Hex roared from overhead.

Aiden stepped back out into the sudden madness and a bloodcurdling scream fell from the sails above until it became a body slamming down upon the deck. The archivist glanced up and found Val swinging about roughly from a rope looped around the mast, The Banshee's wild rocking tossing her about the yards and sailcloth like a ragdoll.

Fancy yourself a sailwarder now, asshole?

Bodies lay everywhere. Instantly, Blackhall's Banshee had become a potter's field. And one soon to be given to the sea, the way things were going.

You have to do something.

And the thought came to him that he could use the wind. If he could hold her, mayhaps he could provide some cover from the barrage of arrows. *Key word 'if.'* Wind spells were considered exceedingly dangerous due to their unpredictability and horrid penchant for going awry. But he didn't see much else in the way of choice. Not in the time he had.

He glanced down at the nearest deckhand. The poor sod had taken an arrow through the neck and was still in the process of bleeding out.

You'll have to do.

"I'm sorry," Aiden whispered, running a ring razor across each palm. "The gods be good, I hope you had some manner of the gift in you."

He clasped the arrow and placed a hand against the deckhand's throat, easing the arrow free from its lodging. The rasping deckhand looked him dead in the face as his blood began to gurgle and spurt and pour all the faster. Aiden pressed his hands into the deckhand's blood spill, coating them as much as could be had before rising to his feet.

Eyes closed, he slammed his bloodied hands together and threw them out wide, sifting through the toiling winds, repositioning his fingers like a mandolin player at strings, hungry to catch her cadence. "Sing to me, lass." He shifted with the wind, his fingers dancing. "Come on then, sweet thing. Name me your song."

"LOOSE!" he heard Hex command.

The water rose up past his leathers, soaking his trousers halfway to the knee, as crew members began to rush past him to and fro. But he ignored it all. He couldn't stop now. He was starting to feel her anger, her lament, her affliction. A hum began to vibrate through him.

Aiden paced a few steps backward, sloshing out of the rising water, then another two across, toward the prow. He was on her trail now, her strings finely tuned, and ready to be plucked.

Cannon thunder rumbled again.

And he sensed the beast's company just as he always had when a serious strain of magic was at play, only this time he let it slither nearer the surface. A sudden cramp bit into his calf and the itch returned to his belly scar, screaming up from some misplaced void within.

"AIDEN!" he heard Val shout, though behind his eyelids it came from all directions.

His fingers quickened, and he began to sing along with the humming vibration, the lyrics finding his tongue as though from a dream, lyrics that he had never known possible, from a language he'd never heard before, and his eyes burst open.

Just then, for an instant, everything bent crooked and reality slipped from its axis.

Time was dead in the ether, warped and spun out of proper sequence.

All was caught within the field of a single breath.

He could still feel all of his senses but, somehow, he had become completely untethered from his body, watching, winding, haunting, a phantom cut amidst the gale's twisting ire. He had decrypted her song. But there was also something else there.

No. Not something else.

Dread erased the faintest sense of accomplishment.

Someone else.

And their presence was cloaked by a cold sulfuric hate…and a familiar pain, sharp and focused, fixed through some bygone accord.

He hadn't decrypted shit. The thing that now possessed him had.

Tetherow.

A vortex of blood was flowing to his conjuring hands from every opened corpse in count across The Banshee's entire expanse, pissing from their bodies to his calling like a fountain in reverse, and a standing wall of ocean began to rise up around the ship, absorbing the latest volley and cannon fire.

Everyone outside of his spell and specter remained perfectly still, staring at him in utter disbelief.

Impossible.

It was a display of power like nothing he had ever seen before. Not from Stella, not from Rhymona, not even from one of Perciya's most renowned discipline masters. This wasn't just aeromancy. Hells, it wasn't even hydromancy. This was a hemomancer's pull, no mistake about it, and a hybrid version at that, somehow melding all three mantia together at once.

But hemomancy was a discipline of magic long since forbidden by the universities, and thusly a discipline he knew exactly fuck all about.

Nevertheless, it was killing him all the same. Like a phantom limb, he could feel his lungs begin to fill up from the conjuring's pressure and the blood begin to rise in his throat. The thing inside was drawing too much —far too much.

The light drained from his eyes and lines of blackened crimson trailed down from his nostrils and ears.

No more! The scream came up sour red vomit as he snapped back into his body and buckled to his knees.

The conjured blood flow came splashing down thick and copious across The Banshee's long, fractured hardwood like a series of great beastly tentacles, and the archivist plunged face forward into the great wide grinning abyss.

CHAPTER THIRTEEN

T he bastards were everywhere and growing uglier by the passing. And the mists had become dense as soup in some parts. So much so that scurrying about was no longer the best course of action. Thusly, Rhymona and Casilvieri kept close as they hugged the walls opposite the windows, back to back.

The sound of glass shattering and a struggle from up ahead sent Rhymona's heart sprinting. She screwed her fingers around Fucker's spine like she was wringing a wet rag.

"Mum!" came a child's voice within the chorus of clicking sounds.

"Don't stop, darling." A woman's voice answered.

"Keep going, Highness!" A man's followed.

"Julia," Rill said.

Up ahead in the break of mists, they could see figures scuffling and scraping about. There was no telling how many. Queen Deadbeat and the little one came out of the chaos first. They were followed by one of the knights, but one of the blighters appeared behind him with animalistic speed, tackling him to the stones and tearing out his throat.

"Highness, this way," Rill yelled as Larissa and Julia neared.

Rhymona toed forward a step, Fucker clutched impossibly tight, and stared hard at the ghoul now making a gory mess of its catch. She recognized the fallen knight as the man Remy had named Captain Aldridge.

And the ghoul as the perfumed girl that had hugged Remy in the King's solar.

The girl looked up at her, fresh new milky-white stare, blood dripping down from her chin onto the knight gurgling his last breaths of air, and she smiled.

What the fuck? Rhymona mouthed.

More of the knight's blood spilled out of the ghoul's mouth, and she pushed up slowly from the knight's corpse, the dribble running down onto her gore-stained dress.

"Morgan, let's go," Rill ordered.

A clicking sound arose from the perfumed ghoul behind them, but Rhymona left it to the mists as they scrambled back whence they came.

More clicking sounds and death screams resonated from the halls ahead, and they came to a stop.

"This is impossible," Larissa murmured as she held her daughter close.

Rill turned his nose up and glanced over at Rhymona. "You smell that?"

Rhymona breathed in deep. She would recognize that particular stench anywhere. *Sulfur. Fresh. Ward magic.* "Rotten eggs."

Merillion trailed the wall and stopped at a chamber door. "This one here."

A bloodcurdling screech echoed past them from the corridor up ahead. It sounded as nasty as they came, and it was far too near for comfort.

In a blink, Rill had the lock picked and the unlikely group shuffled into the chamber's darkness. The only light came from the sister moons, through the multicolored stained-glass window at the opposite end. It was like looking through a kaleidoscope. Purple shifting blue shifting green shifting yellow shifting red.

"Maidens know," Julia said, pinching her nose. "It stinks in here."

"Quiet, darling, they'll hear us," Larissa replied.

Rhymona found an oil lamp on a desk near the door, turned its key, and it sputtered to life, bringing a shade more clarity to the room as she walked toward its center. It was surprisingly unblemished, especially given the bedlam going on just outside. Rhymona found herself tiptoeing as she neared the window. She dared a peek outside, and through a pane of red she unbound the scale of the lichlord's army ranging far outside the castle walls.

They were legion, numbering in the thousands, and this was only a fraction of what loomed beyond that.

Swiftly Rhymona turned away from the window, holding a finger against her lips as she straightened against the wall. An eerie silence stretched the span of the chamber. She couldn't see the bastard, but by the others' expressions, she knew one of the wall crawlers was peering in at them.

Rhymona held her breath. Only moving again after the others relaxed. Warily, she drew the curtains shut.

"We need to barricade the door," Merillion whispered.

"No, what we need is a fucking miracle," Rhymona returned. "Where the fuck are we, anyway?"

"This was one of our guest chambers," Larissa answered. "And must you be so indelicate?"

"Indelicate?"

"I'll ask that you curb your language around my daughter, if you can manage it."

This bitch and her polite society rhetoric. Rhymona glanced down at Julia before turning away to comb the walls, muttering all manner of indelicacies. Merillion searched the other side.

"What are you two doing?" Larissa asked.

"Here," Rill breathed. He washed his hand down the stones, and it glistened a faint shade of gold.

"Do that again," Rhymona said as she approached. Merillion complied, revealing a familiar large X with a small triangle at its center. "It's a portal spell. And I think I have an idea where it's going to take us. I saw the same sigil back in Palatia." *Twice in a few days. Not good.* Where portals were concerned, one was luck, two was a problem, but three was a fucking agenda.

"And where is that?" Rill questioned.

"A shop in the lower quarters, though there is a chance it might put us behind most of the blight."

"You can't be serious," Larissa argued. "We can't leave the citadel."

Rhymona eyed the Queen from head to toe and back again. "Look, no offense, but you can do whatever the hells you like."

THUMP! Something hard slammed into the door, followed by a clicking sound.

"Shit," Rill said as they all turned to the noise in unison.

THUMP! The door groaned.

"That won't hold them for long," Merillion said.

"Your choice to stay and find out whatever that is," Rhymona whispered, "but I'll take my chances." It had worked before, after all. And it was some rotten luck to be sure. But the gods know, any luck at all counts for something. Especially when it's mostly shit.

"Fine, fine," Larissa relented.

"Fantastic," Rhymona said, "now who's up for giving blood?"

THUMP! The door splintered and an angry shriek followed.

"Fucking hells," Rill groaned as he shook his coat off. "How much?"

"Half inch deep, four fingers north of the wrist." Rhymona handed Larissa her trusty flask.

"What is this for?" the Queen asked.

"Thought you might could use some flavor."

"Some what?"

"It was a joke," Rhymona returned. "It's for the blood spill. You drew the short straw." She turned to Merillion. "Ready?"

THUMP!

"Fuck it," he said, placing one of his many knives against the inside of his arm.

"Look away," Larissa instructed Julia.

"Tell me when," Rill said as the blood poured down his arm into the flask.

"Give it a good ten count," Rhymona replied as she ran the ring razor across her palm for what felt like the hundredth time in the last week and studied the fading sigil. *Just like last time.*

THUMP! THUMP!

"Now!" Rhymona said. "Bring it over and start pouring over my hand, into the wound." Larissa followed the requests precisely. Rhymona had to admit, for a Queen, Larissa Waldgrave was proving herself rather keen at taking orders.

Once the flask was emptied, Rhymona pressed her palm flat against the wall, forcing the sigil back to life. Immediately the wall began to melt away, and it wasn't but a few seconds more before the same murky puddle of water from Palatia appeared.

THUMP! THUMP! THUMP!

"You first, Cas," Larissa uttered, clearly terrified and mistrustful.

Merillion grabbed his coat, covering it over his wound, and stepped through.

"In you go then," Rhymona said. "Once I go through, the ward will seal."

With a desperate sigh, Larissa took Julia by her hand, and they both disappeared inside the portal.

And suddenly she was alone.

Only she wasn't.

Her lips bent downward.

Her fucking hand hurt. Her fucking neck hurt that much more from the blighted fuckface atop the battlements. And her fucking head—well…

THUMP! THUMP! THUMP!

Fia's dark form found her from the corner of an eye, as she always did when The Hood came round for a visit.

The magus remained perfectly still, concentrating on the watery blur of her dead sister, forever cast as the child.

THUMP! THUMP! The door buckled inward.

Rhymona breathed in and closed her eyes, willing her haunter away.

THUMP! THUMP! THUMP! went the beat of her heart and Lancastle Citadel was gone once more.

CHAPTER FOURTEEN

M*y Queen?*
      How's that for subversion? Rembrandt Lanier, Queen of the Dracari. No doubt Father would be fulsome proud.
The scent of rain washed over him as the memory of a violet-scaled dracari flashed before his eyes. She was at once breathtaking and terrifying—her spirit and buoyancy offset by her many jagged fangs, her knife-like talons, her long, pointed antlers, and her piercing, otherworldly silver orbs. He briefly had the sense of flying as they twirled and cut about the stormy heavens, Myrenna and her Queen. A ripple of lightning passed alongside them, and there was a sudden joy found within it. Remy felt warm and fuzzy without reason. But he quickly understood that to their like, this was an experience to be treasured. Dragons loved thunderstorms just as much, if not more than humans took to the sunlight.

"I've sealed this stairwell and every one west to the abbey," Effie announced.

"Well done. At least, we'll face them head on then," he said as he watched the Eldn flame die out atop one of the half-disintegrated blight.

"The last I saw of the lichlord, he approached from the northeast courtyards," she added.

Remy had never seen the cloth maiden so verbose and confident. In the few times he had actually taken notice of her, she always appeared rather meek and nervous. Though he supposed at the present, given her truth, her reserved nature made all the sense in the world.

"...*And that is where we must go...*" Thira spoke.

"On your orders, Majesty," Effie said, lowering her head into a slight bow.

"...*The balance has been tipping the other way for far too long now...*" the watchman said as they briskly paced the corridor toward the next stairwell and the awful din up ahead. "...*And one of them has found a way to exploit it. A y'deman named Malthus Tetherow...*"

"Tetherow?" the cloth maiden uttered. "The philosopher?"

"...*The very same...*" Remy confirmed as they came upon the stairwell entrance and began ascending. "...*In his day, he may have been best known for his theories and credos, but he was also quite a powerful magus just the like. Storied, as the Midarans say. And with good reason, as it were. He was clever enough to split his soul between the planes and resilient enough to maintain some measure of his sanity thereafter...*"

"A mortal man split his soul? How is this possible?"

"...*Would that I could name it. Fixation, obsession, hatred, come to mind...*" Thira's words became hard as tempered steel. "...*All it takes is one little inkling of an idea. One little seed with a push and revolution sprouts. I won't pretend to know the man's thoughts or where he had to put himself mentally to survive the nether for all these cycles, but I know he is not to be underestimated because of it...*"

"I should say."

"...*Whatever may come...*" Remy stopped to take Effie in, "...*I am glad to have you by my side once again...*"

"Always, Majesty."

"...*I take it the others are amidst the winds...*" he continued as they took another plot of stairs. A series of names passed through at the inquiry, Eldnumerian all.

Hrathgon. Astur. Emyria. Agault. Dregvash. Velperian.

"I am afraid it's been many cycles since I have seen any of our kin. I came to Lancastle on Velperian's order after the fall of King Whit. I was tasked to watch over the royal children, to protect what remained of the godsblood as best I could."

"...*And so you have...*" Thira granted.

"You should know. There is another in count now as well."

"...Yes, yes. Desmond Lanier yet still lives. I am aware..."

"No, Majesty. Not Desmond. Marsea. The princess...she is with child."

"What!" Remy's voice cracked through Thira's dominion as he came to a halt and rounded on the cloth maiden.

"She doesn't yet know. But she will soon. She is nearing her fifth week."

Marsea, you idiot. Remy raked a hand through his matted curls. "Is it his then? Is it a Harver bastard?"

"To my knowledge, Vaustian is the only man she has ever lain with."

CALM YOURSELF, PRINCE. WE HAVE FAR MORE PRESSING MATTERS TO ATTEND JUST NOW.

That man has stolen everything from us and now he has managed to poison our lineage with his seed too?

AND HE IS NOW A CORPSE FOR ALL OF HIS OFFENSES, IS HE NOT?

It's not nearly enough.

IT WILL HAVE TO BE ENOUGH. YOU MUST EMPTY YOUR HEART OF THESE OLD HATREDS AND PURGE YOUR MIND OF SUCH LESSER BOTHERS. YOUR OLD LIFE IS DEAD, REMY. YOU NEED TO UNDERSTAND THIS. WHAT IS DONE IS DONE. YOU MUST LET THE PAST LIE.

And what if I can't?

A KING MUST BE MORE THAN HIS FELLOW MAN, argued Thira, plucking some old Uncle Rho wisdom straight from his own memories.

"Hudlow, you craven scab bastard!" a voice bellowed from somewhere outside the stairwell. "Get back to your fucking post or I will kill you myself!"

It was the last voice Remy needed to hear in that moment, and his grip constricted around the hilt at his side. But, of course, it was the voice of Raelan Harver. How could it be any other?

Remy filled the dark space of the stairwell entrance, Effie just beyond his shoulder, as Hudlow skidded to a halt before them and fell back on his ass. In the mists, a stone's throw further, Remy found the last of the Harver brothers barking orders down the line of navy and gold liveried archers.

Remy's mouth became a hard line. *I could be done with them. All the Harvers. Right here and now.* His watchman's blade was begging for blood and his heart screaming for fifteen cycles worth of vengeance.

NO, Thira bade with stark finality. *DO NOT ACT SO FOOLISH AND FEEBLEMINDED. YOU ARE NOT THAT ANYMORE. LANCASTLE STILL NEEDS HIM DESPITE YOUR ANIMOSITY. WE STILL NEED HIM. HE IS THEIR LEADER. THE ONLY THING KEEPING THE MOST OF THEM HONEST. THE ONLY THING KEEPING THE LINE FROM FALLING APART. AND IF THAT IS NOT ENOUGH TO STAY YOUR BLADE, I WILL REMIND YOU HE IS YOUR SISTER'S FATHER.*

Remy thought on his own fatherless childhood, chased by the threat he'd aimed at the helpless father and daughter within the Brymshire bloodbath.

WOULD YOU ROB JULIA AS YOU WERE ROBBED? WOULD YOU WISH YOUR WORST PAIN ON THE PERSON YOU LOVE THE MOST? ALL YOU HAVE BEEN THROUGH? ALL OF THE OSTRACISM. ALL OF THE INSECURITIES. ALL OF THE JUDGMENTS. HAVE YOU TRULY LEARNED NOTHING FROM IT?

Raelan Harver turned on his heel at the end of the line and briefly froze. "Lanier?" he mouthed before resuming his march. "Remy, is that you?" There was a smear of dried blood down one side of his face. "The gods know. You are the absolute last face I expected to see back—" Raelan stopped abruptly midway down the line and directed his blade out at them. It was a ghastly horror of a thing, having seen hard use freshly, every measure as bloodied and nicked up as its wielder. "Hrathgon's horror, the fuck is with your eyes then?"

"Gods!" one of the soldiers behind Raelan gasped and a few of the nearby archers trained their arrows on them, muttering curses of their own.

A sliver of starlight cut across the stones between them.

"I don't suppose you've ever heard of the Eldnumerian?" Remy asked.

"The Eldnu-what-now?"

"Thought not," he sighed. "Dracari soul bond ringing any bells?"

Raelan gawped at him as though he were speaking damned Wngarthraine. And the gods only knew confusion was not a flattering look on the top man of Lancastle's Own.

WE DO NOT HAVE TIME TO CUT PLEASANTRIES.

"It means I'm possessed by a bloody dragon, yeah. Not important. We're here to help. So let's just leave it at that."

Raelan inched his sword lower. "Fuck it. I don't reckon it could get much worse the way things are anyway. Two thousand soldiers, two thousand of the Vael's finest, undone in minutes."

Raelan Harver was a tall, intimidating sight to behold, especially with a blade in his hand, but in that moment, Remy felt a fear in him, a nervy animal fear, like that of a lamb amidst wolves, a fear like that of a man that had brushed too closely against death.

"...Your men have never seen anything like this before..." Remy said as he followed the General's gaze out over the parapets at the whole of Lancastle. The chaos was somehow uglier than what he remembered of Palatia. He supposed familiarity was a different form of horror—perspective being what it was. In Palatia, he had been utterly bereft of perspective, fully immersed in the madness, crashing and slashing from ghoul to ghoul and corner to corner. There hadn't been proper time to devise a strategy. His every breath had been entirely governed by one rash Rhymona Curie decision after another. But here and now, with a bird's eye view of the slaughter, what he had gone through back in Palatia was made that much more dreadful. Twixt patches of mist, the bloodbath spread as far as the eye could see.

In the faraway distance, Lancastle's hamlets were burning, fingers of smoke rising high above the misty pall, scratching long, angry nail marks across the starry heavens. Just below, Lancastle's once picturesque courtyards were teeming with conflagration and battle and body parts and the bastard blight running themselves a gory mess up the curtain wall.

Off to the north, a screeching bright white ripped his attention from the butchery below. *"...And there it is..."* Remy turned back to Effie, and they shared a look before starting away toward the flash of light.

"Where are you two going?" Raelan called after them.

"...Where do you think?..." Remy replied. *"...Just keep the ghouls off us. We will handle the lichlord..."*

"Yates, you hold the line here," Raelan ordered. "Braemoor, Ashford, Graelish with me. Mosshart, send a quad, you hear the horn."

Remy glimpsed over his shoulder to find Raelan and the named bowmen in tow. They passed through a tower and onto the battlements overlooking the northern courts. Remy stopped at the edge and found the lichlord amidst a mob of freshly turned ghouls. Despite Yvemathira's presence, a chill wandered through him at the sight of the creature. It had once been a man just like him, after all. It had once had a family, friends, hopes, maybe even a true love, but now—

The fiend glared up at him between strands of long moss-gray hair, winter incarnate, as though it had been there waiting for him all this time, and it leveled its icy sword upon him.

"He doesn't care much for you, does he?" Raelan remarked.

"...*No, I would not expect he does...*" Remy answered, grim as gravestone. "He knows he's about to have his shit handed to him."

"Chuffing hells, Lanier. I say, is that really you in there?"

"Would that I could name it," the watchman said.

"You've fucking changed," Raelan returned with an air that almost resembled respect.

Oh, you have no idea.

The wind began to pick up again, a hair below a bluster.

"Majesty, we cannot banish it without knowing what its phylactery is...or where."

"...*Such is the way of things...*" Thira answered. "...*But I was not thinking to banish it just now...*" The watchman turned to his brethren. "...*There is another way...*"

It took the cloth maiden a beat before the color drained from her face. "You mean to bind it?"

Bind it? Remy echoed.

"...*In the time we have, it is the only way, I am afraid...*" Thira returned. "...*We must stop the bleeding...*"

"Then it must be me," Effie said sharply.

"...*Absolutely not...*"

"My Queen, after all you've sacrificed for us over the centuries, it's the least I can do. I failed you once. I will not do so again."

"...*Myrenna...*"

"Forgive my boldness, Majesty, but The Vael needs you. Now more than ever. And it needs Rembrandt. You know this to be true. It has to be me. I beseech you. Please allow me to make amends for Nocthun."

Thira held the cloth maiden's eyes, and Remy felt a sudden twisting pain in his chest for things he knew nothing about. "...*You have always been forgiven, Myrenna...*"

"I may have your forgiveness, Majesty. But I do not have my own."

"...*Despite your feelings to the contrary, you were always too selfless for your own good. I do hope you know that...*"

"So they say."

"...*I will find a way to free you...*"

"Of that, I have no doubts."

"The hells are you two on about?" Raelan asked. He appeared the very image of unscholared bewilderment. "Free you from what?"

"...*Just keep the ghouls distracted...*" Thira bade. "...*And once you hear the snap, head for cover...*" He cut back on Effie one last time, fighting back a deep, stabbing sorrow. Remy was only just now beginning to understand the level of sacrifice Myrenna was about to make. "...*Ready?...*" His voice came with an edge.

Effie nodded.

He touched a hand to the side of the cloth maiden's face and gazed directly into the pits of her ghostly eyes. "...*We will speak again, Myrenna...*"

"See you on the other side."

At that, Remy bowed low before circling into a full sprint down the battlements in the opposite direction. A large clot of ghouls topped the wall at the lichlord's behest near the next tower down. *This is absolutely barking mad*, Remy thought. He could hear Effie begin her chant behind him as Raelan gave the orders for his bowmen to loose. Before the watchman could form a tactic for his approach, a tingling sensation settled inside his offhand.

RALLY UP, PRINCELING.

Thira.

"...*Over here, you bastard!...*" Yvemathira roared down at the lich as the tingling sensation became a screaming sphere of conjured Eldn flame.

Thira.

The blighted on the battlements before them numbered somewhere in the dozens. Most were attired in Kingswatch blue, but there were a few civilians peppered within, the majority of which appeared to have gone to the rot days ago. Though, none of this mattered to Yvemathira, Queen of the Dracari.

ALL IN, she said as the watchman hurled the glowing mass over the battlement.

All in, he echoed, relinquishing control, as though there was any other choice in the matter.

Together, they were a feller's axe, a butcher's cleaver, a skinner's knife, a cutthroat's shiv, a watchman's silver, a fieldhand's sickle, bloody Death herself, as he hewed through the initial wave of blight like a buzz saw off its mount.

The Eldn fire was boiling in his blood with each cut and thrust as the blighters swarmed him from all directions. Smooth as silk, he spun past the first of the second wave, muttering a Chandiian curse in its ear. He sliced through the second ghoul and brought singing silver up through the jaw of the next in line. The gods be good, he'd never danced with a blade so richly in all his life.

Suddenly he felt a different sort of sensation, a radiating aura, similar to what he'd experienced in the courtyard with Curie. It was a presence, like a piece of himself outside his own body. The connection was so powerful he could practically taste it in the back of his mouth, all sulfur and rust. And before he could cobble the bits together, he made a dragging motion with his offhand, and the curse burst out the other side of the first blighter's head, azure and angry.

The image of it was surreal as the ghoul blood glistened with Eldn fire. The watchman seized the azure-flecked blood spill in midair and sent it shrieking forward into the approaching pack as it crystallized. The nearest ghoul dodged it by some manner of ungodly fortune and the blood spike impaled the next in line.

"...*Thas'kon ech valla yll sepp...*" he growled as he buried his blade through the face of the blood-dodging blighter, forcing it down on its knees, and left the sword wedged through an eye socket. Concurrently, the speared ghoul burst to bits before him, and Remy caught the airborne blood slop once again as the gore spatter from the second fallen ghoul surged past him akin to a wave of arrows into the blighted mass ahead, causing a domino effect of exploding ghoul parts.

It was grotesquery at its most depraved, but the way Thira manipulated the sea of blood was nothing short of masterful. Like poetry in motion. Resembling the strokes of a painter across a most unsuspecting canvas. And, the gods only knew, but somehow, he was composing this barmy level of carnage—by Thira's grace and guidance—he could feel every movement and every twinge of agony in his muscles as he wrought a grisly path through the unending waves of ghouls. The dracari queen was a fever inside him, beyond elemental, straining his body to its utmost limits, until all that shown atop the battlements around him was a ring of black and crimson appendages.

A deep, primal sound forced its way out of him and the sea of surrounding ghoul blood obeyed, forming something like a slithering serpent as he turned back to check on Effie.

The cloth maiden's hands were steepled and emitting a silver light as the ancient ritual began to slice itself free from The Pale.

Remy retrieved his sword from the kneeling ghoul's skull and glanced over the edge at the lichlord. But of course, they had stopped coming for him. The ugly bastard had become keen to their game and sent the house surging after the cloth maiden.

The castle wall was covered in blight beneath them, a mountain of gore, hundreds and hundreds of them, folk he used to see daily about the courts and cobble, scratching and crawling atop each other, mindless to their own dogged demise. Not a single stone showed through the heaving shroud of flesh. Raelan and the bowmen had been reduced to a desperate pair, swatting and stabbing down at the ghoul wall with everything they had.

THIS IS GOING TO HURT, Thira warned as Remy's entire left arm became engulfed in Eldn fire. Remy felt his blood begin to boil as he cast his arm out wide and let the conjured blood serpent pass through it. It glistened with streaks of azure as it slithered to the edge of the battlement and disappeared over the side.

A moment later there was an explosion like cannon fire and blood sprayed skyward.

Cradling his aching arm, Remy watched as the ghoul wall began to topple. The lichlord screeched, and Remy scowled ugly back down at it.

From the corner of his eye, he caught Effie as the binding concluded and the silver light began to consume her body like a spill of honey. Jaw clenched, he watched as the cloth maiden darted forward, stepped up through the crenellation, and leapt off the wall.

DOWN! Thira wailed and Remy dropped low, closing his eyes and covering his ears.

A crack like the moon snapping in half followed his descent and all of Lancastle shook in its wake. A gust of winter shrieked through the battlement breaks overhead angry as the mother of all banshees. Remy buried his face into the fetal position as sound itself died inside the ringing in his skull. He couldn't even hear the sound of his own screaming. The wind burst tore holes in his leathers and opened gashes across his exposed skin.

One second.

Two seconds.

Three—

Eternity in a burning glass.

A burning glass conjured from the coldest layer of the nine hells.

And just as quickly as it started, it was over.

The watchman rolled over onto his backside, his breathing ragged. His thoughts were the only thing he could hear outside the muted ringing. When he opened his eyes, he found the blight collapsing atop the battlements. Most of them were missing their upper halves entirely, rent in twain by The Spellbind's surge. Ash rained down from the heavens precisely as it had been in The Spellbind with Rhymona. All to sight was cast in dark gray as though he had become caught inside a sketch made with charcoal.

Shivering and stiff as a board, he groaned to his feet and staggered to the battlement's edge gazing out over the ledge. The wall below was one massive wine-colored blood-stain. Beyond that, the surrounding court-yards were a pit of cinders. Everything that had been within when The Spellbind opened was now gone, evaporated, sucked into thin air. Living, dead, it didn't matter. The summoning had consumed all. Effie and the lichlord included.

Another vision overcame him as Thira's emotions began to swell. Remy's knees suddenly became weak and he propped himself against the stonework.

Yvemathira had been mortally injured at the end as she plummeted from the stormy heavens, dark fluids wetting the air twixt severed albino scales. Her left side and wing had been grazed by a ballista bolt, and it was all she could do to keep her rider from being crushed beneath her massive body as she came crashing down, barreling to a stop against the elder tree.

The flame-haired rider pushed up from the wet grass with a notice-able limp, Eldn fire burning in his offhand, a kindleglaive gleaming with malice in the other. Even with the bad leg, he cut a most intimidating figure, wedged inside his marred gravestone armor, his long velvet cloak thrashing about the roiling tempest that took them. A dust cloud mob approached on the horizon, dozens upon dozens on horseback, but the rider did not stop in his advance. He kept hobbling out toward them, a creature possessed. Remy understood this rider's name to be Darazko LeDrange and he understood the man would defend his dragon until his last breath.

I'm sorry, Thira. It was all the prince could think to offer.

AN ANIMAL THAT CEASES TO USE THEIR TEETH WILL EVENTUALLY LOSE THEM.

Remy understood the phrase as something LeDrange had once told her. The Chandii warrior had warned her time and time again that her benevolence toward the Midarans would one day come back to bite her.

WE ARE NOT OUT OF THE WOODS YET.

The watchman pushed up from his lean, his eyes sweeping over his dead father's kingdom until it landed on Raelan and the surviving bowman. Both stood bloodied and hunched, favoring their wounds. But still alive. A patch of bluecoat archers appeared from inside the tower beyond.

All right then. Let's get to work.

CHAPTER FIFTEEN

For a beat Rhymona took note of her surroundings, letting them breathe to life all around her, and she recognized the space as the abandoned shop she and Toff had arrived in during their escape from Palatia.

The shop was cast in a ghostly shade of white-gold from the crackling ward scratched across the opposite wall. To her left, Rill lay on the floor clutching at the hilt of the sy'chii that had been plunged into his upper chest, blood welling between his fingers. To her right, Queen Deadbeat was on her hands and knees, pleading and crawling toward her daughter and the slender hooded figure that presently held a knife to Julia's throat.

"Not another step or she gets the red smile," the hood threatened. A pair of large golden pools gleamed out from beneath the cowl as the figure eased it back over her head.

Rhymona's chest became tight at the sight of her, and a name screamed out from its plot upon the flesh of her right thigh.

She knew this one. But, of course, she did. This one had all the classic Luiryn family hallmarks, most prominently the awkward inimitable lopsided grin. This one counted the eldest of the Luiryn siblings. The lost one. The one Rhymona had been told a thousand, thousand times had long since found an anchor in the darkest depths of the Graylem Ocean.

For so many cycles after the fall of House Tully, Rhymona had prayed that her aunt would come for her. Her aunt, the ambassador. Her aunt, the hardest warrior House Luiryn had ever produced. Her aunt, the legend, of which there had been numerous chronicled tales of unmatched heroism. But over time what little hope she had of her aunt's arrival had bled into the void she had forged in her mind to sever her emotions from the horrors that continued to claim her company. And then one day, it was simply too late. It no longer mattered if she was ever rescued or not. For there was no way back from all the cruelties that had found her. At least not fully. And any slip of happiness that would ever come to call her name would thereafter find itself haunted right alongside her. In that place, inside that dank, forgotten crypt, is where the ghost of Dysenia Luiryn had lain for all these cycles—fallen—dormant—lifeless—

Until—

"Aungh..." Rhymona's first attempt at a response came out as little more than a choked grunt.

Drowned or no, Dysenia Luiryn certainly displayed the part of a proper sunken sea hag. She was waif-thin, wet and ragged, with shit-colored hair that clung to her face like some manner of used-up slag. Anything but the valiant champion their House had always painted her as.

"Aunt Dys?" She tried again, her voice cracking.

"Morgandrel," Dysenia's voice poured out like poisoned honey. It was nothing at all how Rhymona remembered it from her childhood. "Or should I name you Mad Mona then? From *The Warlock's Heir*, if memory serves. Everyone's darling favorite Penny Perfect. Rhymona Curie, heir to the iron crown. Rhymona Curie, warrior princess. Rhymona Curie, Ashira's chosen. Oh, but you don't exactly fit the inspiration now do you?"

"It was you?" The puzzle pieces began to click into place as they came to her. "You were the one that tried to kill Remy in Palatia?"

"And you're still sleeping with the enemy, I see. Still acting as the beaten family mutt." *Still?* "I'd rather hoped by now you'd be done playing have-not to these ungrateful shit-heels."

"You knew I was alive?" A forgotten pain ruptured to life inside her. She imagined a long wooden stake being driven straight through her bosom.

"Of course, I knew. I found out some months after the coup the Alyfains had spared you. But by that time, this bastard here," she nodded down at Merillion, "and his brethren had already made of you a right proper little house pet, hadn't they?"

At that, Rhymona's eye twitch decided to join the reunion, and what little that had returned of old Morgandrel Tully in the past few minutes very quickly began twisting itself back into Rhymona Curie.

"And they took it all from you, didn't they?" Dysenia kept on. "What was it they got on naming their woeful little house pet?"

"Fuck you."

"No, no, that wasn't it," Dysenia offered a passively quizzical expression. "I want to say Table Scraps Tully? That sound about right to you, Rill?"

"Blow me," Merillion grunted from his pool of blood.

"Yeah? And what did I tell you back when? You keep sending your men after me, you were going to keep finding corpses. Now look at you. You've gone and made one of yourself."

Rhymona scowled. "You knew I was being bullied and beaten and forced into servitude? And you just left me to them?"

"Oh, spare me the pity parade. Honestly, you're nowhere near as compelling as you think you are. You don't think there are a thousand girls out there right now just the same as you were?"

"I lived in a fucking stable, chained to a feeding trough like a gods damned animal, and you just left me."

"I left you to see what you would do," Dysenia spouted. "To see if you were actually worth saving. To see if you were strong enough."

"Strong enough? *If* I was strong enough? Strong enough for what exactly? What the fuck were you actually expecting from me? I was a child!"

"And so you were. And I watched how you suffered and how alone you were, and for a stretch, it gutted me to bear it. Trust it true, there was that. It was not easy, despite what you might think of me. But it became clear after a time that they were never going to kill you. No, no, no. Not their precious little house pet. They liked you just as you were. But that being what it was also meant I couldn't quite trust you. Not completely."

Rhymona had taken her fair share of daggers over the cycles, but this one sank the deepest, intending to exorcise every shred of decency yet still left her. "Damn you!" her tongue conjured the bloody nine. "I was your niece! Your family! Your blood!" Rhymona clamped down hard around Fucker's spine, fingers hurting for splinters.

"And you still are, Morgan. Nothing will ever take that from us. And look at you now. Through it all, here you are anyway, a tough old cunt that doesn't take shit from anyone or anything."

Rhymona took a hard step forward.

"Mmm, oh, no, no, no, I wouldn't do that right there." Dysenia inched the blade a hair deeper into Julia's neck drawing a trickle of blood.

"No!" Larissa wailed, drawing the attention of the room. "I beg of you!"

"Oh, and how the mighty have fallen," Dysenia purred.

"Please don't take her from me!" the Queen pleaded.

"You lot don't keep your fucking voices down, I'll be the least of your problems."

Suddenly all the sounds of the blighted army just outside the shop's walls resonated.

"I must say, Morgan," Dysenia continued, "you've got yourself a rather messy quandary here with these Lanier whelps, don't you?"

Rhymona's eyes fell upon Julia, who appeared absolutely terrified in her fresh puddle of piss. Verily, the image was not too far off from the one Morgan portrayed for most of her young life after the Alyfain coup.

"From what I can tell, all they've caused you for your efforts is headache after bloody headache. Quite honestly, it's a miracle you've even made it this far."

Sadly, that bit was truer than not. But the Lanier whelps, as they were, had shown themselves more of a family to her than anyone else in recent memory and certainly more so than Dysenia ever had, especially considering the fresh details of the past few minutes.

"Take it from Old Muggins here," Dysenia added, "misplaced loyalties are a real bastard mother you piss around in their pulp for too long."

"Not for nothing, yeah," Rhymona said, "but you're about the last arsehole on the moon I'd take advice from regarding misplaced loyalties."

"Mmm, and there's that Luiryn spirit. Bet I know what you're thinking too. You're thinking you've finally found some folks you can relate to, yeah? Some folks that listen. Some folks that need you. That you've finally found some place where you can belong. But deep down you know you don't belong here. Deep down you know they are just like the rest of them. You know they are just using you. Do you think they would be so accepting if they knew who you truly were? What you truly were?"

"Go eat glass, bitch," Rhymona snarled. *Preferably until your fucking tongue falls out.*

Dysenia snorted. "Oh, now that's a fun one. I must say, Morgan, your cracks are an absolute riot. All Caladria there. But let's get serious for a moment, shall we."

"Let the girl go, and I'll show you just how serious I can be." She brought Fucker to the fore.

"Hmm, not exactly the reaction I was hoping for." Dysenia took a slow step back, forcing Julia with her, chased by a second. "I can see I've misjudged you, Morgan. Hells, I've had the shit humbled out of me enough times I could put up a decent standing farmstead with it. Truly, I might have never been more wrong about anything in all my life than I've been about you. You're not weak. I see that now. You're a dark horse. Hard. Tough. Gutsy. Angry. But I wasn't wrong to leave you, no matter what wretched circumstances came to find you. And you've proven that in spades time and time again. You merely surviving all these cycles has made you into a better version. A stronger version. A fiercer version. You're like a tortured artist in that way. Like some manner of misery glutton. Honestly, it's as though the more you suffer, the more adversity you face, the less control you have, the better you somehow become and the more you somehow defy the odds."

"Are you insinuating that because you allowed me to be starved and tormented that I am now somehow better off for it?" A dark tremor quaked through her entirety.

"Take it as you like. It made you a survivor, didn't it? It made you survive for *you*. Because *you* wanted it."

"You think this is the life I wanted? A life without a proper family?"

"They did that to you!" She pointed a condemning finger at Merillion. "They took our family!"

"And then you left me to them!"

"The gods know. We don't have time for this shit. I understand there are going to be hard feelings between us. A lot of hard feelings. Truly, I'd think you a simp if there weren't. But some things are bigger than we are. If you only knew what was coming, if you only knew what I know, you would realize how pointless all of this quibbling is. Let me show you, Morgan. Come with me and see for yourself."

"Let the girl go," she returned.

Dysenia shook her head and the knife edged higher as Julia raised her chin to avoid it. "Gods dammit, Morgan. You still don't get it. The girl doesn't matter. None of this shit matters. Listen to it out there. Lancastle is a fucking crypt."

"It matters to me." Rhymona locked eyes with Julia. "She matters to me." *And Marsea and Toff.*

"Then you're a fool," Dysenia hissed. "And you dishonor your House and tarnish the memory of your parentage."

"Yeah, and I'm a hypocrite too, just like my craven auntie."

"You would choose these cretins over your own blood?"

"My own blood? All told, I'd choose a stable of diseased cocks over you at this point."

Dysenia's lopsided grin returned. "That's how it is then?"

"That's how it is."

"That's always been your problem, Morgan. Ever since you were little. You've never been able to see past what's right in front of your face. All that anger, all that ability, all that potential, and you choose to waste it protecting these over-privileged nothings. These insignificant eaters. You choose to remain their slave."

"At least the choice is mine to make."

At that, Dyseina's expression bent ugly as the night is dark. "Tell you what, niece. Blood to blood, I'm going to do you a favor since you seem utterly incapable of making the call yourself. I'm going to allow you to take back some measure of ownership over your life. You love your wretched masters so much I'm going to allow you to decide which one is more deserving of your continued servitude." She backed away another step and a wand thrummed to life in her free hand. Save for the crackle of magic at its tip, it appeared like any old ordinary twig plucked up from the forest floor. "You choose which one you want to save. The Lanier Queen or this Alyfain knobend."

"You don't want to do this."

"Say a name or I say for you."

"Don't you dare." Rhymona came forward a stride.

"Choose, Morgan. I won't ask again." There was something horribly hateful in her aunt's tone.

Rhymona swallowed, shame burning at the backs of her eyeballs.

"For the things you believe in the most will fuck you the hardest in the end if left to chance," Dysenia cited Tetherow's *N'therN'rycka*. "The trick, I've found, is not giving a shit."

"Let them go, Dysenia. Do me this one favor."

"Wrong answer," Dysenia said and there was a blinding flash of gold.

A hard, wet sound followed to her left and the Queen's neck snapped back as though some invisible force had yanked at her hair. Rhymona turned to find the entire left side of Larissa Waldgrave's face suddenly missing as the insides of the remaining half began to empty itself like an overturned bucket. What was left of her tongue hung out loose from the charred opening as blood and brains and fragments of skull gushed down the mantle of her furs and onto her dress. Gurgling sounds replaced the hush as the heavy side of her head wilted away like a windblown flower, and she collapsed dead to the floor.

Julia shrieked and pushed away from her captor, stumbling forward into Rhymona's midsection.

"What an ordeal," Dysenia mocked as she sheathed her knife and pressed her hand against the sigil, opening up a rippling portal. "I see you again, Morgan, I can't promise I will be so forgiving." And just as quickly as the portal had formed, she was through it, and gone as a hillside haunter.

"Mum!" Julia wailed as she let go of Rhymona and fell to a heap at her mother's side.

Rhymona could feel the heat of tears leaking out from behind her eyes —and breakdown calling her name—and her body wanting to crumble into a thousand pieces. It was never-ending, this rabbit hole she'd found herself in. And it never got any better. And every new day, it hurt that much more to bear it.

"She's at the heart of all this," Rill labored. "You must go after her."

Rhymona took in her old master. "What?" She barely felt the word leave her mouth. "I can't—"

"You can and you will."

"This is all wrong." Rhymona turned a defeated half-moon and paced the room. "This can't be how it's supposed to be."

"Morgan," Rill grumbled.

"I don't want to do this anymore."

"Morgan."

"I can't do this anymore."

"Morgan!"

"What?"

"You need to take the girl and go."

"Go? You're fucking bent if you think I'm going after that hot platter of crazy bitch."

"Listen to me."

"What would be the point anyway, Rill? I mean what am I expected to do here? Kill her? Revenge is a game for those who have already lost. Was it not you that taught me those words?"

Fresh banging from outside drew their attention. It sounded like a loose shutter flailing in the wind, back and forth, slamming against its structure. For half a moment it stopped, then more knocking and thumping came from all around them. Clicking followed.

"Are you really going to make me give you the fucking hero's speech on my bloody deathbed?" His words ended in a coughing fit that loosened up his top row of false teeth. "Damned things." He dug bloody fingers inside his mouth, pulled the molding out, and flung it across the room.

"I can heal this." Rhymona knelt by his side.

"Like hells."

"I've managed worse."

"Morgan," he looked her dead straight.

"You won't escape this, Rill."

"Don't reckon I plan to." His words were slurred and his face sagged like a cheap mask. "Now you get that girl and you get on through that fucking portal there. That's an order."

"The gods know, you were always a miserable old shit, weren't you?"

"Yeah, and I'm a fucking dead man just the like. But you know this shit with your aunt has to be you right? You have to be the one that ends it."

Rhymona shifted away from him and her face wrinkled up in the darkness as the pounding and hammering came louder and the clicking of the nearby blight became a halo all around them. She glanced back at Julia. The girl was whimpering a prayer over her mother's corpse. Then her vision fell on the fading glow of Dysenia's sigil.

"I'm so fucking sick of this shit," she muttered as she came to her feet and stomped over to the youngest daughter. *First Desmond. Then Marsea and Toff. May as well complete the fucking set then.*

Bowing, the door cracked as it began to give under the ghoulish onslaught.

"Julia, we have to go," she said, stretching her fingers to widen the same old wound across the center of her palm.

The girl blubbered something indecipherable as devastation continued to flood from her eyes.

Rhymona refused to look her proper as she pressed her hand into the blood spill from Larissa's opened skull.

"What are you doing?" Julia cried.

"There's no other way," Rhymona answered callously. "The monsters will be in here soon."

"You must go with her, Jules," Merillion added as he came to a hard lean against the shop's dilapidated sales counter. "She'll need all the help she can get."

Sweet Julia once again fell into sniffling tears, and it broke Rhymona's heart to bear it. Marsea had spoken so lovingly about the younger sister during their many tavern talks. But the gods knew, this one was far too close to home. Far too close to her own age when she had lost her mother. Far too undeserving of such a cruel fate. To watch your mother murdered before you. At least, Rhymona had been spared that bit. But, still, she knew every horrible emotion this girl was wading through and every fresh pain that would follow for cycles yet to come.

But there was no time to attend them just now.

There was never any time for anything anymore.

Not in this version of the Vael.

"We have to go." Rhymona offered Julia her trusty boot knife. "She's yours to name, if you'll have her."

Trembling, Julia took the hilt in her hand and nodded.

Rhymona trudged over to her aunt's sigil and slapped her hand flat against the stone-cold surface, reaching within to call the portal back to life. It was all she had left in her. But it would have to be enough.

A thrashing arm appeared through the front door across the shop as the central paneling began to fissure. Blackened blood leaked through the opening as the blighted mass crushed the first ghoul against the hardwood. A bulbous eye, the color of curdled milk, darted wildly about the room, its grisly maw gnashing for flesh, even as its own came sloughing away against the jagged break in the door.

Julia hurried to Rhymona's side, drying rheumy eyes with the end of a sleeve.

"You'll have to go through before me," Rhymona said.

And, so she did, without a word of complaint, without even the faintest hesitation.

Despite the girl's liquid eyes, Rhymona could tell, Julia Harver was going to prove a tough fucking cookie.

Her attentions shifted back to Merillion as he eased the knife from his chest.

Mist began to pour through the crack in the door, seeping around the pulp of heaving ghoul flesh, ready to burst through at any moment.

Another coil in the downward spiral. And another portal to scurry through. Her third in as many days. She was collecting them just as quick as she was saving Lanier whelps, it would seem.

But it didn't have to be that way.

Rhymona stared at the ugly fucker being squashed through the crack in the door like a square peg through a round hole. She could simply stay. She could stay and let the mist swallow her up and maybe brain a couple of the bastards before they made a fresh meal of her. At least then there would be a finite threshold to her pain. There would be an end to her suffering. And she could finally be with her sister once more. And her mother and her father. She felt their names prickling on her right thigh. And...

"The world still needs you," Rill said, as though he could hear her thoughts. He tossed the knife toward her, and it came to a halt at the toe of her boot. "I know a few pretty words won't be enough to erase a life-time of shame and servitude, Morgan, but that gutterwitch aunt of yours wasn't all wrong." He coughed and spit up another mouthful of blood. "There is something greatly powerful inside of you. Something special. Something beyond the means of the most of us."

A distant explosion drew both of their attentions and a beat later the building shuddered, the stone walls cracking, the windows vomiting shards of glass inward, the cobwebbed shelves emptying themselves for the first time in ages.

"I took a fucking knife for that girl," he wheezed. "Now you make it count for something."

The entryway door groaned as Rhymona reached down to retrieve the knife and the gnashing ghoul collapsed through the crack in the door's upper half, accompanied by a second broader monstrosity attired in the King's navy.

"Fuck oppression," Merillion howled. "Fuck adversity."

Fuck it all, Rhymona thought as she turned inside the portal after Julia Harver and her hellspawn aunt to the gods only knew where.

CHAPTER SIXTEEN

R eal classy, lady, you bringing your spawn out to a shithole like this," some nondescript fuckwit slurred from the crowd as they passed from the docks to the innhouse tavern.

Rhymona halted at the entrance, scowling through the firefly swarm, and found the fat bastard sitting across the porch puffing on a cigarillo. "Yeah? Well, we heard you were out here giving tale to some rousing conversation and thought we'd come have a look-see."

"The hells did you just say to me?" He made to stand, but the slag on his arm urged him to remain with her.

Not here, baka. Not with the kid.

"Fucking prick," she muttered as she turned back to Julia, and they started forward again into the smoky alehouse shroud.

"Yeah, that's what I thought," the fuckwit called out after her.

"Sorry for the language," Rhymona offered as they cut through the cramped swell of alkies, shufaheads, and resin fiends. Music, wild and lively, played from the other end of the teeming expanse. A pair of women held the stage, one strumming a lute, and the other sawing ferociously at violin strings, their talents far greater than anything this ill-bred lot deserved. A purple and gold banner above them read, *'The Maidens of Mischief.'*

This fucking world, Rhymona thought. Not an hour ago they were running from ghosts and ghouls and now here they found themselves watching the fucking Maidens of Mischief in a tavern full of oblivious drunkards. *O, but the night was still young, wasn't it?*

"It's fine," Julia said. "I know it's just how you talk. At least that's what mum said. She said Southland hicks can't help it."

Rhymona cycled through a few rather harsh things she could name about the girl's mother, but thought the better of it.

"Seasea told me about you once too. She said you were one of her night friends and that she had to sneak out because mother wouldn't approve of her consorting with your ilk."

"And she was likely right," Rhymona answered. "Let's hold here."

She halted at an empty table stripped of its chairs, and inspected the tatty old coat she stole from the cottage whence the portal placed them. It was big on her, but at least it concealed most of the bloodstains smeared across her tunic. Julia joined her, donning an equally ugly tawny-colored cloak, and for a surreal moment, they both just stood there, side by side, watching the musicians play, as though all the world beyond weren't hurling toward a most violent end.

But the gods only know, what an awfully peculiar pair they made, she and Julia Harver.

"Seasea said she trusted you," Julia said once the song came to an end. "She called you fierce, fearless, and doubly clever."

"Did she now?"

"She said you were helping her, teaching her about all sorts of things, and that you were a lot alike. She said she wished I could meet you."

Now why would you go and say a thing like that, darling Marsea? "Your sister is an odd duck, isn't she?"

Another song began with a lute solo. The violinist set her instrument down, smiled out at the crowd, thanking them for the warm reception, and thereafter began to sing.

"Well odd," Julia said. "But I still love her anyway." Neither one of them looked at each other, they just kept staring forward. "Remy said she went through a portal with some bad people to save his life. Is that true?"

Rhymona nodded. "It is. She would do anything for you and Remy. She loves you both dearly. She was always so worried about what might happen to you. Julia and Remy this, Julia and Remy that. Some nights you were all she could talk about." *About how the world was ruining you far too fast and much too young.* "Prize well, she saved my life too, going through that portal. And I made a promise to her. That I would protect you and Remy. So you see it's my sworn duty now to keep you safe until she returns."

"Your sworn duty?"

"Hand to heart." The magus placed a fist over a breast.

"You shouldn't make promises you can't keep," the girl said.

"You're absolutely right," Rhymona was quick to recover, feeling the worst side of contrived. "And yet I made it anyway, didn't I? I may not be much, but I'm a woman of my word." *Baka, baka, baka.* "We're a team, you and I."

"I guess."

"No, we are. And every team worth their weight needs a secret word, yeah? In case one of us gets in trouble."

Julia glanced at her. "You mean in case I get in trouble?"

"Yeah, I do," Rhymona met the girl's gaze. "But you see someone coming at me, I'm going to expect you know what to do with Old Trusty there."

Julia looked down at the boot knife that she had kept concealed against the flat of her inner arm, like the magus had shown her in the cottage the portal spat them out in.

"I don't want you to have to use it," Rhymona added. "You only use it as a last resort, you hear?"

Julia nodded.

"But that's why we need a secret word. A word between us girls. Of course, we will tell Marsea and Remy too when we find them. But, for now, it's just ours. Sound like a plan?"

"All right."

"You should pick the word."

"Me?"

"Yeah, you. And make it weird. Something you might not hear every day, but something you would never forget either."

A light danced across Julia's eyes like a shooting star. "Like munchkin?"

"Munchkin?" *The fuck?*

"What? You said it should be weird."

"I certainly did. And you bloody well nailed it, didn't you?" Rhymona smirked. "Munchkin it is then."

"Thank you, Rhymona," the girl said.

"For what?"

"For...I don't know...for trying?"

Rhymona hadn't heard anything so adult come from a child in all her days. She watched the songstress dance circles to the crowd's delight before she began to sink into her solo. And it was in that moment the magus decided that the gods willing she would do everything within her power to reunite the girl with her siblings. Even if it meant her own life to do it.

———

RHYMONA SPENT the last bit of her coin on a room upstairs. It was precisely the quality of quarters one would expect from an establishment named Bottom's Up. Though it housed a bed and a chair, and only faintly ponged of last night's poor decisions, so there was a thing.

Had it been only her, she might have gone after a big ass bottle instead and suffered a corner in a back alley somewhere, but the girl deserved better. She'd just lost her mum, after all. She deserved an actual fucking bed behind an actual locked door for at least one fucking night.

The magus took a drag from a half stick of shufa she had bummed from one of the townie's downstairs, and watched from a chair across the room as Julia Harver slept. Her eyes fixated on the boot knife lying useless atop the mattress beside the girl.

Tears stung the raw surface of Rhymona's face as they trickled down. She didn't attempt to wipe them away, though. Instead, she leaned into her numbness scratching her fingernails down the old blade wound that ran the length of her inner left forearm. She pretended her ring razor had been released. The gods knew. She wanted to release it. She could feel it begging from the metal band around her middle finger. *One quick little flick, Morgan. That's all it would take.* Her thumb brushed across the notches in the ring. One blade smooth, the other serrated. Oh, but how she wanted the jagged one. Old Hagtooth. Right across the wrist. Kiss the veins. Just a little bit. Just enough. *A scratch a day keeps the demons away.* But, of course, she knew the depths of her truth. And, likewise, the pit of her urges. All too well. One little cut would never ever be enough. One little cut always led to another. And one little cut would lead her back to the world downstairs where she would proceed to the quickest bottle and the rowdiest bunch. Where she would then drink herself barmy and start talking shite to as many folk as would listen. Where she would then throw her fists at the first arsehole fuckwit that looked her wrong. Likely that mouthy cunt she'd passed on the porch on the way in. If ever there was a face that needed a fist in it, it was undoubtedly his.

But she knew she had to stay strong. She had to maintain. If not for herself, then for Julia and for her silent promise to keep the girl safe until they found Marsea and Toff. Thusly, she sucked in one last decent pull of shufa and blew it out, feeling her eyelids become heavy. She had hoped it would be quality shit. *When in Courowne*, as the old saying went. Fortunately, she'd somehow managed to find the right townie. The gods only know, how she needed to be put down.

If only for a few hours...

If only for a single hour...

If only for...

Her shoulders relaxed, and she sank down into the chair as Julia shifted slightly deeper into her pillow.

Sorry, I couldn't do us better, kiddo, she thought before some bastard form of oblivion came forth to swallow her up whole.

"ACTUALLY, IT'S A DAERISH TONIC," Rhymona said. "You know how it is with the daerish? They drink to die."

Marsea made a sour face. "Mmm, yeah, not for me," she nudged the bottle back across the table.

"You asked."

"Only because I need to catch up." The princess smiled from under her blood-red cloak. Her hair was matted to her forehead from the rainfall and her eyes leaked mascara long past her jawline. "And I find your company far more tolerable whilst drunk."

They shared a chuckle at that.

"Well, I certainly can't argue that logic," Rhymona said.

"Oh, fuck it all then." Marsea brought the bottle to her lips, scrunched her nose at the smell, and turned it up.

"There's a honey."

"Uggh," the princess groaned, wiping her mouth with the back of an arm.

"And what may I ask ails our dear, lovely princess this day that she needst seek the fellowship of wretches and rot-gut?"

"What do you think?"

"Far as I'm concerned this is on you."

"On me?"

"You're a grown-ass woman, aren't you? You've got a mind of your own. You can make a damn decision, can't you?

"Yeah…"

"So just walk. You're out here now, yeah? The hard part's over. All you have to do is stay the fuck out here. Simple as that."

"It's not that simple."

"It is."

A procession of murmurs trampled over the gravedigger's silence that fell between them.

"I can't just leave Julia with that woman and…him. I won't. I've already told you."

Rhymona studied her company keenly as the girl slugged back another dram of Daerynger. She was finding it remarkably difficult to argue with a girl that loved her sister like Marsea Lanier did Julia. Were Fia still alive, she would have kept as close as possible for as long as she could manage. "You could always sneak her out here with you."

Marsea shook her head. "You're mental, you know that? I would barely be able to take care of myself out here, much less a little girl. Besides, I highly doubt Jules would ever be game to such a dare."

"I thought you told me she was a little spitfire."

"Oh, she is, prize well. And she's also the worst part of eight. But she's not a runner. The maidens help her, she's a fighter like her father. Anyway. None of this is actually why I've asked you out here." Marsea slid the bottle back across the table.

"That right?" Rhymona said before she raised the bottle to her lips.

"We've been meeting for quite a while now."

"We have."

"So I suppose, that being the case, you could say I'm maybe, kind of, sort of, potentially starting to feel like I can trust you."

Rhymona had never seen another creature so raw and uneasy before. She almost felt sorry for the girl. Almost. "Well, all things honest, I wouldn't advise you do that."

"I'm being serious, Rhymona."

"As am I," the magus said before chugging down a few more gulps and slamming the bottle back down between them.

A few heads turned in their direction.

Marsea remained perfectly still, their gazes entangled.

"This may sound horribly pathetic," the princess said, "but you're the closest thing I have to a friend."

"Mmm, yeah, that does sound horribly pathetic," Rhymona said with a crude smirk.

Marsea turned her cheek.

"What happened?" Rhymona kept on. "You and the Ve'Lir girl get in a little tiff over which maiden was best or something?"

"Effie?"

"Sure. You're mates, right?"

"I mean, we're friends…I suppose. But I wouldn't exactly call us close. I couldn't talk to her about half the things we get on about."

"I don't know whether to be flattered or insulted."

"Take it as you like. But know that to me you're different from all the rest. Somehow, through whatever past experiences you've gone through, you get me. You understand my circumstances. As close as anyone could. You understand the difference between living in privilege and being privileged. And you treat me as an actual person, not as a princess or a prisoner or some such pawn to be wagered. It's for these very reasons and a thousand more that whether you choose to accept it or not, you are my friend."

Rhymona snorted. "Am I being threatened with a friendship right now?"

"I don't know, is it working?" Marsea gripped the bottle.

"The gods know. This is so perfectly you, Marsea."

The Lanier princess was fighting a bashful smile. "Can we be serious, please?"

"Be serious she says, bottle of black in her hand."

"I know you mentioned joining the Royalguard last time," Marsea said. "Were those words just?"

"I don't fucking know. Why?"

"Because if you were…" The Lanier princess took an even sip. "…I thought I might convince you to go after my brother. I thought I might convince you to bring him back home."

"Bring him back home? The boy who deserted a kingship for a potter's field? Are you taking the piss?"

Marsea leaned forward, eyes hard as steel. "Not even a little. Remy is stubborn. He thinks he knows what's best. But he doesn't. He won't survive out there. He's…" she thought for a moment, "sensitive. And he's an idiot. And he's nowhere near proper swordsman enough to handle himself in a duel, much less an actual battle."

"Oh, ye of little faith."

"I'm just being honest. Have you ever seen him wield a blade? It's like watching a blind man swat at flies." Marsea leaned back in her booth. "I will pay you. Whatever you want. I will pay it all, your enlistment fee, your travel expenses, all of it. As long as you bring my brother home." The princess fished a sack out from under the table and dropped it next to the bottle of Daerynger. "Here's a taste."

Rhymona loosened the string to check the contents. It was full of gold marks. Nice, new, and shiny. Never touched. Never used. Fresh from the furnace, as they say. The magus's eyes floated back up to Marsea. "To what end?"

"What do you mean to what end?"

"Your brother. It's obvious he wanted out. He left of his own volition. Why bring him back to the place he fled? What purpose would it serve? Why should I risk my fucking neck out there for a bloody fool's errand?"

"You probably shouldn't, all told. Hence the coin."

"Come on, Marsea. What is this?"

"I fucked up, is what it is," she said. "I betrayed our pact. I chose Vaustian, and I shouldn't have. The council…they did something to him. Raelan and Ganedys…they did something to him. And I ignored him when he needed me most. I ignored him when all he needed was his sister. He tried to tell me about them. And I pushed him away. I called him a liar and a fool. I abandoned him. My own blood. My only brother…" Her eyes were dry and drowning. "I mean to make us right again. If it's the last thing I do. I know it's selfish. But I...we...we were supposed to be a team. No matter what. And I ruined that."

Rhymona clutched the bottle, clicking her rings against it in rhythm. *Tink, tink. Tink, tink. Tink, tink.* Just like the old days back in Toberon with Halion at her side, taking suicide missions if only to pass the time.

"I meant what I said, Rhymona. You are the closest thing I have to a friend. Or at least what I understand of what a friendship should be. And you are the only person I know that might be both willing and capable of pulling off such a task."

Rhymona kissed the bottle, grinding glass to teeth, as she sucked its contents to the dregs. "Fucking hells."

"Say you'll do it." Marsea's eyes were big as the sister moons behind her big ass granny glasses.

"All right, just give me a fucking second to think. And you can knock off all the sappy, woe-is-me bollocks for fuck's sake."

Marsea's grin widened. "Is that a yes then?"

Fingernails dragged across her temple as the alcohol settled in. "Gods' teeth, Marsea, let me pretend for half a fucking second that I'm actually thinking about it, yeah."

"The stars save me," Marsea beamed as she swung around the booth to wrap the magus in a hug. "Thank you so much."

"Understand though," Rhymona said against the crush of the princess's tiny arms. "You and I, we are not mates, yeah. We're merely two ships passing that happen to have compatible present paths and agendas. Nothing more, nothing less. All business."

"Of course," Marsea promised, "all business."

Oh, the lies we tell.

CHAPTER SEVENTEEN

D emons live inside. Devils live around. And the demons, they'll get their pound of flesh, one way or another. But prize well, there is nothing more dangerous walking this moon than an empty devil. – Malthus Tetherow, *The N'therN'rycka*

AIDEN COULD ALMOST SEE the faces of his mother and father. They were confined to the seat of their thrones by the weight of the gold adorning their heads. His sister and brother were also crowned—and noosed with bejeweled collar-shackles to either side. Only there was some confusion in his mind over who he thought they should be and who they actually were. As such, their faces had become warped, almost boneless, lacking any distinctive features at all. He imagined Marsea quite tall and leggy and commanding in a flowing gown, her hair pinned up in the latest highborn fashion. And Rembrandt wore the finest of leathers. He would be near a man grown now, bearded and strapping, no doubt with a fetching lass attached to his arm. For reasons beyond his measure, the fetching lass began to sprout long auburn locks, thereafter taking the form of his sister Tam.

House Lanier, they were.

Only this wasn't how it was. Not even close. No, in his reality, he'd become a ghost and the king a desiccated corpse, fifteen cycles grave-bound.

With the thought, his vision's integrity began to unravel and blackened blood began to leak down their faces from somewhere beneath the bands of their crowns. Their mouths opened wide in a silent scream, unnaturally wide, as though in violent protest, and an arm rose from each of them ending with a finger of condemnation stabbing out straight at him.

All save the king.

Crows cawed down at them from the rafters. More than a murder. More than a massacre.

He could feel more fingers from the black behind him, and he could smell the rotten breath from their stretched open mouths.

Aiden didn't turn away, though. He watched as the king began to waste and wither, his skin rotting away, his hair falling out, his body shrinking, until he crumbled into a fleshless pile of bones and the blood-speckled crown clattered down to the stones below, spinning end over end, and coming to a stop at his feet.

The archivist stared down at it, the crowsong halting all at once, and a chill crawled the length of his body.

A series of clicking sounds began to echo inside the darkened expanse behind him and as he made to shift toward them—

SALT-WATER SPLASHED across his face and Aiden gasped back to life, choking and coughing, falling to his side as he cupped manacled hands to his face.

"All right then, collect yourself, lad," said a bald man decked in gold and black. He was leaning against a chart table watching the archivist, clearly unimpressed. "You put on quite a show out there, didn't you? In the least, the others are telling me you are the man responsible."

Aiden blinked through brackish tears and shimmied back up against the wall as the goldcoat that had splashed him vacated. "Where am I?"

"You are inside the Captain's Quarters aboard the warship Belisarius." The bald man answered in the elegant parlance owned by those who had spent the lion's share of their cycles consorting with the upper crust. He was tracing his thumb down the edge of a sword. "I am Commodore Ender Visbane."

Aiden wiped his sodden face against his sleeves and looked up at the Commodore with one eye open. Here was a polished turd if ever he'd seen one.

Visbane wore a scowl as long as the chart table he presently propped against. He appeared roughly sixty cycles old, and it was quite plain that his better cycles were well behind him. Physically, he was the quintessential Midaran everyman. Average height. Average build. Probably average income. Probably even more average wife with equally average features. Entirely average. Entirely forgettable.

"I have your betrothed in the brig," he continued. "The old man as well. He tells me you are Desmond Lanier. As in the Empress Magwyn's nephew Desmond Lanier, apparently back from the grave. And here I thought I'd heard every excuse a pirate could give across the gods' great ocean. Though I must confess, I am rather keen to hear your version of it. One does wonder after all, how the betrothed of a dead prince would find herself in possession of such dangerous weaponry as ka'rym chii steel."

At that, Aiden recognized the blade in Visbane's hands.

"And prize well, sailwarder," Visbane added as he came to firm footing, leveling the mae'chii at Aiden, "the Gold Sail Code punishes omission just as harshly as outright deceit. If I suspect you're lying to me, I will not hesitate to slice you open cock to throat and feed you piecemeal to your few remaining shipmates."

Now there's a sunny picture for the morn. He wanted to say he had done worse before, but for once, he might not have. Outside death itself, he imagined this was about as shit as shit situations got.

"Their claims are true," Aiden said. *Stiff upper lip.* He straightened himself into a respectable sitting position. In the least, one that didn't show him as a complete pushover craven wantwit.

"And so what? I suppose you expect me to believe you've been in hiding all this time? The gods know, how long has it been?"

"Too long, I'm finding," the archivist kept his chin up like a proper royal twat. He knew how to work Visbane's type. He was a rigid, hard-looking, "yes sir, no sir" bastard. A military man to the letter. All bark. Vincent Damned Ashborough with a fancy coat. Yeah, he knew the type well, and he knew he had to stay just as hard. Moreover, he would have to truly act the role of Desmond Lanier, the role of a man who had been as a King all his days.

"No offense, but you look scarce better than something the Crown Prince of Lancastle would wipe his pampered ass with," Visbane said. "But let's say I entertain this obvious drivel. Why in vaelnation would a Crown Prince ever associate himself with bloody pirates?"

"I blame my idiot guide for that bit," Aiden grumbled, turning his gaze away. "The geezer that never shuts his yap. By sea, he said. It would be much faster and far less troublesome than the King's Road. Far less trouble my eye. Look where it's got us. Though, to have it true, between you and me, he's done considerably worse before."

"Mmm. Your idiot guide claims he is a spy for the Emperor. I trust you were not aware."

"What?" Aiden kept his play rolling, though it seemed shaky at best. "I'm afraid you are mistaken, Commodore."

Visbane sheathed the mae'chii and fished something from his pocket. It was a shiny gold coin far larger than the typical Commonwealth currency. "Do you know what this is?"

"It appears to be a coin."

"Yes, but not just any coin. It is a coin only given to the Emperor's most trusted. Your idiot guide offered this to spare your lives."

"I don't know what to say. I had no idea."

"At any rate, the three of you will be brought before the Emperor soon enough. For your man's sake, I hope he is telling the truth."

"Does that mean my cock and throat are safe?"

"For now," the Commodore answered. "Though I am curious to know where you've been all this time and how the Crowned Prince of Lancastle came to become such a polished sailwarder. I must say, all these cycles at sea, I've come across my fair share of powerful spellslingers, but never have I beheld a display like you put on."

Say one thing about Aiden Ashborough, say he could lie with the best of them. And if he had learned any one thing about lying, it was that sometimes the best lies were the most obvious truths.

"As I'm sure you are aware, I was stabbed during the coup of Lancastle. I was bedridden for days afterward, but fortunately, I had the best physicians in the Vael attending me and they nursed me back to health.

167

However, my poor mother fearing for the Crown Prince's safety thereafter faked my death and had me stolen away to the Southlands. There, I was brought up a student at Perciya University where I learned how to wield my gift and protect myself. So that once I returned to my kingdom, I would be prepared." The gods know, how this story was coming far too easy to him.

"Who looked after you? Who trained you how to sailward?"

"The university staff looked after me, of course. And I learned sailwarding from a Professor Anholdt." A professor that died around the time of Aiden's third or fourth semester. Though he had never actually met the man, Aiden had heard plenty of tales regarding Professor Anholdt's strange seafaring exploits. A convenient enough fabrication. Or so he hoped.

"The name rings a bell," Visbane offered as he set Val's mae'chii atop the table and came to a lean in the same spot as before. "And, so it was you met your betrothed at university?"

"And, so it was." Aiden made to stand.

"Not yet," Visbane said. He knocked on the mae'chii's scabbard. "Where did this come from?"

Aiden calmly lowered himself back down. "If I'm being honest, I haven't the faintest. Val has always had the thing, ever since I met her. She said it was a gift."

"A gift from...?"

"Her grandfather, I believe."

"Is Val a sailwarder as well?"

"No."

"Is she alumna?"

"She is not."

"And yet you met at university?"

"A friend of a friend, you know how it is..."

"I see." Visbane circled around the table, hands clasped behind his back, and gazed out the middle window. "She doesn't much fit the queenly mold though, now does she?"

Is this really the conversation I'm in right now? "Might be why I fancy her so much."

"You are aware there is a war on in the north?"

"I am. And that is precisely why I've decided to come home."

"Commodore," a goldcoat greeted from the doorway. He glanced down at Aiden momentarily before returning his attention to Visbane. "We've found something."

Aiden recognized the satchel and a lump formed in his throat. *Fuck.* He could feel his skin go pale as crow shit.

Visbane turned to face the goldcoat as he overturned the flap and revealed the *Arcanum Volume IV*. "And what have we here?" Visbane asked.

Aiden had never seen it in such poor repair, which was saying something considering how rough he'd been on it since Stella passed it on to him.

The goldcoat set the soggy ruin down atop the Commodore's table.

"Does this belong to you, sailwarder?" Visbane asked as he approached it.

Play it to your advantage. "It does," the archivist said, maintaining his sullen look.

"Open it, Lieutenant," the Commodore ordered.

The goldcoat parted it carefully, and Visbane studied it for a moment before his eyes shifted back to Aiden. "Well, this is not your typical codex, now is it?"

"What makes you say that?"

"For one, it's written in Chandiian."

Evidently, the good Commodore is a fucking linguist then. Didn't see that shit coming. "You know the Chandiian script?"

"Enough to recognize it when I see it, though I am quite curious how such a relic would have found its way into your possession."

"Mother was part Chandii. My adoptive mother, I should say. She left it to me."

"An ashaeydir sword and a Chandiian codex. Crown Prince or no, you lot certainly offer your fair share of intrigue, don't you?" Visbane worked a finger between the damp cuts of parchment and turned to a different page. "Hmmm. Yes, I suppose that will be all for now." He turned to another page. "Lieutenant, please escort our guest here to the brig, if you would."

CHAPTER EIGHTEEN

I
t was the last show of the annual Harvest Light Festival, and
Valestriel's sisters had abandoned her yet again. For the third
bloody night in a row. And right before the fireworks were set to
begin too.

Solindiel sang off drinking with her soon-to-be swordbrothers, and
Nymuriel sauntered away with her dandy new boy toy. Admittedly, their
leaving broke her heart far more than it should have, but with Soli-shan
shipping out to the boot camp trenches in a few weeks, it was likely the
last festival they would all have to spend together for quite a while. Shame
on her for wanting to spend more time with her stupid, selfish sisters. No
doubt they would expect her to go fussing to mother yet again. But what
would have been the point? She would only get the same old tired speech.
That she wasn't a child anymore. That she was sixteen and should be
more than capable of making her own decisions and watching after
herself. That holding on to such trivial sentimentalities was utterly
useless and an inexcusable weakness.

Oh, but how she should have known better than to invite these sorts
of feelings in. Though she could no more help their presence than she
could make her sisters stay. Thusly, she found herself trampling through
the sea of painted faces and colorful Harvest Faire robes, her head hung

low, kicking at rocks and mumbling curses, until she was well past the most of it and into the lesser loved parts of town.

"The fuck's your problem?" a voice slithered forth from the shadow of The Wayfarer Inn, chased by the slosh of liquid shifting inside a bottle.

Val stiffened as the figure cleared its throat. "Scraps?" she offered the darkness.

"I really fucking hate that word," Morgan responded. There was certainly no mistaking it now.

"Sorry, I know," Val made her best attempt at recovery. "You just startled me is all."

"Yeah?" Morgan started from her perch atop a bale of hay. "And what are you doing out here all by yourself anyway? Shouldn't you be down at the faire fawning about some dashing, rich fuckwit, or some such rubbish?"

"Pardon the language, but honestly, fuck the faire." Val was being bold indeed. But she knew to watch herself around those in the Ashaeydir Guard, especially the women, and doubly especially Morgandrel Tully.

"Fuck the faire," Morgan echoed with mild amusement. "I like that. Bloody useless tradition I say. The face painting, the garish robes, the ridiculous wigs. You all look like a herd of done-up corpses."

"Are you drunk?" Valestriel asked as she inched closer, and in the starlight found that Morgandrel had an exposed sy'chii resting across a thigh.

"I'm certainly something," Morgan grumbled from behind her long, greasy cellar banshee mane.

"Something that needs company?" Val came to a lean against the wall beside the swordswoman, riding the willful pull of a wild hair.

"I'm not so sure that's a great idea." Morgan sheathed the sy'chii in its leather hold across the small of her back. "Nights like this don't usually end so well for old girl."

A skinny silence danced about them, their gilded orbs suddenly coupled in could-bes and what-ifs.

"Well, maybe this night's different," Valestriel dared.

"Doubt that," Morgan countered before tossing back another swallow. She held the jug against the back of her hand with a pair of fingers hooked inside its ringed handle.

"That a challenge then?"

"A challenge?" Scraps chuckled. "Ramble on back home, Val. I think I feel a scene coming on and you're better off as far away from it as possible."

"Fine then. Your loss," Valestriel murmured.

Morgandrel stared at her with a look that hummed of options being weighed.

Val pushed away from the wall. "Nip for the ramble then?" A last gasp effort.

"You won't like it."

"I don't like a lot of things, prize well, but I'm not afraid of a little fizzy water. Besides, if it's good enough for you, it's good enough for me."

"All right, suit yourself," Morgan offered her the jug, "but it's your funeral."

Valestriel swallowed a lump she hadn't realized had been forming and took the jug up awkwardly by its base. "What is it anyway?"

"Grandpa's old cough medicine." Table Scraps brushed her hair out of her face and peeled back that ghastly lopsided smile of hers. "You might want to take it easy first sip, yeah. Fucker packs a mean punch right about here." She drilled a hole with a finger at the back of her jawline. "Put your teeth straight through the back of your head, you're not careful."

Valestriel brought the bottle slowly to her lips and tongued the remnants of Morgan's swig from the rim, if only to get a sense of her bravery. Table Scraps wasn't fooling. It tasted exactly like cough medicine. She eased the jug up with both hands and let the contents wet the outside of her lips then licked it clean as a screamer went up into the distant heavens and burst into a dozen bright red tendrils. Fuck it. Eyes closed, she turned the bottle all the way up, taking down a great big gulp as a second screamer followed, then a third.

It burned like firewater all the way down. But she handled it, swallowing over and over again as it settled somewhere in her center, and when she opened her eyes up to the sea of stars above, she found purple and blue and green and red thunder grasping out for all eternity. Over and over and over again. Each one wholly different from the last, reaching further and further.

Say what you will about tradition, there was something undeniably empowering about watching a proper fireworks spectacle. It was at once hopeful and stimulating and, for lack of a more profound description, almost heavenly.

As promised, a moment later, the back of her jaw, in the ridges just below her ears, began to buzz something vicious. Though, truth be told, she didn't mind it so much. Not under such a brilliant display as what presently rapt them.

Minutes passed...

Mayhaps hours...

Or even ages...

And when she came back to, she realized there was something warm brushing against the back of her other hand. She glanced down and found to her astonishment that the warmth belonged to that of her newfound drinking companion. Valestriel hadn't the faintest inkling of when it happened or if it was even purposely placed, but nor did she care. She inched her hand inside Morgan's as though by command, and her eyes trailed up to meet the others as their fingers slipped snugly in between one another.

"What?" Morgan said, the word reeking of grandpa's old cough medicine.

"Nothing," Val breathed. Her heart was drumming obnoxiously loud, masked only by the war of fireworks.

Morgan gazed back out into the battle.

How? Valestriel's mind was scrambling for understanding. How had she never seen *this* girl before? Morgan's hair was now drawn back into a ponytail. She was poised and fierce and stoic and absolutely stunning. And in the starlight, she was practically radiant, her pale lilac skin shimmering against the onslaught of exploding colors, a patchwork of freckles like flecks of glitter across the bridge of her nose.

She felt Morgandrel's fingers squeeze tighter against hers, and for reasons beyond her comprehension, Valestriel brought the back of Morgan's hand up to her lips and pressed down gently, ruining what was left of her lipstick, before smearing it across the white foundation of her cheek and clutching it there tightly.

CHAPTER NINETEEN

V alestriel had never beheld such raw power before.
She'd borne witness to her fair share of extraordinary acts
over the cycles, from Morgan's healing wizardry to Merillion's
dexterous knife-wielding techniques, but neither one could hold a candle
to what Aiden unbound aboard Blackhall's Banshee.

Clung to the mast above him, she watched in horror as he drank from
everything around them, rearranging the balance of all within his
vicinity to structure something of a protective barrier between The
Banshee and the goldcoat fleet. Oh, but how his armor was fleeting. She
could hardly describe it still, and she had thought about naught else since
their capture. It was as though he had somehow peeled back the veil of
reality from the laws of nature, from the laws of time and space, and, in
fact, dared to fuse all three back together against their proper
constitution.

A tug against her shackles drew her from her stupor, and she glanced
over at her cellmate. The dirty, rotten scoundrel bastard Xavien Ledgermaine. They were in the bowels of the warship Belisarius where the brig
they presently found themselves was scarce larger than a kennel for dogs.

"What, old man?" she snapped.

There were only a few of them left now from The Banshee's crew.
Most died during the endless bombardment that followed Aiden's bat-

shit incantation. Those remaining were given the choice of being cut down or walking the plank.

Hex had her throat opened promptly upon capture, before the entire crew; though it stood to reason with the amount of arrows she had sticking out of her she wouldn't have survived much longer anyway. In the end, the red smile was almost a mercy.

Keats, on the other hand, was nowhere to be found. More than like he was injured or cast overboard at some juncture during the shelling. However, it was doubtful the Royalguard would have spared him the plank had he been taken. What she knew about Midaran military punishment for defectors, a drowning was probably about the cleanest expiry he would have been offered.

Val had managed to survive only by the grace of Lady Luck. Aiden's spell gave her barely enough time to climb down from the sails and pull them both to cover inside the mess hall before it got really messy.

When they were found, Ledge got to yakking post haste, hamming up every ounce of charisma he still had left to him. He showed the goldcoat officers some queer trinket she couldn't quite make out in the darkness and explained that he was a spy for Emperor Drezhal. And that the sailwarder was Desmond Lanier, nephew to Lady Magwyn, which in fairness he truly was, and that Val was his Royal Highness's newly betrothed.

And with that last bit, she knew they were properly fucked. It was the very crown of shite ruses. Idiocy to the nth degree. No one in their right mind would take a dodgy old clip like Ledgermaine at such an obvious crock. And yet somehow, for reasons she could probably never fathom because it was classic Midaran absurdism at its absolute fucking finest, the ruse kind of maybe halfway sort of actually bloody worked.

At least, they weren't dead. Yet. Though the longer she remained shackled to Ledge the more she was beginning to wish she was.

"You think I like this any more than you?" Ledge dug in. "You think I want to be in here with your ilk? Think again. But like it or not, like me or not, we're in this thing together. We're allies in this, you and I."

Valestriel pursed her lips to keep her anger from spilling back out. It was really quite useless in her present predicament anyway, wasn't it?

"And we'll want a damned good story to tell. This fellow Visbane, he's a real son-of-a-bitch. Got my fill of his antics at the ports. Tales in the hundreds. But end of the day, he's an old dog."

"That a fact?" Yep, she was in a mood. "And so what's the plan then? You old dogs going to toss a pint and shoot the shit over it?" Val scoffed. "You're a fool if you think you're just going to talk your way out of this. The man ordered the slaughter of an entire crew without even showing his face."

"And he could have lumped us in just the same," Ledgermaine returned, "but he didn't, did he? And do you know why that is?"

"Midaran lunacy."

"That." He let out a raspy chuckle. "Always that. But, moreover, we got his attention, didn't we? And there is nothing in this world quite like good ol' fashion intrigue."

Valestriel let out what felt like her thousandth sigh in the past hour. *And here we have it, another puffed-up once-was with a superiority complex.*

Ledge's voice lowered. "A man of Visbane's record and repute, it's all he's got left these days. Give it a think, yeah. I know he's at least my age. I know he's been at the sail for decades. No doubt he's already surpassed the peak of his societal reach, and his better days are now long behind him. So what does that leave?"

"You're pinning our hopes on the chance that he's simply bored with all of this?" It was everything within her not to get up, wrap her chains around the old man's neck, and squeeze until she heard a pop.

"I'm pinning our hopes on greed," he corrected. "That our story is just daft enough, just tricky enough, just stimulating enough to work. And that mayhaps the good Commodore fancies himself a fat purse at the end of his long, arduous journey."

"The maidens know. Do you even hear your own bullshit anymore?"

Another chuckle. "Truthfully, at this point, I've found it's better not to think about it."

"Mmm, scoundrel's code and all that then?" she added.

"Sure." He winced as he adjusted his position. "You know it is possible I'm not all the piece of shit you paint me as."

"A likely something only a piece of shit would say."

"What's your problem with me, girl?"

Val snorted. "Bigotry begets bigotry, I suppose."

"*That* a fact?"

"You talk down to me and name me filth based on my heritage, without a clue into mine actual person, and yet you expect my unbiased pleasantries in conversation? Piss on that."

"But of course, you're right. Fair is fair, after all. And I believe you are due some measure of gratitude for your selflessness aboard The Banshee." He looked her straight. "I am in your debt, Val."

She could sense the false Midaran charm shimmering in his weathered sea-green eyes, but in the least, there was some effort there. And like it or not, he wasn't wrong; they were in this shithole together for the time being. There was really no use being a cunt about it any longer. The whole affair was becoming quite tedious anyway.

"Fine," she mumbled. "But understand, I still don't fucking trust you."

"Can't say I blame you there."

"Right." *Fucking asshole.* "So *if* we're to be allies, as you say, then it stands to reason I'm going to need some actual answers out of you. Some proper clarity, if you catch my meaning."

"I reckon you will then."

"Tavernmast?" She couldn't think of a better opener so she just chased it with the first thing that came to mind. "What in the actual fuck? You were playing at some sort of barkeep slash necromancer slash—"

"No slash. No necromancer. I was a barkeep, plain and simple."

"The hells you were. You were speaking damned drac-tongue at that jar of demon shit. And you called a dead man into that girl's body. Or so I presume that's what happened. And that doesn't even cover the fact that you were using the place as some sort of creepy cellar murder dungeon."

"I believe the proper word is Chandiian. I was speaking Chandiian. And *I* wasn't using the place as anything. *I* didn't put those prisoners down there. Nora did."

"Nora? Who the fuck is Nora?"

"Eleanor Redding. The Madam that runs Heart House. She's Arys's granddaughter. Or so the story goes. She and Stella were close back when. And so we became acquainted through Stella. Long story short, when I'm in town, I scratch her back, she scratches mine. As for the prisoners..."

"Rot, rot, bloody rot. As I recall, they weren't exactly Tavernmast's finest. Let's have the Redding bit. Is he dead, or isn't he?"

"Arys Redding the man is dead. That jar of demon shit, as you so eloquently put it, is a phylactery of sorts for what's left of him on this side."

"Which begs the question. How exactly did the nether get on this side of The Pale in the first place?"

"As the tale goes, Redding's left hand became infected with nether-rot from a summoning gone sideways so he hacked it off before it could spread and dumped it inside the jar, binding it with a soul spell thereafter."

Valestriel snorted. "And you believe that?"

Ledge shrugged. "I know there's some truth in it. As a former Oathsworn myself, I had access to their archives. As such I know Arys Redding was called Dead Arm in his day, having earned the name from concealing his bad arm under cloak whilst in public. Now, whether or not that thing in the Heart House cellar is actually Redding is up to you to decide, but you saw it clear as me. Something that calls itself Redding comes back when blood-conjured, something that has far more knowledge about affairs than one ought, so take from that what you will."

"You were Oathsworn then?"

"Aye, ages ago. But I've since renounced my vows—after we brought Desmond back. I thought it better to distance myself. The gods know. We had no idea what we were dealing with, the last of us. We were, every one, arrogant fools to believe we could stand up to such a monstrosity."

"You're talking about the nether?" He was an old man, rambling at this point to be sure.

"The nether. The world eater. The unmaker. Whatever you wish to call it. It's something far beyond how we describe things, and it only takes that which makes it stronger. Honestly, how we were able to keep such a miscreation at bay to this point is anybody's guess."

"You know what it is, don't you? The nether."

"Of course, I fucking know. Isn't it obvious? It's us. Somehow. It's everyone you've ever known to pass from this world. It's where our gift goes when our bodies fail us. And where the gift goes, the soul shall follow."

"How? How do you know for sure?"

"Stella. She was well practiced in black magic, and in my opinion, the most singularly talented magus left amongst us. She was the one that pulled Desmond back, after all. She'd pulled others before him too. I once

178

asked her to describe the nether to me. But she said it was not something to be described, rather it was more of a feeling. She said it felt like the physical manifestation of a nightmare...like the darkest depths of wildland winter...like swimming naked in freezing water."

"Come famine and sorrow, hunt, wither, and splinter the damned who defy the dead hounds of her winter."

"How's that then?"

"It's what Darrow said to us in The Spellbind. Right before the nether claimed him."

"Bit odd, that."

"You've heard it before?"

"Aye. It's from an old poem. *The Madman's Rime.* No one knows who originally wrote it, but to this day, it's considered to be one of the longest poems ever penned. Many have since speculated prophecy from its many words."

"Not ominous or anything."

"Aye, and you'll want to be real damn careful deconstructing prophecies. It's always been my experience that one man's prophecy is another man's ploy."

The sound of approaching voices drew their attentions and the archivist appeared, flanked by a pair of goldcoats. They led him into the cell across from them, and Val was at the bars immediately.

"You're still alive," she uttered once the soldiers vacated.

"Still alive," Aiden echoed. "Whatever you said, it was enough." And he split one of his trademark shit-eating grins. "Betrothed."

"Oh, fucking hells, here we go," Val groaned.

"What's the matter, my betrothed?" he kept on.

"Thanks for this," she hissed at Ledge.

"Would you rather be drowning with a hole in your gut?" Ledgermaine returned.

Val muttered a few choice curses under her breath in return. None of which were in common tongue.

"Fuck, I'm old," Ledge added with a wince as he came to the bars. "I say, you look a proper wet dog, lad."

"And there goes my one remaining feeling," Aiden replied.

"So what happened?" Val asked.

"Aside from the cold shower?" Aiden started. "We're headed to

Courowne. We're to be brought before the Emperor." He held Ledge's eyes. "Why the hells did you tell him you were one of Dalivant's spies?"

Ledgermaine sighed. "Seemed a fine idea at the time, considering."

"And are you?"

"You know the answer to that."

"Fuck all."

"It bought us another day, didn't it? Sometimes, most times I've found, that's about the best we get."

"And what do you reckon happens when they find you out?"

Ledgermaine shook his head. "We can't worry about that now. What's done is done. Besides, this is about something much larger than a little white lie from the troupe geezer, wouldn't you say?"

"And no doubt there's another meandering tale to follow," Val muttered.

A pair of grim stares found her.

"What? So I'm the asshole here? I mean, we get it, right?" She looked at Ledgermaine. "You're a dead man." Then Aiden. "You're literally a dead man. And I'm a wonderful little mound of piling anxieties. Hu-fucking-zzah. What are we going to do about it?"

"Magwyn will take you in the moment she sees you, of that I have no doubts," Ledge began. "But Drezhal will be a problem. I can't see any way around that. He is a mad dog that lords over Courowne with an iron fist. To have it from your Uncle Rho, he has become more and more the tyrant over the past few cycles, utterly devoid of compassion."

"But, of course, he has," Aiden grumbled. "You know, pissing in the wind here, but it would be just grand if we could get one fucking story where the king isn't absolutely barking mental."

"Right. And about that. Don't call him king, yeah? He rather prefers Emperor. He believes himself the ruler over all of the Vaelsyn Empire and distinguishes his sovereignty over the other kings and lords by naming himself Emperor."

"And the other kings willingly accept this?" Val asked.

"Other kings?" Ledgermaine returned. "What other kings? Lancastle is governed by a band of lowborn jackals. Valenforth is a fat, drunken buffoon that wouldn't know his ass from his elbow on his best day. The dwarven royal family hasn't been seen for half a century, mayhaps longer.

And the y'deman council bent the knee ages ago. At this rate, he'd sooner find trouble from the wilderfolk or your people."

"Right," Aiden began, "so since we've all managed to make it this far somehow, are we up for the elephant in the room conversation?"

The archivist gave Val a once over before shifting his haunted icy orbs to Ledgermaine.

"Tetherow," he said. "How do I burn him out of me?"

"Haven't the faintest, I'm afraid," Ledge answered.

"What do you mean you haven't the faintest? You managed to get him inside of me."

"*I* didn't. If you want to get particular, Stella did. I was more of the, shall we say, emotional support..."

"The dull-witted knave, more like," Val murmured.

"Then we find another gravedancer," Aiden argued. "Surely, you must know others."

"How many cycles have you spent in the company of giftborn?" Ledgermaine countered. "And how many dark-dabblers do you know? Actual proper dark-dabblers you trust not to accidentally summon a demon cock in your ear?"

A very specific name came to Valestriel's mind at that, and her heart stammered as the words left her lips. "I know one." She met Aiden's icy blues. "And so do you."

CHAPTER TWENTY

Despair wore on the watchman like plated armor as Remy marauded forward, one plodding step at a time.

He'd split off from the others some time back, burning through countless corpses and slogging numbly from mist patch to mist patch and bloodbath to bloodbath, as the remaining Royalguard survivors made to clear the citadel halls in groups. Three floors he'd combed, each one worse than the prior. So much so that Gray's old blade had become an utter ruin from the hunt. It was now chipped and blunted, and the hilt's leather wrapping had become ground down to its metal spine.

At some point, he convinced himself that the act of killing a blighter was nothing at all akin to killing an actual living being. Or maybe it had been Thira that convinced him. It was becoming more and more difficult to discern—her thoughts from his.

Eyes down. Chin up.

Onward.

He tried not to look at the dead properly anymore. It made what needed doing a little easier to stomach. He had come across far too many familiar faces. Faces that had names. Faces that belonged to memories. More faces than he cared to admit. Bluecoats, castle staff, noble guests, and such the like. Ghosts who deserved a damned sight better than what he gave them. Ghosts from a time long forgotten. Ghosts he'd buried when he deserted all those many quints ago. Ghosts he'd rather remained as such.

Only...

He hadn't found his mother yet, had he?

Nor had he found his little sister.

He arrived at the end of another stairwell and the beginning of another dark, hazy corridor.

The men. The big, ugly bastards. Their slayings he found easy enough to put away. They were merely shapes in the void. Masterless shapes serving little purpose in the wake of their lichlord's banishment.

It was the women and children that fucked with him. For it was the women and children he couldn't chance ignorance upon.

Just in case his fears were counted true.

Remy trudged inside the guest quarters hallway, unveiling another familiar face, forgetting yet again to look away. It was that of Lord Cleverly. The chamberlain was propped up against the wall just outside the stairwell landing, missing an arm below the elbow and much of his legs. The arm had been taken with a blade, but the legs had been all blight. The scene quite reminded him of Miss Allison's wounds.

At some point, the chamberlain had shit himself. He smelled worse than a wngar's asshole, as Curie would say, which was truly saying something considering the unending trail of corpse stench he'd trudged through over the past few hours. Honestly, Remy couldn't blame the poor bastard in that. All told, had it been him being eaten alive, he'd have pushed out a few turds like as not.

Cleverly made to swipe at him with his one whole appendage, clicking angrily, but given the chamberlain's corpulent build and mutilated state, he was hardly able to move himself from his present position. Remy gazed pitifully at the thing, jabbing the point of the blade against Cleverly's shoulder to pin the riled creature back.

"You were always such a tosser," Remy murmured. "But you didn't deserve this." He drew the blade back, leveling it at the fiend's face, averted his gaze, and thrust the steel forward through a cream-colored eyeball.

Cleverly became quiet, slouching slightly, and Remy let out a heavy sigh.

Movement from down the corridor wrested the watchman's attention, and he slid the blade free from the chamberlain's skull, shifting toward the disturbance. He held his breath, listening intently. A moment later, he heard a scraping sound inside the veil of mist. *The hells?* He fixated on it. Something scratching across stone; thereafter accompanied by a wet, crackling sound that mimicked the wheezing rattle of someone on their deathbed.

"I haven't got all day," he grumbled, sensing malevolence.

Just then the company exposed itself at the edge of the mist. It appeared like a girl in the soft kiss of sunrise.

His azure-flecked orbs widened.

The gods be good. She stuck to the bloody ceiling...crawling toward him as though such a thing were the most natural affair on all the moon, her long black hair hanging down like vines.

The watchman's jaw hung as the creature descended onto the wall and remained there, sticking to its surface as though a banshee possessed, its clicking call emanating from the space behind her tongue.

He could just barely make out a sliver of face between the clumped strands of her blood-matted mane. But that wasn't what stopped his heart. No, that bit was brought on by the scent of her perfume, faint as it was. Perfume that had wrapped its arms around him not so very long ago.

"Aeralie?" he rasped.

Her nether-blackened feet peeled away from the wall, reaching forward over her head, bones crunching throughout her entire torso as the rest of her body followed, bending into a slow-moving somersault maneuver. Between curtains of hair, her face was screwed up into an expression he had never beheld of another human being before. Milky-white eyes took him in as a broken-toothed smile split open the crimson stain that comprised the lower half of her face. Her gown, once a fine shade of lavender, had become a tatter, smeared in the foulest tints of red and black, and her naked hands and arms were coated past the elbows in all manner of unsightly gore. Bare feet sloughed worn skin off against the stones beneath her, leaving a river of black ichor with bright cherry eyes that popped like pus-filled lesions in her wake.

I'm sorry, Aera. Quite suddenly he regretted how hard he had been on her during their last conversation.

:End of the line...sunshine,: she croaked in a familiar eldritch tongue.

Remy's skin crawled. *That voice?* Instantly, his mind hearkened back to Westerly's laboratory in Palatia. *We banished you.*

YOU MISUNDERSTAND OUR COMPANY. Remy could feel Yvemathira's spirit begin to return to their bond. *THIS ONE HERE IS THE ONE WE SEEK.*

"Tetherow."

:Still kicking...I see...: Aeralie wore a carrion grin at the telling. *:It won't...be long...now.:*

It had been unsettling enough hearing Tetherow's guttural voice strain from Lieutenant Shore's suspended corpse, but to hear it come out of such a delicate flower as was Aeralie...

"You won't win," Remy returned, struggling to keep himself collected.

:This is not...about winning...boy. But you...already know that.: The girl toed a blackened step forward, her hideous arms tucked neatly behind her back.

Azure flame ignited inside the watchman's offhand.

:And...would you...look at that. The boy wields...dragon's fire.: She coughed up a thin cloud of ash. *:And which one...are you...I wonder?:*

Remy remained silent, his knuckles flaring bone-white around the hilt of his sword. He could almost feel the Eldn flame burning within his stare.

:No matter. The boy won't...be enough...to sustain you. He is weak...like his father.: Aera's deranged smile lengthened. *:The last thing...your father... ever did in this world...was soil himself. Blind. Mute. Castrated. He begged... for his...death.:*

Castrated?

THEY ARE ONLY WORDS, Thira said.

:You'll do the same...before the end.: Her tone became more aggressive. *:Your maidens...your gods...your hells. There is only one...hell. The one you all made...when you stole...from the maker. Over and over...again. Freedom... was never enough...for you lot. Was it? You all had to be...titled...and then lords...and kings. But then...that wasn't enough either...was it? You also had to be...gods...too. But it only made you...hypocrites...and killers...and monsters.:*

Remy held his burning palm out at the ghoul and she halted.

:Your victory...here...is only...a bandage. A bandage..for a death-

wound...: Ash spewed from her mouth at the passing of the final word and she listed forward, sinking hard onto her knees, before dropping limp to the floor before him.

Remy blinked down at her, frowning. He closed his fist to quench the flame spell and took up the hilt in both hands as he settled the sword's biter against her temple. The scent of patchouli washed over him one last time as he drove the blade through skull until it kissed stone.

———

"The bastard's toying with us," Remy said from his windowsill perch, staring blankly at Aeralie's freshly undone corpse. "He's been playing with us all along, hasn't he? He means to see us all in ruins."

IT WOULD CERTAINLY SEEM SO.

Remy ran a hand through his dark, unruly curls. "How? How can he just do this? And how can he just talk through them like that. Like they're fucking puppets or something?"

"*...The same way I speak through you...*" Thira forced her words through him. *YOU AND I ARE BOUND THROUGH THE GIFT. THE BLIGHTED ARE ALL CONNECTED THROUGH THE NETHER.*

"How do you mean connected? I thought the lich controlled the blight."

THE LICH DOES CONTROL THE BLIGHT. AND THE NETHER CONTROLS THE LICH. AND TETHEROW...

"Controls the nether," Remy finished, shifting his attention into the hellsborn expanse outside the window. "So this all ends with him."

I AM NOT SO SURE.

"What does that mean?"

I COULD SENSE SOMETHING ELSE THERE. INSIDE THE GHOUL. IT WAS FAINT. BUT STRANGELY FAMILIAR.

"In what way?"

I WISH I COULD SAY.

"So what's the plan then? Where do we go from here? Lancastle is a shambles." The devastating view from his post was more than evidence of that. "It will likely take decades to return her to proper livability. Not to mention the fact that there is a Spellbind opened right in the heart of her."

MATERIAL CONCERNS, PRINCELING. KINGDOMS COME AND GO. SURVIVAL IS ALL THAT MATTERS NOW. THE SURVIVAL OF THE GODSBLOOD. YOUR BLOOD.

"And Marsea's."

Marsea. Seasea. Sister.

For cycles, they had been inseparable. Everything to one another. Like two sides of the same coin. They were each other's comfort blankets, each other's sounding boards. They had even made a pact with one another. That no matter what, they would be there for each other. Sure, it was a silly, pinky-swear child's pact, but they never treated it as such, and as such it held firm for cycles. Some days, most days in fact, it was the only thing that even kept him going. But then Marsea grew a pair of tits and started to feel womanly urges and suddenly Vaustian appeared, like a bloodhound, the fucking mangy mongrel, and he slowly began to put thoughts in her head. Thoughts against her family. Thoughts against him. And then one day she was simply lost to him, as though she had been replaced by someone else entirely. Their pact had been ripped to shreds overnight and their bond had been forever tarnished. All their talks, all their plans, all their promises. Gone to the winds. And so he could no longer trust her. And there wasn't another soul left to Lancastle he could confide in. There wasn't one single soul that gave a shit about his problems or worries.

Thusly, he decided to put his dead father's kingdom behind him...

But now—could it be that he had been wrong about Marsea all this time? That he had underestimated her? That she had been playing at some sort of long game against House Harver that required the utmost level of secrecy? Her cheekiness with Curie in Alistair's Courtyard certainly seemed to argue in favor of such a possibility. And knowing his sister and her protective nature, if she thought the game dangerous enough, she never would have included him in such a ploy.

The gods knew, but she was always so cautious.

Though, what had that cautiousness ever bought her?

What had it ever bought him?

Remy's gaze fixed on the fade of Y'dema as smoke clouds from the blight burnings waned amidst the morning heavens.

IRONICALLY, THE VERY THING WE NEED TO PROTECT MOST

FROM THE NETHER MIGHT BE THE ONLY THING CAPABLE OF STOP-PING IT.

"We have to find her," said Remy, wondering where his sister was in that very moment, and wishing for all the coin in the commonwealth the gods would grant him even the faintest inkling. "We find Marsea," his gut went on boldly, "and we might just stand half a chance."

CHAPTER TWENTY-ONE

Daylight found her haunting the haxan dream once again. The one in the dark, twisting labyrinth with all the crimson mirrors and the tall, skinny witch god.

Rhymona learned long ago that the mirrors were a trump card of sorts. They offered a doorway out of the dreamscape in case shit went sideways (which they almost always inevitably did). All she need do was find a mirror and she was out, back to the woken world, back to the Vael and the same old sad song fuckery that danced amongst her doleful denizens like a plowman's plague.

The discovery of the mirrors' reward made her less fearful of the deformed reflections she found in the place of her own. Everything from antlers sprouting out of her skull to eyes showing nether-black and big as a barn owl's to her skin warping and withering and flaking away as it had during her climb from the dead man's rift.

But, as with all things worthwhile, a price must be paid, and in the instance of her dreamscape, staring her demons dead in the face was always the price of leaving.

By comparison, this version wasn't so bad. Fucker was lodged in her head down to the space between her eyebrows, just as she'd done Vaustian. She felt her face begin to sag as she mocked her demon in the dream language. Then an eye strayed, rotating in its socket until the pupil disappeared entirely. A bright red boiling tear trickled down from her milky-white orb, scalding her face, and she could feel her body begin to panic.

The panic was a good thing.

The panic meant escape.

She reached out to the fiend in the mirror, let out a mad cry, and burst awake upon its burning cold contact, her hands searching every aching inch of her face before skirting across the top of her scalp.

No blood upon her cheek, no hatchet in the skull.

She breathed a sigh of relief, riding the echo of her scream, as her conscious mind caught up with her nightmare version.

"Oye, shut the fuck up!" a voice rumbled from the next room over.

Lucidity returning, her watery eyes arrived upon the empty bed and quickly swam the space of the room.

"Julia?" she rasped.

No response.

She rose up from the chair, a dizzy mess, still a little high from the shufa, and called out again as she stumbled into the upstairs hallway, scratching soggy dream crust from her eyes.

Gilded morning light spilled down the walkway from the open window at the corridor's end and a salty sea breeze whispered past like a hillside haunter. An image of Aiden at the Kanton pier invaded her senses, but she pushed it back down and pressed on toward the landing.

"Julia!"

The inn slumbered silent as a daydream save for the gentle pluck of lute strings resonating from downstairs.

She staggered down the hallway, chasing after the song, walking the walls with her hands, and shambled down the stairwell like a peg-legged cripple.

"Julia?"

And there she was, at a table with the lute player from the night before, raven-haired locks wild as a briar patch, yet otherwise cozy as could be.

Rhymona exhaled, and eyed the lute player hard. To have it true, she appeared anything but a musician. In fact, by her dress, she looked far more suited to a library or lecture hall. Scholar's robes on, long blond hair pulled back into a ponytail, and crystal-clear eyes like miniature frozen ponds behind a pair of egg-shaped reading glasses. In a queer sort of manner, she rather bore a striking resemblance to Marsea.

"Did you not hear me calling?" the magus snapped, doing her best to save face.

"Sorry," Julia answered sheepishly, her mouth full. "I was eating."

"Yeah, well you scared the fuck…udging mess out of me, yeah." Rhymona hated the way she was lecturing at the girl, but someone had to do it.

"You know you can curse around me if you want," Julia said. "It's fine."

"You can't just go around trusting anyone you meet," Rhymona glanced over at the lute player, "no offense."

"None taken," the woman said. "Wish I'd had a mother that cared enough to scold me when she thought me the fool."

"She's not my," both Rhymona and Julia started before meeting eyes.

"She knows she's not supposed to be wandering off, is all," the magus finished.

"I had this," Julia produced Old Trusty from under the table.

"And she made well sure I knew she did," the lute player added.

Rhymona shook her head and plopped down in the chair next to the princess, pinching off a piece of the girl's crumpet.

"Hey!" Julia cried. "Get your own."

"This is your amends for running off and not telling me," she said before popping the piece into her mouth. "Don't do that again, savvy?"

"Savvy," Julia answered with a flawless highborn eye roll.

There's one for the collection, Rhymona thought, having caught the same eye roll from each of the girl's older siblings on numerous occasions.

The woman chuckled. "Aren't you two quite the pair? Name's Lizet, by the way."

"Rhymona," the magus said, easing back in the chair. "Hmmph, damn, that wasn't half bad." *The gods know. Bread, I have missed you.*

"There's a few more left. You're more than welcome."

"I've no coin to—"

"Just think of it as a courtesy with the room," Lizet said. "Besides, they'll go bad if someone doesn't see to them." She stood and rested her lute atop the next table over before trailing over to the bar.

"Well, in that case, far be it from me to turn away a free breakfast," Rhymona said.

191

"Julia was just telling me you were visiting from up north," Lizet said as she returned with the plate.

"That's right," Rhymona answered, palming two of the remaining three crumpets. "You can probably guess as for why."

"Oh yes, the tales are plenty these days. Tales of the blight and their lichlords and the like. Spooky shit there, yeah. And by the looks of you two, I'd say you rather left in a hurry."

That's one way of putting it. "We did." Rhymona's eyes wandered the room as she took a chunk out of a crumpet, the night before still prevalent in the form of overturned chairs, strewn about tankards and bottles, and puddles of varying substances along the hardwood. A young couple slept against each other on the floor next to a dusty old hearth.

"Apologies for the mess," Lizet flushed a light shade of pink. "It's been some time since my sister was in town. I'd say the homecoming got a little out of hand."

"The violinist?"

"The violinist," Lizet echoed. "She's been out on the road for a spell with her troupe."

"The Maidens of Mischief?" Rhymona asked reading the banner above the stage.

"The Truly Triumphant Traveling Troubadours," Lizet answered. "Alas, The Maidens are no more, save for the occasional reunion show."

"Well, you were both quite talented anyway," the magus continued.

"Agreed," Julia added, finishing her crumpet and eyeing the last one on the plate.

"I appreciate the kindness," Lizet said as she moseyed back over to the bar, grabbed a dishcloth, and set to wiping the nearest in a line of mugs.

"You have to clean this place by yourself?" Julia asked, as though such a task were utterly incomprehensible.

"I'll have to get started by myself, yes," Lizet replied. "My husband got called off on some urgent matter to the Nobles and I promised my barkeep the day off." She glanced past them. "Also, that's him drooling on himself in the corner over there so…"

"Well, maybe we can help then," Julia said.

"Julia," Rhymona started. "I don't—"

"That would be wonderful, honestly," Lizet returned. "First rule of innkeeping: Never turn down a helping hand."

Brilliant, now we're playing at barmaids.

"I can't offer you coin, but there's the room upstairs, if you all need a place for a few nights."

"Deal," Julia blurted out, her chair scraping back as she came to her feet.

"Jules. Hold on a tick."

"Please," the girl produced a pouty face for the ages. "Just for a night. You don't even have to help. I'll do all the helping."

"It's not that. I just..." She stared at the girl. *You just what, baka? Give the girl a fucking day already. She just lost her mum and mayhaps more. Let her help, let her pick up a few dishes, let her sort it out in whatever way she might. Besides, you'll need time to form a plan going forward anyway.* "All right," she muttered.

"You mean it? We can stay?"

"I said all right, didn't I? But only for today, yeah."

"A girl arguing to do chores?" Lizet said, her grin spreading. "My father would have found the floor at the sight of it."

BETWEEN THE THREE OF THEM, they had the place back to respectability by morning's end. All told, it was the least she could offer for the meal. But Lizet proved a wealth of generosity beyond even that, sparing them some clean clothes and a wash bucket to freshen up.

By midday, she and Julia almost appeared as wholly different people. Well, at least she did anyway, sporting an off-white tunic and baggy brown trousers in lieu of her typical black leathers. Slightly less unbecoming, some might say. And thanks to Jules dousing herself in a cloud of Lizet's perfumes, she even smelled different, like a basket of island fruits, most of which she couldn't recall the proper names of. Though better a harbor-end whore than a privy, she reckoned.

Patrons began to make their rounds sometime midafternoon, and Rhymona helped Lizet tend the bar until her husband Lucian returned.

Come to find out, Lucian Calderwood was a physician that left to make a house call that morning. To Rhymona's surprise, he appeared considerably older than Lizet, possibly in his fifties, but there existed an immediate warmth and care between them that could not be mistaken for anything other than love.

Given all the bullshite going on in the world these days, a little tenderness and fancy were, quite honestly, nice to take in.

"Can I see what you really look like?" Julia asked some hours later after they had retired to their room.

"What I really look like?" Rhymona turned from the window to the girl on the bed scraping a chip of cobblestone down Old Trusty's edge. "This is what I really look like."

"No, I mean…well, you know what I mean."

Rhymona unleashed a wry smile. "I don't know, if I turn, I might lose control, and then I might just eat you up, and wear your skin about the heathens downstairs. Haven't you heard the tales?"

"That's all rubbish. Ashaeydir don't eat people, at least not most of them. And those that do, don't wear their victim's skin."

"Well, aren't you the clever one?"

"Seasea told me all about the ashaeydir. She's read all the books and tales."

"Has she now?"

"At least she said she has, and I believe her over almost anyone."

"And did she tell you how it is we ashaeydir change our skin?"

Julia swallowed. "No, not exactly."

"Well, I suppose you'll have something new to learn *her* up on next time you see her then won't you?"

Rhymona sat on the bed next to Julia. "Place your finger right here." She tapped a faded scar slightly below the back of her ear.

"Does it pain you?"

"It did at first, though the pain is but a memory now, just like any other old scar."

Julia lay the blade and stone down on her pillow, scooted in close, and poked the slightly raised circle of flesh. "It's squishy."

"It's called trezsu. It's a material from Ashira. My ancestors harvested it some centuries ago and found a way to bind it to the bloodstream. I don't rightly understand it myself, or recall all of the fancy terms for how it works, but once bound, it allows its host to reflect light so they can appear to change their skin pigmentation and even their hair and eye color."

"What a madness!"

"It has its advantages, I'll grant you. But now you know. It's not actually special to the ashaeydir at all. We happened to find the trezsu first and somehow determined a way to manipulate some of its properties. You could have the trezsu implanted just the same as me, any Midaran could, but trust, it takes a skilled surgeon to see the procedure through properly. It's not a pretty sight if the surgery goes bad."

"What happens if it goes bad? Can it kill you?"

"Nothing quite so serious as all that. But let's just say, some folks discovered some terribly interesting colors and others found far more than they ever wished they had."

"Oh, no."

"Oh, yes. Nasty as a curse from the cruelest bog witch."

"But why is it behind your ear? Seems a rather odd place."

"The implant is typically positioned in areas that are easy to avoid contact but can also be reached at any moment. As such, most soldiers in the ashaeydir guard have it implanted behind the ear."

Julia offered a slow nod. "Remy said you're a pretty good fighter too."

"I do okay." *Relative to the amount of rot in the belly.*

"Mayhaps you can teach me a little."

That'll be the day. "Mayhaps."

"Only enough to defend myself."

"Fighting is not an easy thing, Jules. At least not quality fighting. And it's not a thing to be taken lightly. There's a lot more to it than the act itself."

"Maidens' bones, now you sound like father."

Rhymona winced at the comparison to a Harver, a string of indelicate thoughts leaping for her tongue, but she fastly decided it wasn't worth upsetting the girl.

"All right." She slapped palms down to her knees, stood up, and rounded the bed to the other side, away from the window's view. "Better get in a good once over, yeah. I'm only changing for a few seconds." She placed her hand against the implant. "Ready?"

Julia rolled to the other side of the bed, straightened the rumples in her dress, and sat attentively, a true lady of courtly inheritance. "Ready."

Rhymona swept a finger across the tiny patch of marred flesh and Julia drew in a quick breath, her expression filled with wonderment.

"Good gravy," the girl uttered.

"Bloody terrifying, I know," Rhymona murmured. It went without saying really, but if this were the last time she ever wore her true skin, it would be too soon.

"But your hair is still white."

"Yeah, it's permanently white now, I think. But that's a tale for another time."

Footsteps passed from the hallway outside and Rhymona pressed the trezsu implant a second time, returning to her preferred form.

"Your eyes," Julia said. "I wish I could have eyes like that."

"No, you don't. Trust me. They're far more trouble than you know."

"But they're quite bonny, aren't they?"

"There's a laugh," Rhymona snorted. "You do know what bonny means right?" *Dramatic and mercurial, a Harver through and through.*

"Of course," she said.

And then it happened, another slice of Harver unpredictability.

Julia's intrigue melted down the span of her face to her drooping shoulders and the tears returned as though summoned from the shop in Lancastle a day past.

"Jules." Rhymona took a step closer. "I didn't mean to upset you. It was only a jape."

"I'm sorry," Julia managed, wiping feverishly at her eyes. "I don't know why I'm crying..." But try as she might, her sadness would not be undone so easily, stealing away her voice, and escalating to sniffling and sobbing in an instant.

Rhymona advanced another step, her knees pressing against the edge of the mattress.

I know why you're crying, she thought as she brushed back strands of raven-black hair from Julia's face. *All too well.*

And she'd take it all away from the girl in a heartbeat if the gods did so permit.

Julia leaned forward and Rhymona let her in, tears spotting the bosom of her shirt, as she stroked a hand down the length of the girl's locks.

She could mend almost any physical wound the moon over. But this manner of affliction was beyond such endowments. This wound would have its time with the girl and then some, and then one fel night far too long away from her present count it would pass by one of two methods.

It would either break her or make her hard as the stone.

Have a care, Morgan. You're not so hard yet yourself, now are you?

"I'm here," she whispered. "For as long as you need."

From the corner of her eye, amidst the chamber's shadows, she caught the shape of another sad little girl ruined far before her time.

"And for as long as you'll have me."

CHAPTER TWENTY-TWO

T he sunlight struck her first, hot as a blade fresh from the
furnace, and Valestriel squinted up at the screaming bright mass
as though she had been living in a cave all her life. Fortunately,
the open air was quick to follow, flowing through her loose, frizzy curls
and lifting her face from the belowdecks swelter. She inhaled the sea and
the sun both like a proper line of spriteling dust, every ounce of it she
could handle, and she let it out slowly.

She'd never been to Courowne before, though she had heard plenty of
tales about its unmatched magnificence from her sisters. The Jewel of the
South, they named it. Even still, as she crossed the Belisarius's main deck,
she found that no collection of words would have ever been enough to
describe the port kingdom's true spectacle.

Courowne's harbor put the whole of Six Ports to shame. Here there
were war vessels, over there mid-sized fishing boats and scattered skiffs.
And the people were everywhere, countless, like a colony of ants, shifting
this way and that, performing this little chore and that one, a continuous
rolling wave of moving bodies.

Past the docks rose the great sun-washed sea wall, lofty enough to
defend against even the cruelest of tides, and beyond that were a series of
white-gold towers and spires rising high into the beaming heavens. Each

was adorned with a flowing golden banner that bore the black bird sigil of House Dalivant in its center.

"Welcome to pisscoat territory," Ledge muttered from behind as they were led from the Belisarius to the docks by Commodore Visbane and six of his best, three to the front of them and three in back, each one armed to the teeth.

At once, Val felt the pull of a thousand eyes turn upon them, each watching with their own measure of curiosity. Oh, and how the emperor's sentinels glared.

Val's vision swept across the sea of faces until it caught the scowl of a dwarf woman that had a babe cupped to her bosom. Quickly the sellsword averted her gaze. The stare was so intense Val couldn't help but wonder if the dwarf could somehow see through her trezsu implant's mask. Dwarves were maddening little buggers after all, known well for their most peculiar abilities.

Faces, worn and leathery, blurred one into the next as the docks gave way to a sliver of beach and then to the whitewashed stone cobbleway.

At some point, Val decided it best to simply ignore all the watchers. So she kept her eyes pinned to Aiden's backside, concentrating on a purple linen patch that had been sewn onto the right shoulder of his robe. It stuck out like a sore thumb against the dusty black cut surrounding it.

She thought of Morgandrel and wondered if this was how she had felt for all those cycles spent as House Alyfain's servant girl.

Where are you now, Morgan? Her thoughts began to drift. *Are you still here? I found Aiden. And he found me trouble. But I guess you already knew that he would. The maidens know, even shitfaced you tried to spare me the burden, didn't you?*

"Hail Drezhal!" one of the emperor's sentinels bellowed as they came to the kingdom's edge. He certainly cut a daunting figure in his gold and black Dalivant House livery, a full head taller than any of the other nearby soldiers, shoulders like that of a mountain range, features sharp as an axe.

"Hail Drezhal," Visbane returned with considerably less vigor. "I heard about your old man, Captain. You have my condolences."

The sentinel shrugged. "He went out in battle."

"A suitable end for The Iron Black, I'd say," Visbane added, all business.

"It is at that. And what has the good Commodore brought us this time?"

"A would-be king and his betrothed," Visbane answered.

"Would-be king, is it?" the younger Marlowe eyed each of them one by one. "Which one? The geezer or the bender?"

"Which one do you think, asshole," Aiden returned, chin high. "Honestly, can we hurry this along, Commodore? I'd rather like to see my aunt and be rid of these chains."

Marlowe scoffed. "Who are you then?"

"Desmond Lanier. You may have heard of me."

Marlowe looked to Visbane. "Is this wretch serious?"

The Commodore remained nondescript.

"Impossible," Marlowe declared. "Desmond Lanier died cycles ago."

"Oh, but how the moon wishes it so," Aiden said as he implored the good Commodore forward with a lordly glance of annoyance.

Visbane pressed on with Marlowe lumbering at his side. One of the soldiers jerked the chains forward and they fell back into stride. By now, in the least, most of the common folk had lost interest in them and gone back to their dailies. Given Marlowe's initial reaction, Val deduced that this sort of pageantry, dragging pirates through town and the like, must be something of a common occurrence.

Onward they trudged, passing through one ripe smell to another. There were rotting fish and baked goods then body odor and horse leavings and a few more Val was rather reluctant to venture a guess about. It wasn't long inside the sea wall that they passed a butcher's block. It appeared to have seen action freshly. A shirtless fellow with a bandana draped around the lower half of his face was red to his elbows in the latest victim as he emptied a bucket of water across the staging and thereafter dropped to his hands and knees and began scrubbing.

Aiden glanced over his shoulder at Val and they shared one of their odd little looks. She could tell he was struggling with something, but they couldn't risk making a scene. Not as they were. Not if they planned to stand half a chance against what was to come. No. For now, they had to remain strong. And that much shrewder.

The further inward they traversed, the more she found Courowne's character to be the same as every other Midaran kingdom she had ever toured. There were the outer hamlets of course, which housed the poorer folk. Many appeared fisherfolk and craftsman and honest hands, but peppered there within were the beggars and the corner whores and the shifty tradesmen. Outside the harbor front market, the most of their haunts were brothels and shufa dens and seedy pubhouses, though a couple blocks in and the streets cleaned up considerably. It wasn't quite nobility opulent, but it shown a mite more respectable. Painted signs hung in front of shops and the women kept their tits in their blouses. The goldcoats too became thicker in count, though such was to be expected as the greater palace walks drew nearer.

Partway through The Middles, as Ledge had named it, Visbane and Marlowe turned down a much narrower alleyway. The buildings to either side blocked all from sight save the sky and the soldiers before them. The path left just enough space to walk side by side. It was tight enough that she began to feel a slight onset of panic. Fortunately, the alley soon opened up to arguably the most breathtaking view she had ever beheld.

A great expanse of lawn appeared before them, green as the lushest clover, stretching several fields long, twice as wide, and exceptionally manicured. The marble walkways within were immaculate, white as bone, breaking off into little patches of garden and pillared courtyards that centered around a statue of some bygone vinteyaman royal or another. It was no secret, even in the ashayedir circles, that amongst the Midaran royal houses the Dalivant's were by far the most ostentatious and thought far too highly of themselves.

Case in point, off to the left of the estate lawn there flourished a hedge maze that ventured on as far as the eye could see until the old moss trees came to linger. Val couldn't help but wonder if Drezhal or his Lady had ever once bothered a stroll within. To the right, there was the tourney ring and stables and beyond that a barracks and training yard.

Then there was the palace itself a little further in, utterly incomparable to any other castle Val had ever seen or heard of, shimmering like a massive diamond that had come crashing down from the heavens. Its color almost translucent, resembling that of the shiniest pearl.

"Hail Drezhal!" a patrol greeted as they passed through the bulwark and onto the palace grounds.

Fuck Drezhal, Val echoed as she took in the lads in the training yard. Not a one was a woman. Though there was scant surprise here. In contrast to the Royalguard proper, ladies were not permitted to enlist in the goldcoat legion. More Dalivant chauvinism, the fucking prick. It went without saying really, but half an hour in and she was already well over the 'Hail Drezhal' bullshit to be sure.

A sudden commotion broke out from the back of the procession, and she turned to find Ledge on the ground.

"On your feet, old man," ordered one of the goldcoats.

"Would that I could," Ledgermaine labored.

"I said get up," the goldcoat snapped.

"I need a break. Bum leg and all. Unless you lot intend to carry me on the rest of the way."

"Tell your man to get on his feet," Visbane ordered Aiden.

"The state of him," Aiden said. "He's a rundown old tosspot. He needs rest and likely more, thanks to your archers. Either way, it has little to do with what we're trying to accomplish here, wouldn't you agree?"

"You would leave your man behind?"

"We've more important matters to attend presently, I would say."

Really digging into the whole wanky king gig now, aren't you? Val thought.

"Very well," Visbane said. "Fallon, Latham, get him to the barracks and keep him confined to the infirmary. We'll have the truth of he and the Emperor's rapport soon enough."

"Sir," the pair answered in unison.

"Shall we on then?" the Commodore issued Aiden a hard, irritated glower.

The archivist offered his shackled hands forward as if to say 'after you.'

Val glanced back at Ledgermaine. He caught her with a puzzling wink before one of the goldcoats took him up under a shoulder.

Ledge, you mad old codger. What are you up to?

CHAPTER TWENTY-THREE

D espite its minimalist décor, the pillared expanse of Courowne's palace throne room screamed of untold wealth and indulgence. *What a waste*, Aiden carped, disgusted by the degree of utterly useless extravagance.

Her high arching stones were white as the heart of winter, as were the many statues and busts lining her lofty, cavernous interior. Banners of black-trimmed gold ran down like twin rivers behind the dais, where in between loomed the largest shield the archivist had ever beheld. It was tall as a man and twice the width. Aiden couldn't help but wonder if it had once belonged to some great creature, mayhaps a wngar or some manner of ancient swamp beast. Alas, wherever it had come from, it was now little more than a lifeless decoration, painted gold with the black bird sigil of House Dalivant across its face.

The chamber's belly was not unlike that of a cathedral in that there were rows of pews facing the platform. They found Emperor Drezhal in the middle of the stage sitting atop a towering throne of marble, his fine lichen-green silks shimmering smooth as Lake Gallea under a midsummer lull. Next to him, an arm's breadth to the left, stood the Lady Magwyn, a look of bewilderment veiled across her searching countenance. Both lingered tall, ten steps above another soul in attendance.

Light murmuring trickled through the pews as Commodore Visbane lead Aiden and Val down the center aisle between the perfumed clouds of the nobility to the edge of the lowest stair where they were forced down upon their knees.

Drezhal appeared to be a man in his middle cycles, mayhaps late thirties to early forties, though decidedly far too young still for the silver-gray curls that held up his bejeweled bone-white crown. Aiden rather thought he made for a handsome figure, which only exacerbated his annoyance toward the man that much more. Station and affluence were one thing, but a chiseled jawline and perfectly bronzed skin were a bit much. No man should have every advantage in life, after all. Such weighted fortune was precisely how monsters were made.

The archivist's vision trailed back over to the bride. Next to Drezhal, Lady Magwyn appeared about as plain as they come, buckteeth inching between delicate pouting lips. Though there was the sense that she had once been at least mildly attractive in her younger cycles. She wore a high-necked gown that matched in color to her husband's robes and an emerald studded tiara that screamed for attention against her stark black curls. After a moment of tarry, she took a step forward and another, her mouth widening that much more with each descending step toward them, her stare never once averting from his.

"Commodore," Emperor Drezhal greeted.

"Hail Drezhal," Visbane saluted followed by a chorus throughout the attendees.

"So this is the purported Desmond Lanier, is it?" Drezhal scoffed. "Did your betters never teach you proper etiquette, boy? Frankly, I've seen street urchins with more class."

"I have no betters," Aiden returned. "Only folk worth my time and folk that can piss the fuck off." *How's that for your fucking etiquette, asshole?*

A collective breath erupted from behind them, and a murmuring hum began to make the rounds again.

Drezhal inched to the edge of his throne, clearly affronted, and a raven came down from the rafters to rest easy upon his shoulder. "You dare address your Emperor with such an insolent tongue?"

My Emperor? "I come to your hall in rags and chains so that I might merely speak with my bloodkin, and unprovoked you greet me with childish insults. Is this how you receive all of your guests, then?"

"Bloodkin? There's a bold one from the corpse prince. Assuming that is you in there, after all." Every word that left Drezhal's mouth spewed forth with snide inflection.

"You somehow believe yourself my better because you've an audience and a staircase with a fancy chair?"

"You're damned right I am your better," Drezhal answered crossly. "Look at you. I can smell you from here. Like a tavern piss pot. Sullying my palace stones with flies and stink as we prepare for the Midwinter Gala, bringing scandal into my home, besmirching my wife's name, and yet—"

"I say," Magwyn interjected from the space between them, "what is this bit of quibble meant to accomplish?"

"You believe this imposter then, do you?" Drezhal hissed.

"I can't say for sure just yet," Lady Magwyn answered. "But there is undoubtedly a resemblance here."

"Go on then," Drezhal sneered as he leaned back into his throne. "Let's make us a proper show of it." The raven settled down on the arm of the chair, its head shifting this way and that, taking it all in.

The Empress descended the final few steps slowly, her delicate movements refined and noble, almost frighteningly so. Aiden found himself in awe of her as she came within arm's reach. There was a power behind her saggy, shapeless figure. A dangerous intelligence that he would never make to cross. At least, not intentionally. But there was also something else. Something deep within. Something eerily familiar. Something that gave him pause.

A vision returned to him, like the gutter of a windswept candle. It was had from the perspective of a child sitting atop a woman's knees. The woman glanced down at him revealing that inimitable bucktooth smile. She appeared considerably younger then, but it was undeniably her. *You have a funny smile, Aunt Maggie*, the boy said. *And you have a funny nose*, she returned, her smile growing ear to ear, as she pretended to pluck it from his face and hold it between her fingers.

"It's really you, isn't it?" Lady Magwyn asked as she gently cupped a hand against his face. Instinctually, his cheek sank into her palm. "The gods know, but you look just like him, don't you? A bit on the skinny side, but here you are." Her inquisitive face softened. "Wherever have you been all these cycles?"

Aiden started to raise his manacled hands up, but Magwyn crooked her head. He glanced past Magwyn's shoulder at Drezhal, glaring with intent, and took her meaning.

"They have come from Six Ports, milady," Visbane offered. "We found them aboard Blackhall's Banshee."

"Blackhall's Banshee?" Drezhal echoed from on high.

"I thought given the circumstances and the persons in question, it should be dealt with from the highest order, Majesty," Visbane continued. "They made quite a compelling story of it, all told. You should have seen the conjuring this one cooked up. All my seasons at sea I've never seen anything like it. He pulled forth a wave from the ocean's depths tall as the sea wall, nay, taller, and bloodlet half The Banshee's crew in the process."

"Bloodlet half the crew?" Drezhal snorted. "I say, are you sure it's not senility finally catching up with you good Commodore?"

"I've a score more witnesses that can attest to it, Your Majesty, with far fewer cycles than I. We saw what we saw and we saw it true. The gods only know. To name it mere sailwarding would be an insult to its quality. And to its horror."

"As you say, I do hope Hex was counted amongst the lot."

"She was not, Emperor, but the Golden Fleet saw to her ruin all the same. She was sacrificed to the sea, red smile waiting."

"And what of your turncoat quartermaster?"

"Suffice it to say, Keats was not found, Lord Emperor. Though I suspect he did not survive."

"You suspect? I certainly hope your suspicions are better founded in that than was your belief in his undying loyalty to mine Empire."

Like a scolded child, Commodore Visbane lowered his gaze in shame.

"And who is this one here?" Drezhal cut his eyes upon Val. "You look a harbor-end whore if ever I'd seen one."

"She is my betrothed, fuck you very much," Aiden answered drawing another sequence of gasps.

Drezhal shot him a withering glance. "I don't give a rip who you claim to be, boy. One more outburst like that and I'll have your tongue removed and nailed to the back of your skull, is that clear?"

Aiden met his Aunt Maggie's eyes, reading her directive, and nodded.

"I'll have the words then," the Emperor said.

"It's clear," Aiden mumbled.

"It's clear...?" Drezhal made a coercing motion with his hand.

"Emperor," the archivist finished.

"Brilliant." The Emperor shifted upright in his throne. "And where does our mysterious betrothed hail from I wonder?"

"Nowhere of import, Majesty," Val said.

"We're all from somewhere, dear. And you've come all this way, haven't you? You have an audience with the Emperor of Courowne and the Southern Hollows. You may as well tell us your story." A row of perfectly aligned teeth split the lower half of his face. "What's another lie for the posh folk, after all?"

"I was a sellsword," Val answered. "A wanderer."

"Val," Aiden started.

She met his icy blues. "It's fine."

"Val?" Drezhal echoed as he rose to his feet. "Now we're getting somewhere, aren't we?" He descended a few stairs, arms tucked behind his back. "Tell me Val the Sellsword, were you guilded?"

"No," she answered, holding her gaze upon Lady Magwyn's feet. "Never. I was masterless."

"Masterless," Drezhal chuckled. "None of us are masterless, dear. We are all slaves to something." His lips arched into a devilish grin. "Well, almost all of us." He stopped a few stairs north of them. "My, my," he addressed the rows of spectators, "it would seem the alleged crown prince of Lancastle certainly knows how to pick them, doesn't he?"

A wave of amusement circled the hall.

"She had this on her person," Visbane brought forth the mae'chii and offered it to the Emperor.

Drezhal took the scabbard, unsheathed the blade, and studied it as though it were some manner of long lost relic. "I know this symbol," he remarked after a beat. "It is the insignia of House Alyfain." His dark orbs flicked down at Valestriel. "How came you about such a unique treasure?"

"It belonged to my grandfather," she replied. "He left it to me."

"Your grandfather? How quaint. And who might I ask was your grandfather?"

"Beg pardon, Emperor," Aiden cut in, "but what exactly does any of this have to do with our being here? I say, if it's all the same to you, I should like to catch up with my aunt that I haven't seen in well on a decade."

Drezhal came forward, joining his bride, and placed the tip of Val's mae'chii against the archivist's neck. Aiden turned his chin away from it as much as his woeful positioning would allow. "There you go again, presuming to have mine trust."

"Drezhal," murmured Magwyn. "He is your nephew."

"He is a heathen."

"He is Desmond Lanier, my love. It may displease you to hear it, but that doesn't make it any less true."

"How can you possibly know this?" the Emperor gritted.

Magwyn met Aiden's eyes. "I just know." She placed her hand atop her husband's arm coercing it away from the archivist's throat. "You must trust me."

"Then he should know there is another member of his illustrious family here at court," Drezhal said.

Another member? Aiden's stomach turned a few more knots at the prospect. *Brother. Sister. Mother.* "And who would that be?" He'd rather hoped his voice had remained somewhat composed, but the truth was he barely even heard the words leave his mouth.

"Why, your *other* uncle, of course," Drezhal clarified, snapping the mae'chii back inside its sheath. "The traitor, Rhonyn Waldgrave."

Traitor? "What?"

"Oh yes, the ambassador has rather made a mess of his storied legacy."

"How so?"

"He has become a threat to the commonwealth and The League of Royal Houses," Drezhal expounded. "And he is now a war criminal for his transgressions."

"War criminal?" The archivist glowered at Drezhal. "That is a severe allegation, Emperor. What has he done? What grounds have you to make such a claim?"

"He was in direct opposition to The League and the Royal House Pact. A pact your father founded, I might remind. He became quite violent in his resistance to the latest amendments, brandishing about his sword in protest. I shudder to think what may have transpired had Lady Magwyn not been in attendance to calm him."

And I shudder to think of the amendments you've put in place to produce such a reaction. "So we're to be sent off to the dungeons then?" the archivist asked.

"Desmond," Lady Magwyn uttered, regaining his attentions. "You really should speak with Rhonyn." Her words were laced with all manner of hidden context, but her eyes were what sold the show.

"Are we prisoners here?" he asked her.

"The council and I will need to discuss what exactly you are," the Emperor returned. "For the time being, you will be confined to the cellars. If you go along willingly, I can at least spare you the chains."

Spare us the chains? Aiden glanced at Val and she offered a solemn nod. *The gods only know. This is all just supremely fucked, isn't it?* But what other choice was there? "Fine," said the archivist. "You have our cooperation."

"There. Are you satisfied now?" Magwyn said to her husband, restraint in her tone. "You've got what you wanted." She cast an ironclad scowl at Visbane. "Well, what are you waiting for, Commodore? Remove their bloody chains. Immediately."

CHAPTER TWENTY-FOUR

K eys rattled at the end of the cell block followed by the sound of a lock turning and voices that slowly faded into noth- ingness.

"Well, Dalivant was certainly something else," Val offered once the goldcoat guards rambled out of earshot.

"Yeah, a massive wanklord," the archivist muttered.

"A massive wanklord that recognized an ashaeydir House sigil. The maidens only know how he put that bit together."

"Desmond?" a voice rasped from the shadows across the walkway.

"Rhonyn?" Aiden ventured forward, pressing his face between the cell bars.

Chains jangled inside the pitch whence the voice came. Gods' wounds, but the firelight did the man little in the way of favor. Both his hair and beard were short, greasy, and quite disheveled. Though his appearance was not nearly the most off-putting detail about him. No, that would belong to his horrid stench. He reeked liked burned flesh from the crow's foot brand that had been seared into the side of his face. "I daresay, this is not at all how I saw our reunion coming to pass."

"Your face," Val uttered.

"Mmm, that bad, hunh?" Rhonyn managed before clearing his throat.

"Haven't had the pleasure of seeing it myself yet, swollen eyes and all, but your reaction seems about the proper pace of it."

"How long have you been down here?" Val asked.

"A few days," Rhonyn replied. "And you are?"

"Valestriel...Val..."

"So he's actually gone full loon then?" Aiden said. "Drezhal, I mean."

"Where the Dalivants are concerned, the apple doesn't fall too far from the tree. Drezhal's mother proved a tyrant just the same until she started losing her faculties a few cycles back. Now she can't even remember her own name."

"Why the hells would Lady Magwyn align herself with such a monster?" Val asked.

"You know how it is with the Upper Houses," Rhonyn said. "Every fresh face is a new foe found. Allegiances are typically forged through circumstance, necessity, and longevity, rarely emotional compatibility."

"Classic Midaran bosh," Val quibbled.

"This is all fucked," Aiden grumbled for what felt like the hundredth time in the last hour, pacing a circle and scratching his head, before returning to the bars.

"Reckon it's a bit passed its due at this point," Rhonyn said, "but I take it you know who you truly are then?"

"It took some convincing, but yes. Though, to have her honest, I rather preferred life as a drunk, penniless has-been to this rotty bollocks."

"You sound like your father in that."

"My father?" Against its truth, Aiden imagined Vincent Ashborough sitting on the back porch in his worn, old wicker chair, deep in his cups, watching over his vineyard. "I find it hard to believe King Whitman would ever need to drink himself black."

"To the contrary, your father abused the bottle constantly. Though he did well to keep it from you little ones."

Aiden let that one sink in and stew. "Magwyn said I should speak with you," he said after a bevy of heartbeats.

"Did she?"

"Dalivant named you a traitor. He said you were brandishing your sword about the closed council like a madman."

"Not my finest moment, I will admit."

"So, it's true then?" Val asked.

"Dalivant is forcing abdication on House Lanier. He's convinced The League that Lancastle should be left to the rot. And I rather took offense. But prize well, there is more at play here than lost loyalties and theatrics."

"And Magwyn approved of this abdication?"

"To my knowledge, the order has not yet been ratified."

"That's not an answer," the archivist returned. "Do you think she is capable of turning on House Lanier? On us?"

"Your aunt may have married into House Dalivant, a forced marriage, mind you, but she is no turncloak. Keep that one close to heart. She will back you and Lancastle until her dying breath. No matter what the repercussions. Her allegiances will always lie with her blood House." Rhonyn shifted his back against the bars.

"Are you saying she would move against her husband?" Val continued from over Aiden's shoulder.

"I believe that is the far more likely outcome. She's been playing at some sort of long game within The League for quite some time now, undermining this little decree and that one, and she is not alone in her opposition. Trust it true, Maggie is one of the most patient and prudent folks I have ever met."

"Yeah, well I'm not so sure this world has much room left for patience anymore," Aiden remarked.

"A shrewd observation," Rhonyn said, turning back to face them, "and a sentiment I too share."

"Though I've no doubts, if she weren't present in the throne hall, Drezhal would've had us both in a noose rather than a cage."

Rhonyn cleared his throat again. "I can assume by your being here that you haven't been home yet?"

"If by home you mean Lancastle, no, I have not."

"I should say, the state of you, Rissa would've had a conniption post haste."

Rissa. Larissa Lanier. Mother. "How is she? How are they?"

"I wish I could say. As I'm sure you've deduced, I haven't been home in weeks. Since before the blight uprising. Though even then it was like walking on eggshells between Larissa and Marsea. Peas in a pod, those two. Though neither one would ever admit to it."

Marsea. The likeness of a younger blond-haired girl formed inside his mind. It swiftly bled into his memory of little Tam and then into the twisted thing he saw chained to their mother's throne in his dream aboard the Belisarius.

"Remy has been at The King's Wall or somewhere thereabouts for nearly a cycle."

"The King's Wall? Whatever for?" Aiden knew scant little about The King's Wall, in truth. But he'd heard plenty of drunken tavern tales from Cork and his boys on the topic. Enough to know it was little better than life behind a prison cell. And certainly enough to know it was no place for a Crown Prince.

"His choice," Rhonyn expounded. "There was a time I tried to talk him out of it. I did everything save place him under lock and key to keep him home. But it was his choice in the end. Crown Prince or no, mistake or no, a man's eighteen cycles old, he should be allowed to make his own life choices, wouldn't you agree?"

Aiden could barely remember them, try as he might, but he found himself wondering more and more what they must be like now. And moreover, against his dreamscape's horror, what they must look like. The gods knew. They would be fully grown. He imagined a pair of wanky poshers in the finest cut cloth the king's coin could conjure. He thought about how it might be to go shoot the shit with such a pair in Paddy's Pub for a night. He and Marsea and Remy. And maybe Val and Calem. How it might be if he introduced them to Autumn and Vincent. How they would view the rather ordinary life he'd managed to scrounge for himself.

"I suppose..."

"At any rate, they certainly remember you," Rhonyn said. "In the least, Marsea does. All told, she has probably missed you the most. She has suffered your shadow all her days, struggling mightily to fill your elder sibling shoes for both Remy and Jules."

"Jules? Who is Jules?"

"She is your half-sister."

Half-sister?

"Julia Harver. She is the daughter of your mother and Raelan Harver."

A bastard? Mayhaps the Laniers were not so pristine as publicized, after all.
"How old is she?"

"She just turned nine. We celebrated her birthfall last month. It was the last night I was in Lancastle actually. And she's all Harver too. Though Marsea has certainly put in the effort to keep her levelheaded."

Hearing their names spoken on with such care and fondness, Aiden was starting to understand some semblance of the life Redding had promised him he had lost. "I was such a wretched little shit to Marsea back then," he found himself saying, nostalgia in full haunt.

"You were a wretched little shit to everyone, Desmond. But trust, it was nothing most boys don't go through at one point or another. Your father was fearsome tough on you besides, so it came as little surprise that you acted out a prat to everyone else."

"Father..." A fresh image of a crowned corpse in navy and gold flashed through.

"But there beat purpose behind Whit's harsh conduct against you. For he believed he was battling against prophecy."

"Prophecy?" *Lovely, just what we need, more storybook bullshit.*

"A prophecy he received in his youth. A prophecy that belonged to his heirs."

"What sort of prophecy?" Val inquired, joining Aiden at the bars.

"Alas, I only know a portion of it."

"Aye. Well, let's have it then," the archivist said.

"You won't care for it."

"I already don't care for it, being what it is. Prophecies by nature sit ill with me. As do most things missing logic's count. But you've gone and stirred the pot then, haven't you? So let's have it done with."

"Very well," Rhonyn began. "One will die before their time. One must go alone. One will cede love's greatest gift in turn to spite the throne."

Aiden let the words resonate. *Fucking hells, it even rhymes.*

"Rather open-ended, wouldn't you say?" Val returned.

"All the best prophecies are," Rhonyn said dryly. "But Whit never let this one go. As the cycles passed, he only became more and more obsessed with it. And with the reemergence of Ravenholme and *The N'therN'rycka*, around the turn of the century, it only sank its teeth into him that much deeper. So, he put their covenant to the inquisition. His own infernal crusade. And thusly, he began to experiment with his gift and fashioned something like a grimoire with his findings.

"'*Frayed are the threads that cast shadows. Lush is the drear in their unforgiving wake.*'"

"The hells does that mean?" Aiden asked.

"Would that I could name it," Rhonyn replied. "It was what he called the damned thing."

Frayed are the threads that cast shadows, the archivist ruminated. *Lush is the drear in their unforgiving wake.*

"I can say, the grimoire's intention was to fight back against the darkness—against the nether and all of the abominations hidden within *The N'therN'rycka's* pages.

"And trust, I had my reservations just as well. There were many nights that I questioned your father's sanity, putting him to my own inquisition, and many more that I kept your mother from storming his solar and causing a terrible fuss. But that all changed when...well...when you..."

"When I died," Aiden finished, holding his uncle's haunted orbs. *One will die before their time.*

"It gave the prophecy some credence, didn't it? Made all of the horrible shit Whitman had been going on about that much more real. To see your corpse in that fucking coffin...and to think of all the cycles that had been stolen from you..." Rhonyn shifted slightly, leaning a shoulder against the bars.

"Who else knew of this prophecy?"

"Magwyn and Stella for sure. Hells, to have the tale, your Aunt Maggie was there with Whit when the words were given. I'm sure your mother has some shape of it as well. Also, a magus named Ledgermaine."

"We're familiar with the later," Val said.

The archivist could almost hear her eyes roll at the name.

"I pushed them to bring you back," Rhonyn said. "Stella and Ledge both. That's on me."

"Why?" Aiden stopped at the word, the rest following in his head, *should I deserve to live?*

"Why?" Rhonyn echoed. "Aside from the obvious reason that you are my nephew and mine blood? Because fuck prophecy, that's why. Fuck the crone and fuck her pale fucking horse right along with her. She took it all when she took you and Whit. King and Crown Prince both. Leaving my sister and family at the mercy of heathens. That bitch meant to bury our Houses with a sad little spell and she almost succeeded. But not whilst breath still finds my lungs.

"One must go alone? One will cede love's greatest gift in turn to spite the throne? To spite the fucking throne? Our fucking throne? Shit on that.

You reckon given your own doom, a child should have to hear they own such a rotten fate? That one day one of them would be alone and the other would turn against their House? You reckon, you'd let that abide?"

"I—"

Fresh noises from the hallway outside halted their mad symposium.

Aiden and Val watched the door in wide-eyed anticipation. It was a strange rhythmic clicking sound that approached and even stranger footsteps. No voices found purchase. The noises came to a halt on the other side of the cellar door and a faint, metal scraping sound resumed in their place followed by the slow inward creak of rusty hinges.

A hunched figure with a cane appeared in the doorway.

Aiden blinked at the unexpected shape.

"Pion?" Rhonyn said.

"Ambassador," a nasally voice cut through the dreary haunt.

"What in vaelnation are you doing here?"

"There isn't time," Pion answered as he hobbled up to their cell door and went to work with a pickset.

Aiden stepped up close to the man and his breath caught. Another flash memory of a sickly boy crying on stairs. "Runt?" The name just came to him like a whisper on the wind.

The tall, grotesque figure met Aiden's icy blues between strands of long, stringy black hair and smirked as the lock clicked and the cell door eeked open. But the gods know, he wasn't much of a runt anymore despite his deformities.

Pion Harver.

"Is this absolutely necessary?" Aiden asked.

"Your aunt sent me down here, saying it was urgent." Pion spoke in a low tone. "So take from that what you will."

"Maggie sent you?" Rhonyn questioned.

"She did," Pion answered. "She—"

Approaching voices echoed from down the lower corridors into the dungeon hall, and they all turned toward the doorway.

"Follow me," Pion ordered.

"We can't just leave him," Aiden said as he came before Rhonyn's cell.

"There isn't time," the grotesque hissed.

"I can make time," Aiden returned. "Just get him out."

216

"No," Rhonyn said. "It's too risky. You need to leave while you still can."

"I won't just leave you down here. Fuck that."

"My fetters are anchored to the floor and I can't see shit. I'm a liability, Desmond. I will only slow you down."

"Yeah, and you're family too, aren't you? After everything you just said about family, you're going to fight me on this? You're not the only one that doesn't leave family, you know."

The echoes were joined by footsteps that clamored ever closer.

"Don't be reckless on my account, lad," Rhonyn arched in close. "Not here. Not in this place. Not as the world is now. You're the rightful king of Lancastle. You must be able to see beyond what lies plainly before you."

"Rho—"

"The old blood must survive, Desmond. Your blood must survive. The blood of the maker. You have a chance to get out, you fucking take it, you hear me? I don't care who you have to fucking burn in the process."

CHAPTER TWENTY-FIVE

Their escape from the palace cellars passed like a fever dream on spriteling dust. Through stone and field and wood and back to stone again, long into the evening crowds, long inside the mouth of madness.

And then there were the lightning bugs, as though the city had suddenly become invaded by a fairy host. They were everywhere, floating about like tiny flickering bubbles of foxfire. Valestriel had seen the creatures in patches a few times before, in the marshes outside Toberon, many cycles past, but never to this extent. Here they were legion, hundreds upon hundreds of them, drifting amidst the endless pockets of city folk.

Despite his obvious physical disadvantage, Pion navigated the sea of lights and faces expertly, his cane snapping to and fro against every wayward ankle, forcing a path through.

"This way," the grotesque steered, eventually guiding them from the heave and swelter into a narrow alleyway. He stopped at a door midway down and knocked with the handle of his cane. An elderly woman answered, eyeing the three of them closely before silently allowing their passage.

Raucous noises came from somewhere beyond the other side of the wall as Pion led them down a dimly lit hallway to a dark wooden stairwell. "This is where I must leave you," he said. "I've another matter to attend just now."

"What matter?" Aiden asked. "We've only just reunited."

"Oh, you know. Have to see a man about a thing, rot, rot, bloody rot, and a thousand mysteries." He presented Aiden with a key. "Upstairs, on the left, you will find a room with a parted hourglass carved into the top right corner. I will come back for you in the morning. For now, I suggest you just keep to the room."

"Cheers," Aiden said, as he took the offering.

Pion turned away, shuffling back whence they had come.

"And Pion," Aiden called.

The grotesque stopped and glanced back over his shoulder.

"I won't forget this," the archivist said.

Pion's lip curled up. "Do try and get some rest, Desmond. The morrow is soon upon us and there is much, much more yet to be done."

AN OIL LAMP was burning on the nightstand upon entry, casting the room in a cozy amber glow. The space was small, but surprisingly well furnished. And it was obvious someone had taken the time to tidy up freshly. Even the bedsheets looked clean and crisp.

"Dodgy as fuck, that one," Val said.

"Yeah, I think me and Dodgy were mates once."

"That right?"

"Sadly, I remember him better than I do Marsea or Remy. Better than I do mine own mother."

"You named him Runt."

"It just came to me. I think that's what we called him. Or at least what I called him. I don't know."

"And you're sure you were mates then?"

"Sure? Not even a little. But there was some sort of connection between us. Some bit of meaningful something-or-other. I wish I could name it better."

"Well, if nothing else, he's freed us from Dalivant's murder cellar, so he's earned full marks in my book."

"And Rhonyn. I can't believe that was him. The state of him. He and Ledge were once best mates. You believe that?"

"Honestly, I don't know what I believe anymore," Val answered.

"The shit just keeps fucking piling, doesn't it? I mean we've been here what, a few hours? And we've already got all this fuckery going on. And we're not even glancing the Tetherow bullshit yet. We're not even glancing the blight up north. Marsea's up there in all that shit. Remy's up there in it. At the fucking King's Wall, no less. Mum's up there. They're all up there, smack dab in the middle of it. And—"

She gripped the folds of Aiden's robe and pulled him into her lips, splitting his mouth with her tongue until she found his. They brushed against one another, swapping salts and saliva, before she fastly spun away.

Another momentary distraction for the collection. "You taste awful," she groaned into the chamber's open space.

"I hate that you do that," the archivist returned.

"What?"

"Kiss me when you want me to shut up."

"Then maybe you should stop saying stupid shit," Val said, to the chagrin of her own similar concerns. "Besides, what did I tell you back in the brig? We'll find Morgan. And we will. I truly believe that. She knows soul magic. She knows The Pale. And she'll know what to do about Tetherow. She was at The King's Wall too, last I heard. Mayhaps she and Remy somehow found each other."

The archivist beset her with a most incredulous gaze, lips in full purse.

"Don't look at me like that. Stranger things have happened."

"How?" Aiden shook his head. "How are you always so impossibly fucking hopeful?"

"I don't know." She wanted nothing more than to tell him how she truly felt, but instead settled for, "how are you always so impossibly fucking gloomy?"

"Is that how I am then?"

"All day, every day." *Baka.*

"And here I thought I was slowly inching toward optimism. Fuck me, right?"

She halved the gap between them. "Fuck you." *Pathetic girl.*

He stepped up to her and gripped her curls in a fist. "Fuck you then."

She clutched under his jaw, squeezing his lips into a pout. "Fuck me."

"You think this a joke?" he said between her pinching fingers.

"I think it's fucking hilarious," she said before forcing her lips against his again, hairs ripping away from her scalp.

They let each other go and the flesh of their mouths twisted against one another, the softness of their lips bending and curling as their front teeth scraped back and forth with a crooked violence. And they sank past their wants and their longings straight into the depths of their needs, kissing and sucking at each other long and hard and deep and slow.

"And so, what do you see when you look at me, I wonder?" Val panted as they broke for breath.

"I see you," Aiden answered far too quickly.

Valestriel pushed away from him, floating to the other side of the room and into the starlight's cast. She gazed out the window at the cobblestone street below. It appeared dark and empty save for the glow of fireflies. She raised a hand to the side of her neck, feeling for the small mound of scar tissue that housed her trezsu implant. "How about now?"

Hands slipped around her waist and across her belly, and a scruffy chin settled atop the opposite shoulder from her trezsu implant. "Still you," he answered, apparently not without his charms.

Held close, Val wiggled around his embrace to face him, batting her doe-like golden ashaeydir orbs. "You don't have a preference?"

Unflinching, he held her eyes. "They're both you, aren't they?"

"You tell me," she answered, tilting her head slightly.

"What is this?" he asked. "Tell me, what more would you have of me? What more can I possibly say to convince you?"

"I don't know." *But I know you can't be this. I know we can't be. This...*

"I don't care that you're ashaeydir, Val. I'd scream it throughout the gods' green Vael if I didn't think it would bring you trouble."

"You did care. And not so very long ago."

"That was then. And I was an idiot."

She snorted. "Hate to break it to you, but you still are."

"Ouch," he uttered as he backed away from her, clutching a hand to his chest where an imaginary arrow had apparently made its mark. "And here I was thinking, maybe after all of this was over, we could go on an actual proper date sometime."

An actual proper date? The prospect of her courting a Midaran boy was so far-fetched she couldn't even begin to conjure her family's reaction to such a scene. Even for a would-be king Midaran boy. No doubt her father would have had him flayed and fed to the dogs, and that's if Uncle Rill didn't fancy a knifing first. She didn't even want to consider her mother or sisters' opinions. For she knew their reactions would be far, far harsher. "Is that what you were thinking then?" she countered with her best placed smile.

"That's what I was thinking."

"And so, where did Mister Hopelessly-Unavailable-and-Doomed-to-Die get off to, I wonder?"

"I'm quite serious."

Why you? Why me? Why us?

There was something in his icy blues just then. Something that gave her pause—something mystical and far beyond a mere word for description—and everything within her that yet still belonged to Morgandrel Tully quivered in its wake.

Here comes the harbor-end whore.

A moment ago, exhaustion swallowed her spirit and sleep screamed her name long into the high-ranging heavens, but that moment was an age at length, an age and then another. And quite suddenly there was work to be done. She wanted him, she decided. And she wanted him inside her. Inside her ache. Ache for ache. Her body commanded it, eroticizing her pain against her better scruples. And she wanted to stare directly into his bonny blue eyes as he went at her, fucking her agony until it was banished some place beyond blackout numb.

She offered something like a gasp to the moon between them. "Are you hard?"

"What do you think?" he rasped. He almost sounded ashamed. Though, maybe that was just her head playing their games again.

She began to unbutton her blouse. "I think I want you to be hard." *There she is.* "And I think I want you inside me."

He had his shirt off in a blink and she drifted against him, touching his bare chest, running a hand across his naked stomach, over the patch of scarring, down to the swell in his trousers. She felt her nipples rise and goose pimples prickle along the span of her arms. Fingers worked his belt loose and his trousers spilled down around his ankles. She cupped his exposed fruits in the candlelight and stroked his shaft, her palm glistening with pre-cum, and she shoved him backward onto the bed.

She let her blouse slide down her arms, peeled her boots off with the arches of her feet, then shimmied awkwardly out of her britches. She reckoned some things were impossible to make sultry. When she turned back up to Aiden, she found him watching her with a lewd expression scrawled upon his face. Somehow, he had already shed all of his clothing.

They remained still for a moment, taking each other in fully, their flesh marred from the violence of their union— matching chain marks about their wrists—scrapes and bruises in the dozens—lips pink and puffy.

A shared suffering.

You always said you wanted to find true love, didn't you? She sauntered up to him, her natural form laid bare. *Well, here he is, staring you dead in the face.*

She could feel his ache and desperation as a palm wandered across her hip and settled upon her buttocks, enticing her in closer. He didn't care that she was ashaeydir. No more than she cared that he was Midaran. And he wanted this as badly as she did him. She knew this for truth. Even without words. Even without regards. His yearning was just as demanding and obvious as hers.

It was all so damned undeniable, she and him. And that much more inevitable.

His mouth found her tits, licking, flicking, and biting, the roughness of his beard scratching her precisely the way she preferred. She hugged around his head, raking fingers through his long raven-black hair, pressing his face into her body as he burrowed deep like a feeding beast. Impatient hands ran the length of her backside from ass to shoulder, unable to settle, and he began to kiss her softly. All over. In the space between her breasts. Feathery lips. Across her ribcage. Feathery lips. Around her naval. Feathery lips. A current radiated across her skin from all of his bristly attentions.

"I wish we had met at a less complicated time in our lives," she whispered.

He halted at the words, pulling slowly away from her, looking red and raw as he scooted back further onto the bed and she followed the invisible strings, placing a hand atop the bedsheets, chased by a second, then a knee, and its opposite, and she slunk up his body until her cunt grazed the bottom of his shaft.

A pair of fingertips sank into her wetness, her fingers, brushing pulsing heat, and she rubbed her fluids against the head of his cock before allowing him to split her open. She muffled an involuntary moan as she lowered herself against him, arching her spine, forcing every inch of him inside her. It hurt, but in the right kind of way. And in truth, she rather preferred Aiden's brand of hurt to the others she had lain with, ashaeydir all. She felt his belly tighten beneath her sticky hands. And they began as they always had. Going at each other like a couple of wild beasts, as though fucking as hard and angry as possible was the only way to preserve their lives.

Only—

Something began to change about their movements partway through the storm—something unspoken—yet something silently instructed.

In seconds, they'd gone at each other so hard they had practically sweated the stench of the sea and their rusty shackles completely away. Though, what mad love that bewitched them wasn't about smell. Nor was it about sight. Or sound. Or taste. This madness had yet transcended all of those senses, ebbing in their significance for the one yet remaining, unnamed.

She lowered her body against his, skin to skin, her breasts throbbing against his heartbeat, and he took her up at the small of her back, laying her down beneath him. In the shifting of position, he fell out of her, but there he returned a moment later, glancing against the softness between her legs. She inhaled as he entered her and bit her bottom lip as she exhaled. His thrusts were unhurried and deep and almost tender. Tender considering their usual fair.

She watched him, his eyes closed, and placed a hand against his cheek. His icy blues whispered open to her, and she offered up her throat to him. He nuzzled into the softness of her neck, sucking so sweetly, as his thrusting adapted to the energy held between them and became something like a slow rhythmic ritual.

Eventually, his lips found her jawline and then her cheek and her mouth again, and their kisses were just as gentle as their lovemaking. They snogged long past where they would have normally broken off, their lips practically sewn together, not a worry to be found twixt their shallow breaths and moving parts...

Until her straying thoughts drifted back to Morgan, *her* Morgan, and tears began to form at the edges of her eyes, trickling out of her, one by one.

Suddenly his lips thinned and his body went taut then almost boneless as his weight settled down upon her and she was filled with a warm flooding sensation.

His mouth came away from hers and his face swept through her streaks of tears onto the pillow. His body followed in descent, his manhood sliding gently out of her, against her side.

"Not even close to done," he breathed, a hand grazing softly across her belly.

Tears flowing, Valestriel Alyfain licked the awful taste of him from off her lips and turned up a sparkling white smile for the stars above.

"I know."

CHAPTER TWENTY-SIX

I will not let my past define me.

About a third of the way through the bottle, the pain of each needle prick began to fade. Admittedly, once it dulled, she kind of, sort of, maybe, just a teensy bit, began to rather miss it.

When asked where she wanted the thing, Marsea originally indicated the arm of her bad hand. She figured it was already a ruin anyway, what was a little more character? But Beldroth was quick to correct her mistake. It needed to be somewhere about her torso. As grim a notion as it was, limbs were far easier to lose. So she chose her right shoulder blade. What better place than to have the thing watching her back?

And they hadn't even arrived at the hard part yet.

Marsea took another swig, her vision swimming as she watched Broenwjar, who lay on the floor at the foot of the Yule Tree, a patch of darkened bandage on his flank from where they drew his blood for the branding. The whiskey tasted absolutely awful, but somehow it seemed a fitting component to this whole dreadful experience. Though, awful as it was, she didn't exactly hate it.

And the maidens knew she was leagues away from the pathetic, fretful shut-in that was terrified of ever leaving her kingdom's cobble.

What would the maidens make of this fresh version? She couldn't help but wonder. Defiling her body with the devil's scribblings and the blood of dead things? What would her mother think? What would her father think of his only daughter now? The stars rest his soul. What would he think of how her life had become?

Though, truthfully, she had never really met the whole princess mold anyway. She had come to terms long ago with the fact that she would never be the sort of princess to turn heads or draw gasps. Nor was she the sort to turn beasts into dashing princes or any other sort of dull fairytale rubbish. She had no fixed opinion about council chamber politics like Remy, and she could give a fig less about all the regal pageantry spun by her mother and the toffee-nosed hens of court. No, the fates would see her a different manner of princess altogether, it would seem, though much to her prolonged dismay the fates also seemed utterly disinterested in clueing her in as to what exactly that was. And so, in the place of something this ridiculous society might halfway accept, this darkly present-day misfit version of a princess was made.

But weren't all the damsels damned in the end anyway?

"Nearly done," Dagmara announced. "You've done quite well." Those were the first words spoken between them in what felt like an eternity.

"Cheers to that," Marsea said as she turned up the bottle once more before setting it on the table before her.

Beldroth and Klaus had gone out a while back, leaving the two of them and Broenwjar to the needle and the drink and the firelight and apparently the silence. Though Marsea couldn't solely put the blame on Dags for the last bit. She didn't realize how rubbish she would be at participating socially when she had the choice not to.

But rubbish or no, she was missing an opportunity here and she knew it. *The stars save me. You're such a wimp, Marsea. Truly, she's a little old lady. What's the worst that could happen?*

Famous last words, those.

"Dagmara," she began anyway, crossing her arms atop the spine of the chair she sat backward in.

"Yes, milady?"

Start easy. "How did you...hic..." She covered her mouth with the back of a hand. "Excuse me...hic...how did you and Klaus come to meet Beldroth?"

"Beldroth." Marsea could hear the smile in the woman's kindly voice. "He hates that name you know. Beldroth. Absolutely detests it."

"I didn't know," Marsea confessed with a pang of guilt. He'd never once said anything to her about it. "Truthfully I know nothing about him save...hic...that he is not who the rest of the world believes him to be. And yet somehow I feel like he knows everything there is to know about me."

"That is because he likely does."

Marsea looked sidelong over her shoulder just barely catching the elder from the crook of her eye.

"You must understand. Elsymir has lived for centuries. Much of those cycles in solitude. As such, he now bothers himself in everyone's business. Especially those that are not y'deman. And doubly so those of the old blood."

"He disregards his own people?"

"They are not his people anymore. Not in his mind. And they haven't been for some time now. Elsymir was unjustly exiled from the fae kingdoms many, many cycles ago because of his father's actions."

Marsea had a difficult time imagining Beldroth as a youngling, ever answering to a father, ever answering to anyone at all.

"But the rest about that is his story to tell."

"So it is." The drink was making her bold indeed. "And so...hic...why does he now pretend to be Tetherow, I wonder?" Marsea's nose scrunched up as she felt the needle dig slightly deeper.

"It is not so much that he pretends to be Tetherow as it is that he continues the teachings he was once given and yet still holds to heart. But that is merely one old woman's opinion."

"Were you one of his students?"

"As a matter of fact, I was. Back when I was your age. Mayhaps a little older."

"You were a member of Ravenholme?"

"Aye. It was a far less turbulent time in those days. Your grandfather sat the throne. Whitman the First."

"I never got to meet my grandfather, but I've been told father was the spitting image."

The needle pricks stopped.

"Done," Dagmara said as she gently pressed a cloth over the tattooed patch. "Not to toot my own horn, but I have to say this is some of my best work."

Marsea pushed up from the chair and worked the soreness from her shoulder. "Hic…"

"You want to get rid of those, you should try holding your breath and counting to fifty," the elder said.

The princess inhaled, trapping the air in, and began counting.

"You want to see it?" Dagmara asked, as though the answer weren't already plain as day.

Breath held, Marsea covered up as best she could and followed after Dagmara until they came to the candlelit washroom. There was a standing mirror a head taller than Marsea with a crack running across the top left corner. It appeared just as old and rustic as every other piece of furniture in the VanLandingham's cottage. Marsea let her arms down and stared at her partially clothed upper half in the flicker of flame as Dagmara lit a few more candles.

Who are you? Marsea's eyes lowered slowly from between her oily mop of hair to her torso. Her shirt was half on, the sleeve of her left arm disappearing inside the cuff of her leather gauntlet. The right sleeve trailed down the center of her chest from the rumple of cloth around her neck. Her vision stopped upon her exposed breast before trailing down to a line of scabbing near the bottom of her rib cage.

"Here you are." Dagmara offered a hand mirror.

Marsea took it with her good hand, turned around, and held it up to view the reflection of her backside. "There it is," she exhaled. It was almost identical to what she remembered of Beldroth's version, stark and eternal, mayhaps the size of an apple. The ringed hourglass branded with a most steady hand. An easy smile touched her lips only to fade as her eyes dropped to the bruises and cuts that plagued much of her sides and lower back. "It looks better than I imagined it would."

Dagmara gently wiped the area again before placing a bandage over it. "I'm glad you approve, milady."

Marsea handed the mirror back to Dagmara and slid her arm back into the sleeve of her shirt. "What now?"

"Now. We wait for the boys to get back with the fixings. And then… the hard part."

THE STAG HALL, in all its wonderment, was a construct of the old world, the communal world, the world before the dominion of societal hierarchies, refinement, and domestic isolation, the world before the age of sorcery and disposable things. Or so Dagmara had told her. As such it had been abandoned many cycles past alongside the memories of its archaic ideals. Left to wither and collect dust and eventually collapse under the weight of its exile. But the collapse never came, in spite of those with such a penchant for utter negligence, for the ancient ancestors of Vaelsyntheria were keen architects who believed in the authenticity of their labors. They did not build frivolously. They built out of necessity. Thusly, each dwelling was erected with meticulous exactitude. This particular stag hall, named Hyrngaut by the forefathers, was once a den for many families during the wintry days of yore, though its cycles of mistreatment now yielded a cold, murky creature that ponged of wet dirt and mildew and forgotten dreams. All the same, through the decades of darkness, by some apparent jape of the fates, she yet still clung to life. In the absence of her makers' cares, she was thenceforth sustained by the forest—by the Vael mother herself. Mushrooms had sprouted between the fissures of her flooring, crowding the walkways, and thick rope-like strands of ivy had weaved betwixt the tiniest spaces of her wooden layers to keep her upright, synchronously creating a beautiful emerald skin about her outer shell.

Of course, none of this was known by the present-day folk of Vinth. Dagmara had claimed Hyrngaut in the name of Ravenholme some many cycles back, placing a madman's ward around it that would cause trespassers to see and hear the things they feared the most if they dallied too near. To this day, Dags concluded, only a handful of folk even knew of Hyrngaut's continued existence. And it was undoubtedly better left as such.

I WILL NOT LET my past define me.

'Twas the dead of night, nigh on the crone's hour, and cold as the hells' hinges. Cold enough that Remy's old hunting jacket, one of Dagmara's fur skin cloaks, and a bottle of red-eye couldn't stop her bloody shivers.

Marsea watched Beldroth and Broenwjar from the center of the magic circle that inhabited the space before the stag hall's great burning hearth. Beldroth, looking spent as a deathbed rotter, was kneeling before Old Boy at the other end of the hall. One last commune between the bonded pair, she supposed. Maidens' mercy, she couldn't imagine. The pain between them was practically sentient.

It wouldn't be long now. She brought the bottle back to her lips and took a small sip. Just enough to burn. Just enough to keep her quiet. Just enough to distract her for another few torturous seconds. She didn't want to make this all about her. Never that. Never again. But the anticipation was beginning to eat her alive. But, of course, it was. The fucking Lanier spirit and all that. It took every decent ounce she had left to her to keep her expectant tongue at bay, to keep her selfish posturing in check. At this point, she just wanted the damned ritual over with. For better or worse. Come what may.

Beldroth patted Old Boy behind his ear and stood with a sickly groan, leaning heavily on his walking cane. Marsea's vision dropped to one of the pentagram's painted points. Though she could still feel the y'deman's stare on her. It burned almost as hard as the whiskey warmth.

At the table against the far wall, Dagmara was grinding away, pestle to mortar, at some arcane substance that Marsea had more than like never heard of. Klaus, meanwhile, prepped the irons. A kindleblade, Marsea knew it to be named. Waxing it in some solution Dags had made prior to the one she was presently concocting.

But the maidens knew. She was a far cry from the perfumed nights in the court of courts, wasn't she?

"The hour is upon us," Beldroth said as he neared. "Let's go over it one last time."

"I know what to expect," Marsea answered, with far more impertinence than she meant.

"Then speak it true," he grumbled.

Marsea's eyes flitted from Dags to Klaus to Old Boy and back to Beldroth. "Dagmara will begin the spell as Klaus burns the mark off of you." She fished a piece of parchment from her jacket's inner pocket. "Once the signal is given, I will begin to read from this scripture, completely, word for word, from beginning to end, no stopping."

"Good." He said as he took her in. "No matter what you see or hear."

"No matter what I see or hear." And she made sure to show him her eyes.

The bandages were off, and the left side of his face had become completely necrotic from the nose over, showing varying shades of black, purple, green, and yellow. It prevented him from properly using that side of his mouth. But even that bit wasn't the worst of it. Just a mite lower, about his neck, there pulsated a large black growth that appeared on the verge of bursting.

There was no point in asking if it hurt anymore. And there was doubly no point in hopeful talk. That time had long passed. Elsymir Beldroth appeared the very image of death now. It went without saying really, but there were actual corpses that looked more alive than he did.

"Dags," Beldroth groaned. "We're ready."

Dagmara brought the bowl over to them. "Take as much as you can stomach," she instructed.

The contents appeared like herbs in mud and smelled like saltwater.

"Swallow, don't chew," Beldroth said as he took a pinch and chased it with a second.

Marsea did the same and nearly retched it back up on contact. She slapped her good hand over her mouth and forced herself to take it down.

Klaus came over to the hearth and offered the kindleblade to the flame's kiss. Marsea heard him muttering something, some bit of Chandiian prayer she supposed, but she was far too distracted by the horrible taste in her mouth to capture it proper.

Dagmara led Beldroth to the table and he laid flat atop it, lifting up his shirt to reveal his faded ringed hourglass. She offered him the wooden pestle, and he fitted it between his teeth as best he could. Then she glanced at Marsea, took up the codex, and began chanting from it.

Klaus strode past her, the kindleblade glowing angry as smelted hellfire in his gloved hand as he stared his good friend straight. "You ready?"

Beldroth nodded.

"Here we go then," Klaus said.

Beldroth gripped the edges of the table as the knife came near, and he yowled bloody murder around the makeshift bit as the blade blistered into flesh. With his free hand, Klaus pressed down on Beldroth's chest to keep his writhing manageable.

All the while, the princess watched owl-eyed. And Dagmara kept chanting. And the wind howled outside as voices flooded into the hall from the hearth behind her. Voices without bodies. Dozens and dozens of them, reminiscent of the haunter's in Alistair's Courtyard. Marsea's eyes wandered to Broenwjar and her breath caught.

The stars save me.

Beside the beast, on all fours, was Other.

Dagmara slammed the book shut and it sounded like a crack of thunder.

Now.

What?

The signal.

So soon? But I...

Read now, Other ordered.

Marsea fumbled with the parchment, her shaking hands holding it inches away from her nose. Dagmara's chanting intensified. As did Beldroth's screams. Why were her glasses suddenly so foggy?

Her left foot slid back, and her right foot inched forward as a lap of waves vibrated within. She felt her hips settle, and words began to pass unto her tongue and release. Words she hoped were correct. Words she could no longer hear. Words that faded from sight between watery blinks. Words that...

Remy!

The parchment vanished.

Wait...Remy? How are you...?

She felt a growl loose from within. A growl she couldn't possibly produce.

Where am I? What is this?

"Broenwjar thae quolo," a voice called from the dissipating haze. Somehow, she understood the words. *Stay calm.*

Clarity formed in the mold of a dense forest...

Remy collapsed to his knees, head hung, and she began to lick at her bloody paws, chunks of flesh and bones surrounding her.

Another voice drew her attention and she glanced up to take it in. Night flickered to daylight in an instant and she found two figures in the distance.

The one facing her, Marsea recognized as Elsymir, though he wore a warped leather mask that almost appeared like wood or burned skin, as though attending a harvestide masquerade, and the other...

He removed his cowl as he turned toward her, and Marsea nearly stumbled in her chanting.

Father!

She couldn't be sure if she actually spoke the word inside the chant or if it was imagined.

Don't stop reading.

A grin like she had never seen her father make found his face as Broenwjar padded up to him.

"Old Boy," Whit called as he knelt before her, grazing his hands through the beast's thick coat of fur, and patting him lovingly on his flank before returning to his feet.

Marsea couldn't believe what she was witnessing.

The Lanier prince couldn't count much north of her current age; still, his dark curls had already begun their turn to silver in places. The maidens knew, but it was uncanny how much he favored Remy in the face. Though he certainly cut a far more masculine figure from the neck down.

Whit strode after Elsymir and they halted at the edge of the forest. Broenwjar joined them as the three of them gazed out at the whole of Lancastle in the distance. By the view, Marsea placed them somewhere not far outside of Mythris Pointe.

Suddenly her adrenaline began to spike, and she found herself on the run. The forest closed in around her as she moved. She was being chased. Hunted. A wolf darted across the path before her and a second and third could be seen off to her right.

The maidens wept.

The pieces were beginning to fall into place now. These memories belonged to Broenwjar.

Don't stop reading! Other hissed once more from the void.

One of the pack cried out from behind and took a tumble. Broenwjar halted in his flight and spun about to his fallen brother. A massive horror of a creature came stomping up to finish the job. She hesitated but for a moment, glancing after the fleeing others one last time, before tearing in the opposite direction toward the great behemoth.

A wngar?

Marsea couldn't believe what she was seeing. It was thrice the size of a Midaran, twice as wide, ugly as a wildkin savage, and wielding a big, nasty, spiked club. In spite of all that, she dove in at it, fangs bared, just before the wretch was to bash the fallen wolf's head in. The wngar caught her one-handed by the neck and flung her into a redwood.

The impact took her breath and crippled her, and she lay there broken as the wngar smashed its club down into her brother's skull.

Broenwjar! Marsea found her voice whimpering, lost in the beast's lament. *I'm so sorry.*

Keep reading!

The giant turned its attentions on her next, and she found she couldn't move. The rush of blood thundered in her ears as her body rejected her commands. It smiled a hideous smile as it neared. By the cruel cast of the sister moons, she unveiled a more defined glimpse of her foe. Its head was shaved on each side, leaving a wild patch of flaxen in the center, and it wore a braided tuft of blond hanging low from the misshapen jut of its chin. A frayed corpse of a cloak stretched down over its backside to the length of its knees and varying shades of stitched animal hide adorned its person from neck to toe. Its face shown a medley of scars, ink, and exposed bone, a muddle that had rendered the original version beneath nearly unrecognizable.

The devil burned in its eyes. But as it came within striking distance, something hit it in the back and a shadow appeared between the trees, fleet as a fox. Suddenly the wngar was driven to a knee as deathly silver flashed along a hamstring. The wngar roared and swiped its great club after the shadow, but the shadow was gone again in a blink. Furious, the wngar spoke out in Wngarthraine, as it tried in vain to put weight on its wounded leg.

For a moment, there was complete stillness. Then Marsea saw the shadow again, and another glint of steel as it approached from the wngar's stern. The shadow grabbed hold of the giant's shirt collar with one hand and plunged its sword deep into the nape of its neck with the other.

The mae'chii's tip appeared through the front of the wngar's throat and the monster clutched at the wound as it collapsed to a hand and then face first into the muck.

The shadow pushed up from the giant's backside once it was down, twisted the blade, sharp end out, and sliced it down the side of the wngar's neck as he leapt to the ground.

Her vision was becoming dim as the shadow approached, splashing dark fluids off its blade before sheathing it. His face was about as ordinary as they come in the ashen starlight. Not a one of his features was in the least bit distinguishing. But she knew the figure without a doubt.

Elsymir.

Her back began to tingle and then burn, like a hot iron was being pressed into it, and she caught the stench of scalded flesh. Suddenly she could feel the parchment again, rough against her fingertips. And the words crossing her lips. And she could hear Beldroth howling through the pestle between his teeth. And Dagmara chanting. But all she could see was Old Boy at the edge of the circle, bowing low before his new master. Unable to stand it any longer, Marsea collapsed to her knees before him, and wrapped her arms around his big, furry neck, letting the rest of the moon fade away around them.

The maidens keep us.

"Thae quolo, Broenwjar." Her tear-filled eyes closed as she hugged him tighter. "Thae quolo."

CHAPTER TWENTY-SEVEN

Thira remained dormant. Still. Somewhere deep inside of him. Detached. Walled off. Silent as the stone. Somewhere he couldn't go. Somewhere he didn't dare.

Remy could only feel her presence through faint sporadic vibrations. Just enough to let him know she was still there with him. Though he had to wonder what all remained of that which endured. For what he felt when he wandered too near those vibrations was a solemn sort of emptiness, as though her very being had been hollowed from the inside out.

'Twas the cruelest form of agony, hers.

Pain within the absence of pain.

Pain with only a memory to define it.

A heart most haunted, once and evermore.

A soul benumbed, eternally starved of rescue.

What right did he have to beggar even the smallest fig of her cares after this fresh loss?

As such, he did his best to remain decent and give her space. All that was going on, he still had a thousand questions for her. But, of course he did. Who wouldn't in such a scenario as what presently found them? But he decided to hold them back for as long as possible.

Still, his mind wouldn't settle. He'd finally made it home. Finally. And yet, it felt nothing at all like a home. Not a one of his family or friends could be found. Marsea was the-gods-only-knew where, hopefully safe, and mother and Jules had apparently vanished. Over a day gone by, and not a soul left to the kingdom could speak to their whereabouts. A potboy barely off his mum's tit claimed to have seen the queen in the guest quarters during the lichlord's offensive, swearing up and down, swearing himself snot-faced and hoarse, but of course, there was nothing there for it. They scoured every chamber a dozen times over to find only ghosts and shadows.

All of this and no Curie either. No Casilvieri. Not one soul he even partway trusted. Truth's witness, it was Curie's absence which troubled him the most. The gods knew. He hadn't realized just how much he had come to rely on her over the past few days. What was the old saying? *You don't know what you've got 'til it's gone.* The watchman would never openly admit it, but he actually missed the mad woman's company. She was something special indeed, it turns out. Something like an actual true friend. Thusly, as with his mother and sisters, he prayed to any and all the gods that would listen for her protection.

"The creatures are still dangerous, make no mistake," Mosshart said before what remained of the small council, "but without a master to control them, they've become a much easier herd. The murder pits and archery lines should see their numbers dwindled to nothing by afternoon, and we may even see the high courts restored to order by sundown."

"Order my eye," Chancellor Ellory chimed in. "What in vaelnation do you suppose we're to do with the contaminated area? It's swallowed near half the upper kingdom."

"We've placed barricades—" Mosshart began.

"The affected areas are to remain forbidden for the time being," Raelan interjected. "We will have soldiers posted outside each surrounding entrance around the clock. No one goes in without authorization. Not until we fully understand what it is and if it's safe to enter. For now, we will concentrate on what all we know can be salvaged."

Remy remained silent at the head of the table staring long into a spiraling chip in the wooded surface.

"Salvaged?" Pryce spat. "The kingdom is in tatters. What exactly are we attempting to salvage here?" The councilman was always far more outspoken than he ought to be.

"No one's asked you to stay, Godric," Raelan grumbled. "As far as I'm concerned, you can sod off back to whatever wallowing cesspit you crawled out of in the first place."

"Are we under military rule then?" Ellory croaked. "Is this now a dictatorship?" The old man cleared his throat. "Highness?"

Remy's eyes flicked over to the Chancellor's, their pits screaming all manner of unholy azure terror. Ellory immediately lowered his gaze.

Silence descended, save for the crackle of firewood from the great hearth.

"What are the totals, lieutenant?" Raelan repaired the conversation a moment later.

"Roundabouts a thousand, sir," Braemoor answered in a thick country twang.

"And civilians?"

"No tellin', all things honest. Could be quints 'fore we have the numbers. Reckon four to five thousand, addin' the outer hollows. Most o' the reports comin' in are pretty damn bleak, though. The few survivors we've come across are young'uns and elderly. Folk put in hidin' 'fore it all went to pot.

"Bunch o' hicks were holed up in the Golden Fleece Innhouse in Helmuth and managed to defend it. Mostly drunks and degenerates, bastards too ornery to die, but damned if they didn't down a shitload o' ghouls in the process."

"Lovely story, lieutenant, so we're landing on roughly six thousand then?" Pryce quibbled. "That's not even half the bloody population. Barely more than a quarter. General, I ask again, what are we attempting to salvage here? The damage Lancastle has taken, it'll be decades before she's fully restored, more than like long after our lifetimes."

"That is quite enough, councilman." Raelan punched a fist down into the table as he stood. "Affairs are already grim enough without your incessant whining. We've all lost something here. I lost both of my brothers in the span of a week. My feckless wastrel of a son has chosen to abandon his family, despite all I've given him. I haven't seen my wife or daughter since the attacks began. My wife, the chuffing queen, I might remind. You don't think I'd rather be out there searching for them? You don't think I'd like to give Vaustian a proper burial? Instead, I find myself in here squabbling with you fucking useless lot. Instead, I choose to stand by my kingdom. The kingdom I love. The kingdom I swore an oath to die for. I risked my neck out there, time and time again, nearly died a dozen times over. Meanwhile, what have you sacrificed in all this? What have you done for your kingdom save cower in a fucking cupboard with your thumb up your puckered asshole?"

Pryce glanced away from the General muttering under his breath.

"Apologies, councilman, I didn't quite hear you?" Raelan kept on, his knuckles boring down into the long table as he lorded over the man seated across from him.

"Another council in disarray," a voice called from the doorway. "I can't say I'm surprised."

"Tenbrooks," Remy said as he came to his feet. "You're alive."

And alive was being generous. The magus looked scarce better than any of the rest of them, appearing quite gaunt and frail.

"I could say the same of you," his expression darkened. "Your eyes—"

At the words, Remy's anxiety suddenly spiked. There was something in the sorcerer's alchemy, something cold and arcane and...

"...*Brother?*..." Yvemathira surged to the surface, and Remy could feel a kindred aura pouring off of Yurien Tenbrooks.

"Sister?" Tenbrooks uttered. "How?"

"...*You?*..." Remy's blood began to boil as Thira conjured the whole fount of the five ancient furies. "...*It all makes so much more sense now. You are the one responsible for all this. You are the one that let the nether cross over...*"

"To show them the truth of their greed."

"...*Have you taken leave of your wits? The nether will take everything...*"

"As they took from us," Tenbrooks said, his silver eyes igniting into azure.

"...*Hrathgon, what have you done?...*"

"You should have listened to me, sister."

"...*What have you done!...*" Thira bellowed.

"I warned you this would happen. I warned all of you." A skinny black stick sparked to life at his side sputtering acid green bile from its end. "Now you will see the error of your ways."

"What is the meaning—"

A coil of magic took Pryce's head clean from his shoulders, sending blood spatter across Mosshart's face, and several events occurred in consequence. A shaking hand rose up to wipe it from her eyes, and a

240

finger smeared it down her cheek as she ripped the knife from her belt with her other hand. Shrieking like a madwoman, she rushed at Braemoor, plunging the blade into his face as they clattered to the floor, she atop him, stabbing over and over and over.

A second blast winged Raelan's shoulder, sending him sprawling backward into the wall and dropping him to the floor. And just like that Tenbrooks was gone.

Raelan let out a demonic screech of his own.

RUN NOW! Thira cried within.

Remy found his foot in the seat of his chair, then his other followed pace atop the table, and before he knew it, he was tiptoeing the length of the great wooden long table, dancing around candles and parchment and mugs to the other end, somehow keeping his balance.

What the fuck is happening?

HE CAST A BLOODBORNE MADNESS SPELL. IF IT TOUCHES US...

Bat-shit mental, got it. He slammed the door closed behind him, and Ellory's screams joined that of Mosshart and Raelan.

Footsteps echoed down the hallway away from him chased with another spark of magic.

THAT WAY.

Remy gripped the hilt of his blade.

NO. WE CANNOT CHANCE IT.

Body-weight began slamming against the door behind him.

AVOID EVERYONE AND EVERYTHING.

The gods fucking know, but it was always something. He pushed away from the door and sprinted toward the announcement of screeching from up ahead. The sounds of the bedeviled council clattering out into the hallway resonated behind him, but he didn't dare look back.

STAY ALERT. Thira called forth a sphere of Eldn flame scarcely larger than an egg. *ONLY IF WE NEED IT.*

In the torchlight ahead, there was a pair of bluecoat soldiers warring with each other. Remy dodged past their tussle and past another ruined corpse before clambering down the stairwell. He saw another flash from the hallway inside the next floor below. From inside the guest quarters. Down he strode, wide-eyed, skipping two and three stairs at a time.

"He went in that one, Highness," a woman said, pointing ahead. Magic emanated from a room long down the corridor, long past the torchlight.

"Everyone, stay back. Clear the area," Remy ordered. Mercifully it appeared no one else had become demented. "And do not go up into the royal halls."

A wind of rotten eggs filled the corridor, and Remy's mind flashed to Palatia as he crept toward the room, slight as a sunken shadow.

He found the chamber empty, and the remnants of a glowing ward not unlike the one he and Rhymona had taken a few days earlier. Morning light spun a wheel of colors amidst the stained-glass window as he placed the azure egg against the blood-marked sigil, flattening his palm against its stone surface, and a portal came rippling to life around it.

HOLD.

"Hold?" Remy hadn't expected such a response.

YOU GO THROUGH. YOU MAY NEVER RETURN.

A sudden sense of dread washed over him. "Then the Fates are assholes."

I JUST WANTED YOU TO KNOW YOU HAVE A CHOICE.

"Not really." He could feel the portal sucking at him, urging him forward. "But just as well."

HARVER WAS RIGHT ABOUT YOU, REMY.

"Yeah? And how's that?"

YOU HAVE CHANGED.

"I suppose we all have," he returned before sinking through to the other side.

He found himself back in the shop off Market Street and Aft. Back at the beginning, as though he were somehow being forced to live the same nightmare all over again. Only this time it wasn't empty. There were corpses everywhere, ghouls mostly, and a crimson-black ichor dripping like viscous honey from the ceiling and down the walls.

Another portal crackled from across the shop, a lone beacon within a hellish tomb.

Nothing else moved inside the clot of carnage.

"Holy shit," he uttered.

And a distant cry of "LOOSE!" filled the air.

THIS PLACE IS A NEST, said Thira.

"A nest?"

LIKE A CROSSROADS FOR TRANSLOCATION WARDS. I COUNT TWELVE SIGILS IN TOTAL.

"Twelve? I only see the pair."

YOU DO NOT SEE THEM. YOU SENSE THEM. SOME ARE MANY, MANY DECADES OLD, CONJURED BY THE OLD TONGUE.

Remy took a step forward and jerked to a halt, staring dead ahead, terror claiming every fel inch of him from the corner of an eye. He began to turn his head toward the waiting horror, but froze halfway, instead opting for nothingness as a substitute.

It felt as though every emotion he had ever invoked was shredding their way through him all at once.

And then there was the burning sickness to bear it.

And the drowning heat behind his dracari eyes.

And the suffocating tingling across his clammy coat of skin.

And the buried ache in his ragged breathing…

No.

But the dress was unmistakable.

No.

The world seemed to spin in slowed motion as he shifted toward it, meaning to take it in.

No.

His legs weakened and his body followed and something ghastly tore out from his throat.

REMY.

Shaking numb, on hands and knees, staring into the watery stones and the fragments of bones and viscera and the endless river of blood spill, he began to drag himself through it until he arrived at her side. *Maybe it's not her.* He hoped against hope. *Maybe…*

A hand found hers. She was cold as a pale winter's moon. His eyes trailed the length of her lifeless arm to her shoulder, upward to her neck, and finally fell upon her face. The wound was so massive and dark it was like staring into a never-ending void.

"Ma…" he swallowed the attempt back down, its taste thick and mucousy, "nnoooohhh…" He lowered himself beside her, curling into the fetal position as he stared into the ungodly void that replaced her beautiful face, canvassing from the hole to the half that remained. He brushed back her blood-matted golden locks and glanced down into the stonework. It was actually her. The sounds that escaped him were barely human, much less actual words.

I should have stayed.

REMY.

I...we...we could have kept you safe. You and...

His breath caught inside the realization. "Julia," he rasped, lifting up from his mother's side and searching the chamber.

"Julia," he called again and again as he scrambled up to his feet and chased about the shop, kicking over bodies, sifting through the piles of flesh and rubble, expecting to find his sister's half-eaten corpse beneath one of them. The gods only knew. He had no idea why he was calling out her name so. Why he still had some manner of hope left for her. He certainly wasn't expecting her to answer.

"She is not here," a shadow said from the doorway, dawn light stealing away its features. "But she yet still lives." The figure stepped inside the shop, nearly breathless, clutching a set of ka'rym chii in her hands. "Or so she did." It was ashaeydir and dressed in a castle hand-maiden's attire, attire that was festooned end to end in all manner of innards.

Though she appeared quite different in her natural form, recognition swiftly came to claim its count. This one belonged to Marsea's insuffer-able flock of lessers. And so, it was that a name found his tongue. "Yuna?" he uttered.

"They went through," the ashaeydir answered, sheathing her sy'chii. "Through that very ward there." She touched a hand to her neck, and her blood-speckled skin shifted back to its midaran make. "I'd been following Rill...Casilvieri..." She motioned to a body propped up against the sales counter. "Tracking his trezsu implant, and suddenly it disappeared from the citadel and reappeared out here. I found him just as the blight were about to...well, look at him...you have the idea. Not that it mattered much. He was already at The Hood's Door anyway. Had enough in him to tell me your sister went through with one of ours and that I needed to follow."

"One of yours? Who? Who did my sister go through with?"

"A soldier named Morgandrel Tully."

Rhymona's with her. Thank the gods. "And where does it go?"

"Haven't the faintest." Yuna dared another step closer.

The egg of Eldn flame returned once more to Remy's offhand. "No."

"No?" Dark curls clung to her face like a wildkin funeral shroud. Lost within were a pair of frantic and fraught eyes haunted by the act of killing things—far too many things.

"Not another step." Her stench hit him and he nearly gagged. "You've coated yourself in ghoul guts?"

"No other choice. There were too many."

"Fuck's sake."

"Yeah? Does it bother you? I've been out here in it for a day and a half now, killing ghoul after ghoul, waiting on one of you rotten bastards to show up and call that ward's name back to life." She leveled her mae'chii at him. "Welcome to the show. Now kindly call it forth, magus, and I'll be on my merry."

"Magus?"

"Don't fuck with me, princeling. I lost my sister and uncle both to this shit. Not to mention the rest of my cadre. She was the one that took them from me. And by the looks of it, she took your mother too."

"She? She who?"

"A dead bitch from a dead House named Dysenia Deadeyes."

"Right. And who does that make you then?"

"It doesn't matter. Just open the bloody portal already. We're wasting time."

"I'll call the ward," the watchman said with an iron-hard glower, "but I'll have your name first. A name for a name. That's your price for passage. It's only fair."

"Only fair?" She lowered the blade. "Tut. Fair is not a thing. Fair is a fantasy. A lie. This world you're either fucked or you're not. End of story."

"I won't argue that, but I'm not into handouts and presently it's the only thing of yours worth half a toss to me. I lost my mother just the same, remember. Your words."

Her gaze lowered. "Solindiel Shadowsong. Soli-shan Sareil of High House Alyfain. Yuna Prentiss." And rose again. "Sharlit Ives. Whisper. Red Marion. And a dozen some odd others. I've had enough to fill a bloody playwright's appendix, all told. So does it really matter what I tell you?"

THIS ONE WEARS HER SOUL STAINED UGLY AS HER SHIRT-SLEEVES.

He looked at her proper and answered simply. "It matters."

Thousand Names scoffed. "Fine. If you must have one, you can call me Sharlit."

He nodded. "Shan. That's meant to be some sort of title in ashaeydir culture, is it not?"

"It is a rank of nobility, yes."

"And what rank is that?" he asked as he approached the dying sigil, stepping over a pair of bodies.

"There is a range of titles it could signify, but in my case—"

"You're a princess, aren't you?" He said, glancing past her back to his mother.

"Something of the like."

Everything within him was screaming at him to stay. For his kingdom. For his people. For his mother. What kind of son would leave his own mother in such a ghastly state, after all? Instead, he strode over to the wall and placed the azure egg against the sigil's embers calling the puddle's boil back from its simmer.

"After you," said the watchman.

Thousand Names cast him a most sinister scowl as she passed through.

He took a breath, minding his mother one last time. "May your luck stones prosper, Lancastle."

And once more. Into the fray.

CHAPTER TWENTY-EIGHT

The portal spat them out into the gloom of a squalid old cottage. Twixt cobwebbed shutters, pillars of pale morning sunlight cut across the hardwood floor providing just enough illumination to unveil someone's downstairs living room.

Remy glanced over his shoulder as the sigil dimmed inside a staircase cupboard, its rotten egg stench quarreling with the room's odor of burnt hair and magic dust.

"I think I'm going to be sick," Thousand Names said, clutching her belly, as she rushed to the front door and let herself out onto the street.

A moment later, Remy heard the sounds of yesterday's scraps slapping down wet and plenty against the cobblestone walkway. He shook his head and surveyed the room between dust particles thick as withered dandelion. The cottage appeared every measure as abandoned as the shop back in Lancastle and that much more in disarray. The floor was littered with trinkets, tomes, candlesticks, and silverware, the walls were in desperate need of fresh paint, the furniture shown spotted and moldy, and what once served as a kitchen table had since become decorated with all manner of charring and blade marks. In the distance, somewhere past Sharlit's troubles, he could hear the rhythmic clanging of a smithy's hammer.

He's gone. Remy thought, studying one of the many ancient portraits that hung on the walls. It was flaking away horribly, inside its rusted gold frame, though he could still make out some of the original scene. It was of a man in a dark gray doublet with pointed ears and long silver-gold hair. A naked sword rested easy against his shoulder.

BUT HE IS NOT FAR.

Where are we? He loosened the laces at the top of his jerkin. Wherever they were, it was considerably more humid than Lancastle. Two minutes in and he felt as though he'd stepped inside a boiling cauldron.

I CANNOT SAY. SOMEWHERE SOUTH. AND NEAR THE SEA.

The watchman took a step toward the door.

REMY, HOLD.

What is it?

ABOUT YOUR MOTHER.

Another flash of the queen's ruined face came to haunt.

I know. He wanted to crumble. He wanted to hold his mother close again. He wanted to tell her he loved her and that he was a selfish fool to have ever left her. *But we have to keep going.* He toed a chalice from out of his footpath and stepped outside the entryway. *We make this right, then we'll make the time to mourn her properly. It's what she would have wanted.*

"What the fuck?" Sharlit grumbled, still bent over, hands cupping her knees. Her mae'chii lay in the patch of grass beside her.

"First time through a portal, is it?" Remy asked as he scanned the avenue both ways. Not a soul to sight.

"How could you tell?" Sharlit groaned before spitting.

"The feeling will pass." He paced toward the sound of banging metal and looked up. Above the rooftops, dawn burned like a midsummer bonfire. A flock of seabirds conversed as they cut across grand Y'dema's morning fade.

So Tenbrooks...your brother lives in him as you live in me?

EVIDENTLY SO.

And dracari can sense each other?

SOME CAN, YES. HRATHGON WAS ONE OF MY CLUTCH. THIS MADE US QUITE CLOSE. THERE WAS A TIME WE WERE INSEPARABLE. NOT UNLIKE YOU AND MARSEA.

He said he did this because of you. To show you the error of your ways. Thira, what did you do?

HE BELIEVES I SENT THE DRACARI TO RUIN BY AGREEING TO

COUNCIL WITH THE MIDARANS. HE WAS VEHEMENTLY OPPOSED
TO OUR ALLIANCE. AND GIVEN THE TURN OF THINGS, I MUST
ADMIT, HE WAS NOT ALTOGETHER WRONG.

So, it's true then, about The Dragonsfall? You and your kin, your battle with
our ancestors, this brought about the Giftborn Age?

I ONLY INTENDED TO BETTER THE LESS FORTUNATE.

And instead, we revolted against you.

SOME FOLKS ARE NOT MEANT TO WIELD SUCH POWER. FOR
SOME JUST A TASTE IS ENOUGH TO TURN THEM ROTTEN.

And some men just want the war. It was something he'd once heard his
Uncle Rhonyn say about Vaustian.

SOME MEN JUST WANT THE WAR, Yvemathira echoed.

The nether. The lichlord. The blight. Hrathgon.

OUR UNION CAUGHT HIM BY SURPRISE, MAKE NO MISTAKE. BUT
HE LED US HERE FOR A REASON, WHEREVER WE ARE.

You mean to say he wanted us to chase after him?

I MEAN TO SAY. I BELIEVE HE CAME TO LANCASTLE TO HARM
YOU AND YOUR SISTER.

To what end?

COULD BE ANY NUMBER OF REASONS, THOUGH MY FIRST
INKLING IS THAT HE INTENDS TO PURGE THOSE OF THE GODS-
BLOOD. OR SOMEHOW DIMINISH YOUR GIFT.

Diminish it?

AS YOU HAVE NO DOUBT SURMISED, THOSE OF THE GODS-
BLOOD POSSESS GREAT POTENTIAL. THEY REPRESENT THE VERY
CROWN OF MAGIC.

Meaning, in his mind, we pose the greatest threat.

PRECISELY. THOUGH FOR ALL OF HIS WIT, MY BROTHER CAN BE
QUITE PREDICTABLE. HARKEN BACK TO THE OLD SCRIPTS AND YOU
WILL FIND MOTIVE. KILL THE HEAD…

And the body will follow. Remy finished. Thira, you speak of genocide. You
believe your brother capable of such atrocities?

HRATHGON HAS NEVER COUNTED FORGIVENESS AMONGST HIS
FINER QUALITIES. CERTAINLY, IF PURGING IS HIS INTENT, HE
WOULD VIEW THIS AS A JUSTICE. AN EYE FOR AN EYE, IF YOU WILL,
A TOOTH FOR A TOOTH…

"The gods know, Pip, if you weren't my favorite person," an effeminate voice said as it cut the corner from the mouth of an alley down the street. "More than like it's just another dodgy asshole stirring up the jackals, looking to make a fast name for himself."

Remy halted, holding his breath as he watched the pair stroll down the avenue in the opposite direction.

"It's not," his podgy goldcoat companion quibbled as they entered what appeared to be some fashion of innhouse. "It's really him."

The sign above the entrance read: *Bottom's Up.*

No doubt a cesspit for open harlotry, heavy hedonism, and a rogue's gamut of general skullduggery. "May as well have a once over then. Find out where the hells we are."

AGREED.

Remy took in a fresh lungful of air. "I'm going to the inn up ahead," he called over his shoulder to Thousand Names as he shuffled forward, back into step.

A few strides in and he found himself breathing in deeper than he had in days. The air was kept by a light breeze, thick with the stain of salt. Nothing at all like home. The contrast of this strange new place by comparison to Lancastle and the other northern hollows was almost surreal.

But the gods only know, how he'd almost forgotten what it was like to draw in fresh air unencumbered by the stench of death and decay.

A tabby cat wandered into his path a stone's throw from the innhouse entrance, cool as you please. Remy stopped and the little furball approached, meowing garrulously. As though they had been mates for cycles, it twisted its paunchy frame affectionately around and in between his ankles.

The watchman prince almost smiled. *What is this place?* Not ten minutes past he was curled up in a pit of ghoul remains next to his mother's faceless corpse, and now here he was playing footsy with some overly outgoing stray.

Remy bent down and ran a hand down the black streaks atop its head. "Sorry boy, you're purring up the wrong tree." He offered only empty palms. "No food here." The cat mewed and nipped at his fingertips, turning on the charm.

"New friend?" Sharlit muttered as she passed him by, doing her best to brush down her horribly disheveled curls.

"Something like that," Remy answered as he started forward alongside her shadow. "All sorted then?"

"Well enough," she said. "Though I suspect I'll need some fresh clothes before the town comes to life. Can't go about looking like I just butchered the neighbors, now can I?"

"I'll say. I'm sure the pair that just popped in up here will know a tailor." Remy shook off his officer's coat. "For now, you may want to wear this." An ashaeydir spy donning the navy and gold? He could almost hear his ancestors cursing in their crypts.

Sharlit took the offer, punching her arms through over-sized sleeves. In the least, it was big enough to hide most of her blood-stained hand-maid garb.

He pulled open the door and entered first.

The place was nearly empty but managed a strange jovial appeal all the same. 'Twas nothing at all what he expected from the name above the entrance.

"The gods wept. What are you two arguing over now?" a blond woman asked as she swept the top of a dais.

"The king of Lancastle, of course," the goldcoat returned, dragging a hand through his unshorn russet shag. "Haven't you heard? He's come to Courowne."

What?

COUROWNE.

Got it.

"There is no more king of Lancastle, Pip," the woman said, leaning the broom against the wall. "Welcome to the Bottom," she said to Remy with a warm smile as she passed toward the bar. "Seat yourselves. We'll be right with you."

"Aye, there is," Goldcoat Pip kept on. "Returned from the grave, they're saying. Desmond fucking Lanier. You believe that? Empress Magwyn named him true. Returned with a betrothed to boot."

Desmond?

"Right, and who is this they you've apparently given all of your trust to?" the woman asked as she tied an apron around her waist.

"Heard it from Old Dick Cotton."

"He means spent-the-last-quint-in-a-dungeon-for-shitting-in-the-

Emperor's-gardens, Dick Cotton," the dandy appended from behind the bar, pouring the goldcoat a cup of dark liquid from a kettle.

"The man's a fool for sure," Pip granted, "but Ned was there and so was Fenton Gilmore and they both corroborated."

"Corroborated. There's a ten-schill word for ya," the dandy said.

"Oh, piss off, Ozzie," Pip grumbled. "Where's Lucian? I'm sure he's heard as much."

"Had another call in the middle of the night," the woman said. "The Strathmore's little one came early."

"Ask him when he returns then," the goldcoat kept on, before taking a swallow from his steaming cup.

The scent of peach tea hit Remy as he filled a space near the end of the bar a few stools down from Pip. "Pardon the intrusion, sir, but did you say Desmond Lanier?"

"Aye," Goldcoat Pip said. "And his betrothed. Val the Sellsword, they're naming her. Dark skin, light curls, strange markings down her arm. They say she looked pretty odd to be the betrothed of a highland lord. And they both looked like they just got done scrubbing out the ass-end of a casern privy."

His betrothed? Fucking hells, Desmond. "And where are they now?"

"Locked up in the palace cellars, last I heard. Along with the turncloak Waldgrave."

Turncloak?

"I reckon the Emperor is still deciding what to do with them given the direction of the Summit."

"And what direction would that be?" Remy inquired.

"Gods' teeth, boy, have you been under a bloody rock for the past quintweek?"

"You could say that." *And, honestly, it might have been an improvement over the truth.*

"The League's discussing House Lanier's permanent removal from the Royal House ranks."

Like hells they are.

A SMALL DISTRACTION CONSIDERING.

Remy channeled the spike of rage into a fist.

"Awfully convenient time for a long-dead Crown Prince to suddenly turn up from the grave, wouldn't you say?" Pip added before turning up a sip of tea.

"Of all the bars on all the moons," a familiar voice called out from across the room.

Remy glanced over his shoulder to find a most unexpected pair descending the stairwell.

And despite everything. The talk of abdication. All of the horrors in the north. All of the pain and loss over the past few days. There remained some bit of goodness yet. Some scant morsel of favor.

And somehow, through the pall, a smile dodged the ache in his heart to find the curve of his lips.

CHAPTER TWENTY-NINE

R emy!" Julia shouted as she ran up to her brother.
"Jules," he returned just before the girl slammed into him,
wrapping him inside a great big hug.

"Scraps," Soli-shan mumbled at her.

"Solindiel," Rhymona scowled, her hand dropping to Fucker's eye.

"How it is you haven't danced your last at the end of a rope already is
beyond me," Soli-shan said, always so superior.

"You want, I could certainly learn you up as to how it is." Rhymona did
little to conceal her rancor as she approached.

"That right?" Solindiel was quick to her hilt.

"Oye," Remy interjected, "that'll do right there then. We're all on the
same side here, yeah."

Same side, my arse. Rhymona spit the sour glance sideways. *I'd sooner
face fuck a bear trap than rally beside Soli-shan Sareil.*

"For the record," Ozzie announced from behind the bar, where he was
wiping a mug with a dishcloth, "I'm on whatever side doesn't fuck with
these two catty bitches."

"Aye," the fat goldcoat agreed.

Rhymona and Soli-shan shared a chuckle at that.

"Catty bitches," Solindiel echoed. "Thank the gods Father never heard
that one."

"Or Rill," Rhymona added.

"Especially Rill," Soli-shan agreed, splitting an exceptionally hideous ghost of a smile. "May he find some measure of peace in The Great Hereafter."

Rhymona pounded a fist against her chest three times in unison with Solindiel and pointed to the heavens. Such marked a long-honored ritual held between soldiers of the Ashaeydir Guard when remembering the fallen. It was meant to signify pride, unity, and reverence, which, for the most, meant exactly fuck all these days. In fact, where most of the guard was concerned, Rhymona would sooner piss on the ritual than see it out proper, but in the case of Old Merillion Alyfain, he had actually managed to earn some bit of respect in her eyes. In the least, enough to see her act out a good little soldier lass this once.

"I'd heard you returned," Soli-shan said.

"Mmm, if only it were under better circumstances."

"Well, I never thought I'd actually say the words, but it's good to see you."

"A tenderheart from the Lady Shadowsong herself? Aren't I the lucky girl?"

"Don't get used to it," Soli-shan said as she sauntered up to the bar. "Pint of whatever and a dram of your hardest."

Lizet gave a nod and went to work, shimmying around Ozzie to the back wall of bottles, grabbing a handle of mead and a mug.

"Oh, honey," Oz said a moment later, covering a hand over his nose.

"Right. Um, you lot wouldn't happen to know a place where a girl can have a wash and beggar a fresh patch of clothes, would you?" Solindiel sprinkled a fistful of coins on the countertop like some manner of spriteling merchant.

"For all that, you can take some of mine," Lizet said as she placed the mug and shooter between them and began scooping the money into a cloth purse. "'Round the bend there, you'll find a room with a wash bucket. Clothes you'll find in the chest at the end of the bed. Nothing fancy, but take what you like."

"Cheers," Soli-shan said, pouring the dram in her pint and gulping it down to the dregs in seconds. She let out a loud belch at the end as she turned the glass over on its head.

Same old Soli-shan then, Rhymona thought. Solindiel was one of a handful she found could actually hold her own when it came to the drink.

"Wash-cloths are in the cupboard," Lizet called out as the swordswoman disappeared around the corner.

Rhymona's lips curled upward as she and Remy met eyes again. "Gods' breath, Toff, you're actually here."

They paced out into the maze of tables and chairs and found a suitable spot away from the others.

"And just barely to have it true," said the princeling. "But that infernal shop won't be denied its due, will it?"

"So you know about mum then," Julia asked.

"I do," Remy answered, desolation thick upon his tongue. "I found her."

Rhymona's mind fell back to the split-second choice her aunt had forced upon her. A choice she didn't make. A choice that in hindsight should have been obvious given Rill's state. But as awful as Rill had once been to her, he was also the reason for her second chance, and apparently, that was reason enough for pause. Still, she couldn't help but wonder if she had chosen to save Larissa, if Dysenia would have actually honored it.

"Lancastle," Rhymona started, pushing down the nasty little guilt gremlin. "Is it…"

"Full Palatia," Remy said.

"Full Palatia?" Julia echoed, her voice every measure as gloomy as the countenance she wore. "Are you saying Lancastle has fallen?"

"The state I left her in, she was well on her way," Remy answered. "With Emyria's help, we managed to banish the lichlord, but more complications arose."

"What complications?" Rhymona pressed.

"Tenbrooks, namely. Your hunch back in Palatia was dead-on. He cast a madness spell inside the citadel. In the King's Hall of all places. Just strolled right in, and once Thira made him, he turned straight to violence. I gave chase of course, but eventually lost him, which is how I ended up back in the shop and now here."

"I knew there was something fishy about that shifty-eyed arsehole."

"Right, well as it turns out old Tenbrooks has a little secret as well. He too houses a dragon soul."

"You're pulling my pisser."

"The Horror of Hickory Hollow himself."

"Hrathgon?" the word felt forced upon her lips.

"Oh, do prize well. And what's more, Hrathgon is one of Thira's clutch."

"One of Thira's clutch? Fancy words those. Now, what do they actually mean?"

"It means I sense him whenever he's close. Or rather, Thira does. I think. Everything's a bloody guess anymore at this point. Though Thira believes he means to purge all housing the godsblood."

"The godsblood? As in *your* blood?"

"As in."

"Do I even ask why Thira suspects this?"

Remy's irises shifted to azure. "Centuries ago, before The Dragonsfall, my brother opposed our union with the Midarans. And so it became my opinion versus his, which was really no debate at all for my folk. My opinion won out because I was named as Queen. But Hrathgon could not accept this, he would not, and eventually, this opposition would lead to his ostracization and subsequent exile. He believed the Midarans would abuse magic just as other races had in the past and history would only repeat itself."

"You speak of the Chandii."

"I do. And of the ashaeydir."

"The ashaeydir?"

"Oh, yes. It is the reason for Ashira's fall after all. And Ilynderos before her. Ashira was once home to the Chandii and the dracari, long before the ashaeydir dropped from the stars to claim and rename her. Back then she was named Ilynderos, back when I was but a whelp. I remember in those times strange occurrences emerging in rapid succession as the nether began to take form. And so it was that my ancestors discovered the nether's truth much too late. That it came into being as a response to our use of magic, hounding after the gift, devouring everything to sight in the process, until it forced us through the godsgate. Thusly Ilynderos became abandoned and we found Vaelsyntheria and what is now known as the Chandii Isles."

"But the ashaeydir are said to have found Ashira completely barren," she said.

"And so they did. Magic left with us, and so the nether, being a creature of reaction, had nothing left to hunger after. But sometime later, your folks began colonizing, spinning their spells, and drawing from the gift again, and once more the beast was awakened."

"The Stranger take me." Rhymona massaged her temple.

"So you see, this has all happened before. And not only that, but several times. Until The Dragonsfall and The Spellbind summoning, I thought the entity, whatever it is, was solely bound to the moon of Ilynderos."

"But it's actually bound to magic, isn't it?"

"Yes. It would seem so. Wherever magic goes, the nether will follow, and the more it's used, the more ravenous the nether becomes."

"So Hrathgon was right then?"

"He was correct, but correct does not necessarily mean right."

Gods, what drek. Like some dumbass shite straight out of bloody Mervold Chronicles. "So what then? He means to end the Giftborn Age now? To make mortals ungifted again?"

"That is my belief, yes. And I believe he is willing to sacrifice everyone and everything to do it."

Damned if you do, damned if you don't. "Brilliant. So everything's pretty much fucked then? As usual."

"I will not delude myself into once again believing he can be reasoned with," Remy continued Thira's words. "But I do believe we can defeat him. He is bound to a man just as I am, and I doubt this Tenbrooks fellow holds anywhere near the quality of gift that Remy does."

"Isn't he just as much at risk, pulling from the gift?"

"Of course, he is, but I sense my brother has more than a few tricks up his sleeve in reserve."

"Such as?"

"Would that I could name them. My brother's deceptions range mixt and many."

"A comforting concept."

"For the time being, I must rest and ruminate." And with that, the azure glow vanished from Remy's orbs.

"Helluva history lesson, yeah?" the watchman returned a moment later.

"Aye."

"Can I assume you also haven't heard the other business of the morn?"

"Any chance it's good news?" *There should be a limit to how much fucktittery one is forced to stomach before breakfast.*

"Good and bad, I'd say."

"Well, there's an improvement."

"Evidently your old mate from uni and his beloved are in town."

"Aiden?"

"Fuck, it's weird you name him that. But yes, according to the goldcoat fellow over there, he's being held in the palace dungeons with a betrothed."

"A betrothed?"

"Good sir," Remy called over to the bar. "What was the name of the betrothed again?"

"Val," the goldcoat grumbled over his shoulder.

Fuck me.

"Another mate from uni, is it?" Remy asked, cheek in his tone.

"Not quite." Her eyes trailed away from him to Julia.

Remy's expression hardened at her reaction. "Who is she then? What are you not telling me?"

"She is..." *Your best friend. Your heart. Your family. Your everything.* "Soli-shan's sister."

Remy blinked through a dumb gaze. "Her sister? But she said her sister died."

"She has two, of course. Nymuriel and Val. She and Nym were quite close. She and Val not so much. Wait. Nym's dead?"

"I suppose. I didn't get a name, all told, but Soli-shan suggested as much. Why in vaelnation would my brother agree to marry an ashaeydir?"

Because I'm a colossal fuckup.

And also because she loves me for some mad reason.

The youngest of the Alyfain sisters always had a knack for sifting through the bullshit, however loud, and centering in on what truly mattered. And she wasn't afraid to fight for those things, however small and mundane. Foolishly, Rhymona wrote off all of Valestriel's chasing and pleading as lovesick naivety and mayhaps some of it was, but not the most of it. The most of it came from the heart and from a goodness far beyond the capacity of most folks, and now it had evidently found her a dungeon cell for her troubles. The gods know she owed Val a massive apology the next time they met. A massive apology and, the gods willing, a massive kiss.

The mere prospect of simply seeing her again sent Rhymona's heart aflutter.

"Jules," Rhymona glanced the girl true. "Would you mind giving us a few?"

Julia met her gaze, nodded, and without a word of protest made herself scarce.

"Well, that was dramatic," Remy said.

"And it's about to get a whole lot more so," Rhymona said. "But I told myself I wasn't going to lie to you anymore and I'm a woman of my word, yeah. So here goes." She dragged hair from out of her eyes and looked him proper. "Your brother and I, we weren't just mates at uni. In fact, we were considerably more."

"More like...?"

"More like we were romantic."

Remy pinched the bridge of his nose. "The gods know. Of course, you were."

"Keep your stomach yet, it gets better," she said, expecting the poor reaction. "I came to find your brother because of a plot put together by High House Alyfain. A house in ashaeydir society not dissimilar in caste to your own. I was a vassal to this house and put to the task. A task named as The Lanier Objective. My assignment therein was to bring your brother back home to Lancastle. An assignment I failed at monumentally."

"All we've been through and you're just telling me this now?"

"I'm telling you this now, because now you're ready." *At least I hope you are.*

"I'm not, rest assured. But at this point, fuck it, right?"

"There's my favorite wittle Toff-woff," a grin grew despite the coming words. "Val, the betrothed. Oh, Val. Valestriel-shan Alyfain. You could say we go back a ways."

"You don't say."

"Don't be a cunt, Toff."

"Then don't make it so dreadfully easy for me."

"Fair point," she said. "Now, Val. She's my girl, yeah. My heart. My lovely lady lass. And every other fancy watchword to wet the gash. You follow?"

"Unfortunately."

"Grand. So, Val, she's what we walking shitshows name a diamond in the rough, yeah. Heart of gold, that one. Mayhaps a mite misguided, but the head's in the right place for the most. And being such a sweetheart, she rather charmed her way into what's left of mine one summer back when. And well, I gave it a proper fucking go, if you catch my meaning."

Remy leaned forward. "You go both ways then?"

"I'm rather offended you've had to ask. But yes. And yes, I've sussed your flavor some time ago. Long story short, Val was always too good for me. Too good for most, all told. And I tried to let her off easy. But damned if she wasn't the most infuriatingly stubborn and willful girl this side of the Vael. Easy was never in the cards with that one. Now for the full circle bit. Being that her family planned The Lanier Objective, and being that she knew about my courtship with Aiden at uni, she..."

"Let me guess, followed in your fuckwit footsteps..."

"More or less." She almost smiled.

"But she's not you, so she and my brother are now apparently...together?"

"Apparently."

"I wonder if he knows she's ashaeydir."

"Val was never much one for keeping secrets, so I give it half and half she's told him." Rhymona rose to her feet. "Trust it true, Remy, I care for them both, and I'm willing to fight for them, whatever it takes. Just as I'm willing to fight for you, Jules, and Marsea. This shit with Hrathgon, I'm all in with you and Thira. Prize well. Come what may. But first things first, I need to find Val and Aiden, I need to know if it's truly them, especially if they're locked away. Mark my words, I'd take a blade for your brother if it came to it, but I'll be damned to the deepest pit of the nine before I abide Valestriel rotting in some puffed-up tosser's piece of shit dungeon cellar."

CHAPTER THIRTY

How does one know where the devilkin goes when the devilkin knows you're awake?:

A rumor of voices passed from somewhere nearby and the archivist groaned awake from his first dreamless sleep in ages. He found himself face down naked on the floor. Nothing new there. Honestly, the like had been a fifty-fifty occurrence since Stella's passing. Though he had certainly hoped to have turned a corner now that he and Val were apparently together. Together. He could still almost feel himself inside her. He and an ashaeydir. And not just together, but betrothed. Or so the story went. Utterly ridiculous, that.

Something like a smile tugged at the corners of his mouth as his eyes cracked open...

...a sickness ensued, stomach acid yellow, warping his smile's shape, as he unbound a lilac-skinned arm bereft of body, the blood from its severed end having pooled around his lips and cheek.

He could practically taste the gift within.

It took a moment to register what he was looking at and a moment more to understand it. But once it hit, it hit hard as a stone ton.

The fuck? He jerked up and out of the crimson stick that surrounded his face, pushing back into the foot of the bed.

The arm was unmistakable. As were the mesmerizing tattoos that once defined it. To the last memory, it was an arm that had been warmly wrapped around him under the bedsheets as he and its owner snuggled and snogged and fucked in full embrace of one another.

And then the smell hit him, the hum of sweat and lust, followed by the metallic scent of blood and the stench of fresh decay.

No.

Terror became him as he scanned further into the dawn-lit chamber. He had never beheld such carnage in all his days. There were dismembered appendages strewn about in all directions, one leg in quarters, and gore spatter slashed and splotched wildly across all the walls and furnishings.

What have you done?

The archivist struggled to his feet, fighting back the coming nausea as he found Val's bare limbless torso atop the white linen bedsheets, crooked trails of viscous crimson where her arms and legs and head were meant to be. The room began to spin and his insides came up anyway as he turned away from the scene. But then something tenfold worse caught his eye from the vanity in the corner.

No!

But he knew what awaited him there in spite of his denial. He could feel the dead horrorstricken stare condemning him in that dark horrid corner nook.

It was the last expression she ever wore.

What did you do?

A helpless, hopeless sorrow washed over him. Through welling tears, he forced himself to look at it and it instantly brought a wobble to his legs and he lowered himself back to his knees to the company of more vomit.

What the fuck.

It was actually her.

Valestriel. The real version. The ashaeydir version. The version he had begun to shag and then accidentally made love to...

Her severed head was propped upright on the table-top, her golden orbs glaring straight ahead through droopy eyelids and a tangle of dark blood-matted curls.

His vision fell and he found his hands and arms stained in her up to the elbows. Further evidence of the crime was painted and plastered across near every exposed inch of his pale shivering chest.

No. He couldn't take it in. *You're in a nightmare. This isn't real. This can't be real. You could never do this...*

You could never...

He spit to clear the taste of puke from the back of his mouth and glanced back up at Val. This time he noticed the writing scrawled above her head in streaking red that had long since dried upon the glass surface as does wax down a candle stalk.

Smeared with a bloody finger across the vanity mirror were a trio of words that eviscerated him like a series of gut punches knife end out, thieving away what little humanity he had left to claim.

Numb, the archivist rose again and found a strange, devilish reflection waiting in the plane beyond. All from within glared darkly in at him. Returned was the same cold, sulfuric hate that had crippled him aboard Blackhall's Banshee during his infamous conjuration. And their icy blue eyes crashed into one another like foes upon a battlefield, the bloody message screaming the hells' furies between them.

Blade in. Blade out.

One. Two. Three.

Easy as you please.

Stella Forgives You.

"You," he hissed against the deathly quiet. "You did this." And he found that his jaw burned with each passing word.

:Oh, but she put up a fight at first,: his reflection responded with a demented grin and a noticeable gap to the left side of his front teeth. *:A little something to remember her by.:*

Aiden glared at his twin with a gravedigger's scowl.

:Don't look at me with such resentments, boy.: He spoke the words true, but it was no longer his voice. This voice carried a callous old-world nuance to it. *:I gave you the life you now own. The life you've seen fit to make an absolute shambles of. And I tried to warn you with the last one what would happen if you let another one in. To that one's credit, she was wise enough to get the hint. But this one here. This one kept filling your head with foolish promises and false hopes.:*

"What the hells are you on about?" The question echoed within.

The shadows moved all around him, drinking in all the color of the dawn light, revealing a world not his own. A world black as the unholy abyss. Coiled within were shifting, serpentine creatures flecked with thousands of blinking crimson eyes that whispered and sniggered in terrible little goblin sounds. It was precisely as the ichor that burst out of Darrow in The Spellbind.

:I'm speaking on your little ashaeydir problem, of course,: his possessor answered. His expressions and mannerisms were decidedly, unmistakably, y'deman.

"My what?"

:The ashaeydir are a disease, a ruin to all they chance upon,: the possessor spat, his hatred nigh on sentient. *:And yet you cannot seem to get enough, can you? Slumming it with whatever filth crosses into your sad little footpath.:*

Aiden wanted to scream. He wanted to run. He wanted to wake up. But he only found himself rooted to the spot. "You've chopped her up... into pieces..." The words felt stupid and ridiculous. And yet here they were.

:On account of the gravedancing, mind you. Can't chance her coming back clean, now can we? She knew far too much about us.:

The archivist was beset by a detached gaze as he became woefully aware that he was no longer in control of his own body. He still moved about, as one does, but they were not movements of his command.

Had it been this way all along?

How long have I been as the reflection?

How many times before?

"Stella forgives you," he mumbled, almost catatonic, as something akin to a memory began to take shape. Some cruel misbegotten horror of a thing. But he *had* gone home back then, hadn't he? He remembered the smells of Gallea's Grace and Ashborough manor as though they were yesterday's passing, of a long dusty road desperate for rainfall and an endless country wind dying for respite, of father's tobacco stench across the front porch like some manner of piss to mark a man's territory, of Tam's fresh bake from the crack of morn inside, sugary sweet and oh so inviting.

:But she was going to be a problem, your Stella. Just as your ashaeydir pity fuck here.: The possessor stepped inside his trousers and came to stand before the mirror shirtless, his chalky white skin in stark contrast to the trails of deep red that marked him up and down like a wildkin war

demon. *:That one's on me. I always had a weak spot for our dear lovely Stella Critchlow. She was one of my better pupils, all told.:*

Pupil?

:Oh yes. A man knows his own teachings when he sees it. And Stella was quite the scholar. As book smart as I've ever seen. She most assuredly deserved better than what we gave her, but she also knew the risks that came along with fostering such darkly knowledge. Rarely do the black arts smile upon their lowly beggars, after all.:

Somehow, she knew he was there, his mother, that fateful eventide. Somehow, she knew he had returned home. Like a sixth sense. He recalled as she ascended the front porch stairs and they met eyes through the opened doorway. It had been months. But she did not smile at his presence. And there wasn't an ounce of her definitive maternal warmth to be felt. Instead, she appeared quite troubled and almost resigned. He despised seeing that look upon his mother's face.

And so it was, for all her ability and honor, for all her cleverness and care, when it all came down to it Stella chose wrong. And for what? She knew better. She had to have known. She should have run. She should have leveled her wand on him and fired it through his gods damned bastard temple. Or in the least, she could have cast a binding spell to keep him at bay. She could have done something. Anything. Anything at all but what she did. Instead, she came inside defenseless. She came inside and...

What was it she said?

"I'm sorry, Aiden." Her voice was a fragile whisper. *"We never should have brought you back."* Heart-shattering words, those. But her tears were far more damning. *"Not like this."* He could almost feel her in his grip again as he recalled taking hold of her and slamming her roughly against the wall. *"I forgive you,"* she said without the slightest measure of resistance, and he split a black smile before smashing her face into the edge of the hallway table.

Guilt and shame poisoned his soul, festering within like a pox of necrosis. "You killed her." His voice was trailing along horridly now, dragged down far too deep inside the muck of long-repressed memories.

:Killed her?: The possessor pushed away from the vanity and retrieved a shirt from near the door. *:Still haven't learned the lesson yet, have you?:* He held the tattered, discolored cloth to his nose and tossed it away.

"What lesson?"

:Oh, do catch up, would you? No one ever really dies, Desmond. Not anymore. The nether will not let us.: He lifted the robe draped over the back of a chair in the opposite corner and punched his arms into the sleeves. *:Turns out we're all merely recycled parts in the end. Jumbled auras. Rearranged energies. Cattle for a god most gluttonous. Insignificant puzzle pieces in a big black vat of perpetual suffering.:*

Aiden recalled Ledge's omen about The Great World Eater.

:Swim around in it long enough and you'll find a decent pattern. Find a decent pattern and you can do just about anything you want with it. You can become just about anyone you please.:

"And so Malthus Tetherow chose this old tosser of all folk, did he?"

Tetherow brushed Aiden's long black hair behind an ear, and one side of his face curled up into a deranged smirk. *:Not so much chose as you were readily dumped into my lap. Desmond Lanier. The Crown Prince of Lancastle Citadel. He of the blessed godsblood. Might I add, for those of us that have been without, you must understand, once you have a taste of the maker's ichor...well, there really is no substitute. It's like going from well water to the top shelf royal reserve. And trust, I was about as well water as they come. May as well have been born in a damned grave for all the world gave me. I lived most of my young life as a slave in shackles. I was beaten daily. Castrated the day my balls dropped. Written off a nameless turd before I was even given a name at all. Left to wallow and waste with the rest of the so-called undesirables. Rot, rot, bloody rot, and a dozen more story-book banalities—:*

"So what? You are judging us now for the sins of our fathers?"

:Sins of our fathers? Oh, come off it.: His face hardened, turning an expression Aiden had never beheld of himself before. *:Your kind are all the bloody same in the end, aren't you? So painfully predictable. You all believe you are innocents in all this. The champions for good. The Great Midaran Dream and all that. Tut. Well, I've got news for you, Desmond. Valor is a lie told by killers and lunatics. And history is always left to be written by the broken and the craven. You people. The gall. The insolence. Too proud to see your own fucking depravities. You are the problem. The curse. The infection. Every last one of you. And you only have yourselves to blame for what's to come. You all cling to the old ways and yet call it progress. And in doing so, you all let the nether back in. Your greed. Your conceit. Your hypocrisy. Your thirst for power and devotion to absurd tradi-*

tions. You have ravaged her with your endless vanities. Vaelsyntheria, once divine. The gods know, she deserved so much better from her denizens.: The archivist had never heard his own voice so vile and twisted. *:Whilst some sacrificed to keep her pure, the most of you leeched from her selfishly, drawing more and more from her spirit until there was scant little left. Until her many wounds had gone septic and become desiccated. And so what did you do then? Did you stop? Did you strive for even the smallest level of accountability? No. Of course not. You then began carving each other to pieces and marketing the blood spill of your own brothers and sisters.:* He shook his head. *:And those folk bold enough to speak out against this, those few folk brave enough to defend the Vael mother and some sense of actual mortal decency, were instead butchered to bits for their morality, their families burned screaming and strung from trees. They were named as blasphemers and tyrants and monsters, and thusly their deaths were dismissed as necessary for the greater good and their lessons were thereafter swiftly forgotten. Your people did this. And they are still doing it to this day. Only the favored shall feast, your lot have gotten on naming it. Well, I've got a game you can sink your teeth into. Oh, and what a lovely little game it will be. All the way down to the last fucking lot of you. The nether will play its part of course. And you all will consume one another, like the mindless, ravenous swine you are, until not a one stands to defy Her and the balance is finally fully restored.:*

It was like he was reciting a verse from the book of Redding.

:Oh, but it took some time to get here, didn't it?: His temperament calmed. *:Some dark centuries. Some lost oaths. Some hard sacrifices. But here we are. And thanks to your Stella and the ashaeydir here I've been given a front-row seat to Vaelsyntheria's grand opus. The humble shepherd I am.:*

It was only then that Aiden noticed the shapes in the blood-stains all around him. Suddenly they had all become clear as ink on parchment, slick with a dusting of freshly conjured magic. They weren't just random blood spatter. Not even close. They were sigils, positioned to perfection. Ancient words with ancient frequencies from ancient artifices. Symbols meant to thieve and defile. Symbols meant for ruin and chaos. And the bedchamber was littered with them. He recognized a few of them from his mother's grimoire as their cruel reality began to sink in.

And so it was, in the end, Valestriel-shan of High House Alyfain was little more than a verse for a possession ritual. *The fucking cunt bastard*

Tetherow. All her sunshine, all her hope, all her love. All for a fiend to seal a soul bond to a feckless, drunkard afterthought.

"You're fucking mad is what you are," Aiden spat in defiance. Yet never before had his words felt so utterly hollow and meaningless.

:Hmm, well, I suppose there is no denying that, now is there?: Tetherow wore the darkness as does a King fisted jewels and fine fur trimmings. *:Spend enough time with the nether and you'll find madness is about as good as it gets. But I found meaning in my suffering and so too will you. We are now bonded, Desmond Lanier. A madness of two. We of the mongrel making. You cannot rid yourself of me as I cannot rid myself of you. The nether has demanded our union. It's inside of you now as it once lived inside me. And so it will grow until it devours everything this corpse has to offer.:*

"And you readily accept such a fate?"

:Oh, with open arms I do. For ages, I tried to control the nether. Paltry efforts by a blind, overconfident narcissist. Of course, you already know how that tale ended. But sometime after my hopeless demise, a realization overcame what scant spirit was left me. An epiphany, if you will. A notion so blatantly simple in its inception that it shames me still to admit how long it took me to unravel it. Why try to control the storm, after all, when you can become it?:

"Extinction is not the way."

:It is the only way! You will see. Oh, there will be those scant few that survive, don't you doubt it. Those clever unlucky few. There always are. But mayhaps they will do better with Her cares than our current lot has.

:Trust I am not alone in all this. There are those that follow, those that believe in the devouring god. The god we made. Those that believe extinction is proper justice for mankind's great many offenses. That starting anew is the only way to save Her. And in doing so, ourselves.:

There was a light rap at the door.

"Lord," a weaselly voice followed.

Runt? Aiden wanted to howl for Pion to turn tail and run or hobble or whatever the hells he did to escape such shite situations as what presently awaited him from this side, but...

:That would be one of them now.: Tetherow twisted his wrist slightly and there was the clicking sound of a lock being turned and the bedchamber door came creaking open.

...too late.

"Lord?" Pion Harver brought the end of a sleeve over his nose as he entered and quickly closed the door behind him. "Quite the scene," he said as he navigated between a pair of leg chunks to the center of the room.

:Not my finest work, I confess,: Tetherow said as he settled down in the corner chair and began to lace up his boots.

You two-faced, craven bastard. Aiden wanted to punch the fucker's front teeth down his throat.

:You've acquired the grimoire?: his voice asked instead.

Pion patted the satchel at his hip, a smug look dancing across his gaunt features.

:I do hope the good Commodore wasn't too much trouble.:

"Not at all. Nothing a round of bitters couldn't settle, my Lord."

:I see.:

"And Desmond?" There was guilt in his beady black-ringed irises at the name.

:He is still with us, though he won't be much of a bother.:

The hells I won't! But the words never reached his tongue for release. They were barely a thought in truth, for the archivist was the passenger now. And even that proved a generous branding. The term prisoner would have rung far more accurate.

:Take it from me, boy,: Tetherow returned. *:Emotions will eat you alive if you let them.:* One side of Aiden's lips quirked up involuntarily. *:Besides, you wanted your comeuppance, did you not? You wanted to be invisible, to suffer properly for your misdeeds. Now you have your wish.:* He stood, thumbing the ring razor about the base of their middle finger. *:Runt.:* Tetherow glanced one final time at his new reflection as he passed the vanity mirror.

"Lord," the grotesque answered, eyes lowered.

:Let's go kill us an empire.:

CHAPTER THIRTY-ONE

Marsea woke up crying, her face sore from it.

She ran her tongue across the notch in her upper lip where the tear salt still found a faint stinging presence, and for a series of heartbeats, she remained perfectly still, listening to the current of blood swimming around inside her head.

The maidens only knew how long she had been sobbing into her pillow.

Something inside her dreamscape had spurred forth some manner of heavy emotions, though any measure of understanding had evaporated with the ghost of her half-dried tears. She could not recall specifically what had sent her well on into such an intense sadness, but she felt the overwhelming urge to tell someone that she loved them—moreover, to tell many such someones that she loved them.

The princess inhaled as she rolled over onto her backside and let the air out. It was thick with whiskey. Though, astonishingly, she seemed to have no ill effects from the night before. She shifted her legs to the side of the bed as she folded the covers away from her body, then her bare feet pressed down against the cold hardwood floor. She rather liked the sensation. As part of her new daily routine, her attentions fell to her bad hand, but only for an instant as movement from the chamber's corner caught her eye.

Broenwjar raised his head from his rest and watched her. She offered the big furry heap a sheepish half-grin and stood. "Morning," she rasped as she stepped over to the window and brushed the curtains apart. A fresh powdery snowfall greeted her. She gazed out long into the unbroken white watching the snowflakes dance and swirl beyond the frosted pane before bending her attentions down on Old Boy. Kneeling to his level, she inspected the scar on the side of his face. "The scars that bind us." She gently placed her bad hand over his marred cheek. "I know you're sad, B. But for what it's worth, I will do everything in my power to make our union just. I will prove myself to you. I promise."

She ran her hand through his thick fur, down to his shoulder, and patted him twice before rising to her feet. She needed to drown away the stain of dried tears before anyone else saw. She refused to be that weak little girl from court any longer. Shielding her face, she shuffled from the guest room to the washroom across the hall and closed the door.

The washroom appeared quite different in the daylight. One side of the curtains had been left drawn and a gentle wintry light illuminated half the space.

The standing mirror called to her from the bright half and Marsea slowly approached, gingerly lifting her shirt over her head before letting it float softly to the floor behind her.

She stopped within arm's reach of her reflection and stared at her naked torso. It was a bit blurry without her glasses, but there could be no mistaking it, her bruises and scrapes were mostly healed. She stepped closer, turning her shoulder to the mirror, and found that the swelling around her tattoo had gone down considerably as well. The redness had given way to a pale pink shadow. Her lips quirked up and she faced the mirror fully again, bringing her bad hand up between them.

The stars save me...

In the frost-colored sunlight, she walked the trails of her sutures, just as she had a thousand, thousand times over the past week. But this time their presence seemed wholly unnecessary. The wounds beneath had closed, showing bright white lines of scar tissue, as though the mangling occurred ages ago. The healing effect almost made the nubs of her ring finger and pinky bearable to gaze upon once more.

Almost.

Marsea clenched her hand into a fist and felt a strength within that she thought quints away.

O, but how the maidens wept. Tears began to heat the space around her eyes, but this time, for once, they were tears of joy.

She spun a graceless half-circle at the improvement and her attentions fell upon the console table across the room, deviating from the wash basin to the straight razor twinkling in the darkness next to it. Her eyes would not be diverted, once it had her. Nor would her thinking. She licked her lips, and her briefly held joy melted as an idea began to unfold. A notion cycles in the making. Like a scream in the quiet. It was a whimsy most queer, but a whimsy she owed, and a whimsy she could not simply ignore.

Not anymore.

Before she knew it, she found herself advancing into the dark half, toward the table, almost tiptoeing, as though she were some damned rebel sneak stealing out after curfew. She felt absolutely absurd with each slinking step forward and yet she couldn't stop herself. It was as though she were a sailor snared inside a siren's song.

The handle felt cold to the touch as she flicked the blade out from its recess. She studied its slender surface as she shadowed her steps back toward the mirror's haunt. Her vision crawled across her blurry reflection, from the lump in her throat, over her breasts, down to the razor-blade whispering at her side.

She swallowed hard as she clasped her long, honey-gold locks in a bunch.

This has been a long time coming, she thought, as she raised the blade and settled it about midway up her ponytail.

A long, long time coming. Her hands held firm and her eyes closed. She sucked in a deep lungful of air and a moment later her blade-hand began to move.

Her mother never would have agreed to such an act. Never in a thousand cycles. Oh, but how her mother was so very far away now. And oh, but how she could feel a weight lifting inside every tiny heartbeat and every strand broken.

Light as a feather, Marsea Munch.

And just as suddenly as it all began, it was over.

Her hands dropped once more to her sides—some random blade in one, her severed locks in the other.

Breath filled her lungs again and her eyes, sharp and silver, yawned wide.

Oh, it looked absolutely awful. All stringy and woefully uneven. A hells-damned mockery of traditional femininity.

The maidens knew, her mother would have become unhinged at the sight of it.

And yet...

Her face brightened despite the lingering creases of pillow-case scars —and her pearly whites broke the clasp of her lips as she adored every last bloody regret her twin conjured.

She let the bundle of hair fall to the floor and ran a hand through her wavy golden mane that now barely passed below her jawline.

Turns out, not every smile is a waste, after all.

CHAPTER THIRTY-TWO

I still cannot believe you took down a wngar like that," Marsea said, as she and Beldroth and Old Boy crunched along through the snowy Kingswood some hours later. She recalled one of Uncle Rho's old hearthfire haunters. Some mad yarn about a farm boy and a beanstalk. "It was like something out of *Mervold Chronicles* or *Devil Cake*. I've never seen anything like it."

"Fortunately, that one was still quite young and arrogant and only about average size," Beldroth said. "I would have been far more reluctant had been one of their warriors."

"You mean to say they come bigger than that one?" she brushed her freshly shorn hair behind an ear. It was at that awkward length now that just wouldn't seem to stay put. She decided she would do her best to clean it up a bit more once they returned to the cottage. In the very least, she would need to trim it back a few lengths out of her eyes.

"Oh, yes. Much bigger, in fact. I've seen some tall as citadel towers. Let me tell you, you see one of those bastards, you run. You run and you hide 'til it's gone."

"You don't have to tell me twice."

"If somehow you do find yourself in combat against one, you go for the neck. It's one of their few vulnerable spots. As I am sure you are aware, wngar are known for their unnaturally thick skin. Most blades

275

barely penetrate the surface. Though let us hope you never have to face one."

Marsea stared up into the barren branches above, finding a few birds scattered here and there, chirping boisterously. "I also saw my father in one of Broenwjar's memories. Though he was much younger than I'd ever seen him before. And Remy as well."

"Your brother and I met briefly," Beldroth confirmed.

"He looked awful."

"He was in Brymshire when the lichlord attacked. From what I could surmise, he barely escaped. By the time I found him, he wasn't in a proper state of mind to say the least."

Marsea turned on her heel to face him.

"Not that I blame him, but he didn't exactly trust me upon our meeting. I gave him as much protection as I could offer, but there were other matters at hand."

"Speaking of which." Marsea held up her bad one between them. "It's nearly healed."

"So it is," Beldroth said.

"Care to explain?"

"It is the power of the gift, is it not? The give and take."

"What did you do, Elsymir?"

"Nothing you wouldn't have done for me, were our roles reversed." He produced something Marsea could only assume was a smile.

"I took from you, didn't I?" she asked.

"To the contrary. I gave. Willingly. Returned, one might say."

"How? I don't understand."

"During the ritual, there passed a short window of time, a trice by the chronicler's count, just before the bond was bestowed, where we existed as a trinity, you, me, and Old Boy. No doubt, you felt it."

Marsea thought back over the strange visions brought on by the ritual. "I suppose."

Beldroth wiped his brow with the back of an arm. "I'd say this is as good a spot as any, yeah?"

"Everything all right?" Marsea asked, sharing a concerned look with Broenwjar.

"Fine. I just need to rest my leg a bit." He came to a lean against a towering oak. "All told, I should have done more. I should have trusted you and your brother, Marsea. I should have come to you both sooner. And I should have better prepared you. But I was reluctant to involve you with Ravenholme—"

"For obvious reasons," Marsea found herself saying. She was rather thankful her stay with Ravenholme had been quite short, to have it true.

"You and Rembrandt. You are all that's left of the old blood. All the generations from before now reside within you and your brother. You are what's left of the masters' promise. All they fought for. All they sacrificed to give."

"No pressure or anything." It was her best attempt at humor.

"No pressure," he echoed. "And on that note, we've one last lesson between us, haven't we?"

Marsea frowned. "I wish you would stop talking like that."

"I know." He lifted a scabbard from over his shoulder and offered it to her. "But false hope is just another cage to haunt. And honestly, if any one soul deserves to hear truths for the rest of their days it's undoubtedly you."

"That's kind of you to say." She shirked off her jacket and took the scabbard in her gloved hand. *Holy crow.* "I can hear it," she whispered as she choked the crudely wrapped hilt to its razor-thin cross-guard and gently drew the blade from its confines. It scraped out like nails down a pane of glass.

"But, of course, you can," Beldroth said matter-of-factly. "It's learning who you are. It's deciding whether or not you are worthy."

"It's deciding?"

"Mmm, swords are assholes you'll come to find."

"I'm sorry. Swords are assholes?" Not exactly the explanation she was expecting.

"To clarify, possessed swords are assholes. What you hold in your hand there is a haxanblade. They are bound to the souls of their makers by some manner or another and in being so they tend to sort of mirror the personality of said maker. I've come to find this one here to be a markedly sour sort."

"You certainly know how to sell a girl, don't you?" Marsea held out the sword and studied it. On the surface, it appeared an artless horror of a thing—dull, ugly, forlorn—as though it had lain beneath the ocean festering for centuries.

277

"And yet what was it Baylet said about every blade worth its weight?"

Marsea's lip twitched up. "I'm not entirely convinced Baylet was including possessed blades as a prospect in his treatise." She gave the sword a good, clean swing. "Do you know who made her?"

"But of course. The Wyrmstower Witch was that which made her."

And the rest followed from the annals of Lancastle Library. *The White Witch of Wyrmswold Hollow. The Giftborn Queen. Nightmare's Lover. Misery's Mistress. The Devil's Darling. Heaven's Bane. She of a thousand burn names. She that could break the earth with a tiny whisper. She that could split the sea with a sylvan song. She of the Haunter's Hallowed. She of the Sister's Salvation.* "That would make her the blade of..."

"Lita Drufellyn," Beldroth finished.

Marsea blinked at the sword in awe.

"Though I've taken to naming her Blind Widow," he added, "after the seer that forced it upon me some many cycles ago."

"Good gravy!" The hilt began to vibrate, sending white-hot tremors up her arm and throughout her entirety. Marsea dropped the scabbard and clasped her wrist with her gloved hand to keep it steady.

"You need to assert control," Beldroth stated. "Let it know you belong."

The vibration began to burn like bloody hellfire. "Shit," Marsea cried.

"Don't let go," Beldroth commanded. "Let its energy flow with yours."

Gritting her teeth, Marsea let go of her wrist, determined to wield the thing proper.

"Believe," Beldroth demanded.

Believe, Other repeated from some dark rest within, and her feet started sliding into the sparring stance Vaustian had drilled into her.

Believe and you're halfway there. Her Uncle Rho's rooting resonated from her cycles in Mistress Veranski's dancing school.

And then she saw it—a glow radiating from within the blade's ashen surface, pink as a summer snapdragon. "It's changing color," she marveled.

"So it is," Beldroth added.

Marsea spun the haxanblade, falling into her warm-up exercises without thought. A faint pink ghost, like the fade of a rainbow, followed her movements as she thrust, blocked, cut, lunged again, and hewed through the air. At some point, she realized Blind Widow was leading her on in much the same manner a masquerade suitor might upon the evening's last waltz. Marsea could feel the sword's guiding touch with each burning pulse as she threaded through the forest, dancing between the trees, and slicing through bands of sunlight. She spun and slashed and chased about until she was nearly out of breath.

"Hmph, you're a natural," Beldroth called out to her.

"You think so?" Marsea returned as she studied her new favorite thing on all the moon.

"A bit more practice and you could certainly be dangerous."

"Is that you having a laugh then?"

"I'm quite serious, actually."

"Two hours a day minimum for the past cycle. I know you don't exactly have the highest opinions of Vaustian or Cas, but they were both quality blade instructors." *And horrid taskmasters.* "Head clear, form honest, eyes on the chest." *Form, form, form. Anticipate, anticipate, anticipate.*

"That does sound like Harver,"

"He might have been a wretch to most, but never to me. Still, between Vaustian and Cas and you and Dags, this all just feels so...I don't know..." It took her a moment to find the right word. "...unearned."

"Unearned?" Beldroth took her in. "You've got it quite backwards, I'm afraid. The sword is not meant as a charity, and it's certainly not a thing to be cherished. I'd more liken it to a curse, all things honest. Make no mistake what this is. The sword, the lessons, the familiar. I am using you, Marsea. I am manipulating you. I am conditioning you. I am stealing from you everything you might have become had you been left to your own choices. I am unmaking you. I am no better than Harver. No better than Casilvieri. No better than any of the rest that took you under their tutelage over the cycles. But I'm doing my best to guide you true, trust in that. A young woman your age, you should have your whole life ahead of you. And yet I'm the bastard out here asking you to carry on what's left of my legacy. That is why we're out here in the middle of nowhere freezing our asses off. Why I haven't doused myself in charonisk at the end of the civilized world and lit a match. So I can finally give your father the tribute he deserved. So I can pass on everything I know that made me strong. Everything I know that kept me alive all these centuries. So you have a fighting chance to survive what's coming. They say failure is the greatest teacher of all. Let me spare you a few of mine. The sword never sleeps. True romance is lonely. Hate can be had by anyone. And love is the most patient form of madness." He struck her with a grim expression. "Prize well, there is no winning here, Marsea. We don't win what is happening right now. All we've done. All of this preparation. It's not for a throne, it's not for reputation or justice, and it's most certainly not so you can risk your life against the nether and the lichlords and whatever horrors the ashaeydir have cooked up over the other side of that King's Wall."

Her grip tightened around Blind Widow's hilt.

"It's so you can survive all of those things. The old blood must survive. No matter what the cost." He took a step toward her, leaning heavily on his cane.

"Why? What's so important about the old blood?"

"It is the only thing that stands between us and our extinction. Your father knew this."

"Father never would have chosen to abandon us. If that is what you are insinuating."

"There will be sacrifices, Marsea, desired or not. Keep this close. To survive what is to come you will eventually have to abandon someone, a lot of someones more than like, and yes some of them will be your family and the folk you've come to love most."

The Lanier princess returned the gravestone expression with one of her own.

"The seer...when she gave me that sword...she said it was a key. And that I would pass it along to a most unlikely individual during my twilight. She said it would be someone I had met before. And that with it, this individual could both open and close The Door between worlds. It was all quite cryptic, as seers are wont for, but I'm betting on you, Marsea. I think this individual is you."

"How does that make any sense? We've never met before."

"Would that I could name it. I've only got my instincts on this one, and this is where it's brought me. So it's either you or I reckon we're all just completely fucked then, aren't we?"

She examined the blade, end to end, side to side. It was practically simmering. "How do you mean a key?"

"I asked the very same question of the seer. And more than like, all the rest you've got swirling around your head right now. But all she could tell me was that the answer lies within our dusk."

"Within our dusk?" Marsea retrieved the scabbard and sheathed the haxanblade. It sank in smooth as though freshly oiled.

"Dags believes it may gain the use of its enchantment during duskfall. That The Door has a connection to the crossing hour and the sword an even deeper connection to the spirit world."

"You've never seen it yourself, this Door?"

"I have not. Nor have I ever seen the seer's blade shimmer as it has for you. This is all uncharted territory for me as well."

"Well, that's comforting."

"Still feeling like it's all unearned then?"

"Ha, ha, ha," she mocked. "Your flavor for humor is positively appalling."

"No arguments there."

"So, what now?" Marsea asked.

"Now, we wait for dusk," Beldroth echoed.

"Then what?"

"Then we start looking for a Door."

HER OCEAN GLISTENED, its currents calm as ever, and the stars above shone bright as a field of daisies. Other was there, waiting for her on all fours, dragging her fingers through the waves, exactly where Marsea left her.

"I'm sorry," Marsea said as she took a step forward. This time she remained atop the ocean's surface.

Other turned toward her and stood to near equal height.

"For leaving you," she continued as Other came near and sniffed a circle around her. "For neglecting you. For ignoring you. It won't happen anymore." Her chin remained raised despite her fear.

"**Kept us safe. Kept us alive.**" Other's voice almost sounded halfway normal, in a smoked a pouch a day for the past ten cycles kind of way.

"Yes, you did. You fought for us when I lost faith…when I was ready to give up."

"**Now you understand us?**"

"I understand a little." Marsea thought she saw something like a smile between the strands of Other's wiry wet curls. "I understand I need you and that we need each other."

"**Always with you.**" Other placed a hand over Marsea's heart. "**Right here.**"

"I know." Her good hand raised and fell atop Other's.

"**Don't forget,**" Other pulled away, drifting back a series of steps, and began dipping her toes beneath the watery surface.

"Elsymir speaks of a Door." Marsea's voice came soft.

"**Red door,**" Other said. "**No walls.**"

"A red door?"

"**Yes.**"

"You've seen it?"

Other glanced up at her. "**Us.**"

"Us?" Marsea's eyes hardened. "You mean to say I've seen it?"

"**Yes.**"

"When? Where?"

"**Don't know. Don't remember.**" Other shifted away. "**You won't let us.**"

"*I* won't let us?"

"**Frayed are the threads that cast shadows.**"

"The *Kingstome*? Was it in the *Kingstome*?"

Other turned back to her, frowning.

"*Marsea!*"

Her name split the heavens, and rippled across the ocean like a mounting tempest, echoing far into the surrounding wash.

"What was that?" she asked, as the waves splashed angrily about them.

Dark shapes began to form in the distance, surrounding them, swallowing the starlight. Tall, thin shapes with arms. Dozens and dozens of arms. They didn't move, but they kept multiplying, bleeding the horizon dry.

"**Trees,**" Other said as the shapes began to sprout nearer and nearer.

"Trees…floating atop the ocean?"

"*Marsea!*" Her name echoed again, faraway and muddled, but considerably more desperate.

"**Fae,**" Other said.

"*Marsea…wake up!*" Elsymir called again. Clearer.

Suddenly she could feel Broenwjar's anxieties intensify, and something attach itself to her as a howl like bloody murder shuddered through the thickening wood, shaking the stars above, and heaving the sea into turmoil around them.

"**Beastie.**"

"What's hap—"

Marsea jerked away from Other in shrieking agony, the tattoo on her shoulder burning all the hells' nine furies between them, as she plunged backward through the forest at breakneck speed. She tried to grab hold of something, anything, as she crashed through branches, brush, and creeper, but nothing would have her. And then, within a blink, she was through it, bursting out of her gift's gloom as though a newborn from the womb. Back into the natural world. Back inside the late afternoon sun. Back within her mantle of corporeal pain.

Only the pain that found her hurt like nothing she'd ever experienced before.

Her body felt ghastly wrong and burned throughout as though fresh from a flogging. She tried to reach for the ache but found her movements did not match their normal constitution.

Oh, shit.

A terrifying image caught at the corner of her eyes, stopping her dead in her tracks. It was the image of a girl slumped against the base of a tree with a scabbard stretched across her lap. She lowered her glance and found herself staring down a disfigured snout at a pair of weathered paws.

No fucking way. The truth slammed into her like a hammer to the anvil. *This can't be real.*

"Marsea, wake up!" Beldroth yelled again, his voice strained and riddled with unnatural clicking sounds.

Marsea turned her head from her unconscious self, and found Beldroth on the ground in the distance, crawling away from their camp, a trail of bubbly black ichor leaking out from behind him like the slime of a wandering slug.

"I'm here," she tried to say, but it only came out as a yip and whimper.

Dammit.

She padded up toward Beldroth at a safe distance and watched as he clawed himself another few inches away from camp. She barked at him, and he glanced at her.

The wound across the bridge of his nose had opened wide. It was far beyond necrosis, converging into his left eye socket, which was now oozing nether ichor down his cheek and into the ruptured abscess on his neck.

This is what you have been keeping in all this time?

"Marsea?" he rasped.

She whined her response, maintaining the gap between them.

"It's...**taking**...me," he managed between terrible clicking sounds. "I can't...hold it **back**..." His head began twitching and snapping about unnaturally. "Get...Dags." He dry-heaved and bent inward into the fetal position and began to shake as the foamy black bile came up, gushing from his eyes and lips and every opened scar. "She—"

The trail of black that had taken the place of his diseased leg came to life below him and Beldroth let out an ungodly wail of misery that ended just as abruptly as his skull cracked apart and his face opened up like a hatched egg revealing a dark viscous shape beneath. Nether ichor poured out from the gaping fissure as his flesh, brains, and bones ran down the form of the alien entity inside resembling a snake shedding its skin.

For a breath, everything stopped.

A scaly tentacle-like appendage uncoiled from somewhere inside Beldroth's long amber robes followed by a second and a third...

And Marsea was off to the races, scampering past her slumped body, still leaning useless against a redwood, darting clumsily between the trees, her innards slamming hard against her chest. So hard she found it difficult to breathe properly. And the maidens knew, running about as a wolf was nothing near the same as that of a human. Everything moved past ten times faster. Though to compensate for this, her senses heightened with each subsequent padfall. She was changing by the second, adapting, developing a stronger sense of her new form and a keener awareness of her surroundings. In spite of her limited woodland knowledge, she somehow knew which turns to take to avoid roots and pits and dangerous drops. She could feel the blood pulsing through her veins, every bead of sweat trailing down beneath her fur, each furious beat of her heart, the invigorating taste of country air, and before long there was the scent of others, of civilization, drawing ever so near.

She kept to the outskirts of Vinth until she neared the VanLandingham's cottage, and as fortune faired, she found Dagmara out in the yard picking in her garden.

Marsea bayed as loud as Broenwjar's vocal cords would allow.

Dagmara glanced but briefly over her shoulder and immediately dropped her clippers and rushed inside. Before Marsea could even make it to the fence, Dagmara was back outside with a satchel and medicine bag over her shoulder and a wand at the ready.

"Lead on," Dags said twixt so many curses as Marsea spun back around the way she had come and charged forward through the tall grass back into the towering forest.

CHAPTER THIRTY-THREE

M arsea!" Dagmara cried out nearly breathless as she approached, training her wand on the thing that once named itself Elsymir Beldroth.

Marsea forced a bark from Broenwjar and a cold, ugly realization fell over Dagmara's face. A moment later the elder fished something from her satchel and tossed it between them and the Beldroth Horror. It emitted a harsh azure light.

Marsea knew the thing to be named a totem. A warded trinket designed to keep certain plagues at bay.

The Beldroth Horror shrank away from the totem with an other-worldly shriek, and a pair of tentacles lashed up into the high branches, lifting it off the ground.

Marsea couldn't believe what she was seeing. There was almost nothing to be found of the original figure. Of Elsymir. Verily, it scarce had any sort of form or features at all anymore. There was some sort of rough humanoid shape beneath the torn amber robes and a mass of slimy black tentacles pouring out from behind and beneath it. But Elsymir Beldroth, her mentor, was no more.

Beldroth clung to the branches like a waiting spider, and Dagmara tossed a second totem below his perch and fired her wand at him to keep him honest. The Beldroth Horror let out a shrill cry as it dodged the spells, coiling itself amidst the treetops before disappearing from sight altogether.

Marsea could still hear screeching in the distance as it moved away from them, its twisting tentacles cracking against splintering wood. And just like that, the monstrosity was gone.

Dagmara knelt down before the princess holding a linen cloth under her nose as she began speaking something under her breath. Magic words, no doubt. Magic words Marsea couldn't possibly hope to understand even if she had heard them properly.

There bellowed a loud heartbeat, thunderous as a war drum, before breath filled her lungs, and for an instant that singular cut of air was all she knew. It was crisp as the winter's kiss, driving deep inside, racing throughout every deadened part of her like a tidal wave before circling back around into her throat and expelling out of her in the form of a violent coughing fit.

The maidens wept!

Random thoughts filtered through as she reacclimated to the structure of her own body. Stupid, selfish, impossible thoughts.

Thoughts like she wanted a bed.

And she wanted Vaustian.

And she wanted to snuggle up against him and make love.

And she wanted to feel him inside of her...

"Drink," Dags offered her a water skin from the satchel.

Reality dug its dirty claws back in, and Marsea took the spout to her lips and quaffed voraciously. *Pining after a dead man. Useless as ever.*

"These totems will ward it off for now." Dagmara stood. "They were painted in charonisk resin. The nether can't stand the smell of it."

"What is he?" Marsea asked.

"He? He is an It now, milady, and it's named a gnaudrylax. One of the oldest abominations of the nether. And one of the nastiest."

"Beldroth...he—"

"He did what he could," Dagmara finished sharply.

"He knew this would happen?" Marsea was still trying to wrap her mind around what all she just witnessed, and this wasn't even including the fact that all the while she was trapped inside the body of a wolf.

"He did."

"Do you suppose he will come back?"

"I don't suppose to know anything at all about such a ghastly creature. But I reckon, at the present, it has bigger fish to fry than a troublesome pair out in the middle of the sticks."

"He...he wanted me to kill him...to kill it...if it ever came to it. I couldn't...I...I failed him..."

"Tosh! Elsymir was hopeful in that regard," Dagmara said. "And it was unfair of him to put that on you. He knew what such a creature was capable of. Godsblood or no, it was never likely you were going to prevent this result from coming to fruition. It takes a great power and even greater sacrifice to annihilate such a monster."

"I should have done more," Marsea said as she came to her feet.

"For as long as I've known him, Elsymir's greatest flaw lay within his hope and belief in others. Do not let Elsymir's weakness become your burden. You did what you had to do. And when it comes down to it, Elsymir would have preferred you survived above all else. Despite what you might think, you did well in this."

Marsea glanced over at Broenwjar as he stared off into the distance, after the ghost of his old master.

"And you're still here to carry on his teachings, aren't you? It's the way of things this day and age, awful as it is. Sometimes simply surviving is the best we get."

DUSK WORE a muted shade of tangerine, its pastel perfection bathing everything in sight. 'Twas a scene Marsea would have quite treasured in the old times, dallying about the upper courtyards with her baby sister and her songs and her ruminations on writing. But such beauty found itself wholly lost on this fresh version. This fresh version was plumb exhausted. A walking collection of bags and bruises sandwiched between aches and pangs. And even that bit was putting it generously. Her nerves had become like shredded ribbons and every step she took brought on a fresh pain from some far-ranging part of her body. And yet, somehow, they smarted even worse if she stopped. So she staggered onward. And she thought about home as a means to drown out her physical ailments. She thought about Remy, and Julia, and mother, and Effie, and then for some reason, Aeralie. All these cycles at odds and now they actually had something in common. They were both broken, fatherless daddy's girls. She wondered if Aeralie knew yet. At least she'd received fifteen good cycles with her father. That was three times what Marsea found with her own.

Marsea took a sip from the water skin, swished it about her mouth, and spit it out, her gloom and resentments right along with it. There was no place for such things anymore. All she had going on, she was full-up and then some.

She glanced over at Broenwjar as the VanLandingham's cottage came into view. He appeared equally as spent, working through his own apparent troubles, and twice as cross about the turn of things. Marsea wished for all the moon she could offer him more than what she presently held.

"Looks like Klaus is home," Dagmara announced as they drew nearer. "He's about to go well deep in his cups if he isn't already."

Marsea wanted to say something to that, something profound and worthwhile, but her mind went woefully blank, so she left it quiet and lacking.

"I might recommend you let me tell him about Elsymir, just me and him, milady," Dags added as they crossed through the garden path to the back door.

"I understand," Marsea managed.

"Oi," Dagmara turned around and placed a hand against Marsea's arm, startling the Lanier princess. "You did everything right today. Everything you were supposed to. Everything you could have." The elder stared her straight and waited for her attention. "This was going to happen no matter what. The way it happened was completely buggered, I'll grant you that, but that was in no way your fault."

"I know," Marsea replied, fixing her glasses, a fresh sadness worming its way through her.

"It was unlucky, plain and simple, and there's nothing more to be made of it," Dags said as she opened the backdoor and took a step inside.

"What was unlucky?" a familiar voice asked.

"Marsea, run!" Dagmara ordered.

The princess toed a step away, her heart in her mouth.

"I will kill him if you run, Marsea," Yongrin called out. "We just want the grimoire."

Marsea suddenly felt the weight of the wretched thing in her travel sack. The damned eyesore would be the death of her, the way things were.

"They cannot have it," Dagmara said over her shoulder, "at any cost."

Something exploded from somewhere inside and Marsea knew the sound had come from a wand strike.

"Not another word out of you or the next one goes through the back of your husband's head," Yongrin hissed.

"You'll know the page, Marsea." Dagmara took another step inward. "You'll know the page, and it will guide you."

The door slammed shut between them as though a great gust had just blown through. Only there was no actual gust. There wasn't even the faintest hint of a light breeze. A flash of magic followed, chased by the sound of a hard thud.

Maidens' mercy!

Marsea turned away and dashed for the trees as a series of flashes and crashes erupted. She imagined Klaus's brains bursting out the front of his skull. One of the windows shattered, announcing the struggle within to the outside world. But Marsea did not turn back. She didn't even look. She couldn't. The decision had been made for better or worse. And this was all so much greater than her now. Folk were risking their lives and dying to keep this thing out of the Tarboril's hands. Folk far more suited to contend with such dreadful affairs than she. But here she was anyway, apparently honoring their sacrifices. It was the least she could do, all told.

She had to try.

Marsea was about midway between the cottage and the woods when the backdoor came flying open again.

"Marsea!" Davrin hollered out after her.

The princess dared a glance over her shoulder and saw he was giving chase.

Shit!

"It didn't have to be this way!" He wore dark leathers instead of his crimson armor, not unlike that of a woodland bandit. Marsea rather thought the fresh attire a far more accurate representation of his true nature.

Just keep moving, she thought. *Your courage will catch up.*

The Maiden's Canticle swam through her mind again and again as she rushed through the tall grass behind Broenwjar's barreling shadow, her breathing thin and growing all the more ragged in the eventide chill.

Maidens, make me thine instrument

Where doubt may dwell, may I find faith

Where despair may haunt, may I find your hope and grace

Where hate may tread, may I find your gentle love

Where the nether grows, in blackest dark, may I find your guiding light

We can take him, Other interrupted. **Us and beastie.**

Marsea began to slow her pace as she passed inside the tree line. "Broenwjar, thae vasjte," she commanded in their special language. *Stay ready.*

Nightmare swallowed the sky, dripping down angry amidst the forest veil like a spill of piping hot syrup. Marsea ripped Blind Widow from her rest as she turned back to face the starlit tall grass.

After watching his performance against Cas in Alistair's Courtyard, she had little hope she could best Davrin in a battle of blades, but if her few woodland dalliances had taught her any one thing, it was that she could put on a show with the best of them, and this time she had other advantages too—namely a big bad wolf familiar that had long since been baptized by the sylvan shadows.

"Tough break for Granny Winter back there, protecting you," Davrin said as he came to a halt. "I always kind of liked her. The old man? Not so much."

Quiet as the maidens' prayer, Marsea held firm to her post.

"Maaarseeea," Davrin sang playfully as he crept past the tree line, a twinkle of starlight catching his blade. "No one's coming for you."

Not yet.

"Maaarseeea." He took another stride closer. "We just want the grimoire."

One more.

"Maaarseeea." He froze, locking eyes with her. "There's my girl."

"Not your girl, asshole."

"I say, you are a boorish little bundle of discord, aren't you? You and your brother both."

"What? Did you expect to find me hiding?"

"You know, for a moment there, I kind of did." He took another step forward.

"That's far enough there." She raised the haxanblade, aiming it out at him.

His handsome face turned up an amused grin. "Well done, princess, well done. And what do you propose to do with that? Do you even know how to use that thing?"

"Turn away," she answered. Hard, heathen words.

"You know that's not going to happen."

She felt the gift's fever coursing through her, starved and screaming for release, pulsing from heart to fingers and fusing into the sword. The hilt began to vibrate in return, just as it had before, its enchantment soaking into her skin, and constricting around her bones, as the blade began to radiate the magical charge of their pairing. It appeared elemental at their marriage, like conjured adrenaline, its bright pink aura blood lit from within by fire, rendering all else to sight dull and faded.

"Fancy trick, that," Davrin said.

"You want to test it?"

"So what, you're a hard ass bitch now?"

"I am what I have to be."

"What you have to be? A soft little thing like you? You know what we name folk like you where I'm from? A mouth. An albatross. A memory. A fucking afterthought. Deadweight. Useless."

"I can show you useless," she hissed.

"Oh, come off it, princess. You're no killer."

"And here he is. Another daft fuckwit trying to explain to me who I am."

"Daft fuckwit?" he chuckled. "Listen, bitch, truth's witness, I couldn't give a sloppy wet shit about who you are. Grand scheme of things, you're nothing to me. Nothing. Nobody. No one. You alive? You dead? Same difference. I'm just here for the fucking book, yeah. Now you toss it over here and we're all set. The deed is done. You'll never have to see me again and you can hop along your fucking merry, rot, rot, rot, happy day, and all the rest."

"But, you know, maybe you're right," she said as a dark shape appeared behind Davrin. "Maybe I'm not a killer as you claim. Frankly, I'm delighted you think so well of me. But that one there," she nodded to the space just over Davrin's shoulder, "*he* most certainly is."

On cue, Broenwjar leapt at Davrin taking him hard to the ground. The blackguard managed to roll away and tried to stagger back to his feet, but the massive beast was on him again with brute force, driving him back down into the dirt on his belly.

"Good boy," Marsea said as she approached and kicked Davrin's sword out of reach. "You know what's kind of brilliant? Having a big ass wolf for a best mate." Apparently, she was all in on the bandit-speak now.

"The hells take you," Davrin grumbled into the muck.

"I mean honestly, Davrin, you come out here chasing after me all helter-skelter. How did you think this was going to go? Did you think I was just going to bite my lip and bend the knee?" Marsea stabbed her blade into the ground. "As it stands, this can go one of two ways for you." The princess squatted down beside him. And she kept Casilvieri close in mind. The way he spoke. And the way Rhymona spoke. And Vaustian. And every rotten, liar bastard that had ever shown her the true nature of man. "You can answer my questions and maybe you wake up tomorrow still in one piece. Or you can continue on being an ornery little shit-stain and find out just how big a belly Old Boy here has for you." She stood. "Oh, and before you go about telling me who I am again, you should well prize, I've tortured men I've loved for far less than what you've done me, so I certainly have no qualms taking it all from you if it comes to it."

"Suck my cock," Davrin growled, slobber caking dirt to his face.

Goodness knows but he was the worst kind of small, wasn't he?

"Broenwjar," Marsea said and the wolf bit down hard into the scoundrel's shoulder.

Davrin writhed and shrieked in agony as Broenwjar's fangs dug deep.

"You let me know when you're ready then," she said as she removed her glasses and began cleaning them with the end of her shirt.

She was acting far too superior. But wasn't this how the world would have her?

For some reason, the first line of Kitessa Koida's poem *Dolly Damsel Ray-of-Sunshine* swept through her mind.

Such as she was. Such as she would become.

She always liked that line. It carried with it such an air of promise.

"I don't know shit," Davrin gasped, clutching at dirt with his outstretched hand. "The ashaeydir, she's the one you want."

"The ashaeydir?" *Plot thickens.* "What ashaeydir?"

"The warlock's assassin," he said, spitting snow and mud from between his teeth. "She's...my sister's lover." The way he said the word 'lover' reeked of repressed disdain. "She's the one that orchestrated all of this. She's the one that summoned the lichlord...she's the one that stole from the nether..."

"Stole from the nether? What does that mean? What did she do?" Marsea couldn't imagine Rhymona being the responsible party to all this horror.

"Haven't a whore's notion. All I know is she's using it to kill Oathsworn."

"To what end?"

"I don't fucking know. She's bloody mad. She hates the gift. And she hates the world. And she wants to unmake it."

"Unmake it? How do you mean unmake it?"

"How else do you think I mean it? She wants to see it burn. She wants to—"

"Davrin?" Yongrin called out from the VanLandinghams' yard, the end of her wand a burning beacon beyond the tall grass. "Did you catch her?"

Shit. Marsea knew what that voice meant. It meant Davrin had been true to his word. And it meant Dags and Klaus were most likely dead. She tore the haxanblade from earth, its steel crackling seven shades of tourmaline horror, and placed its point against the side of Davrin's neck. "You so much as make a whimper and I promise you'll leave this sunset screaming."

Kill him. Other snarled and Marsea could feel the blade's tip lower into flesh ever so slightly, drawing blood.

No.

Kill him! He deserves death. He killed our friend.

I said no.

The blade came away from Davrin's neck, and Marsea paced a step away. She was shaking.

Dammit!

It was another impossible situation. As though there weren't enough to go around already. But she couldn't just let him go, could she? And despite all of her big talk, she had no intention of ever killing him.

Maidens mine, please hear me. What would you have me do?

Everything was spiraling. Again. Ever and always. But there was no time for a proper prayer anymore. No time to think. No time for—

She caught a wisp of movement a few feet away and shifted after it.

What the...?

She stared ahead into the growing darkness, but found only still, empty woods.

And yet she could sense a presence within the hollow.

Breath betrayed her lungs as another shiver snared the furthest corner of her eye, and she whirled around to face it. The haxanblade drank in all the starglow to sight, and there within its shine for the span of a blink she exposed the fel thing before it disappeared behind a tree.

It was something like the shadow of a man, only tall as a wngar and skinny as a knife.

"Davrin!" Yongrin called again, her wand light looming ever nearer.

Pull yourself together! Marsea exhaled. *You're scared. It's only your mind playing tricks.*

You know what must be done.

It was a most horrible conception, what had to be done. As horrible as she could think of. No doubt brought on by Other's feral urges. But it was a potential solution. And it wasn't as rotten as murder. Not really.

The old blood must survive.

Marsea stalked back over to Davrin, doing her damnedest to ignore her squabbling conscience and the plaything woodland presence, doing her damnedest further to resist all things outside her internal ocean, and though her hands trembled, her blood roared, her heartbeats pounded harder, faster, then harder still, and for the thinnest moment all became silent as the crone's hour between them as Blind Widow leapt high overhead and raced down feasting for flesh.

The haxanblade penetrated Davrin's thigh like a hot knife in butter, gorging through leather, skin, and bone, severing the leg halfway above the knee in a single swipe.

Good gravy!

Regret blossomed in the wake of Davrin's mad howling, and Marsea withdrew Blind Widow, blood chasing blade from chunks and pulp, as she shuffled back in disbelief, blinking through the terror.

Surely there should have been some resistance.

No, there definitely should have been some resistance.

He's only a man...

"Davrin!" the wand light hurried closer.

It was as though the blade had taken a mind of its own...

As though the blade made her do it...

A cherry blossom mist seethed off the steel where Davrin's lifeblood coated it, and Marsea gaped at the haxanblade utterly aghast.

You...

It should have stopped at the bone. She hadn't the power to take a limb so easily, not that she had really gone out of her way to test such a theory before. A flesh wound was all that was intended. Not this. But the sword...the sword wanted more.

You forced your way through him.

Elsymir's warning rang in her ears anew. *Possessed swords are assholes.*

Yeah, understatement of the century, that.

Broenwjar growled, scouring the surrounding forest, and Marsea's hairs stood on end as a whisper caught within the place just beyond her shoulder. A smell rank as gone-off fish invaded her nostrils, and she dared to take the eldritch presence in, but then there was a frigid wind, and a rustling in the canopy of branches overhead, followed by the spattering of something warm across her face and glasses.

She wiped at it with a finger and pulled back a substance that appeared like...

Davrin's screaming intensified and Marsea glanced past her hand, into the darkness, where she found the blackguard's severed limb floating above him, spinning round and round, sending blood and unraveling chunks of flesh spewing out in all directions from inside the flapping trouser leg.

Marsea's mind refused to accept what her eyes beheld.

She swallowed down the freshly formed lump of sick and aimed the majestic pink giftlight of Blind Widow out before her as though it were a crackling torch, at last separating the presence from the woodland shadows.

It was pale gray and unclothed, its towering torso stretched as though from a torture rack, with sagging breasts and an endless mane of white that hid its face from perception. Skeletal arms jutted out from within the veil of hair, ending in taloned fingers that crooked and contorted against one another in a strange esoteric rhythm.

Bugger me blind.

In seconds, Davrin's lower leg was completely exsanguinated, and dropped to the ground, a shriveled wet rag, leaving a rippling sphere of gore floating in the air between them.

Instantly, blood began to rise from the other end of the wound, gushing and twisting out of Davrin like a series of misshapen vines into the swirling crimson pool above him. His wretched cries grew more desperate.

"Davrin!" Yongrin called again, her voice too near for comfort. "What the hells is happening?"

"I...I didn't mean it like this," Marsea uttered.

Davrin looked up at her, hateful words in his bloodshot eyes, but only malformed screams left his lips in their place. His body was being unmade before her, mutilated from the inside out.

"Stop!" Marsea bade the creature, desperate to end the slaughter. "Stop this butchery!"

As she spoke, a spear of bright golden magic hissed past, narrowly missing her.

Shit. The princess shifted toward Yongrin, who was passing into the woods from the tallgrass, priming another curse from her wand.

The old blood must survive, Elsymir's voice echoed once more.

End her, Other commanded, and Marsea's grip tightened upon the hilt. Oh, but how it muddied her soul to conjure the woman's name, for where Yongrin Tarboril was concerned, Marsea's gift would settle at nothing short of death.

No. The remaining fingers of her bad hand curled into its glove as another passage from *The Wise Man's Blade* bubbled to the surface. *It is a fine line between recklessness and courage. A clever man knows the difference, but the wise man respects it.*

She thought of her greed with Ganedys, following the fire in her heart, and how it cost her dearly.

But there must be a balance.

The princess glanced down at Davrin's withering corpse, still being wrung dry of its lifeblood, the last of his screams wilting up inside his throat, then gazed up, past the massive orb of roiling carnage, at the devil hag, who despite Marsea's protests, persisted in its macabre task.

No one's **coming for you**, Davrin's voice resonated, bleeding into Other's.

They cannot have it, Dagmara's bade.

At any cost.

I'm betting on you, Marsea, Elsymir echoed.

The moon slowed to a standstill before Marsea felt the pull of her right leg into the space behind her, followed by the push of her left. *Focus on what you know you can control.* Turning, she put one step forward, then another, and again, her strides sending her away from the Tarborils and Vinth, deeper into the woodland abyss.

"Don't stop. Don't look back," she breathed.

For Dags. For Elsymir.

The forest spun about her harried flight as she slipped and stumbled through the sea of trees, ducking branches, vaulting logs, and dodging roots as best she could in the scant shimmer of starlight. Grotesque sounds could be heard in the darkness beyond.

Another streak of gold, like a crack of lightning, coiled out from some rest behind her, exploding into a tree not a few feet to her right, trailed by a third blast that sent splinters of bark stabbing out after her. Still, she kept moving further into the great wild void, fast as her legs would carry her, one nightmare into the next.

Don't look back. Don't look back.

Don't ever look back.

It wasn't long before Broenwjar caught her up, and Marsea fell inside his hulking shadow, her confidence gaining with every footfall she put between herself and the others.

Just keep moving forward, no matter what horrors may come.

You mustn't ever look back.

Some breathless seconds later, a terrible screech riffled past her, like a demon on the wind. Though, from this distance, she couldn't tell who it belonged to, Yongrin or the ghastly wood witch.

Or, mayhaps, it belonged to something else entirely.

What the fuck are you doing?

Where are you going?

Broenwjar leapt a gaping ditch, and Marsea followed course, picking up her pace, recalling the memory of their varg.

Find it, Marsea.

Dig deep.

You can do this.

You will do this.

Don't you dare fucking doubt it.

As the ditch opened up on her, she embraced the beast, crying out as she pushed off from the rut's edge, taking flight, and bounding it by the skin of her teeth, landing hard on the other side, stumbling a few steps forward, then riding the momentum down to her knees, before sliding to a halt in the snowy muck.

Old Boy stopped and glanced back at her—

She met his gaze and stabbed the haxanblade firmly down into the slush between her legs, pushing herself back up to her feet, her bones cracking like an old nan.

Can't stop now.

Her legs started forward again, knees snapping, and she caught Broenwjar up, sprinting past as he watched, though he quickly returned to her side.

She sheathed Blind Widow, as they raced the patches of starlight, girl and beast, and she thought of Dags and Klaus and what had been made of Elsymir. And she thought about all they had given up. All they had sacrificed for her. All they had done just so she could stay alive a little while longer. And then she thought about how terribly short their time lasted together and how if she'd burned a thousand cycles more, it'd still not be enough to repay even one of them properly.

From there, her guilt began to spiral, remnants of the old Marsea unwilling to give up the ghost of ill worth, and the echoes of her mentors gave chase into the dreary pitch around her, their lessons and expectations and contradictions unrelenting.

Frayed are the threads that cast shadows...

I will not let my past define me...

The scars that bind us...

The old blood must survive...

Marsea nudged her blood-speckled glasses back up to the bridge of her nose, a wind of purpose taking hold within the maelstrom of warring credos.

Well, if the old blood must survive, she humored the last of her haunters. *Then, prayers to promise, henceforth and heartstrung, so it shall pass, that the name must die.*

The End

GLOSSARY

GENERAL TERMS

Blight, The – Sentient beings reborn as ghoulish creatures by black magic incantations. They are typically controlled by a lichlord or a necromancer and operate in a hive mind.

Chandii, The – An ancient race highly attuned to the gift. They are also known as flamekin, summerblood, and summerkin of the Summer Isles due to their distinctive bright, fiery orange and red hair. They were once believed to be beast whisperers, familiars of the dracari, and, thusly, dragonriders.

Charonisk – A man-made concoction with similar effects to Eldn fire.

Dracari, The – The race of dragons. Dracthonir is the name of the dracari language.

Dragonsfall, The – The event comprising both the fall of dragons by man and the spreading of the gift into the elements that would result in The Giftborn Age.

Drylax – A physical curse of the nether. There are two known forms: A gnaudrylax, which is a being fully consumed by the nether. This form is fluid and ever-shifting. And a phaedrylax, which is a partially consumed being. This form still experiences some confines of the host's body.

Eldnumerian, The – A Chandiian term. "eldnu" meaning ancient, "meria" meaning master. They are also known as the old ones.

Nether, The – An ancient cosmic entity that feeds off of the soul and the gift. It can be physically manifested on the mortal planes using reverse wards and necromantic incantations. It incapacitates its victims using their fear until madness consumes. The result of the madness, once the soul and gift have been purged from the body, is known as the blight.

Oathsworn, The – The knights of the round. They are a clandestine order formed to serve the realm of men. There is no head or foot. All are equal. The Oathsworn was founded decades ago by King Cameron Lanier. They protect the realm against darkly creatures and the supernatural.

Quintweek (quint) – A fluid term indicating a general passage of time. There are five days in a week. Six weeks in a month. Nine months in a cycle. Ten cycles in a decade. Ten decades in a century.

Ravenholme – Now synonymous with The Covenant, Ravenholme is a rogue guild created by Malthus Tetherow that split from The Covenant (original). Initially, The Covenant was created in opposition to The Oathsworn. Members of Ravenholme believe that the darkly and supernatural should be revealed to the public, not kept hidden.

Shufa – A powerful drug that can be smoked or consumed with food.

Star maidens, The – The angelic beings followed within the Omedran faith. They are also known as the Amendeiya. Within the order of the cloth maidens are Lirae (a house mother), Rin (a handmaid to a Ve'Lir), and Ve'Lir (a cloth maiden in study).

THE KNOWN UNIVERSE (the sister moons)

Ashira – The crimson moon. It is now wasting away and nearly uninhabitable.

Dalynisa – The big blue planet thought to be completely ocean.

Lumos – The smallest of the sister moons. She is known for her pale white appearance.

Vaelsyntheria – The golden moon.

Y'dema – The giant green moon. It was said to be razed by the ashaeydir after the fall of Ashira.

MAGIC TERMS

Blood candles – They are the stored mold of a giftborn's blood. It allows the user to enhance their inherited abilities, sometimes by considerable margins. They are known to be heavily addictive and can be deadly. The use of varying types of blood can alter and sometimes poison the blood system. Though not entirely banned by the Ministry, the use of blood candles is generally frowned upon through The Midaran Commonwealth, especially at the universities of magic.

Blood merchants (warlocks) – Those who hunt fellow giftborn to drain them of their blood for wholesale.

Codices and Grimoires – Tomes and grimoires contain spoken word magic, including spells, recipes, sigils, wards, and bestiaries. This type of magic existed in previous ages, but has become more archaic in the Age of The Giftborn. It is largely considered an inferior form of magic by comparison to gift conjuring.

Eldn fire – A form of magic conjured and controlled by the dracari. It is the most powerful form of known magic and is one of the few defenses left against the nether. It manifests when called forth as azure and white flame.

Giftborn – A person with magical abilities. They can inherently perform great magical feats. The quality varies and is typically bloodline-based. To conjure magic the person must sacrifice something in return. They are less commonly referred to as warders and spellslingers.

Godsblood, Of the – Also referred to as the maker's ichor. It is the term the dracari use to describe giftborn descended of the older bloodlines with a deep connection to magic.

Gravedancer – A giftborn with the ability to resurrect the dead.

Haxanblade – A possessed weapon. This unfortunate soulmeld occurs through a curse or a mishandled enchantment.

Kindleblade – An iron-forged weapon, typically a ritual dagger or a sword, that is enchanted and soulmelded to a master.

Night writing – Raised code substituting for words. It is often times used with codices.

Soul magic (black magic) – Magic that feeds off of the soul rather than the physical body. This form of magic is very powerful, but also that much more risky and dangerous. Too much use can twist and deform the conjurer's appearance. It can whiten the hair, pale the skin, and rapidly age the conjurer.

Spellbind, The – A sliver of The Pale that was long ago cut away. It is a pocket dimension. A place out of time and space. One must be greatly gifted or use a blood candle, sacrificing something of their own health to enter. A studied giftborn can transfer their consciousness to The Spellbind. It can be a place of great healing or great destruction.

Totems – Enchanted trinkets, typically made of whittled wood or carved stone.

Varg – The ability of a giftborn to enter the mind of a soulbound familiar and take command of their actions. This ability leaves the conjurer in a vulnerable, almost corpse-like state during its casting.

Wands – Enchanted weapons created by giftborn to channel magic. They form a bond with a master through a soulmeld and will only react to that user's gift.

Wards – There are two primary forms of magic. Elemental-based magic and Soul and body-based magic. Elemental magic consists of Fire (Pyromancy), Water (Hydromancy), Earth (Terramancy), and Wind (Aeromancy). These forms of magic were common during the Age of Dragons. Soul and body-based magic consists of Shadows (Necromancy), Spirit (Psychomancy), Blood (Hemomancy), and Flesh and bone (Carnomancy). These forms of magic are common in the Age of The Giftborn. Powerful giftborn can merge two and three mantia at once.

MILITARY TERMS

Crownswatch, The – Liveried in crimson, they are also known as bloodcoats and redcoats. These soldiers man the northern highlands from The Straights to The Scar.

Emperorswatch, The – Liveried in gold, they are also known as goldcoats (and derogatorily as pisscoats). These soldiers man the Vinteyama swamplands and the flatlands between the highlands and southlands. They are noted for not allowing women to enlist in their guard.

Kingswatch, The – Liveried in blue, they are also known as bluecoats. These soldiers man Lancastle and her surrounding hamlets. They also man The King's Wall, a massive construct that separates the highlands from the lands now occupied by the ashaeydir.

Lordswatch, The – Liveried in gray, they are also known as graycoats. These soldiers man the lands east of the Morrigar Mountains, from the north to the southland provinces just outside Six Ports.

Royalguard, The – The overarching term referencing any coat of arms inside the midaran military.

WEAPONRY

Helanderan sword – A one-handed sword of varying lengths, edged on both sides, and generally paired with the use of a shield.

Ka'rym chii – A set of ashaeydir weapons primarily indicating a mae'chii and sy'chii.

Mae'chii – A long, slender, single-edged blade.

Sy'chii – A shorter single-edged blade.

Trezsu implant – An implant surgically embedded in ashaeydir soldiers that allows them to alter aspects of their appearance.

ACKNOWLEDGMENTS

In addition to the wonderful folks at Falstaff Books and the previously named friends and family who helped champion *The Royal Nothings* into existence, there were thousands of moments and interactions with people near and far that played a part in the day-to-day planning and plotting of this series, not to mention in my growth as a writer.

It's true what they say, that all writers are writing even when they are not. Pulling from the most insignificant of exchanges, or from an overheard conversation, or an arrangement of words, an unexpected sound, a random picture, a remnant from a dream...

We can find a story in the most mundane of things. But especially in the things that are not.

That being said, it would be impossible to individually thank everyone and everything that played a part in the decade-long process of this story. For you are indeed legion. And I mean that in the most flattering sense of the word. But please know, from the very depths of my talebearing soul, you are not forgotten, and you are certainly not unappreciated.

For those that have read to these words and given this old writer a chance, thank you.

As before, as always, may you count some measure of hope and inspiration from some place within.

ABOUT THE AUTHOR

Drew Bailey is an emerging author of horror and fantasy. Though he attended college to expand his knowledge of Literature and History, it still took him the better part of a decade to actually mold it into something worth chasing after. Better late than never, as they say. The Royal Nothings is his first novel. In his spare time, Drew is a chronic coffee drinker, avid movie watcher, and follows Liverpool F.C. and the Green Bay Packers. He currently resides in Charleston, South Carolina.

STAY IN TOUCH!

If you enjoyed this book, please leave a review on Amazon, Goodreads, or wherever you like.

If you'd like to hear more about or from the author, please join our mailing list at https://www.subscribepage.com/g8d0a9.

You can get some free short stories just for signing up, and whenever a book gets 50 reviews, the author gets a unicorn. I need another unicorn. The ones I have are getting lonely. So please leave a review and get me another unicorn!

FRIENDS OF FALSTAFF

Thank You to All our Falstaff Books Patrons, who get extra digital content each month! To be featured here and see what other great rewards we offer, go to www.patreon.com/falstaffbooks.

PATRONS

Dino Hicks

John Hooks

John Kilgallon

Larissa Lichty

Travis & Casey Schilling

Staci-Leigh Santore

Sheryl R. Hayes

Scott Norris

Samuel Montgomery-Blinn

Junkle

CPSIA information can be obtained
at www.ICGtesting.com
Printed in the USA
BVHW071633270122
627356BV00014B/543